The Cornish Woman

A novel

Mark Bannerman

Pipers' Ash Limited

www.supamasu.demon.co.uk

CHIPPENHAM ♦ WILTSHIRE ♦ ENGLAND
SN15 4BW

Copyright Anthony Lewing 1999
First Published in Great Britain 1999

Canterbury Edition
ISBN 1-902628-95-0

The right of Anthony Lewing to be identified as the author of this work has been asserted by him in accordance with the Copyright, Designs and Patents Act 1988

For My Wife Françoise

ACKNOWLEDGEMENTS

I AM GRATEFUL to many people who assisted me in the preparation of this story, and especially to Graham Ward whose sense of humour and knowledge of the textile trade would inspire any author; to Gary Mitchell, Mevagissey boat-builder, who is an expert in Cornish dialect and history - and who made available to me a book written by his distant cousin Mary Lakeman; this provided a wonderful insight into Cornish childhood during the first part of this century. I am also indebted to Ann Grimwood, a midwife at the Cambridge Military Hospital, Aldershot; to Carol Papworth who breathed her Welshness into my soul; to Detective Constable Barry Sivier for technical advice relating to police procedure; to Vivian Davis for advice on Cardiff and railways of the 1920s; to Doris Davidson for her many constructive suggestions; to Valerie Thame, Valerie Waters and Nita Raymonde, all of whom stimulated my mental processes when the writing got difficult; and finally to Peter Reese, military historian, whose encouragement, technical advice and camaraderie were invaluable.

- Cover illustration by James Ward

PROLOGUE - 1890

HENRY CARTER HAD LOADED THEIR BAGGAGE aboard the old steamship. He, his wife Sarah and their two small infants had yesterday left their London home, and now were amongst the fifty emigrants taking passage on the *Atlantic Queen,* scheduled to sail that evening from Plymouth for Quebec.

As they stood on the quayside at Sutton Harbour, awaiting the order to embark, lightning rippled across the sky. Sarah shuddered. She had always been afraid of the sea, but now, as thunder rumbled, her fear grew to terror. She wanted to cry out: 'Henry, for the children's sake, let's not go. We can still turn back!' But her lips were trembling so much that she was unable to form the words. Instead, she hugged Elizabeth Jane, her tiny baby, more tightly to her. Beside her, Henry was carrying their first-born, 12-month old Edwin. Henry smiled and said, 'It's not the best of weather, my love, but tomorrow, when we're at sea, I'm sure the sun will shine.'

Anger vied with fear in her emotions. How could he be so blind to the jeopardy he was placing them in?

But of course it was typical of Henry. His mind was so often far beyond what was going on around him. He was a qualified engineer in plumbing and waterworks, and he was always dreaming of his inventions. Now she realised what madness it all was ... crossing the sea in this old steamship because his business had floundered. His partner had swindled him, disappeared with the assets, leaving them penniless. All might have been well if his latest brainchild had been acclaimed. Sadly, nobody in England wanted to patent his unique combination of commode pail, French-style bidet and footbath, though he was convinced that within a few years every modern home would have such an appliance.

'We'll go abroad, Sarah,' he'd finally said as he frowned over their rent arrears. 'I've heard Canada is a go-ahead country with plenty of opportunities. The children will have a better future there.'

Still weak from the birth of Jane Elizabeth, Sarah had nodded. In the past, Henry had had dreams which had come to nothing. Perhaps this one would be no different. Perhaps some minor miracle would appear to inject life into his business, or perhaps he would listen to the advice of his older brother Jeremy and join him in the textile trade, which seemed to offer good prospects. Not that she would relish that, for Jeremy had lecherous eyes and hands that touched her too lingeringly.

But during the following days, as Henry made enquiries, his plans for emigration took on the mantle of reality. Apparently cross-Atlantic fares were at an all-time low, due to fierce competition between the shipping companies. Finally, Jeremy, seeing that nothing would dissuade Henry, lent him money for the sea passage.

Now, waiting upon the quayside, baby Elizabeth Jane began to cry and Sarah fed her. With the baby guzzling, Sarah glanced around at the families who were to share the ordeal, seeing apprehension in the faces of the women as they strove to control their children, seeing their menfolk putting on an act of confidence she was sure many of them did not feel.

There were many regional dialects amongst the emigrants. These sounded so alien to her they might just as well have been Chinese. About half those on the quayside were agricultural workers and their families, driven out of England by hardship inflicted by the importation of cheap foreign wheat. Others came from coal-mining, building and metal-working communities. Most had been lured by newspaper advertisements promising wonderful opportunities in Canada. She felt particularly sorry for one young woman who was burdened with two tiny babies. She was pretty, yet there was a furtiveness about her and she had no man to help her. Another woman, badly crippled, was in a wheelchair and needed constant attention from her husband. An elderly man fussed about a cumbersome cello, anxious to avoid damaging it as a group of urchins played tag around him.

Despite the heavy, torrid atmosphere of the day, some of the emigrants wore old coats and blankets in anticipation of cold nights at sea and the Canadian winter ahead. No doubt most of them, Sarah thought, were driven to leave England by circumstances far more desperate than those of Henry and herself.

The *Atlantic Queen* a wooden, screw-driven vessel, was some two-hundred-and-fifty feet in length. The long deck boasted little housing, apart from the wheelhouse and the cabins over the gangways. There were two funnels, the main one above the steam boiler, and a smaller one for the passengers' accommodation and cooking. The four cross-beamed masts were rigged with sail as reserve in case the engines failed.

As well as the emigrants, the ship was transporting a cargo of corrugated iron. The old ship had undergone a refit and workmen were busy with the final tasks as the passengers waited on the quayside. Presently Captain Gilbert came rushing red-faced down Quay Road. He had been delayed at *The Three Crowns* inn. As he mounted the gangway, lightning again split the sky. He dismissed any forebodings with a shrug of his bullish shoulders. He checked his pocket watch and hurried aboard. Soon he ordered the workmen off the ship, then he passed the word that the passengers were to embark.

Sarah's legs were trembling as, clutching Elizabeth Jane, she followed Henry up the rickety gangway. Ten minutes later they stood upon the deck amongst the other passengers, some of whom were waving good-bye to relatives and friends on the quayside. There was nobody to wish the Carters God's speed.

Despite having been fed, Elizabeth Jane was crying, as if sharing her mother's anxiety. For the first time, Henry seemed aware of Sarah's feelings. Still holding his sleeping son, he smiled reassuringly and gave his wife a hug. 'It'll be all right, my love, once we get out into the Atlantic.'

Sarah did not hear him. Her stomach was churning and inside her a voice was crying out, 'You'll all be drowned ... all be drowned!'

Emma Bray had always longed for a family. Her own relations, said to be gentry, were lost in mists of domestic turbulence - and her husband's only sister at Penzance was not on speaking terms. Emma had desired most fervently to put down new roots, but the fusion of her body with John Bray's had not borne fruit - not, that is, until after seven years of marriage and John Bray had left the tin mines to become a fisherman.

When Emma at last announced she was expecting, they were delighted. In each other's arms, they danced around the small kitchen of their cottage in Megstow Quay as grandly as if they'd been in a gilded ballroom. Soon Emma developed a voracious appetite for dried onions. Together, husband and wife prepared their second bedroom for the baby, with a pretty little crib and a nursery-rhyme pattern on the walls. John Bray bought an old rocking chair that would be perfect for nursing the baby. But gradually Emma's spirits slumped, she was harrowed by the conviction that the child would not survive. True enough, she miscarried.

For weeks she languished in misery, eating little, so that her delicate prettiness withered away and the smallpox scars on her cheeks became increasingly prominent. She spent hours on her knees at the village church, begging for the gift of another chance. Night after night, she drew John Bray into her with fierce eagerness, until he was drained.

Their efforts gained some reward. She conceived for a second time and in due course, as if in confirmation, her craving for raw onions returned.

They took every precaution to ensure a successful birth. John Bray wondered if perhaps he had not shown Emma sufficient consideration during her first pregnancy, and he strove to make amends. He would prop her up with pillows when she suffered from heartburn, and every morning, he would serve her breakfast in bed. He would accompany her on gentle walks, comforting her when she had bouts of sickness, providing her with countless onions. Together they watched her body swell; together they felt the baby's first kicks, and the midwife from the village, Tilly Triggs, visited regularly to make sure everything was all right.

One June day in 1890, the sky went a weird purple, lightning and thunder came, and soon the wind drove the sea-spray over Megstow Quay with ferocity. During the afternoon, rain drove people to take cover; and later as the storm bludgeoned the cottage, Emma's pains started.

Battling the wind, soaked to the skin, John Bray stumbled up Megstow Quay's cobbled street to the midwife's cottage. But young Bessy Triggs opened the door to say that her mum hadn't got back from St Mags where she was delivering a child for the Killigrew family. She promised she'd send her over as soon as she got home. As John Bray returned through the gale, the light was fading, and sea-spray stung his face like grit. He had little hope that the midwife would be able to reach Megstow Quay that night. What had to be done, he himself would have to attend to. His neighbours were the Kelvins and he could not abide the woman. Not in a thousand years would he seek her help.

He found Emma shivering, her face white. Her waters had broken. She lay upon the bed, regular waves of contractions shuddering through her. He felt desperately inadequate. He knelt beside the bed, grasped her small hands in his and pleaded with her to take deep breaths. 'In ... in some more ... and now ... out. Again, Emma, again, again.' Gradually the contractions relented and she rested back, her eyes closed. But her reprieve was only temporary. He watched over her for what seemed hours, comforting as best he could as renewed contractions took hold, until at last, she was raising her voice against the racket of the outside storm, telling him that her time had come.

Earlier, as the *Atlantic Queen* got under way, rain was spitting across the harbour and the sea looked black. The ship cleared Plymouth Sound and headed down the Channel, and by now the clouds were low and the sky was darkening. Captain Gilbert, still slightly drunk and unmoved by the threatening weather, retired to his cabin in the stern. The rain grew more intense. On the steerage deck in the depths of the ship, passengers peered through portholes and glimpsed the lights of St Peter and Drake's Point.

'That's most likely our last sight of England,' Sarah heard a man say.

Around her, parents struggled to calm their frightened infants. She was thankful that her own babies were asleep on their bunk-beds. The steerage deck consisted of a number of compartments, partitioned off with wooden screens, but, in the flickering light of the gas lamps, there was little privacy and already the smell from the toilets was permeating the air. Bracing herself against the ship's lurch, she prayed earnestly that they would all survive - but if that was impossible, please, please God, spare the young lives of Edwin and Elizabeth Jane ...

The ship's second-mate, standing next to the helmsman, peered to the south-west, anxious to spot the Lizard Light, but he could see nothing. He was convinced they were sailing too close to the Cornish shore. A strong southerly wind was blowing, whipping up the waves, causing the ship to roll and plunge.

When the full tempest surged out of the darkness, it tore at the vessel's rigging with frenzied claws.

Panicking, the second mate scrambled below to rouse Captain Gilbert from his sleep. As the captain came cursing onto the deck, still pulling on his oilskins, the forward lookouts sighted the awesome whiteness of breakers ahead, but their shouted warnings came too late.

The *Atlantic Queen* gave a violent shudder, causing panic below on the steerage deck. The ship's forward momentum, assisted by the heavy swell, carried her over a chain of rocks, ripping her hull. Somehow the helmsman turned her into open sea again. Through navigational error, the ship had run foul of the notorious Barnacle Rocks. Soon her hull was leaking and the scuppers were awash. Screaming anguished obscenities, Captain Gilbert had three distress rockets discharged.

These were observed from the shore, but the wind had stirred the sea to such turmoil that it was impossible to launch either of the two local lifeboats, despite their willing crews who came running, hooking up their braces, pulling on their boots, eager to face the danger. Eventually they resigned themselves: they could do nothing except seek shelter and listen to the rant of the wind as it sent slates clattering from the roofs and carried sea-spray far inland.

Meanwhile, out at sea, a giant wave drove across the ship's decks and she plunged, weighted by water. Captain Gilbert, clinging to the rails on the walkway above the wheelhouse, gazing shorewards for the help that would never come, was caught unawares. When the ship rose again, he was gone, lost in the heaving waves.

The ship was listing heavily as wind brought a mast crashing down. Many of the passengers had scrambled up the stairs, onto the deck. They could see nothing in the spray-thickened darkness. Time and again, the seas burst over the decks, throwing people against the bulwarks or carrying them overboard, the screams of women and children lost in the clamour of the elements.

Of the four rowing boats on board, only the two on the leeward side of the ship could be launched. Using ropes slung over the cross-beams, crew-members struggled to lower these into the sea. Somehow they succeeded, and scrambling nets were thrown down. In the lee of the ship, the water was less turbulent. Sarah and Henry were caught in the surge of people struggling to board the boats. There was no question of women and children first. In the mad rush, one burly crewman grasped Henry by the shoulder and dragged him down, stumbling over him to claw his way onto the scrambling net. Sarah was pushed forward by the mob, and in panic she realised that she had become separated from Henry. Terrified that she might drop her baby, she clambered down into the heaving craft, glancing up for sight of her husband. The darkness was full of movement, panic and noise and she was devastated by the feeling that Henry hadn't made it into the boat. Perhaps he had got into the second boat. She managed to find space between two other women on one of the thwarts.

The boat was desperately overloaded, some twenty-five persons aboard, its gunwales scarcely above the water. Back on the ship, people were screaming, realising that they were being left behind, abandoned. Were Henry and little Edwin amongst them? She sobbed with despair. But then she heard Henry's voice, piercing the racket of sound, coming from the stern of the boat: 'Sarah! Sarah!'

She called his name, but she had no strength to fight the wind and she doubted that he heard. Clutching her baby, bracing herself against the rise and fall of the boat, she started to scramble through the crammed bodies towards the stern, anxious to confirm that Henry had Edwin with him. She was weeping with relief. Perhaps they all might now stand some chance of surviving this nightmare.

Men took up the oars, got them into the rowlocks, and started to row. As they came clear of the shelter afforded by the listing ship, the sea drove into them, almost capsizing them. Somehow the craft survived that first onslaught, was lifted upwards on a wave, then plunged into a deep watery valley. Water gushed about their legs.

Sarah glanced upward to see a great escarpment of black sea towering above them. The waves broke and crashed down upon the helpless craft, swamping its occupants beneath the mass of water - but again they were lifted, and men toiled at the oars and some progress was made. Then, when they were fifty yards from the sinking ship, another massive wave struck them broadside.

Water slammed into Sarah with the force of a rock wall, lifting her completely out of the boat. She, and those around her, stood no chance. All consciousness was crushed from them as the boat went under. The second boat had met a similar fate.

At least their terror was over. The final seconds of their lives were spent in black oblivion.

Amazingly the boats re-surfaced - awash yet afloat ... but where people had been before, there was now only taunting emptiness. A few heads bobbed briefly upon the turbulent, mountainous sea, then they were gone.

Across the waves, the broken *Atlantic Queen* finally lost her battle for salvation and vanished beneath the surface.

John Bray gasped, 'Push down, me dear!'

She was panting, the sweat shining on her face. Suddenly the rasp of her breathing stopped; she unleashed a long howl and he saw the baby's head emerging, then a shoulder, and together, they made the supreme effort, Emma pushing down while he drew the tiny, blood-glistening body out.

'Tie the cord ... cut it,' she gasped.. 'String's ... in work-box.'

He found the work-box and extracted string and scissors. With clumsy hands, he grappled with the slippery cord, binding it in two places. Gritting his teeth, he cut the cord, praying that there would be no haemorrhaging. He wrapped the tiny body into a blanket, gazing for a moment into its tiny, squashed face, seeing the closed eyes, nostrils, and lips that just for a second seemed to smile at him. Then he realised the baby wasn't breathing!

Downstairs, the cottage door burst inward and the windswept Tilly Triggs stood beside him, looking like a dripping whale. She snatched the baby, poked her finger into its mouth and flipped out mucus. Then, quite ruthlessly, she stripped away the blanket, held the baby upside down and slapped its buttocks. The child coughed, and, as its lungs expanded, started to cry. The midwife re-wrapped the child, said, 'It's a girl,' and placed it in Emma's arms.

John Bray glanced at Emma's sweat-shining face. She was gazing at her baby, her expression reflecting happiness and love, tears running down his own cheeks. John Bray had never known such intensity of joy, of achievement.

Tilly Triggs bustled about with efficiency, placing her hands on Emma, helping her to expel the after-birth, then she tucked mother and baby warmly together and turned to John Bray.

''Tis a hectic night, what with storm and all!'

'I'm grateful to 'ee for comin'.'

His attention returned to Emma. She was hugging the baby, but it was no longer crying.

'John,' Emma gasped, 'she's so still. She ...'

Fear stabbed at him. Tilly Triggs brushed past him and lifted the baby away from Emma. She peered at it. She placed her mouth across the baby's lips, sucking air in and out. John Bray and Emma watched with horrified eyes, until Tilly drew back, shaking her head and saying ''Tis no good.' ... and suddenly Emma screamed: 'Baby's gone! B-baby's gone!'

'No!' John Bray snatched the tiny body from Tilly, cradled it in his arms. 'No ... No ...'

He glanced up, saw Emma's petrified face. Her scream filled the room. He felt suffocated with grief. He could stand it no longer. Thrusting the lifeless child into Tilly's arms, he fled down the staircase, wrenched open the door and escaped. In the black night, the wind, the rain, clawed at him. He stumbled blindly along the street, down onto the beach, crying out with anguish, fighting the storm, not knowing nor caring where his feet were taking him. But the sea struck him, smashing into him, bowling him over, winding him.

He fought the water, his clothing sodden and heavy. He regained his feet and staggered blindly along the beach, his mind filled with the horror of his tragedy. Now, suddenly, he became aware of a dark bulk of something ahead of him, something that was out of place. He senses became focused. He drew closer and realised it was a ship's boat, driven up on the beach.

He reached the craft, gripped its gunwales and struggled for his breath, then he got his leg over the side and hoisted himself aboard. Standing knee-deep in water, he braced himself as waves struck the craft moving it up the sand. For a moment he felt utterly befuddled, then the truth seeped into his mind. A ship must have foundered at sea. Those aboard had tried to escape in this craft.

Groping in the darkness, he concluded that nobody was now aboard. The poor devils must have been washed overboard. There was little chance of surviving in an open boat in this howling gale.

Then he heard the weakest of cries.

At first he imagined, amid the roar of the storm, that his ears were playing tricks, but the sound came again - plaintive, yet unmistakably real. Perhaps the ship's cat had somehow survived. He was standing in the stern of the vessel. As the cry sounded again, he groped around and his hands touched the door of the small rope-locker beneath the after-thwart. He tugged on it. It was jammed tightly shut. Using more force, he finally wrenched it open.

It was then that he discovered the two infants, wrapped in sodden blankets. Suddenly exposed to the wind, they both bawled with all their might.

Feverishly, he tore them free, cradled them in his arms. They weighed almost nothing. He rushed back with them along the beach to the cottage.

Both had dark hair - the boy was about a year old, the baby girl scarcely more than a few weeks.

After the midwife Tilly had recovered from the initial shock of John Bray's laden return, she said, 'The baby's blue with cold. Let's wrap 'er in a blanket and put 'er in Emma's arms!' and that is what they did. Emma was utterly confused, couldn't understand, but Tilly kept repeating that it was a blessed gift from heaven.

With the baby nestled and warm, John Bray turned his attention to the boy toddler, stripping off his clothing and drying him in front of the fire which Tilly stoked up.

Tilly pondered, then said, 'Keep the girl. Everybody'll believe she died with the rest of 'em in the storm.'

John Bray gasped with shock. 'Tilly Triggs! That'd be kidnappin'.'

The midwife placed her hands on her formidable hips, her eyes boring into him like bullets. 'If 'ee takes that baby away now, it'll kill your wife!'

John Bray gazed across at Emma, resting peacefully in her bed, her face relaxed, the baby gurgling gently, snuggled safely against her.

In a voice that reminded him of the temptress Eve, Tilly whispered: 'Nobody'll be any the wiser, 'cept the three of us.' Then in a firmer tone she asked, 'What were you goin' to call your own daughter if she'd lived? Had 'ee decided on a name?'

John Bray ran a troubled hand through his wet hair. 'Emma wanted to call it Rosena, after her mother.'

'Then call this baby Rosena,' Tilly said, 'nobody'll know it's not your own child.'

John Bray swallowed hard, gazed down at his wife and the baby in her arms. At last he gave his head a slow nod. 'Very well. We shall call the baby Rosena.'

Tilly Triggs smiled with satisfaction. 'Rosena ... 'Tis a pretty name,' and then dropping her voice, she added: 'Rosena Bray.'

And so instead of passing the two infants, through Talmouth's Doctor Carey, to the authorities so that any surviving relatives could be traced, John Bray reported that only the boy had been found in the boat. By this time he had buried the tiny body of his own baby in the garden behind the cottage.

Chapter One

THE VILLAGE OF MEGSTOW QUAY, close to the mouth of an estuary, consisted of some fifty whitewashed cottages, their thatches held fast by chains. Along the narrow lanes, they were jumbled tightly together, as if elbowing each other for more space. The village inn, *The Cherry Bowl*, stood half way up the main street, wedged between butcher's shop and general store, and further up was the bakehouse and a cobbler, who combined his normal duties with dentistry. At the end of the street was the bark-house, where fishing nets were cleaned. From the hill, the village was overlooked by the ancient grey-stone church of *St Arthur's*, its tower a reassuring land-mark for those at sea. In the Spring, daffodils and irises carpeted the gardens with rich gold and mauve, but no scent of flowers could mask the ever-present smells of salt, fish and tar.

Each Whitsun, Rosena accompanied her parents, Emma and John Bray, to the fair at Talmouth. Emma would wear her prettiest bonnet and powder her cheeks to hide her smallpox scars. John Bray, handsome in his jaunty fisherman's cap, would lock up the cottage at Megstow Quay and they would walk along the beach. At low tide, this was a series of coves, separated by rocky headlands. The Brays would pass cool pools, seeing the small sea-creatures stranded there - crabs, sea slugs, mussels, winkles. Sometimes they would explore the shadowy caves, gazing up into the dark recesses, listening to the echo of sea and Rosena imagined she could hear whisperings. There was a legend that a witch had once lived in these caves.

Eventually they would leave the beach, climb a cliff path, and cross meadows to the fair at Talmouth Green.

Rosena would gasp at the sight of the bearded lady, the jugglers and acrobats and the Punch-and-Judy show. Deafened by drums and trumpets, she would ride a horse on a carousel, or watch her father and mother roll half-pennies and sometimes win prizes of gingerbread. There were performing bears, donkey races, fortune-tellers, and endless booths selling sweetmeats.

But in the year of 1898 when Rosena was eight and still unaware of the mysteries of her birth, there was something new at the fair. The Brays found themselves crammed into a tent, packed tightly on boarded seats, surrounded by working people whose language was crude. Everyone was impatient for the show to begin. Before them was a roped-off square and Rosena asked what it was.

"Tis a ring for the wrestlers,' John Bray said.

"Tid'n a ring, Father. 'Tis a square.'

Rosena waited for an explanation but none came. How could a square be a ring? The strange thing was, nobody else seemed at all concerned.

The crowd booed as a wrestler called *The Taunton Terror* climbed through the ropes. He had issued a challenge to the local menfolk. He was wearing a black mask and was stripped to the waist. Amid bawdy shouts he flexed his powerful muscles. He was billed as world-famous, the pride of Taunton.

He took on two bulky Talmouth lads that afternoon. Neither lasted long. The Terror tore into them, grappling furiously, cutting loose a torrent of kicks and blows. Feinting and ducking, he threw and tripped his opponents, dropping on top of them, crushing their breath, twisting their limbs until they cried for mercy. This was very different from the familiar Cornish wrestling, where men remained on their feet until thrown. This was new and brutal ... and the crowd loved it.

Rosena had never seen her father so excited. He even stood up for a better view, but was pulled down by those behind him. Rosena looked at her mother who was smiling, happy to see John Bray enjoying himself.

After his second victim had been carried out, *The Taunton Terror* removed his mask, revealing a face with high cheekbones and eyes which lifted at their outside edges, reminding Rosena of a Chinese devil. He bowed grandly to the crowd, treating their abuse as if it was adulation. With a sweep of his arm he eventually quietened the mob, and proclaimed that he would fight again tomorrow, if there was any worthwhile opposition available.

There was a deep hush. No one dared even a titter in case it was taken as a challenge. Rosena could hear the groans of The Terror's last victim coming from behind the tented wall. Suddenly John Bray lifted his hand. 'I'll fight 'ee ... this time, tomorrow!'

Rosena gasped and she could hear her mother pleading, 'No, John!' Meanwhile, The Terror was nodding, and with great show he walked to the ringside, and shook John Bray's hand in acceptance of the challenge.

'Don't do it, John,' Emma was sobbing.

But there was a stubborn jut to John Bray's jaw and Rosena knew that he would not go back on his word.

As they left, he hoisted Rosena onto his shoulders. Emma Bray was angry with her husband. "Tis total madness!'

'Can't you understand?' he argued. "Tis a matter of pride.'

She muttered something about the stupidity of men, then trudged home in silence. 'That devil needs puttin' in his place!' John Bray muttered to himself.

Next morning, to escape the ill feeling between her parents, Rosena wandered down to the beach and gathered scallop shells. Her mother made earrings and necklaces which she sold at market. Now, the tide was out. Her father had once called this place a sunny, sandy, salty, seaweedy paradise.

She had gathered twenty shells, slipping them into her child's bucket, when her mother called her and she knew they were going back to the fair.

The tent was packed. John Bray was the only challenger that afternoon, and his wife and daughter were seated close to the ropes. Rosena glanced at her mother, seeing how she sat tight lipped, the smallpox scars standing out on her taut cheeks. When a man climbed into the ring and announced the name of John Bray, there was a tremendous cheer.

Suddenly the cheers changed to boos as *The Taunton Terror* made his entrance. To Rosena, he seemed a giant, the muscles of his chest glinting with grease. But it was his face, now unmasked, that frightened her the most. His Chinaman's eyes were narrowed, his lips twisted in an expression of hate.

As the bout commenced, he charged and caught John Bray a blow across the cheek, causing him to fall. The fisherman was up immediately, only to be caught again by The Terror's flashing knuckles. There was a fearsome crack - and Rosena screamed. Blinded by tears she turned her head away. Mother and daughter clung to each other. Rosena was convinced that her father was about to be killed. The grunts of the two men, mingled with the thud of falling bodies, continued for what seemed an age. Then suddenly the roar of the crowd rose deafeningly, and her mother cried out, "E's got him!'

Rosena dared another look, seeing her father's back turned towards them. It was glistening with sweat and blood. He had one knee firmly planted on the back of his prostrate opponent, and had forced his arm up to the shoulder blade. With a jerk he forced it even higher, bringing a screech from the Terror.

'Submit! Submit!' the crowd chanted.

Suddenly the fight was over. John Bray relented, rose and stood back. For ages, The Terror did not move, then gradually his legs stirred and he clambered totteringly up, his arm hanging limp, his head drooped. This time he did not acknowledge the jeers of the crowd. He raised his face, his pain-glazed eyes locking with those of John Bray, his lips forming vicious, threatening words that only John Bray heard. He waited, his finger pointed accusingly. When he was satisfied that his words had been understood, he climbed between the ropes and disappeared through a canvas flap.

Men were scrambling into the ring, congratulating John Bray. Rosena realised that, just as The Terror had fine muscles, so indeed did her father - but Emma hustled her from the tent. They stood alongside a deserted booth until John Bray eventually appeared, clutching his prize of a pound note. His face was bruised, his eye blackened, but he was smiling. When he had pulled on his shirt, he wanted to celebrate his victory by buying his wife and daughter toffee apples. Rosena accepted. Emma shook her head, saying she felt too ill.

When they reached home two hours later, Emma soothed her husband's bruises with ointment, still grumbling at his stupidity. Afterwards she told Rosena, 'Before your father became a fisherman, 'e worked down the tin mines. And before that, 'e was a wrestler. But when 'e married me, 'e gave it up - till today!'

'I'll never fight again, me dear,' John Bray promised.

Emma snorted with disbelief.

Something was troubling Rosena. 'Father,' she said, 'what did The Terror say to you when 'e left the ring? I saw 'is lips movin'.'

John Bray frowned and said nothing, but Emma prompted him: 'Yes, what did 'e say? We must know.'

He hesitated, then said, ''E swore 'e'd get 'is revenge, even if it took the rest of 'is life!'

Emma clicked her tongue in dismay. ''E's an evil man,' she said. ''E'll come back, I'm sure.'

'Don't go frettin',' John Bray said. 'More'n likely 'e's just a big bag of wind.'

Emma was not reassured. She warned Rosena not to wander far from the cottage.

For a long time memory of *The Taunton Terror* brooded over them, but during the next thirteen years until Emma Bray's death of scarlet fever, he did not return. Nor was his name ever mentioned. It was as if it was an oath, the mention of which would soil their tongues beyond cleansing.

Chapter Two

ALTHOUGH TOM LETHBRIDGE was twenty-seven, the same age as Rosena, he liked to assume an almost paternal manner. 'You should be more reserved, me dear,' he would say. 'Tid'n fittin' for a Cornish maid to speak with strangers, particularly men.' There was a twinkle in his eye, for he did not wish to clip her wings, yet he worried about her. Knowing this, had tempered her rebelliousness. Nonetheless she'd stamped her foot and thrown a scrap of seaweed at him.

Rosena had an unaffected grace sometimes mistaken for naivety. There was a healthy radiance in her face and her skin showed the duskiness common in many Cornish folk. Her eyes were compassionate, set well apart and strikingly hazel; they were quick to show the glisten of tears in laughter or grief. Her nose too was slightly up-turned, her chin firm, her mouth hinting a mobility that reflected her changing emotions. And in the spring of 1916, she possessed a restless spirit which not even she could explain.

This hot Sunday, after she had attended church with her father, she left the village and followed the path to the beach. She still wore her best cotton dress, printed with tiny roses; and a pretty bonnet decorated with imitation cherries. To walk after church was a habit of hers - a time when she spared herself from housework and could be alone with her thoughts. Today the words of Reverend Godfrey remained with her. He had spoken on the evils of war and the crippling sacrifices of human life which were being made across the Channel. The whole of northern France was pitted with trenches, dugouts and shell-holes, and men were dying every day. 'The lesson must be learned,' he had pleaded, tearfully. 'before it's too late.' Rosena also wept. She grieved the loss of young, male lives.

She remembered how army recruiters had come to the village, and there had been a band and much flag-waving. Within a few months casualty lists appeared in the local press. Three men from Megstow Quay had fallen; one had been in her class at school, and several more had been wounded. The villagers built a bonfire on the clifftops and burned an effigy of the Kaiser Wilheim II, the German war-lord.

Zeppelins had dropped bombs on London, and there was fear of invasion. In the West Country a black-out had been imposed and coastguards watched the sea for enemy submarines. Rosena yearned to make some contribution towards shortening the war.

Today she removed her shoes and hid them in the rocks. She hoisted her skirt up and waded through the shallows, the small waves creaming her tawny legs. Not very lady-like, Tom would chide, but he wasn't here to see her, though this evening he was coming to supper at the cottage and she suspected he would broach the subject of marriage. He was a fisherman from the next village, St Mags. As assistant coxswain on the local life-boat, he had proved his courage more than once during rough seas. It was not his fault that a crippled leg, received at birth, prevented him from going to war.

She sighed aloud. What would her answer be if he proposed? She didn't want to say she would marry him, but neither did she want to lose him. She enjoyed the comforting knowledge of his presence. Sometimes he seemed like a second, kindly father, even though he was no older than her.

Her father had long reproached her for not taking a husband, reminding her that everybody respected Tom. What was more, he had his own cottage, given to him by Squire Perhaver.

Rosena wasn't sure what she wanted from life, but somehow she felt the need to escape from Cornwall and see more of the world, although she knew she would never desert her father.

The sea stretched in lines of green, parallel with the shore, growing darker towards the horizon. As she waded through the shallows, a feeling of abandon grew in her and she felt as free as the herring-gulls which circled overhead. She started to sing and the sea swirled about her knees, sending an icy finger up inside her leg, giving her a delightful tingle of excitement.

Several times she scrambled across the rocks that separated the bays. Eventually, she left the sea and walked to the base of the cliffs. She paused beside the old wreck of a ship's rowing boat, then she started to climb the steep path upward. She placed her bare feet carefully on the rocky path, the climb making her pant and presently, the slated roof and pointed gables of a big house showed above the cliff-top. This she knew was Perhaver Manor, the house where Tom had been raised.

When she finished her climb, she gazed across the terraced garden to the back of the grey-stone building. For five years it had remained unoccupied, its windows un-curtained. In the village, tales were told about the high jinks and depravity of the Perhaver family whose home it had been. John Bray had advised his daughter to close her ears to such gossip for it was not fit for an innocent girl, but Rosena was fascinated by the talk. Enviously, she had wondered if the ghosts of the Perhavers still enjoyed their outrageous behaviour.

This Sabbath, she saw that the house had been transformed and the paraphernalia of workmen, ladders and scaffolding, were stacked neatly in the grounds. Curtains once again showed at the windows and the house had been re-painted. Gardeners had cut back the rhododendron bushes, restoring the lawns and planting tulip-beds. At the far end, a tennis court had been prepared.

Rosena had read in the newspaper that Perhaver Manor was to become a convalescent home for soldiers. Soon there would be an influx of young men arriving who had suffered and needed comforting. A Miss Florence Lebone of Truro had appealed for young ladies 'of good reputation' to assist in welfare work.

Rosena decided that she would write off, volunteering her services.

That evening, as their grandfather clock chimed seven, the cottage gate clicked and Rosena realised that soon she would have to make a decision. Her heart fluttered. Would she be promised by the end of the evening or not? The thought of marriage to Tom Lethbridge did not excite her, yet she reminded herself that he was a good man.

Sensing her agitation, Cedric the red-and-blue parrot squawked discordantly, hanging on the cage bars, plumage fluffed, looking murderous. She slipped a cloth over the cage to quieten him.

Her father, now greatly overweight, and with his hair gone white since the death of Emma, said, 'That bird'd whip the eye out of anybody 'e didn't fancy!' He had given Cedric to Rosena on her eighteenth birthday, having paid good money for him to a Spanish seaman. He'd never imagined that the creature would turn so vicious. But Rosena could soothe him and feed him from her lips.

She checked her hair in the mirror, then responded to the knock at the door. Tom Lethbridge stood there, clutching the bunch of red tulips from his garden. He was a tall, well-built man and now his Cornish-brown face was beaming with happiness. 'Pretty flowers for a prettier girl,' he smiled.

She took the tulips and pressed her face into them, savouring the scent, then she kissed his cheek. He had been a friend since childhood, but she had never associated him with passion or romance.

There was about him a rich aroma of tobacco and fish. Handling and frequently gutting the catches, Rosena knew that they all smelt of fish. They didn't notice it half the time, but visitors did.

Tom had grown up at Perhaver Manor where his mother had been in service, but she had died when he was two. Thereafter, Squire Perhaver ensured the boy was well cared for by his cook, Mattie - and when the manor was closed and the Perhaver family went north, the squire had given Tom one of his cottages at St Mags, knowing that he was now capable of earning his living as a fisherman.

Rosena led the way into the parlour. The room was small, decorated with brass candlesticks and small ornaments. She had polished the big copper kettle till it gleamed. The table was set for supper. Tom ducked his head as he entered, favouring his crippled right leg and John Bray greeted him with a smile and a nod towards his best brandy.

'We should've been at sea today,' Tom said. ''T'was full of fish just waitin' to be netted.'

''Tis the best season we've had for many a year,' her father commented.

Hearing the two men chatting, she wondered if Tom had more in common with her father than he did with her. Even so she was conscious of his eyes drifting in her direction and twice she met them and smiled. She was ashamed of her feelings, but she told herself that marriage to him would be like a gentle trap. He would never leave Cornwall nor consider a different way of life.

She bustled around, carefully arranging the tulips in a vase.

The meal was a success - Nattlin pie and tatie cake, followed by apple pie with clotted cream. The men ate with relish, coming for second helpings.

Afterwards, she cleared the dishes and started washing-up. Tom followed her into the kitchen, found a tea cloth and began the drying-up. Living alone, he was no stranger to domestic chores. Rosena knew he was gathering his thoughts.

'Me dear,' he at last said, 'I've known 'ee a long time ... and I love 'ee dearly.' He dried two plates, stacked them. 'I'd like 'ee to be my wife, Rosena.'

Now he had spoken the actual words she felt dizzy. He reached out and steadied her. 'What's wrong, me dear?'

'Tom ... I ... nothin's wrong.'

'Rosena, your father 'as given his consent. I know I could make 'ee happy.'

She turned towards him, her hands were wet from the dishes but he didn't seem to care. He took her in his arms and hugged her. 'I do love 'ee,' he repeated. 'Will 'ee say yes?'

She felt the solid warmth of his body. She knew he was as reliable as the shore-line rocks but ...

'I do appreciate your kindness,' she started, tears building in her eyes. 'But I can't be your wife ... not yet.' She paused, knowing that she meant 'not ever'. 'Tom, I don't feel ready.'

'But, Rosena ...' He was taken aback, though the warmth of his embrace did not slacken. After a moment his hands slid up to her shoulders. He held her away from him, gazed into her face. 'You'm certain?'

'Yes, Tom.'

He sighed heavily. 'I'll not rush 'ee into anythin', Rosena. I'll wait, and when you'm ready, I'll be ready too. I promise.'

21

Ten minutes later when they returned to the parlour, she had dried her eyes. 'Rosena's not ready for marriage yet,' Tom said sadly. He reached out and gave her hand an understanding squeeze. 'But I'll be here when she changes 'er mind.'

John Bray's face dropped. 'You'm a good man, Tom,' he said. 'You deserve a good wife.'

Tom gazed at Rosena. 'I'll 'ave a good wife one day. I'll be patient.' Rosena wavered but she did not speak. Instead she lit the oil lamp and drew the curtains. They all had a glass of brandy and they did not talk of marriage again, but when Tom eventually left, his face was downcast. She saw him to the door, watching him limp away.

Her father was displeased. 'Your mother was stubborn, but you beat 'er 'ands down. Take care or you'll be left on the shelf.'

She didn't reply, but she felt relieved that uncertainty no longer weighed her down.

On the following Thursday she rose early, raked out the range and re-fuelled the embers. She cooked a breakfast of eggs and piping hot potato cake, and presently saw her father off to work. She emptied the slop pail and fetched water from the village pump, then she swept the cottage thoroughly. She washed her father's shirts, put them through the community mangle and chatted to Stella Bines, the cobbler's wife, who awaited her turn. Rosena was fastening the shirts to dry on the furze bushes near the cottage, when Harry Ansell the postman appeared, looking smart in his blue uniform. 'Letter for 'ee from Truro, me dear.'

'Oh 'Arry, I've been expectin' that!'

She opened the envelope, feeling breathless with sudden excitement.

'What is it, me dear?' Harry's eyes were crinkled with curiosity.

''Tis from a Miss Lebone,' Rosena explained. 'She's organisin' volunteers to 'elp at the new nursin' 'ome for soldiers up Perhaver Manor. My application's been accepted.'

Harry arched his eyebrows. 'You got to be careful. Wounded or not, soldiers are all the same. They only want one thing from a woman.'

'I want to do somethin' to help the war effort,' Rosena said, and she fetched him a glass of lemonade. She had a feeling that the influx of young men would be like a window to the outside world.

Harry looked at her. She was a warm-hearted, sensitive girl. Her sensual, graceful movements were uninhibited and innocent, yet he knew she would awake lust in men's minds. He said: 'I 'opes no man'll ever take advantage of 'ee, me dear.'

She laughed. 'I might take advantage of them.'

At the quay, John Bray sat on a mooring bollard. He cursed the rheumatism that troubled him these days. He yearned for the fitness he'd had when he'd been a champion wrestler, fitness preserved by hard work in the tin-mines, and, later on, when he'd become a fisherman, by hauling in heavily laden nets.

Close by, but somehow apart from him, were three other fishermen, busy repairing nets - John Doble, Edward Godolphin and Will Lanyon. John Bray smiled as he heard Will Lanyon comment on the fate of the village baker, Seth Trew: 'People won't buy 'is bread no more.'

'Should think not,' said young John Doble, snorting with disgust. 'Wouldn't fancy 'im kneadin' the dough, not after where 'e's bin.'

A week ago, Seth Trew had tottered from *The Cherry Bowl* after a binge. The night had been dark, he'd lost his way and somehow fallen into the bin where villagers emptied their slop-pails. The smell had lingered on him and had driven away his customers.

'Bet 'e won't be so careless next time!' Will Lanyon said, but John Bray did not join in their laughter.

The sun glinted on the water of the little harbour where the luggers of the fishing fleet were moored - two-masted, black-tarred craft, devoid of superstructure. Their drabness contrasted with the exotic ring of their names. John Bray's lugger was called *Silver Cloud*.

Now, as he bound up breaks in the net, his thoughts drifted to Rosena. He wished she'd accepted Tom's proposal.

She was a perfect housekeeper, and there was always a good meal on the table when he came home. She filled her days with activity. The only respite she allowed herself was to read her books, and go for Sunday-morning walks.

But it was time she found a husband. Of course he'd miss her if she married, but he hated the thought of her being chained to him until he died. He hoped she'd give him grandchildren. Emma would have loved that too. To have a family had been her great wish - but in the end she'd had to be satisfied with one child, lucky to have that.

Emma's face loomed in his mind as it had been on the night of a shipwreck in 1890, when she'd suffered in childbirth. Ever since, the knowledge of his sin had been locked inside him. With Tilly Triggs the midwife now dead, he prayed that he would eventually carry the secret of Rosena's birth to his own grave and nobody else would ever know. He shuddered, then forced his thoughts onto more pleasant things.

Chapter Three

TWO WEEKS LATER the first wounded soldiers arrived at Perhaver Manor. They came in ambulances. Some were on stretchers, some in wheelchairs, others walked with crutches. Some had undergone amputations. Others had terrible gas burns. Most wore blue uniforms, with khaki caps, white shirts and red ties.

The warm, West-Country sun was shining brightly when Miss Florence Lebone led her brood of lady-volunteers up the driveway to the house. Rosena, walking at the back, was wearing a violet-coloured dress with purple ribbon threaded through its neckline, and a straw-hat with imitation cherries. To her embarrassment, their arrival attracted a raucous cheer, and some remarks which were not at all decorous. Miss Lebone assumed a superior air. 'Look them straight in the eye, girls,' she advised. 'Don't flinch ... and when you talk with them, insist they call you 'Miss'.'

Rosena felt she would wilt shyly before this male onslaught. But then she reminded herself that these men had been through the equivalent of hell. Many were younger than she was, and, in reality, their banter was good humoured - and she told herself that they deserved any indulgences which might lift their spirits.

Soon, the volunteers were carrying trays of refreshments from the kitchens to the lawn. The volunteers were welcome, for they gave well-earned relief to the members of the Voluntary Aid Detachment. The latter, known as 'VADs', were dedicated ladies who assisted the more qualified Queen Alexandra Nurses. Further assistance was provided by a few local girls, employed as auxiliaries.

Chairs and tables had been set out upon the grass, and men sat around, some in their own wheelchairs, playing board games, smoking, reading, talking. Now the shyness had left Rosena and she was determined to make herself useful. Inwardly, she was weeping at the sight of the terrible injuries inflicted upon young male bodies, but Mrs Lebone had said, 'You mustn't show sentimentality. That's not what we're here for.'

After tea, Rosena and the other helpers joined the patients on the lawn, playing games, chatting and admiring family photographs. Rosena found herself sitting with a man from Yorkshire who had been blinded in the Somme Offensive. She read to him from Dickens's *Tale of Two Cities,* which she'd brought. He seemed to appreciate the story, though presently he went to sleep.

It was then that she noticed another man watching her. He was sitting nearby, his crutches propped against a table. She realised he'd been sketching her.

She found herself gazing into his grey eyes. He was handsome, with dark hair sleeked back and a luxuriant moustache.

Suddenly he smiled. 'I 'ope you don't mind,' and his voice was rich Welsh, 'but you look ... angelic. I couldn't resist sketchin' you. If I 'ad my oils 'ere, I'd paint a full portrait.'

Her cheeks flushed. She said, 'Whether or not I mind, depends on 'ow kind the sketch is.'

'No picture can do you full justice,' he said seriously. She could see that he was strongly built. He did not rise; his leg was too stiff, but he held up his work for her to see.

'You've made me look b-beautiful,' she stammered, 'which I'm not.'

'But you are beautiful, Miss. You're too beautiful to stay 'idden 'ere in Cornwall.'

His words had made her tingle. She felt desperate to extend the conversation. She said, ''Ave 'ee done other drawin's?'

'Oh yes ... but they're not pretty.' He held out the pad and she moved closer and took it.

She turned the pages and was horrified. The drawings were vivid and real - scenes from the trenches, of men with hideous wounds, their faces contorted with agony, of barbed wire, of corpses. At the bottom of each drawing he had signed - Gareth Williams.

She returned the pad. 'It must be awful in the trenches,' she said, realising how inadequate her words were.

'Far worse than any drawin's can depict,' Gareth murmured. 'I 'ope it don't distress you too much, Miss.'

She shook her head. ''Tis only right we should know what you've suffered. You must've been glad to get away from it.'

His expression was full of hopelessness. 'I wish the war was over - but my mates are still there, those that survive, and I feel that I'm lettin' them down, being 'ere.'

Rosena didn't know what to say.

He took a tin of tobacco from the pocket of his blue tunic. With fascination she watched him expertly roll a cigarette. His hands were thick with fingers that were blunt at the ends - not at all as she'd imagined an artist's hands should be. After he'd lit up and taken a draw, he said: 'My leg's much better. In a few weeks I'll be sent back to the Front.'

The prospect of a brave man returning to face death, gave her a choking feeling, but suddenly Mrs Lebone appeared, full of jolly bustle, indicating that the volunteers' visit was over. The afternoon had melted into the softer haze of evening, and across the lawn a flock of house martins was swooping, feeding upon the tiny insects that thickened the air.

Gareth looked at Rosena. 'You'll come again, won't you? What's your name?'

'Rosena,' she said. 'Rosena Bray.'

'Ro-sena,' he said, rolling her name on his tongue. 'A good name is better than precious ointment. That's what it says in the Bible.'

Miss Lebone was listening, so Rosena said, 'But you're supposed to call me 'Miss'.' Her officious words seemed stupid.

He laughed. She imagined him singing hymns with the same Welsh richness. 'Yes, Miss Ro-sena,' he said meekly. 'I must obey the rules. But you call me Gareth ... and please accept this.' He tore the sketch of her from the pad. 'A gift, it is.'

She took it. 'I'll treasure it.' she said. And then a strange thought came to her. I seem to make a habit of meeting men with crippled legs. Firstly Tom ... now Gareth Williams.

That night, at the cottage, she felt excited. The next visit to Perhaver Manor was on Wednesday. 'Gareth,' she whispered to herself, 'Gareth, Gareth, Gareth.' She loved the sound of his name. He had said she was beautiful. No man had ever called her that. For a long time she gazed at herself in the winged mirrors of her dressing table, unpinning her dark hair, allowing it to cascade down. She viewed herself from different angles. Then she studied the drawing. Presently she slipped it into a drawer. She didn't want to show it to her father. It was something that was intimate between her and Gareth.

'Me dear,' John Bray said at supper, 'you'm flushed. What 'appened up Perhaver?'

'Nothin' 'appened, not really,' she said - but inwardly she hoped it soon would.

On her next visit, she found Gareth sitting at his usual place on the lawn, sketching. Having touched his hand, she left him and set about her duties as a volunteer. Industrious by nature, she worked, carrying trays from the kitchen, pausing often with a cheerful greeting for the patients. She had brought some books and gave them out. She was mindful of Gareth's gaze following her and her entire body felt as if it were glowing.

He sat, waiting for her to join him, a faint smile on his face. She came, with a board and draughts. He gave her a rose. She held it to her nostrils, laughing, then gently kissed it, wishing it were his lips.

They pretended to play draughts, moving the pieces but not giving the game much attention. They somehow contrived to let their fingers touch. Presently, when Miss Lebone was at the other end of the garden, he placed his hand completely upon hers and, feigning surprise, she looked at him and he laughed and then so did she.

Presently she asked, 'When did you get wounded, Gareth?'

'Six months ago, it was. Shrapnel shattered my leg. But I was lucky. No gangrene - just splintered bone. I've 'ad three operations - the last one on my twenty-eighth birthday.'

'You'm married?' She tried to sound indifferent. He seemed not to hear. 'Gareth, 'ave you a wife?' she repeated.

He gazed at her and laughed. 'Who'd 'ave me? I've been too busy fightin' for King and Country. I'm in The Midland Rifles. They put a lot of us painters and sculptors into one regiment. They probably felt we'd unleash all our frustration against the bloody Hun.' She noticed how his mouth remained slightly open, his full lips quivering. 'I've 'ad a lot of mates killed.' He placed his sketch pad on the table before her.

Turning the pages, she said: 'You truly capture the men's expressions and the fear in their eyes.'

They sat in silence. Presently he slipped it into his pocket. 'Well, enough of that,' he said, smiling. She noticed him staring at her hands and she felt ashamed. Years of working with other women on the quayside, gutting fish, ripping out the offal, sometimes when the weather was bitter, had made her hands red and chapped. She slipped them beneath the table.

She felt Gareth was gently mocking her, but he said, 'Tell me about yourself, Miss Ro-sena. That'll be interestin'.'

She said, 'I've lived a very unadventurous life.' She related the simple recollections of her childhood. She told him how, on the hilly road to school, the children were often made to dismount from the bus and push the vehicle up the gradient, the strain being too great for the horses alone, and this had always seemed a huge joke. She told Gareth about her mother, Emma Bray, and how her life had been made misery by her ugly smallpox scars. She told him about the grief she'd suffered when her mother had died of scarlet fever. He murmured soothing, sympathetic sounds. 'In the Bible, it says, 'Be of good comfort, my daughter. The Lord of 'eaven and earth gave thee joy for this thy sorrow.'"

He's seen so much death and lost many of his close friends, she thought. He understands how cruel bereavement is.

After she'd finished telling him about herself, they sat looking into each other's eyes, and she felt they didn't need words to communicate. She noticed how his eyes were grey, yet the pupils darkened to black almost hypnotically.

'Ro-sena,' he murmured, her name rolling slowly from his tongue, 'let me show you round the 'ouse. Some wonderful paintin's, there are.'

'But surely walkin' is difficult for 'ee?'

'With your 'elp, Miss Ro-sena,' he said, 'I can do anythin'!'

She laughed. She noticed how little strands of ginger showed amid the darker hairs of his moustache.

When they stood up, she was surprised by his tallness and powerful, muscular body. Most of the other men were emaciated, but Gareth clearly possessed the physical strength to tolerate hardship.

They went into the house and up the grand staircase of curving marble. 'Squire Perhaver and the present-day Perhaver family live in Yorkshire,' Gareth explained, which she knew but of course didn't say. 'They've allowed their paintin's to be displayed 'ere to keep our morale up.'

They gazed at ancestral portraits - men with white beards and wing collars; beautiful women in fine gowns, with jewels glinting.

'They do say,' he said, 'the gentry used to get up to high jinks along these corridors.'

I know,' she responded. 'Father told me that such gossip wasn't fittin' for an innocent girl's ears.'

They sauntered along, the sun streaming through the high windows, her arm around his. The house had been renovated most thoroughly, with its elegant doorways, great fireplaces, and sculptured ceilings gleaming.

On the first floor, there were impressive pictures of battles, of men in uniform and graceful horses with arched necks. Gareth revealed his great enthusiasm for works of art. He explained about colours and perspective, about how the composition of pictures was based on a series of triangles. Much of it she did not absorb. She was too busy enjoying his voice and the closeness of his body as she lent him support.

'An artist's brush is like a magic wand,' he told her. 'It gives life to dead canvas.'

Eventually, as they stood on the landing of the second floor, he showed her the picture of a young Ensign, resplendent in his plumed bicorne hat, red-and-white uniform and dress sword. He was standing with his bride on their wedding day. The face of the girl was brimming with happiness, and she matched the man's elegance perfectly. Her gown was of soft satin, embroidered with rich gold thread. Beneath the painting was a plaque stating:

> Ensign John Perhaver, 32nd (Cornwall) Regiment, and his bride Alice.
> Ensign Perhaver was killed six months later at the Battle of Waterloo.

''Tis truly sad,' she murmured.

He nodded, holding her arm tightly. Presently, they returned to the ground floor, and he showed her large rooms equipped to accommodate a dozen convalescents. Two female auxiliaries were remaking the beds, whispering and giggling as they worked. Most of the patients were well enough to be outside.

On their way back to the gardens, she was so attentive to Gareth, that she overlooked a step, her toe caught and she fell. Gareth dropped his crutch and helped her up, his face showing concern.

''Tis all right!' she gasped, embarrassed. As she smoothed her skirt down, she noticed that he was walking quite easily. 'You do seem all right yourself,' she said. 'You don't need my support at all.'

He looked rueful. 'I wasn't goin' to lose the chance of 'avin' you 'old my arm,' and they both laughed.

'You'm a good actor,' she said.

They went out onto the lawn, and some of the men were playing football, even some who were on crutches. Some fell over, but they were soon up again.

'There's a concert next week,' Gareth told her. 'Would you like to come?'

'Yes,' she said. She'd have jumped over the moon if he'd wanted.

'It's grand bein' with you, Miss Ro-sena,' he told her. 'Like a tonic.'

She realised how little she knew about his past. 'You know all about me,' she said. 'I want to know about you, Gareth.'

'Oh well,' he murmured, 'let's sit down then.' They returned to their seats upon the lawn.

Gareth gingerly lowered himself and placed his crutch on the table. She wanted to help him, to fuss over him, but he was able to manage himself. He rolled a cigarette, gathering his thoughts. He lit up, took a long draw.

'I grew up in the Rhondda Valley,' he said. 'We were a coal minin' family, you know. My brother Owen was killed in a minin' accident. Left a wife and a little'un.'

She wondered if she'd been right to make him recall the sadness of the past. 'Oh Gareth. It must've been awful.' She wished her powers of expression were more adequate.

He pursed his lips, nodded, then went on. 'I 'ad this flair for artistic work. My family couldn't understand it. They reckoned I should be down the pits, not paintin' fancy patterns on canvas. Anyway, when I was eighteen, I 'ad a bust up with my dad, left 'ome. I went to Cardiff, stayed with an artist friend and 'e taught me the techniques of the great painters. Afterwards, I travelled to London, worked in Covent Garden, 'umpin' crates in the vegetable market. I earned enough money to go to art college. After a year, I sold my first paintin' - but then the war started and I joined the Midland Rifles and went to France. And, after certain unpleasant events, I ...' He paused.

'Yes,' she prompted.

'I met you! And, Ro-sena, I love the look in your eyes when you're ... embarrassed!'

She felt joyous. She wanted to listen to his soft, Welsh voice for ever. 'Do you ever go 'ome to see your parents?' she asked.

'I go back, but not to my parents. We've never patched things up. When I go back, my sister-in-law Bronwyn gives me lodgin's. She owns a boardin' house in Trethomas. It belonged to 'er mam before 'er. Good job she 'ad an income, losin' Owen and all.'

Rosena nodded, then she asked, ''Ow long will 'ee be here at Perhaver?'

'Doctor says I'm to 'and in my crutches tomorrow and use a stick, so I must be gettin' better.'

'I'm glad.' But she only half meant it. She didn't want him to go away.

Chapter Four

THAT NIGHT SHE DREAMED that they were again gazing at the painting of Ensign Perhaver and his bride. The pair were looking so happy, little imagining that he would be dead within six months, but suddenly, in the dream, it was not Ensign Perhaver and Alice in the picture, but her and Gareth, and on the plaque, the wording had been changed to read:

Gareth Williams and his bride Rosena ...
Gareth was killed six months later on the battlefield ...

    She cried out, waking herself. Alarmed, her father came rushing from his bedroom, making the old timbers of the cottage creak beneath his weight.
    ''Tis a dream,' Rosena gasped, 'only a dream.'
    He offered to fetch her a drink, but she declined. For a while he stayed, wanting to comfort her and not knowing how, but presently he murmured, 'Get some sleep then, me dear. You'll feel better come mornin',' and he left her.
    She lay back on her bed. She tried to dismiss the dream from her head - but it had seemed so real. It plagued her, sending dark whispers through her mind.
    She was desperate for Gareth. If she closed her eyes, his face was there ... his grey eyes, sometimes twinkling, sometimes vague as memories haunted him ... his bushy eyebrows, his full lips, his teeth, his moustache flecked with sandy hairs.
    She no longer restricted herself to the visits of the Help Society, but went every day to see him. Every second spent with him was precious, and everybody was so kind at Perhaver Manor, seeming to understand her feelings. Of course her father realised that she had fallen in love, and one Sunday he surprised her by suggesting that he'd better meet this Welshman and see if he was worthy of his daughter.
    'You'll like 'im,' she said, her eyes sparkling joy. ''E's the finest I've ever known!'

That afternoon, Gareth stood gazing out from a first floor window. He watched Rosena and her bulky father approaching along the driveway.
    'That Rosena Bray do seem to be gettin' hot on 'ee, bringin' her dad and all.'
    Gareth frowned. The girl standing next to him was Jenny Killigrew, eighteen years old and from St Mags. She was an auxiliary. Her voice was

light and fluttery, and she frequently pursed her lips, as if to invite a kiss, and Matron was always grumbling at her for being too familiar with the patients.

'Bein' poorly seems to make men randy, 'specially you,' she murmured, hugging herself close to Gareth's back, pressing her young breasts against him. 'And you always get what you wants. You should've been an actor not an artist.'

'To be a good lover,' he said, 'you 'ave to be a good actor.'

'You mean you don't mean all they things you say?'

'At the time, I do.'

He shrugged her off. She sighed, then said, 'I guess you won't be satisfied till you've 'ad that Rosena - proper, I mean. Another one of your conquests, eh?'

''Twon't be in a broom cupboard, Jenny Killigrew,' he retorted.

She giggled, then whispered, 'You'll soon realise she won't hold a candle to me, though.'

Gareth laughed. 'Go make somebody else's bed for a while.'

'I'll do as I please. You don't own me!'

'Do as you bloody well like,' Gareth muttered to himself. 'All women are fools, anyway.'

Jennie Killigrew was right of course. He wouldn't rest until he had tasted all the delights Rosena had to offer.

By the time the Brays had reached the back-lawns, Gareth was sitting in his usual place, prepared to meet them. Other patients were waiting on the lawn for their visitors, while some men were knocking a ball over the tennis net, laughing as they missed their shots.

'Gareth,' Rosena announced, 'I'd like 'ee to meet my father.'

Gareth bowed his head in greeting. 'I'm honoured, Mister Bray. Ro-sena's told me so much about you.'

The two men shook hands, John Bray set his considerable weight down at the table alongside Gareth, and soon they were discussing the war. Rosena felt proud of Gareth. He was so handsome, so confident. How could anybody not fall in love with him immediately?

She decided to fetch a tray of tea, and when she reached the kitchen, she found Jenny Killigrew at work. The girl gave her a resentful glare. 'I've only just put kettle on,' she said. 'You'll 'ave to come back in ten minutes.'

Rosena nodded. What was wrong with the girl?

To pass the time, she left the kitchen by the side door and walked along a path she had not previously taken. She reached a large conservatory, and through its open door glimpsed something that shocked her.

Propped up in a wheelchair, was a man without either legs or arms. His eyes gazed ahead, totally blank, and one of the VADs was feeding him with a teaspoon. More men lay in their beds, their faces ghastly white. Others were hidden behind screens, and she could hear the clink of surgical instruments.

She backed away, shaken. What right had she to be happy when others suffered like this?

Carrying the tray, she returned to the lawn in sober mood, but Gareth was exuberant, talking with John Bray as if he'd known him all his life, and her mood soon lightened.

'Rosena 'as promised to come to the concert party next Friday,' Gareth explained. 'It'll be very good, I'm sure.'

''Twill be the first concert party I've ever been to,' she admitted.

'Well, make sure you get 'ome before too late,' her father warned.

Gareth smiled. 'I'll make certain of that, Mister Bray. Rosena is a very precious person.'

And so they talked on, and Gareth produced his sketches. He'd added to his collection with some of the local scenery. Eventually John Bray indicated that it was time to go home. He was out at sea tonight, and Rosena knew that she must cook him a meal before he left. Shortly they were saying their farewells. As her father turned away, Gareth gave her a smile, his grey eyes glinting a secret intimacy, his lips moving in a soundless whisper she was convinced was, 'I love you.' She smiled happily and suppressing an urge to kiss his lips with a passion for everyone to see.

Shortly, as the Brays plodded homeward along the sands, she asked, 'What do you think of 'im, Father? Don't you think 'e's wonderful?'

John Bray was slightly ahead. He didn't answer. She grew impatient. She desperately wanted her father's endorsement of the love she felt.

'You do like 'im, don't 'ee?' she demanded.

At last John Bray stopped, swung around. 'Don't trust 'im, Rosena,' he said. ''E's far too glib. Mark my words. 'E'll use 'ee if 'e can, then be off.'

'Father!' she could hardly believe her ears. 'You want me to find a husband. When I do find a man I love, you speak ill of 'im!'

He reached out, rested his hands on her tremulous shoulders. 'Me dear, I just don't want to see 'ee 'urt, that's all.'

She howled with anguish, pushing him away. She ran back to the cottage, half blinded by tears, her father languishing breathlessly behind. Within a half hour, his meal was on the table. She served it without speaking, then she went upstairs to her room and slammed the door.

When John Bray went to bed, she pretended to be asleep. Next morning, for the first time ever, he left without her kiss and once she was alone, she regretted her behaviour. If anything happened to him out at sea, she'd never forgive herself. She knew he meant well, but he didn't seem to understand that she was old enough to reach her own decisions, that when she married it would be the man of her choice, not his.

The night of the concert came. Rosena sat next to Gareth on a wooden bench, and the audience was packed so tightly that nobody noticed how she drew his hand into her lap, raised her pelvis and allowed him to gently caress her. She became aware of her nipples hardening beneath her dress. They joined in the sing-song. *'Pack Up Your Troubles', 'It's a Long Way to Tipperary'.* There was a magician who actually sawed his lady-partner in two, and the audience screamed for the surgeons to stitch her together again, but none appeared and shortly the lady walked onto the stage in one piece, without even a tear in her sequined costume. She bowed to thunderous applause.

The next act could have been an anti-climax, but it wasn't. The comedian's jokes were really crude, but Rosena laughed. She'd never realised that people joked about bodily functions in that way.

After the concert, Rosena and Gareth found themselves standing alone in a corridor and suddenly Gareth's arms were around her and his lips were on her lips - and her heart and every part of her tingling body seemed drawn to the sweetness of his mouth. Oh God, she thought as she whirled through space, I want Gareth - completely. But suddenly they were no longer alone, and he took her hand and they walked with the others into the gardens.

'Come again tomorrow, my petal,' Gareth whispered. 'Doctor says I can go for a walk, if I've got somebody to look after me.'

She nodded. She pressed herself against him, drawing his lips to hers, not caring who saw. 'I'll do whatever you want, Gareth,' she whispered, and then she left him, running home, praying that tomorrow would come quickly. It would be the first time that she would be alone with Gareth outside the convalescent home. Her father would not approve. But, she decided, her father would not know. Why make him worry about her even more?

Next afternoon they went down the cliff-path, and beneath them, the warm sun was turning the sea into a carpet of glinting diamonds. They reached the beach, removed their shoes and left them in a secret, rocky place. He was hot and removed his blue jacket, resting it across his shoulder. He loosened his red tie and undid the top button of his shirt, and they walked barefooted with their arms around each other, his hand cupping her breast, touching her in a way no other man ever had. He carried his stick but hardly needed it. She was wearing her violet-coloured dress and her pretty bonnet. Sometimes they waded through cold pools.

'I could walk to the end of the earth,' Rosena exclaimed.
He sighed. 'I wish I could, but my leg wouldn't let me.'
'Poor Gareth,' she murmured.

They turned back towards Megstow Quay, splashing through the shallows. She had hoisted her skirts; he had rolled his trousers up. The coolness of the small waves did nothing to cool his passion and he sensed that he wouldn't have long to wait now.

Suddenly she pointed to something on the water. 'An injured gull,' she said. 'Its wing looks hurt.' She waded to the bird, seeing how exhausted it was. 'There's fishin' twine tangled round its wing. 'Tis all blood soaked.'

She made gentle cooing sounds, reached down and took the bird in her hands. It did not struggle but allowed her to untangle the twine. The wing didn't seem to be broken and she replaced it in its rightful position and smoothed the ruffled feathers. She cradled the bird like a baby. Presently she held it above her head.

'Doesn't want to leave you,' Gareth observed. He watched her, knowing what a lovely painting the scene would make: The tawny maiden, dainty bonnet on her head, skirts tucked in, standing in the foam, her compassion focused on the bird she was holding towards the heavens.

All at once it flapped its wings and rose away from her, soaring and gliding above the sea and Rosena smiled happily.

He swung his gaze around. 'I'm tired, Ro-sena. Let's sit awhile. Look, there's an old rowin' boat up there at the top of the beach. Let's go there.'

She nodded, followed him meekly up the sand, sensing that he was feigning tiredness and that his mind was on other things. An old, long abandoned boat was in the shadow of the cliff. It was a total wreck, its rotting timbers showing the flaking whiteness of paint. He climbed over its side, supporting her as she followed. She was conscious of her heart beat as he spread his jacket for her to sit down on the boat's curving bottom. 'Mustn't get that pretty skirt messed up,' he said as he sat next to her. Then, in a whisper, he added, 'Quite a little nest 'ere. Just you and me. Lie back, my petal.'

She'd dreamed of this moment, but now she hesitated because the warning voices of her father or Tom were in her mind, but she forced them away. She unpinned her hat, placed it carefully on one of the cross-seats. 'My God,' Gareth murmured, 'I mustn't crush your cherries!' She smiled, loosened her dark hair and allowed it to fall about her shoulders, then she rested herself back. High above her, she could see gulls swirling around the cliff-top, but their cries seemed a thousand miles away.

He smoothed her cheeks with his fingers, then drew the hair away from her face. 'As brown as the forest, your eyes,' he murmured, 'and much, much more beautiful. Oh, Ro-sena, love ... I've waited so long for this,' and then his lips pressed down upon hers and she accepted them with welcoming softness. No man had kissed her like this before - lips, tongues, hungry to mingle, the homely scent of his tobacco seeping into her every sense.

She scarcely realised that his fingers had pulled open her blouse. She half raised her hand to restrain him, too late to prevent him drawing down the top of her bodice so that cool air touched her where it had never done before. She submitted to his gaze, closing her eyes, letting his voice wash over her ... 'Oh, my petal, you are so ... beautiful. I would dearly love to paint you ...' And suddenly a warm, exultant feeling filled her, and her shyness was replaced by a pride in her body which he so admired.

He touched his lips to her hardened nipple, drew it deep into his mouth, sending her skimming into the heavens. He caressed her. She felt as if she was burning. He loosened her skirts, drawing them upwards until his fingers found the elastic top of her knickers, hooked on and tugged them down across the smoothness of her belly, but she resisted him, not raising her bottom. An image of her father's stern face probed into her mind. If he could see me now he'd go mad.

'Gareth,' she groaned, 'this is my first time. If I let 'ee have your way ... will 'ee promise to marry me?'

'My petal, there's nothin' I want more!'

Her resistance crumbled. The sudden ruthlessness of his strong hands startled her as they moved downward to her lush quim, and she cried out as her maidenhead became a chalice from which he drank to the full.

Chapter Five

THROUGH THE SUMMER DAYS, she watched his recovery continue. Soon he had dispensed with his stick completely, but not with her arm. She had surrendered her virginity, but so sure was she of him, that she felt no remorse. Sometimes the fierceness in his love-making frightened her, but she concealed the rips in her clothing with needle-work and believed that he would become more tender once they were married.

She enjoyed their long walks, their conversations and laughter. Often, she was content to sit, watching him as he sketched. He did some more drawings of her. He longed to have his oils here, so he could paint a full portrait, but he'd left them in Cardiff with his friend.

'To paint you, Ro-sena,' he told her, 'would be my master-piece.' His eyes glowed at the thought. Presently he said, 'They've given me a week-end leave. I want to visit my sister-in-law at Trethomas. She's got a little girl. I like to make sure they're all right.'

'Of course.' Rosena remembered how his brother had been killed in a mining disaster. How good it was of Gareth, she thought, to make sure his dependants were coping. 'Can I come too?' she suddenly asked. 'I'd love to meet Bronwyn.'

'No,' he said. 'T'wouldn't be fair. Her boardin' 'ouse is that full, she can scarcely lodge me, let alone a visitor.'

Rosena was disappointed, but she did not argue.

At the weekend, with him gone away, her first inclination was to walk aimlessly on the sands, dreaming of him, but instead she concentrated on work. At home, she cleaned the cottage from top to bottom with an energy which left her father amazed. On Saturday afternoon she was at Perhaver Manor, applying herself assiduously to her welfare duties, and on Sunday she attended St Arthur's Church and prayed that the day would pass quickly. Gareth returned in the evening, and they were together again come Monday. 'Bronwyn's workin' far too 'ard,' he told her. 'She's got six guests. Grateful for my 'elp, she was.'

During the following month, August, they saw each other every day except for two weekends when he visited Trethomas.

She wanted the whole world to know about their love. Even her father reluctantly realised that he couldn't staunch it. She wished Gareth would speak of marriage, but he did not. Still, she trusted him profoundly, even at the moments when he seemed to drift away from her, his eyes vague. Something was clearly troubling him - something in which, she sensed, she had no part. Perhaps he was tormented by memories of the war, but she did not press him. When he's ready, she told herself, he'll speak the words I want to hear.

The medical-board had been convened in the old dining-room of Perhaver Manor, and when Gareth entered, the three officers were sitting at the far-end table. He closed the door and stood, seemingly ignored, as the officers discussed in low, confidential voices an earlier case.

After a moment one of the officers reprimanded him. 'You forgot to salute, Rifleman Williams!'

Gareth brought his hand up to his cap. Black hatred for the three officers swept over him.

'Sit down, please!'

He moved towards the table and perched on a chair, feeling uneasy. He only recognised one officer - Major Griffiths who was in command of the convalescent home. The other two, a red-tabbed colonel and a major were external consultants who had come down from London to conduct the medical board.

The colonel, a rotund man, was gazing at Gareth's file. 'A displaced knee-cap,' he said, 'and compound fracture of the fibula! It happened in France. You did it in a fall. Still, the surgery seems to have worked.' He thumbed backwards through the pages. 'Doesn't say how you came to fall, Rifleman Williams.'

Gareth cleared his throat, thinking: Mind your own bloody business, but his lips said, 'I slipped, sir... climbin' through a window.'

'God, it must've been an upstairs window to shatter your leg like that!'

'Yes, sir.'

The colonel gave him an odd look, then he grinned. 'Sounds as if he was escaping from some irate Frenchman who'd just caught him in bed with his wife!'

'Lucky the leg was the only thing he injured,' Major Griffiths sniggered. 'Let's have a look at the injured member. Drop your trousers.'

Grudgingly, Gareth complied. He was directed onto an examination couch. The colonel peered at the deep scar on his leg, probing it with cold, efficient fingers. He made Gareth stretch his leg out, feeling the bones and ligaments, checking its alignment. 'Well, it's healed well,' he commented. 'There shouldn't be any permanent disability. Does it give you much pain?'

'Yes sir,' Gareth lied. 'Terrible.'

The colonel nodded thoughtfully. 'Of course that's to be expected. Anyway, most of us have to put up with something. Get dressed, Rifleman.'

Gareth scowled, then pulled on his trousers. The colonel returned to the table, and re-examined Gareth's notes. 'A member of the Midland Rifles,' he said. 'Let me see, they've not seen any action yet.'

'No sir,' Gareth acknowledged.

Major Griffiths intervened. 'I've seen your drawings, Rifleman Williams. You must have a very good imagination, not having been at the Front yourself.'

Gareth dipped his forehead in resentful acknowledgement.

For a moment the officers conferred, speaking in low whispers. He felt angry as they sniggered. After a moment they all nodded and the colonel said, 'Fourteen days leave, Rifleman Williams, then back to France. Stick to mesdemoiselles in future. They don't have jealous husbands.' He made a gesture of dismissal with his eyebrows.

Gareth remembered to salute but his moustache twitched with fury. He hated their arrogance. He left the room, closing the door more loudly than was appreciated.

Next day he gave her the news. 'Medical board passed me fit to fight for king and country again.' He jutted his chin out slightly in the way he knew impressed her.

Sadness settled over her. 'They shouldn't be sendin' you back. You've suffered enough already.'

Quietly, he said: 'In the Bible it's written that greater love hath no man, than to lay down his life for 'is friends.'

'Your faith will give you strength,' she said.

They were sitting on the cliff-top where prolific gorse penetrated the senses with its coconutty scent. He was smoking a cigarette. They gazed down at the sea and everything seemed so serene; then she thought about France and how the war was tearing it apart, and she shuddered.

'They've given me a few days' leave before I go to France,' he told her. 'I shall 'ave to go and see Bronwyn, make sure she's all right.'

She nodded. She reminded herself that it was right for him to fulfil his family obligations. 'Gareth, will 'ee come back here before you return to France?'

'There won't be time. But the newspapers say the war won't last more than a few weeks now.'

'When it's over,' she said, 'you'll come back - for always?'

'I'll come back,' he said, 'and ...' He took a draw on his cigarette and flicked it away.

'Yes, my love?' she prompted, inwardly praying that he would speak of marriage.

'And I'll paint the most beautiful picture of you imaginable, and it will be hung in a gallery for everybody to enjoy.'

Frustration exploded inside her. She burst into tears. Even so pride still prevented her from pushing him into making a proposal. After a moment she regained control and dried her eyes. He'll do it when the time is right, she told herself.

The prospect of him leaving, even for a short time, was ghastly. He had become part of her life and her every moment of the day revolved around him. She imagined he understood the bleakness in her soul. He held her close, soothed her with gentle words, then they kissed and the kiss was salty with her tears. Now, as his hands tore at her clothing, she made no attempt to resist. 'I'm yours, Gareth,' she whispered. 'Always will be.'

He left a few days later and she went with him to the railway station at Talmouth, saw him aboard the train. It was a wet September day, matching her feelings. Rain splattered against the station roof in gusts.

Gareth looked smart in his khaki uniform with its polished buttons, but she noticed how the old vagueness was with him again. However, Rosena had enough warmth for both of them. She had always worn her heart on her sleeve, and never more so than now.

He hoisted his kit-bag onto the luggage rack, leaned from the carriage window and grasped her hand. She looked immensely pretty in her cherry-topped bonnet and red flimsy scarf. A few spots of rain glistened on her cheeks, or had she been crying? What a wonderful picture she would make, he thought yet again.

She wanted to talk of the future. She'd sought desperately to discover the reason for his reluctance to mention marriage, and suddenly she imagined she'd found it. Once, when speaking about his sister-in-law, he had said there was no fun in being a widow ... 'Poor Bronwyn nearly went mad.'

Going off again to possible death in conflict, it must be that he was unwilling to subject Rosena to a similar prospect. Once he was safely back, everything would be different.

'Gareth,' she said, 'I shall pray for 'ee every hour. I'll wait for 'ee. There'll be no other.'

He smiled, raised her hand to his lips and kissed it. The engine was hissing impatient steam. The guard blew his whistle and raised his green flag.

As the train jerked into motion, she released Gareth's hand.

She waited, her ears bludgeoned by the grind and squeak of the carriages, a lonely figure, waving until the train disappeared. She realised she'd forgotten to ask him for his sister-in-law's address. The only address he'd given her was care of the British Expeditionary Force in France.

As she left the station, trudging through spitting rain to the bus, her mind was filled with Ensign Perhaver and how her dream had put Gareth in his place to die upon the battlefield.

Chapter Six

GARETH CHANGED AT CARDIFF, and, with reluctance, ignored the brazen smiles of the ladies standing outside General Station. The lips of a loose woman drip honey, he consoled himself, but in the end she is bitter as wormwood. He crossed the town in a tram. At Queen Street, he boarded another train and arrived at Merthyr Tydfil at four o'clock in the afternoon. From here, he took a bus to Trethomas..

Now, back on home ground, his spirits lifted. Around him were familiar scenes of terraced, slate-roofed houses, coated with coal dust, the dreary colour relieved only by the advertising hoardings at the end of each row. Behind the houses, tall chimneys tainted the air with acrid smoke and colliery-workings loomed against mountains of grey slag.

Several times Gareth passed people he knew and gave them a wave. He basked in the respect and gratitude they showed men in khaki, all heroes in their eyes. There was no point in telling them he'd been nowhere near the Front Line.

The boarding house, at the end of Parry Street, had three floors. A card at the window said **NO VACANCIES**. When he knocked, the door was opened by six-year-old Gwenda, a bright-faced girl with hair the same russet as her mam's. 'Uncle Gareth!' she exclaimed. She looked to him for a kiss but he didn't oblige. He had always found children tedious.

He stepped inside and dumped his kit-bag in the narrow hallway, the appetising aroma of cooking wafting to him.

The house, with its highly polished brass, emanated an air of cleanliness, and through the doorway of the front room, he could see several guests talking over tea. They were indifferent to his paintings on the walls - paintings in oils of Barafundle Bay, and Stackpole Quay ablaze with blossom. Bronwyn's clientele mainly consisted of visiting mining-engineers and travelling salesmen, all too concerned with money to appreciate art.

He found Bronwyn in the kitchen, preparing the evening meal - lamb stew and dumplings. She was a short, ample woman with a fiery nature. Now her face lit up. She wiped her hands on her apron, and was in his arms.

'Why didn't you tell me you was comin', love?' she gasped. 'I'd 'ave been ready for you. 'Ow's the leg?'

'All right now, it is.'

Presently he drew back, his face sober. 'Bronwyn, sendin' me back to France, they are. It's ten days before I go.'

'Oh God no ... so soon.' Her anger showed. 'When's this bloody war goin' to stop? Every week the papers say it won't last much longer, but it still goes on.'

'They need me over there,' he smiled, 'to sort the Huns out, you see!'

'Well, do it quick,' she said, 'then the men can come 'ome and everythin'll get back to normal.'

She checked her saucepans. 'My sister Megan's helpin' me out,' she said. 'She'll keep 'er eye on this lot for a while. But we mustn't be too long.'

He smiled. She understood his need. When they were in the third-floor bedroom they frantically pulled off each other's clothes. She cursed and laughed as she got his puttees in a tangle, but at last she had them off, lying in a knotted heap alongside her stays at the side of the bed, him swearing as he kicked the chamber-pot.

They made love on top of the eiderdown, a flurry of bouncing bodies and ecstatic groans, and afterwards they lay in each other's arms, getting their breath back, her face tingling from the rub of his moustache. 'Gareth Williams,' she sighed contentedly, 'I swear that if I 'ad any more 'oles in my body, you'd have steam puffin' out of me like an old ship's boiler. Thought you'd 'ave been out of practice, after all this time like.'

'No, not with a woman like you to dream about. Buxom Bronwyn, the best little cracker in town, that's for sure.'

She laughed. 'Takes you to bring it out in me,' she said. 'Biggest mistake I ever made was marryin' Owen.'

'Didn't take you long to realise that,' he nodded. 'Can't 'ave been many wives who were unfaithful on their wedding day.'

'All Owen could talk about was coal mines and bloody cricket,' she sighed. 'Once you took a fancy to me, 'e didn't stand a chance.' Her thoughts suddenly returned to the saucepans downstairs. 'I mustn't stay 'ere any longer. I got work to do, love.'

He watched her rise from the bed. He'd always relished her plump little body, a truly comfortable woman, with breasts that fitted so snugly into his hands, but he knew she couldn't hold a candle alongside Rosena. Unaware of his thoughts, Bronwyn enjoyed his eyes upon her as she dressed. 'I wanted to give you a nice surprise,' she said. 'I wanted to come and see you, at the nursin' home, I mean. But I couldn't get away with all these guests 'ere.'

He exhaled with a sudden gush 'No. T'was best you didn't come,' and then, as he recovered from the shock, he added, 'Wouldn't 'ave been fair to expect you.'

She frowned, suspicion clouding her eyes. 'There've been no other women, 'ave there?'

'Bronwyn ... 'ow could there be, with you waitin' back 'ere! More than enough woman for one man, you are. Anyway, with a busted leg, 'ow could I?'

'If there was, Gareth Williams, I'd kill you ... and 'er too.'

'Don't be bloody daft.'

She smiled, naively reassured, and Jenny Killigrew's words flitted through his mind ... You should've been an actor not an artist.

Bronwyn buttoned up her blouse and pinned her russet hair back. As she went to the door, she said, 'You 'ave a sleep, love. I'll call you for supper.'

After she'd gone, Gareth rolled himself a cigarette. He lay back upon the bed, naked and temporarily sated. For some reason his thoughts dwelt on his brother. Owen, with his face pitted by coal chippings. What had Bronwyn seen in him? He wondered if Owen had ever suspected what had gone on behind his back. Whenever he was working nights down the pit, Gareth had slept in his bed. Bronwyn had never been sure who Gwenda's father was - but Owen never seemed to doubt she was his.

And then one morning the alarm-hooter had sounded from the mine, and word of a massive 'bump' and men trapped below had spread. Apparently thousands of tons of coal had shifted a mile down, releasing gasses along the shafts, and as hopes for survivors faded, Gareth's pathway was cleared.

After the funeral, Bronwyn was in a state of shock, her conscience troubled by the way they'd treated Owen. Gareth had been impatient. He wasn't going to let sentimentality stop him from getting what he wanted.

Eventually Bronwyn came round, as he knew she would. At that time, he believed she was the one woman who could satisfy his lust, because she craved for him as badly as he did for her. To prove it, she gave him money to supplement the meagre earnings from his paintings.

Six months to the day after the bodies of twenty-three miners had been laid to rest, and just three weeks before he received his call-up papers from the Army, Gareth and the widow Bronwyn, stood together at St Godfrey's Chapel and were joined in holy matrimony.

Rosena sat at the kitchen table, the parrot Cedric perched on her shoulder, reading Gareth's brief note. He had written from Southampton, in haste because he was waiting to board a troopship for France. He was well, his leg was fine, and he was glad he'd been able to help Bronwyn for a few days. A man was lucky to have a sister-in-law like her.

> *But, my petal, I long to kiss you. I dream of when I can paint the most beautiful portrait of you. I'll write if I can, but at the Front it may be difficult, so don't worry if you hear nothing. I will come back as soon as possible.*
>
> *Love G.*

Rosena pressed her lips to the words, and slipped the letter into her apron pocket, then she rose, causing Cedric to squawk in annoyance. She found a large caraway seed which she placed between her teeth. The bird, knowing the game, plucked it from her with surprising daintiness. She returned him to his cage.

She found writing paper, and in her most rounded writing she composed a reply for Gareth. She wrote, expressing her innermost feelings as she'd never dreamed she would to anybody.

Once she'd finished, she addressed the envelope care of the British Expeditionary Force. Within fifteen minutes she had slipped the letter into the village post-box.

She felt fit to mope, but it would not help, so, as usual, she found solace in hard work, both at home and at Perhaver Manor. And every week she would buy *The Talmouth Chronicle* and read about the war.

Despite everybody's optimism and the United States' entry into the conflict, the Germans were not finished. Their aeroplanes ruled the skies above the trenches.

The Germans had launched great offensives in Picardy and Arras to drive back the Allied forces. The loss of life had been staggering. It was to be repeated as the Allies fought to stem the tide and mount their own offensives, this time along the entire front.

Meanwhile life at home went on, and as the mild autumn passed, huge shoals of pilchards appeared in the coastal sea. The fisherman took full advantage, going out night and day. During daylight hours, a man would be posted on nearby cliffs, to direct operations by shouting through a hailer. By indicating the locations of the shoals, the boats were able to manoeuvre and spread their nets advantageously.

Next to the village quay was the large shed, and this became a hive of activity as the massive catches were landed. Rosena worked hard alongside every other able-bodied person, toiling with feverish haste, gutting and salting the fish before it lost its freshness, packing it into barrels. Most of it would be transported to fish-markets inland, and to the ports for shipping to the Army in France. Fish oil would be used for lanterns and heating. Much of the offal they cut out was packed separately, to be spread across the fields as fertiliser. The smell impregnated everything, catching in the throat. No visitors in their right senses came near the village.

Rosena became oblivious to the smell as she cut open one scaly body after another. As a child she'd been horrified by the glassy eyes of caught fish. But long ago necessity had made her impervious to their reproach. She expelled the offal with the expertise gained from practice. Even so, her hands were reddened and sore from many cuts.

One morning as she worked alongside the baker's wife Mary Roskelly, she realised they had company, and turning she saw Tom, still in his sea-boots and oil-skins. He'd been out at sea all night. Recently he had worked a lot with her father, sharing John Bray's boat *Silver Cloud* which was bigger than his own. His sombre expression warned her that something was wrong.

'Rosena ... 'tis your father. 'E's had a funny turn.'

'Oh, God!'

He held up his hand to calm her. 'Now don't worry, me dear. I got 'im 'ome. I think 'e's all right now.'

She gasped, 'Thanks, Tom. Thanks.' Her heart was hammering as she ran to the cottage, Tom limping along behind.

'In fact we all 'ad a shock,' he was panting. 'While we were fishin' 'twas like a monster was comin' up from the depths. A German U-Boat surfaced close by, caught us in its searchlight. We 'eard German voices shoutin', then they fired their gun across our bows, nearly capsized us. The shock of it was too much for your father. 'E made a chokin' sound, would have toppled overboard if I 'adn't caught him. 'E 'ad awful pain in his chest. Thank God that submarine submerged again and left us alone.'

John Bray was sitting in the parlour, a blanket covering his immense body. As they rushed in, he looked up, his face filled with bewilderment. His breath was coming in wheezy, shallow gasps. 'I don't want a fuss,' he murmured.

Rosena knelt on the floor, grasping his hand, and gradually his breathing steadied. Tom made him put his feet up on a stool.

'You'm feelin' better?' she whispered, her eyes pleading for reassuring words.

'I'm all right, me dear,' John Bray murmured. 'Just a dizzy turn. Damned Huns had no right to scare us. I 'ad this pain in my chest, but it's easier now.'

''E's been overdoin' things lately,' Tom said.

Rosena noticed how her father's skin showed blue against the whiteness of his beard. 'We must get the doctor,' she said.

'Tid'n necessary,' John Bray objected, but she held up her finger to shush him, then she turned to Tom.

'There's a telephone at the inn. Could 'ee call the doctor at Talmouth?'

Tom nodded and left on his errand. Rosena fetched her father a cushion, making him comfortable. She put the kettle on and made some tea. Presently Tom came back. ''Tis a wonderful invention, the telephone,' he said. ''Ow is 'e?'

'E's dozed off now,' she said.

They sat quietly, listening to the steadier breathing of John Bray. She felt ashamed of herself. Her head had been so full of her own affairs. She'd never paused to consider the danger that fishermen faced ... or that one day her father might be struck down by illness, weakened by the weight his heart had to support. Presently she turned to Tom and said, 'Thanks, Tom. Don't know 'ow we'da managed without 'ee.'

'Done no more than anybody would,' he murmured. ''Ow's things with 'ee, Rosena? 'Ow's your Welshman?'

''E's a good man,' she replied with sudden pride. ''E's away, fightin' for his country.'

Tom pursed his lips. She'd embarrassed him which she hadn't meant to. 'I'm sorry,' she said, annoyed at herself. 'I didn't mean ...'

'I'd be there too,' he frowned, 'if I wasn't crippled.'

His presence was a great comfort. She closed her eyes. She felt exhausted, the stress of the last hours taking its toll. As she lapsed into sleep, he fetched a blanket and covered her.

An hour later she was awakened by the slam of a motor-car door from outside, and Cedric's squawking. Both she and Tom stood up. Soon, Doctor Tancred bustled in, unbuttoning his tweed coat, opening up his bag of medical instruments - a round-bellied, genial man who wore leather gaiters.

John Bray's eyes opened and he saw the doctor. 'Good of 'ee to come out,' he said.

Doctor Tancred put on his stethoscope and turned to Rosena. 'I want to give him an examination,' he explained. 'And you can do something for me. A nice cup of tea will go down like oil.'

'Of course.' She hastened away to the kitchen.

Presently, when she returned with a freshly brewed pot, the doctor was examining John Bray's ankles. 'Very swollen,' he commented.

'Am I goin' to die?' John Bray asked, a wry indifference in his voice.

'If you do, after all the trouble I'm going to, I'll be most annoyed. You've had a heart attack, a mild one - but it's a warning. You've got to slow down, lose some weight, take life easier.' Doctor Tancred replaced his instruments in their bag, then he accepted a cup of tea from Rosena. 'I mean it,' he said. 'He'd best stay in bed for the next three days, cut down on the smoking and alcohol. I'll call back tomorrow and bring some medicine. You'd better get some rest too, young lady. Won't do a ha'peth of good if you keel over.'

After Tancred had drunk his tea, Tom saw him to the door.

Rosena turned to her father. 'Like 'e said, 'tis a warnin'. You've got to stop drivin' yourself so 'ard.'

John Bray looked at her from beneath his bushy eyebrows, a smile tugging his lips. 'I'm like 'ee, me dear,' he said. 'Couldn't ease up if I tried.'

Chapter Seven

A YEAR AGO THE ARMY Recruiting Office had turned him down. Tom wondered if he should re-apply. ***Your Country Needs You,*** General Kitchener pointed out from the posters splashed all over the place. After all, Tom thought, what difference did a crippled leg make when you advanced into German bullets? It just meant you couldn't turn tail so quickly. Rosena's damned Welshman had a bad leg, and they'd sent him back. Trouble was, there were bad legs and bad legs. Tom's had been twisted at birth and was shorter than the other, giving him a permanently lop-sided walk. Mind you, it didn't cause him much pain, apart from having to wear civilian clothes, when he should have been in khaki.

He stayed with the Brays until early afternoon, dozing in the parlour rocking chair. John Bray was much better, trying to shrug off the previous night's events. Rosena would have a hard job restraining him.

'I'll 'elp 'ee as best I can,' Tom said, pulling on his cap and stepping out into the sunshine for the walk home. 'I'll stop by tomorrow.'

Rosena nodded. She kissed his cheek, then waved good-bye and watched him limp up the street. His cottage at St Mags was three miles away. He was a strong man, physically and morally. She admired his courage and the way he forced himself to walk quickly as if to prove that being crippled was of no consequence.

Tom took the cliff-path to St Mags, and, climbing, he passed the ruin of the tin-mine engine house, with its broken chimney and giant wheel; beneath this, he knew, old shafts reached far out beneath the sea. Higher still, he crossed a meadow, where the waving grass moved fitfully. For a while he paused, bracing himself against the cleansing breeze. The view was breathtaking. From the great cliffs, black and grey fins of rock thrust seaward, packed slab upon slab like playing-cards, across the expanse of sand darkened with sea-weed. Above this, oyster-catchers swirled, watchful for a tasty snack.

Suddenly he heard the rasp-like sound of somebody panting. Looking ahead, he saw a figure approaching along the path. It was Jenny Killigrew, the young girl from his own village. Something about her haste was unnatural. She ran head down, raising her skirts, frequently stumbling. In her blind rush she almost collided with him before she drew up, gasping for breath. Her face was tearful and swollen.

'What's wrong, Jenny?' he asked.

Her eyes were glinting with madness. 'None of your business, Tom Lethbridge. Let me be. You'll know soon enough, anyway.' She brushed past him, running on.

All at once, realisation dawned in him and he hastened after her. She had clambered down a grassy bank and was poised at the very lip of the cliff. There was a frightening intent about her. She'd raised her arms as if they were wings, and her legs were bent in readiness to jump. He screamed: 'Jenny!' and hurled himself down the bank. He made a grab for her, clutched onto her clothing, ripping her blouse as he strove frantically to restrain her. She clawed her nails across his face, but he strengthened his hold, dragging her back, falling with her to the ground.

For a moment he sprawled on top of her, feeling the shudder in her, both too exhausted to speak. At last he murmured, 'Why?'

'God!' she shrieked. 'Why didn't 'ee let me be?'

He eased clear of her, but kept a tight grip on her arm.

'You'm hurtin' me,' she complained.

'Well,' he demanded, 'promise you'll not try that crazy thing again.'

A change came over her. The tenseness flowed out of her. She sat up, not trembling any longer, her breasts bared amid the tatters of her blouse, her skirt torn half way up her leg, her hair hanging across her face like a wet dish rag.

A defiant, cunning light crept into her eyes. 'I promise I'll not try it again. I don't need to do it now.' Her voice had lost its flutter, was unusually deliberate.

'What do 'ee mean?'

She licked her lips, drew a tremulous breath. 'Because ... because, Tom Lethbridge, you just raped me!'

Gareth stumbled as a rat squirmed from the rotting duckboards beneath his boot. He went down, splashing ooze about him. The rats had lost their fear and would snatch the food from men's hands as they ate, but revenge often came as men impaled cheese on their bayonets, lured the rats to sniff at it, and then pressed the trigger.

Gareth's trousers were soaked. He dragged himself up, cursing as he felt around in the slime to recover his rifle. Above the trench, the night-sky was in constant turmoil, with bursts of flame from the German heavies and the scream of shells cleaving the night-air to explode behind the British line. The air was thick with the stench of cordite. He checked his gas bag, glad that the respirator's goggles were unbroken. He didn't want to cough himself to death with lungs full of chlorine gas, like those poor devils on the Somme.

Now he would no longer have to invent images of the horrors. In fact, if he survived, he'd never speak of, or even sketch, the death and the suffering he'd encountered. The whole experience was beyond any hideousness he'd imagined possible.

His battalion had been moved from reserve and attached to the 25th Infantry Division. After they'd disembarked at the rail-heads, they'd marched along roads, littered with burned-out vehicles and German corpses. They'd averaged twenty miles a day and eventually crossed a belt of low, dreary upland beyond which fields dipped away towards a river where the Huns were entrenched.

They reached some trenches where the barbed wire was on the wrong side. The Germans had vacated these only hours before. Rain had turned the trenches into foul-smelling ditches. The Huns had hardly left the place in slick handover condition, though generally speaking the enemy trenches were better appointed than the British ones. A German corporal sat with the top of his head blown off. When somebody prodded him with a boot, he toppled stiffly into the mud. At least there appeared to be no booby-traps.

That night Gareth, his insides churning, had been in the party sent forward to ram iron stakes into the ground and unroll spools of concertina wire in defensive barriers. While they worked, the Germans sent up flares which floated gently down on parachutes, lighting up the area as if it were day, and any second they'd expected machine guns to open up.

Now, a week later, hunched in his sodden goatskin coat, he'd been to the latrine. In truth, it didn't make much difference where you went because everything was swilling around in the slime. He rejoined Corporal Russell and six others under a flimsy shelter of corrugated-iron. They were sprawled on sacks of lice-ridden straw and were busy scraping out bully-beef from their mess tins. Gareth had little affection for his companions. He, being 'one of them artists', was a convenient butt for banter.

This dug-out, an old shell-crater, had the grand title of 'HQ, No. 3 Post'. The rain was drumming with such intensity upon the corrugated-iron roof, that talk was difficult. He edged close to the candle which glowed falteringly from the upturned lid of a polish tin. He squatted down and rummaged in his knapsack, found his writing pad and rested it on his knee. Because he was afraid, he expressed himself with rare sincerity.

> *My Dearest Rosena*
> *I can't tell you where I am, because I don't know. If you recall the sketches I did and then imagine something a hundred times worse, you will understand what it's like.. The thought of those beautiful days we spent together, wandering hand in hand along the beach, now seems like a wonderful dream. When I close my eyes, I see your face, smiling and happy. and I yearn to capture your entire wonder on canvas.*

As he finished writing there was an massive explosion, throwing him forward into the mud. Earth showered down. The candle went out. He braced himself, expecting the roof to cave in. Gradually the reverberance of the blast subsided, and he became aware of men shouting, groaning, cursing; and, further away, the explosion of more shells.

'God!' somebody said, 'that was bloody close!'

A match flared to show men's anxious, dirt-smudged faces. Corporal Russell got the candle re-lit. Outside an officer was shouting, 'All right! Nobody hurt. Get things cleared up.'

Gareth realised that the letter was still in his hand. He found his knapsack and extracted an envelope. Slipping the letter inside, he sealed it and then, using an ammunition box for a table, he addressed it, his hand shaking. .

'Stand up!' Corporal Russell shouted.

The gas curtain over the entrance had been drawn back. The cherub-faced Lieutenant Carter stepped through, accompanied by a sergeant. 'At ease,' the officer said, with a crisp return of salute.

Edwin Carter was their company officer. Gareth was irritated by his curly, dark hair, bright blue eyes, and smile like an angel's. No matter how alarming the situation, the man never showed a glimmer of fear, and amid all the grime, his uniform always appeared immaculate.

'Gentlemen,' he announced, 'tomorrow, shortly before dawn, we are to go over the top. At last we've got a chance to give the Hun a kick in the teeth!'

Gareth felt renewed fear. Ducking shells in a trench was bad enough, but climbing out and setting himself up as a target for enemy bullets was utter madness.

'If you've got any mail to send home,' the sergeant was saying in his dour Yorkshire voice, 'I'll take it now.'

Gareth held up his envelope.

The sergeant took it and noted the address. 'Bound for sunny Cornwall, eh? I bet it's nowhere near so beautiful as this lovely place!' He was turning away, when the lieutenant spoke up.

'You from Cornwall, Rifleman?'

'No, sir,' Gareth responded. 'I made friends with a young lady when I was in 'ospital there.'

Lieutenant Carter grinned. 'A lovely county. I shall be going there soon. On my honeymoon.'

For some mad reason the men who'd been listening clapped their hands in delight. 'Can we all come to the wedding, sir?' somebody enquired.

Corporal Russell, embarrassed by their impertinence, said respectfully: 'I 'ope you make it in one piece, sir.'

Lieutenant Carter stood hands on hips, a confident smile on his clean-shaven, rosy-cheeked face. 'I shall make it,' he said. 'No Hun's going to stop me.' and then he and the sergeant ducked out of the dugout.

Gareth swore beneath his breath: 'Bloody fool!'

In the dug-out he shared with two other officers, Edwin Carter sat on his bunk, wondering how much longer he could keep up this act of bravado when inwardly he was sick with fear. He had been drinking tea from a mess-tin, but as a shell exploded nearby, he was trembling so much that he had to put it aside. His greatest fear was that he might fail the men who looked to him for inspiration and reveal the doubts that assailed him, doubts that told him that what they were doing was total madness. Why couldn't his men understand that in reality he was as much in terror and doubt as any of them?

Presently he took up his pen and pad. He had written to Elspeth, his fiancée, earlier in the day. Now he remembered that it was Aunt Beryl's birthday in a week's time. At least writing home would distract him from the thought that tomorrow might be for many, himself included, the last day spent on this earth.

Dear Aunt Beryl,

Many happy returns! I hope this arrives in time. I will get you a present when I come home. The local shops do not have a very good selection of gifts. Thanks for the jersey and socks you sent. The sweets too were most welcome.

Here, we make the trenches as comfortable as possible, though it is rather muddy. We work by night and rest by day, though tomorrow we are taking part in an attack upon the enemy. With luck we'll be able to drive them out of this section.

The country around here is flat and low lying. The houses and farms are deserted apart from cats. The Germans are close by, and no doubt are as tired of the war as we are. Hopefully it will all be over soon.

I am looking forward to my wedding day. I am very lucky to be marrying a person so beautiful and loyal as Elspeth.

There is something else I must say. When I lost my parents, I was truly blessed to be brought up by you and Uncle Jeremy. I can

>never adequately repay your kindness, except, hopefully, by being a credit to you. I will try my hardest. You must not worry about me. I am keeping well, get enough to eat, and have the benefit of wonderful comradeship. God bless.
>
>>Your loving nephew
>>Edwin

A continuous thump dragged Tom Lethbridge from sleep. He tried to untangle nightmare from reality, finally concluding they were one and the same. A bright sunbeam shone at an oblique angle through his bedroom window. It was time he roused himself if he was going to sea.

The noise was getting louder. Somebody was hammering on his downstairs door. Images of what had happened reared into his mind ... the girl's morose silence as he'd forced her down the cliff path to St Mags. At the Killigrew cottage, her mother had opened up - a woman of long-faded prettiness whose hair was drawn back and tucked behind large ears - and her mouth had sagged at the sight of her dishevelled daughter. Mrs Killigrew had stared uncomprehendingly as he'd explained Jenny's attempted suicide. He'd allowed Jenny to shake clear of his grip and push past her mother into the cottage, and almost immediately the door had been slammed in his face. He'd stood on the doorstep, stunned by the reaction, sensing the horrendous trouble which could follow. He'd tried to think logically, but grim conclusions festered in his mind.

The Killigrews had never been reasonable people. They harboured a permanent grudge against everybody, particularly the better off. And if the girl's twisted mind somehow believed that she had been raped, he'd be the only person to know the truth.

As he'd returned to his own cottage, he'd tried to console himself. The girl had a reputation for flaunting herself amongst the male population. Indeed, a month ago, she'd tried to tempt him with her ripe body, but he'd quickly rejected her.

If it came to his word against hers, he prayed that sanity would prevail, but the prospect of the inevitable slur on his name made him groan.

Cursing the frantic thumping, he rose from his bed and pulled up the sash-window. 'Will 'ee stop breakin' my door down, for God's sake!'

Beneath him were five men. All were brandishing sticks and grouped aggressively around his street-door. In the forefront was Silas Killigrew, Jenny's father, 'You best come down, Tom Lethbridge,' he shouted. 'We da want a word wi' you!'

Tom recognised the other men: Jenny's two younger brothers, James and William, and two of Silas's drinking-mates from the village pub - both confirmed alcoholics. "Tis more'n a word we da want with 'e!' William Killigrew shouted.

'I'll come down,' Tom said, closing the window.

He paused for a moment in the bedroom. He found his pipe and lit up, taking a slow draw, gathering his thoughts. He could hear the raised voices of the men from outside. They reminded him of a pack of impatient hounds, baying at a fox-hole. He went down the stairs, pulled the bolt back on his door and opened up. He came eye to eye with Silas Killigrew. The air was tainted with beery breath.

'Explain yourself, Tom Lethbridge,' Killigrew demanded. 'Jenny told us what 'ee did, you filthy bugger!'

Tom removed his pipe from his mouth. 'If it 'adn't been for me,' he said, 'Jenny'd be dead now. She'd 'ave jumped clean over the cliff!'

'Likely tale!' Killigrew sneered.

'She's told us what 'appened, clear enough,' James Killigrew cut in angrily. 'She told us you were so woman-'ungry, you couldn't keep your 'ands off her! 'Ow you tore 'er skirt and 'ad your way with 'er ...'

"Tid'n true!' Tom shouted, showing anger for the first time.

Silas Killigrew scowled at him. 'Don't you call my daughter a liar, Lethbridge!'

'Yeah,' one of the others yelled. ' ... just 'cos you can't 'ave that Bray girl you da lust after!'

The whole bunch surged at him, swinging their sticks, but Tom stepped forward, placing his hands on Silas's chest, forcing him back into the others. James Killigrew actually fell, but was up instantly.

Tom drew himself up to his full height, looming over them, his eyes glowering with such fury that they were taken aback. 'If you have any complaint against me,' he shouted, 'take it to a court of law! See where that da get 'ee!'

Silas Killigrew was not going to be brow-beaten. 'Best thing for you, Tom Lethbridge, is to clear out of this village. We don't want the likes o' you here. If you 'aven't gone be tomorrow, we'll spread the word of what you did and let other people decide what 'ee deserve!'

Tom glared at them. Having spent their last loud-mouthed hours drinking, he was pretty sure Jenny's lies would already be common gossip in the village.

'Clear off,' he snapped. 'I've got work to do!' and he stepped back inside and slammed his door, hearing their irate voices raised. Shortly they quietened, and from his upstairs window, he saw them hurrying off down the street. They'll be back, he thought, and there'll be a few more with them.

Within an hour he was at sea, putting his boat around the headland into Megstow Quay Bay. Here he joined the main fishing fleet, assembled in readiness to gather the harvest from the sea. Friends waved to him with their customary cheerfulness, and he wondered how they would change once the gossip spread. When he was out upon waves, spreading his drift-nets, his thoughts turned to the Brays. Somehow their reaction towards him seemed more important than anybody else's. He mouthed a prayer. Please God, let me give them my version, before they hear lies from somebody else.

Chapter Eight

THE COLOUR HAD RETURNED to John Bray's face. He was shrugging off his illness, refusing to behave like an invalid, though he had taken the medicine the doctor dropped by. Already he was talking about re-commencing work. On the Monday morning, Tom visited. He lacked his usual cheerfulness, but Rosena gave him a warm smile which brought some relief to his face. He glanced at John Bray sitting in the rocking chair. 'How be you today?' he enquired.

'Fit as a fiddle now,' the older man responded. He glanced at Rosena. 'Don't need all this fussin'.'

Rosena poured Tom some tea and said, 'Something's troublin' 'ee for sure.'

He nodded glumly. 'You've not heard any gossip in the village?'

Rosena shook her head. 'Didn't go out yesterday.'

Relief surged through him. At least he could break the news to them himself. He turned away, looked with unseeing eyes through the kitchen window, his every sense focused on his next words. 'Yesterday, I was walking 'ome across the cliffs when I saw Jenny Killigrew rushin' towards me.'

Rosena nodded. 'The girl who works up Perhaver.'

'That's 'er. Well, as she pushed past me, she looked really strung up, as if she was at 'er wits' end. So I followed after 'er. When I caught up, there she was, about to throw 'erself over the cliff.'

'No!' Rosena gasped, and her father removed the pipe from his mouth.

'I jumped at 'er,' Tom continued, 'pulled 'er back from the edge.'

''Ow grateful 'er parents must've been,' Rosena murmured.

'No. They wadn't.'

'Why not?' she queried.

''Twas because Jenny Killigrew claimed I ... I raped 'er!'

'What!' Rosena gasped.

Tom met her hazel eyes. 'She said I raped 'er.'

For a moment there was a stunned silence. But he was nodding, his face glum.

'Why should she say that?' Rosena said. 'She must be mad. Surely 'er parents don't believe ...'

'They believe 'er all right,' Tom cut in. ''Er father and 'is cronies have threatened me. Told me to get out of the village.'

Rosena stepped across to Tom, rested her hand on his shoulder. 'Poor Tom,' she murmured. ''Tis an awful thing.'

'Will 'ee go, Tom?' John Bray asked. 'Will 'ee move out?'

Tom's mouth settled into a stubborn line. 'She's tellin' a pack of lies. I won't let 'em force me out!'

There was a sour taste in Gareth's mouth, which not even a swig of rum could dispel. A sense of imminent death was in him. He'd once worked at a slaughterhouse and sensed it in animals as they were dragged in. He wondered if, when they went over the top, he could cut and run, but then he recalled rumours of officers shooting down their own men.

In its trench, the platoon fixed bayonets. The Company Commander, a fierce-looking major, walked down the line, saying, 'The attack will commence at 0500 hrs. Remember, every Hun you kill is a point scored for our side!'

Gareth gazed at his luminous watch, wishing he could hold back the minutes, but he could not and all too soon a single blast on a whistle sounded. Along the trench men, made clumsy by heavy packs, scrambled up the ladders and over the parapet. Gareth wondered if he might 'accidentally' allow his puttees to unwind, thus preventing him from advancing - but no, that would make him an easy target for the enemy. Perhaps he could feign death.

He'd suspected that they would immediately be fired upon, but this was not so. The stillness persisted. Men quickly advanced, clambering through gaps in the wire. Ahead, No Man's Land was shrouded in pre-dawn mist.

Once beyond the wire, each platoon formed its own skirmish line, and Lieutenant Carter scurried up and down, encouraging his men. The air carried the acrid taint of stale cordite and was dank. Gareth felt clammy, his hands slippery as he gripped his rifle. He glanced around furtively. He thought, perhaps the Huns are up to the same tricks as us, mounting their own assault! He crouched down, trying to present the smallest target possible, wishing he was deaf and unable to hear the word, 'Forward!' as it came whispering along the line. He had no option but to start walking, and Corporal Russell appeared on his left, murmuring, 'Keep up, man!' Bayonets thrust forward, they advanced down the shell-scarred ground, the decline giving them unwanted impetus. A scurry to his front sent panic stabbing through Gareth, but Corporal Russell's voice came: 'Only bloody hares out for a morning frolic!'

As they progressed, the first indication of dawn flushed a paleness into the gloom. Their line became distorted as men negotiated shell craters. Gareth encountered a dead cow, its stench catching in his throat, and he undertook a detour. They went another two-hundred yards, getting nearer to the enemy positions.

Then machine guns opened up and the air was full of metal. Men cried out, went down. Something struck Gareth's helmet, knocking it back over his neck. As he replaced it, a stick-bomb blasted off to his left, having him dropping awkwardly across his rifle, almost sticking the bayonet into himself. The rattle of machine guns continued, sparking the mist with angry flame. He heard somebody groaning and saw Corporal Russell sprawled a few yards away. As another stick bomb exploded, Gareth glanced around. A short distance ahead was a crater and, desperate for shelter, he crawled forward. Suddenly Russell unleashed a deep agonised cry. He was totally exposed to shrapnel and bullets. Gareth cursed, then snaked his way to the wounded NCO. The front of Russell's uniform was sodden with blood, his eyes fixed on Gareth. He tried to speak but only produced frothy blood.

Gareth saw a means of saving his own skin. He didn't give a damn about Russell, but he threw aside his rifle, got his arms beneath the NCO's armpits, and dragged him forward, shutting his ears to the man's agonised cries.

A moment later they dropped into the crater. Above them, around the rim, there was a bright yellow flash and an awful explosion. Gareth could hear men shouting, amid rifle fire and the blast of grenades. Russell had lost consciousness, his breath faltering.

Suddenly Lieutenant Carter peered over the crater rim, peering down. 'We're going forward again,' he yelled, and then: 'Are you badly hit?'

'Yessir!' Gareth cried, not differentiating between Russell's plight and his own. Anyway, perhaps he was hit; he wasn't sure.

'Well, stay where you are.' Carter ducked as another explosion shook the ground. 'Stretcher parties'll be along soon!' He disappeared, and Gareth heard him urging his men forward.

Gareth fumbled with his field-dressing, going through the motions in case somebody else peered into the crater. He tried to unfasten Russell's tunic, but the buttons were too slippery with blood to grip. But that blood was covering Gareth. Nobody, seeing him, would suspect that he was unscathed. However all his scheming was wasted; at that moment a stick-bomb hurtled over the rim and landed in the mud close to his boot. It hissed like molten metal being plunged into water. In terror, he scrambled back, dragging the unconscious Russell as a shield. Suddenly the bomb exploded, its devastating, mutilating blast trapping everything within the crater.

Through the smoke, Edwin Carter saw the orange of bursting shells; and there were Germans retreating, heaving grenades as they went. Desperate to find refuge in their trenches, they were streaming through gaps in their own barbed wire which British artillery had blasted. The cries of wounded men mingled with the snap of rifles, and the roar of machine guns and detonating bombs was pierced by the shouted commands of officers and NCOs. All around, men were dropping.

Edwin waved forward the surviving members of his platoon. He mentally ticked off their names: Higgins, Evans, Smith, Mills, Avery ... He could see their white faces, the glitter of madness in their eyes - yet still they complied with his commands, moving forward like clockwork dolls. A hundred yards to the left a further wave of khaki advanced, men of the Sussex Fusiliers. Edwin hoped that they would link with his platoon; then together they could overrun the enemy trenches.

They were thirty yards from that objective when the ground erupted with Germans leaping from hidden fox-holes. A trap had been sprung. Men struggled hand-to-hand. Edwin glimpsed a man lunging towards him behind the cold thrust of bayonet, and fired his pistol, seeing the man's head explode in a flurry of brains and blood. He jumped across the body before it hit the ground, shrapnel bouncing off his helmet. His platoon was being decimated in front of him and there was nothing he could do.

Agony slammed into his left arm, throwing him forward; his pistol flew from his hand, its lanyard whipping across his throat. He hit the ground hard. Another man tripped over him, and lay unmoving with his legs trailed across Edwin's back.

He raised his eyes, saw the earth in front of him leaping and spitting as bullets raked it. He tried to rise, but the pain was too great and he dropped back. His left arm felt as if it had been ripped from its socket. His ribcage seemed crushed; he couldn't breathe. As mist and confusion thickened about him, he lost consciousness.

When he again opened his eyes, he realised that the battle had moved on. He pressed his right hand into the ground and pushed himself into a sitting position. His left sleeve was sodden with blood, but at least his arm was still attached. Corpses were sprawled all around, scattered, mutilated, the colour of their uniforms indistinguishable.

Ignoring his pain he got his legs beneath him and forced himself up. He tottered, dazed by the surrounding horror. Why had he survived when so many had perished? His pistol was dangling on its lanyard and he reclaimed it. To his left a scurry of movement caught his eye. About seventy yards away, British soldiers were scrambling through the broken wire and descending into the German trench beyond. Had the battle been won?

Gunfire still crackled, but it seemed distant and behind the original German line. He went forward, striving to find a path between the bodies. He heard a man calling for water. He located a young Rifleman, his head propped against the body of a comrade. His helmet was gone, his hair shining with blood from a scalp wound. Edwin crouched beside him. He uncorked his canteen and pressed it to the Rifleman's lips, murmuring, 'They'll come and pick you up soon - the stretcher bearers. You'll be all right.'

The young boy gulped water down, then gave him a weak smile. They both knew that he'd be dead by the time further help arrived.

Five minutes later Edwin found a gap in the wire. He hoped that the men of the Sussex Fusiliers had already taken the trench, crushing German resistance. Once through the wire, he staggered up a grassy bank, reached the lip of the trench and gazed over. There was nobody here, but his view was limited by the dog-toothed design of the trench which was divided into a series of firing-ports. There could be an entire Hun regiment in the next section, but he prayed not.

He found a ladder and climbed down. Pistol pointing forward, he moved to his left along the duckboards, hoping that if he met men of the Sussex Fusiliers, they would not mistake him for the enemy. The trench was deep, with entrances to dugouts and high parapets. He glanced up, seeing the dark swoosh of shell fire smudging the sky.

Suddenly there was a explosion, so close it set the duckboards shuddering. The shell must have landed in the next firing port.

He went around the dog-leg and saw a young German NCO crouched on his haunches. He was gazing with incredulity at his severed limb which was a few yards away. Suddenly he pitched sideways. Through the splintering of ribs, his intestines were spilling out, like stuffing from a rag doll, yet he was still alive. His eyes locked onto Edwin's pistol. 'Kill quick,' he gasped.

He was dying in agony, yet Edwin hesitated. He gazed into his pleading eyes. 'Kill bloody quick!' The man was terrified that Edwin would not comply. Edwin extended his revolver and the German's lips seized onto the barrel, the steel clicking against his teeth. Edwin clenched his eyes shut and pulled the trigger. The explosion reverberated in his ears. Opening his eyes, he saw how the German had fallen back, trails of his brain splattered around.

He reloaded his pistol with trembling hands. Five minutes later he encountered an advance party of the Sussex Fusiliers as they moved along the trench. He came within a second of being shot. 'Fucking hell,' a sergeant yelled, 'we thought you was a bloody Hun, sir.'

A grey-haired major came up, calmly puffing on a pipe. 'Signal's come through. We've got to fall back.'

Edwin could hardly believe his ears. 'Fall back?' he gasped. 'After all the men we've lost getting here?'

A harassed-looking corporal appeared on the far rim of the trench, pointing behind him. 'Enemy approaching, sir! There's bloody thousands of 'em.'

The entire party, Edwin included, clambered onto firesteps to peer over the trench wall. There was a collective gasp. The whole treeless landscape was seething with grey bugs getting progressively closer, wave upon wave of them.

'Yes, I think it's time to fall back.' The major said. He pointed the stem of his pipe at Edwin. 'You'd better get your arm treated, that's if you don't want to lose it.'

The British had retreated to their original trenches, crippled by staggering losses. Bodies littered No Man's Land and in the early evening stretcher parties went out. It had begun to rain quite hard.

By this time, Edwin had been rushed to the casualty clearing station. When his arm was eventually examined, the weary doctor said, 'You're lucky. A nice little Blighty-wound.'

'I don't want to be sent home,' Edwin complained. 'I can't leave my platoon.'

'From what I've heard, there's none of your platoon left,' the doctor commented. 'Anyway you don't have any choice.' He scribbled a note, passed it to an orderly and moved on.

Presently, Edwin sat close to some German prisoners who were smoking cigarettes, thankful to be no longer part of the conflict. He thought of the man he had shot. It could so easily have been one of these.

He regretted not being allowed to return to his platoon. He felt he was betraying the men who'd walked to their deaths, trusting his judgement.

There was only one compensation in being sent back to England. His marriage to Elspeth could go ahead - but would he ever feel normal after what he'd seen and suffered here?

It was almost dark when a medical orderly gazed down into the crater in which Gareth Williams and Corporal Russell were sprawled motionless. Suddenly a hand moved, blood trickling between the fingers, clawed upwards, then fell back. The orderly beckoned to his companion and a stretcher was lowered into the crater. Russell was decapitated. He'd caught the full impact of the blast, and had acted as a shield. The orderly placed his ear against the chest of the second body and discovered a heartbeat. They lifted him onto the stretcher. It seemed unlikely that their patient would survive the journey back to camp, but they went through the motions. The orderly at the back-end of the stretcher complained: *'Ich weiss nicht warum wir unsere hälse für das Britische schweine riskieren.'*

It was a fine day for drying. Rosena fastened her father's shirts along the furze bushes, feeling the chill bite of oncoming winter in the wind. She hoped it wouldn't be too rough at sea, for the village fleet was fishing beyond the Isles of Scilly. Since recovering from his illness, her father had lost a little weight but she saw in him an uncharacteristic tiredness that concerned her. At least Tom Lethbridge would keep a caring eye on him while they were at sea. As usual, her thoughts drifted to Gareth. She had not heard from him for three weeks - and in his last letter, she had sensed a frightening finality.

She had finished securing the washing when she heard somebody call. Turning, she was surprised to see Jenny Killigrew standing by the gate. 'Mum said I should come and talk with 'ee,' the girl said.

Rosena felt resentful. She had not seen Jenny since Tom had told them of her shattering accusation. True enough tongues had wagged in the local community, but despite the loud-mouthed indignation of Silas Killigrew, the story had been dismissed as implausible - the overfanciful imagination of a young girl who already had a reputation for hallucinating.

'What is it?' Rosena called.

The girl drew the wind-swept hair from her face with a nervous jerk of her hand. 'Can I 'ave a word? Won't take much time.'

Rosena wondered if she might be able to discover why the girl had behaved so outrageously. 'Come in,' she called, and Jenny nodded and followed into the cottage's kitchen. 'I'll get 'ee a warm drink,' Rosena said and she put the kettle on to boil.

Jenny sat down and rested her arms on the table.

Cedric was squawking so Rosena slipped a cloth over his cage. 'You say your mum sent 'ee?'

Jenny was ill at ease, so different from her arrogant manner up at Perhaver. Now, she was deeply agitated. ''Tis me father,' she said. 'He's always on at me ... I ...' She faltered. 'Oh, God!' and tears were suddenly in her eyes. She dropped her head onto her arms.

Resentment left Rosena. She rested a comforting hand on Jenny's shoulder. She thought, perhaps she's ill and can't help her strange ways. She gave the girl a handkerchief to dry her eyes. She poured the tea into mugs. 'This'll make 'ee feel better.' And then, as Jenny sat up, Rosena gently asked: 'Why did 'ee try to kill yourself?'

'Never did no such thing.'

'Then tell me why you'm here.'

The girl took a tremulous breath. ''Tis me father. I thought 'e'd understand, seeing it wadn't my fault - but Mum said 'e'd go mad, said I should come and talk to you before 'e found out. She said you'd be able to help me, seein' as your head's full of book-learnin'.'

Uneasiness spread through Rosena. ''Ow can I help 'ee?' she asked.

'Mum said 'ee might be able to tell me 'ow to get rid of it.' Jenny said, then added, 'Tom Lethbridge's bastard, I mean!'

Shock swept through Rosena. ''Tid'n true,' she gasped. 'Tom Lethbridge would never ...'

''Tis true,' the girl argued. 'I swear it! Mum said ... you'd tell me 'ow to get rid of it before my belly starts to ... swell. Please 'elp me ... please!'

Rosena was lost for a reply. She tried to think logically. She knew there was a woman in Truro who undertook such operations, but the thought of it horrified her. One girl, she'd heard, had been punctured internally and nearly died.

And yet, she thought, if the child is born, Tom will be ruined. Nobody would then doubt the girl's story.

'Either that, or maybe you could make Tom Lethbridge feel responsible for the awful thing 'e did.'

Rosena's heart was pounding. 'I'll think about it,' she said, anxious to be rid of her. 'Come back Monday morning. We'll talk again.'

Jenny dabbed her reddened eyes with the handkerchief. 'Thanks, Rosena Bray. Thanks!'

Chapter Nine

JENNY HAD PLUNGED ROSENA'S mind into chaos. At first her anger was turned against Tom. Had he deceived everybody? But that afternoon, as she worked at the packing shed, she felt ashamed of her hasty judgement. The girl might be lying in a further attempt to attract attention or get money. At least, Rosena decided, she must give Tom the chance of reacting in his own way before she condemned him.

Rosena herself had a problem. Jenny would come back on Monday anticipating assistance. The prospect of helping her to terminate her pregnancy was abhorrent to Rosena - and the truth was she had no information about the woman in Truro, apart from what she'd heard from gossiping tongues.

She didn't see Tom when the fleet returned that evening. Her father came home, tired but in good spirits, and after supper he went to bed. Rosena didn't mention Jenny's visit, and after she had cleared away the dishes, she went to her own room. For hours she could not sleep, and come morning she had no clearer idea of what she must do.

Today was Sunday, and at eleven o'clock she knelt with her father at the hill-top church, and prayed for guidance. After dinner she told her father she fancied a walk, and she would go to St Mags and visit Tom. John Bray was pleased. He wondered if his daughter was at last shaking off the memory of the Welshman.

She took the cliff path, passing the old engine house with its chimney raised against the sky. She stood for a while close to the spot where Tom claimed the girl had so nearly committed suicide. The drop was awesome; five-hundred feet below, the sea foamed angrily about the jagged rocks. The thought of leaping into space made her tremble.

She found Tom in the garden behind his cottage, chopping wood. As she approached, he straightened up and put his axe aside. A moment later they were sitting in his kitchen.

'Tom,' she said, 'Jenny Killigrew called yesterday. She says she's expectin'.'

He breathed in sharply. 'She's not sayin' ... I'm the father?'

She gave a dejected nod.

'Oh God ...' His face was a picture of anguish.

'Tom ... 'tid'n true, is it?'

He seemed not to hear. After a moment he swung round. 'Rosena, you don't believe 'er?'

His eyes were on hers. She lowered her head. 'No,' she said.

'Why did she come to you?'

'She said 'er mother told 'er to come, because I might be able to 'elp 'er.'

'How can 'ee 'elp 'er?'

'She wants the child aborted,' she said.

'Oh God, no!' .

'If the child isn't yours, Tom,' Rosena said, 'whose is it?'

He sighed heavily, shaking his head. 'I don't know.'

For a long moment they were silent, each deep in their own thoughts. At last she asked: 'What am I to tell 'er when she comes? She expects me to 'elp 'er.'

His fierce look stifled her words. 'Rosena! Don't 'ee dare push Jenny Killigrew towards abortion!'

'Tom ... I never intended ...' She wilted before his wrath.

''Twould be murder. It can't be contemplated!' He was pacing about the small kitchen.

'Tom,' she said meekly, 'if a child is born, nobody'll believe 'tid'n yours.'

'Except you, Rosena, except you.'

She rose, went to him, slipped her arms around his waist, rested her head on his heaving chest. 'Except me,' she whispered.

'Tomorrow, when she comes,' he murmured, 'tell 'er that if she wants to go away, perhaps into a convent for the birth, then start a new life somewhere else, I'll pay whatever she wants.'

'But, Tom,' she whispered, 'if 'ee do that, people'll say you've accepted the child as your own.'

'It'll hurt my pride, Rosena,' he said. 'If word leaks out, it'll turn people against me. Perhaps I'll 'ave to sell up and leave this place, after all. But at least I'll not 'ave the murder of an unborn child on my conscience.'

She admired his courage. Pressed against him she could feel the pulse of life within him, the increasing pressure of his hands on her back, hugging her tighter, and a sudden warmth went rushing through her veins. Its intensity frightened her so much that she swung away from him, brushing his cheek with her lips, a breathlessness upon her. Previously she'd believed that only Gareth could arouse such stirrings in her.

If Tom sensed her emotion he didn't show it. Kindly he asked, 'Can I get 'ee a bite to eat?'

All she could do was nod.

She sat down, watching him as he moved about his kitchen, cutting cheese, slicing bread, sorting tomatoes to find the ripe ones, pouring water from a jug.

When they were sitting, munching away, he said, 'I'm sorry you've been dragged into this mess.'

'If I can help 'ee,' she said, her mouth full of cheese, 'I'll be glad to.'

'You know what to tell 'er, then?'

'Yes, Tom.'

When she reached home, her father was sitting with the newspaper spread before him on the table. 'Prime Minister's made a speech,' he announced. He peered over the top of his spectacles. 'In Germany, the 'arvest 'as been poor, and with the Allies blockadin' their sea-ports the civilian population's nigh starvin'. There's been demonstrations. There's even talk of the German navy stagin' a mutiny. The only folk doing well are their industrialists. Every German penny is being spent on the production of munitions.' He looked at the newspaper and quoted from the Prime Minister's speech, pausing over the longer words: 'Meanwhile, Allied troops 'ave been called upon to hold firm for days and nights in morasses and under ceaseless thunder-bolts from powerful artillery, and then to march into battle through an engulfin' quagmire, under a 'ail-storm of machine gun fire.'

'Poor Gareth,' Rosena sighed. 'Please God may it all finish soon!' For some time now, she had determined to think positively, to banish from her mind gloomy thoughts of Ensign Perhaver and his bride. She took solace in the saying: no news is good news! Now she contemplated no possibility other than that Gareth would return.

That afternoon, at Perhaver, she kept her spirits buoyant by concentrating on work and helping with the latest influx of young wounded men. She sought information of Gareth, but she met the same shake of the head and the explanation that the Front Line had become very complex.

Once home, she had an early night, her thoughts centred on Jenny Killigrew's visit the next morning. Of course Jenny might insist on going through the frightening process of abortion - but now Rosena knew that Tom's feelings were as strong as her own, she would do everything in her power to prevent such drastic action.

Next morning, she saw her father off to sea. She occupied herself with household chores while the hours ticked by, constantly pausing to gaze through the window for sight of Jenny. At eleven o'clock she made herself a some tea and sat, reading the newspaper. How encouraging the news was:

> *Less than six months after the Germans launched their great offensive, the Allied Armies have turned the tide, have broken the enemy's assaults, and are today advancing victoriously. The German population is calling for an armistice.*

She leaned back, Gareth's Welsh voice whispering through her mind. How much would all the conflict and suffering have changed him?

Suddenly she glanced up. Cedric started his squawk just before the gate sounded, causing her mind to slip back to Jenny Killigrew.

A familiar, homely voice called out. It was not Jenny, but Harry Ansell the postman, not even bringing letters, but just calling for a chat. By the time he'd departed it was past noon. At two o'clock, Rosena concluded that Jenny was not coming. Of course the girl was unreliable, but Rosena had felt sure she would come. Through the afternoon, she became concerned in case Jenny had taken matters into her own hands.

When Tom visited that evening, after a day at sea, they agreed that if the girl did not appear within the next two days, enquiries would have to be made at the Killigrew cottage. At first Tom declared that he would go himself, but Rosena convinced him that this might make matters worse. Silas could well turn murderous, particularly if he'd found out about the girl's pregnancy.

So Wednesday arrived, and in the cool, grey afternoon Rosena took the familiar path to St Mags across the cliff-top. Tom was out at sea. The Killigrews' home was halfway down the village street, conveniently close to the local watering hole. The cottage looked run down, with the thatch broken out from its holding chains. Even the curtains were filthy and tattered, behind windows hazed with an accumulation of salt blown over the years from the sea. She raised the door-knocker, let it fall, hearing sound echo through the inside room as if it was devoid of furnishings.

Martha Killigrew opened up, her hair in tousled disarray, forcing its way out from behind her large ears. There was a smudge of flour on her cheek. 'What can we do for 'ee, Rosena Bray?'

'Is Jenny 'ome?' Rosena asked.

'What's it to you?'

'She came to see me on Saturday, said you told 'er to come.'

'Did she now, the little vixen? I told 'er no such thing.'

'But ...' Rosena stood perplexed. 'Where is she now?'

Martha Killigrew gave a disdainful sniff. 'I wish I knew. Perhaps you put some fancy ideas in 'er 'ead.'

'Where is she?' Rosena persisted impatiently.

'Well, if 'ee want the truth, she left 'ome yesterday mornin'. Went off with young Jack Turnwell. I forbade her to see 'im, but she da always do the opposite to what she's told. Anyway, she ran off wid'm. 'Er father flew into a rage when 'e found out. Jack Turnwell's on leave from army. She left a note, sayin' they was goin' to be married, even if they 'ad to go all the way to Gretna Green.'

Rosena was amazed. She remembered vaguely hearing about young Turnwell, how he'd virtually come to blows with Silas Killigrew after he'd warned him to stay away from his daughter - but that had been a year ago, and she'd forgotten all about it until now.

But now a strange change had come over Martha. It was as if something had cracked inside her, forcing aside her haughty facade. Misery bubbled out of her. 'The girl's given us so much worry,' she sobbed. 'When Jack Turnwell left the village to join the army, we thought that would be the end of the trouble. Now we've found out 'e's been comin' home and meetin' Jenny behind our backs. God knows what they've been up to. Silas went livid the first time 'e found out, gave the girl a good hidin'. You wouldn't credit the row we 'ad in this cottage. And off Jenny and Jack Turnwell go ... and who knows if we'll ever see'm again.'

Rosena tried to absorb this latest twist in events, then she said, 'Mrs Killigrew, I'm really sorry. You must be out of your mind with worry, Jenny expectin' a baby and all!'

'What baby?' Martha gasped.

Rosena felt shock throb through her - shock at her own stupid tongue. 'Perhaps there was no b-baby,' she stammered. 'I must've been mistaken.'

She felt suddenly sick of Jenny's crazy antics, of her mother's strange ways, of Silas and his violence. 'I 'ope, Mrs Killigrew,' she said, 'that Jenny'll find 'appiness with this man, and that she'll cease to be a burden for you.'

Martha said. 'I best tell 'ee the truth - about 'er and Tom Lethbridge. Come inside.'

Mention of Tom stimulated Rosena's interest. A moment later she was in the shabby kitchen. The half-completed makings of a cake stood upon the stained table. A stove was leaking smoke into the room, creating an eye-watering fug. But Martha Killigrew seemed not to notice. ''Tis best you know,' she said, her arrogance completely gone. 'Jenny is a wicked girl. She's always played up to men. 'Er father took 'er across 'is knee and gave her the hidin' she deserved, and that's when she ran out and up along the cliff path.'

'That's when she meant to do away with 'erself,' Rosena said, 'and she met Tom?'

'She had no intention of throwin' 'erself over the cliff,' Martha Killigrew went on. 'Wouldn't 'ave the guts to do that - though she'd fancy the drama of it all!'

'And all this talk about rape?'

Martha snorted dismissively. 'Just a way of gettin' even with Tom Lethbridge. You see ... she never forgave him for givin' 'er the cold shoulder a while back. She thought this was the way to pay 'im back, or perhaps get some money out of 'im ... But she forgot about that when Jack Turnwell asked 'er to run away with 'im.'

'So she wasn't pregnant at all?' Rosena asked.

'If she is, tid'n Tom Lethbridge who's the father.'

For a moment they sat without speaking, the only sound the spit of the stove, the truth seeping through Rosena's mind.

'Now 'ee know everythin',' Martha at last said, 'maybe you'll be glad Jenny's run off. At least she won't cause more trouble round 'ere.'

Rosena reached out and touched the other woman's hand. 'Thanks, Mrs Killigrew. I 'ope Jenny'll realise 'ow wicked she's been, causin' all this concern. I 'ope, wherever she is, she'll find peace of mind.'

Martha gave a sad nod.

Chapter Ten

'IT'S TOO DAMNED LATE to change your mind,' his Uncle Jeremy declared. 'After all, the wedding's tomorrow! Guests have come from all over the country. I'm afraid, Edwin, you'll have to go through with it, even if it does mean spending the rest of your life trying to change her into an honourable woman. After all,' he paused, a lecherous glint in his eye. 'there's many a less pleasant task.'

Both men watched Elspeth moving about the crowded room, laughing with people, particularly males, a glass of wine in her elegant hand. She was full of coquettish, Yorkshire charm, fluttering her long eyelashes. Her family had made a fortune in business and had climbed the social ladder. Now she revelled in being the centre of attention.

A sense of depression settled over Edwin. He knew that many a man would give his eye-teeth to have her. It was true that whilst he'd been in the trenches and later in hospital, amid all the blood and suffering, the illusion of her waiting faithfully at home had been like a guiding star. But now everything had gone sour.

Of course his Uncle Jeremy and Aunt Beryl wanted the match to take place for more than one reason. Elspeth's father owned Huddersfield's foremost textile mill - Emsfield Fabrics. He had set his mill working overtime to feed the Army's insatiable appetite for khaki. Uncle Jeremy knew that it would be a monumental business coup if, through marriage, he could fuse Emsfield Fabrics with his own company, Carter-Wilson (Textile Warehousemen).

When Edwin had come home, recovered from his wound, the marriage plans had gone ahead, and today it seemed that Yorkshire's entire nouveau riche, had descended on London for the wedding. A mountain of presents awaited attention at St Carlton's Hotel in Leicester Street, where the reception was to be held, and the gift from Elspeth's parents, a fine Lanchester motor car, was due for delivery tomorrow. But there was one fly in the ointment: Edwin had discovered that Elspeth had been deceiving him.

But perhaps tomorrow, after vows had been exchanged, everything would be different. Perhaps a leopard could change her spots.

The mahogany pews of St Peter's Church in Belgravia Square were packed next day, the colourful dresses of the ladies tempered by the black morning suits of the men. Now, as time moved close to noon, the excited murmurings gave way to an expectant hush. The organ had completed its overtures, the organist gently massaging his fingers in readiness for the entrance of the bride. Edwin, despite dark patches beneath his eyes, looked immaculate in his grey morning suit, silver-grey cravat, lavender waistcoat, and white gloves. He waited at the head of the aisle. his top-hat beneath his arm. Just behind him, was the Groom's Man, his cousin Geoffrey Frenchcombe.

Of course mid-summer would have been preferable for the ceremony, but the two families had agreed that the war had already delayed things long enough. Anyway, it was as fine a winter's day as had ever been.

Suddenly everybody heard the sound of the bride's carriage as it drew up outside. There was a pause, then the organ roared into life, its triumphant power flooding the *Bridal March* into every cranny of the church. Elspeth made her entry on her father's arm, moving up the aisle with slow majesty. Edwin took a glance over his shoulder. His chest should have been swelling with pride, for his bride was a vision of loveliness. She was radiant in a fine-gauze veil and frothy gown, and her bouquet, a Victorian posy, was decorated by streaming ribbons. Her train was held by four girls, also in frothy gowns, with circlets of flowers on their heads.

Edwin felt as if his veins had stiffened with ice. A vision flashed into his mind, a vision of silky underwear being shed, of naked bodies writhing together on a bed, of throaty laughter turning to ecstatic groans - Elspeth's ...

She took her place alongside him, passing her bouquet to a bridesmaid, the heady sweetness of her perfume wafting to him, but their eyes did not meet, and, as the opening hymn finished, the officiating vicar, clutching his prayer-book, stood before them. He spoke with such a resonance that he might have been God Himself ... 'Dearly beloved, we are gathered together here in the sight of God and in the face of this congregation, to join together this man and this woman ...'

Edwin's attention wavered, his ears only catching odd phrases here and there as the vicar spoke of Holy Matrimony ... 'Is not in any way to be enterprised, nor taken in hand unadvisedly ... to satisfy men's carnal lusts and appetites, like brute beasts that have no understanding ... First. It was ordained for the procreation of children ... for a remedy against sin and to avoid fornication ...Therefore if any man can show any just cause, why they may not lawfully be joined together, let him now speak or else hereafter for ever hold his peace.'

The vicar paused. The challenge was thrown to the congregation and greeted with quickly stifled coughs.

Edwin felt wet with perspiration. He watched the vicar open his mouth to continue. 'I require and charge you both, as ye will answer at the dreadful day of judgement ... that if either of you know of any impediment why ye may not be lawfully joined together in Matrimony ye do now confess it. For be ye well assured that so many as are coupled together, otherwise than God's Word doth allow, are not joined together by God; neither is their Matrimony lawful.'

Somehow the next second hung suspended in time, as if they had all been turned to salt like Lot's wife..

Suddenly, Edwin's voice came of its own accord, but was drowned by the sudden commotion of incredulous titterings from the congregation, which was soon stifled by the demands of those eager to listen.

Edwin had turned, squarely facing the sea of astonished expressions, and all at once, with the decision made, his confidence grew. 'At this point in the service,' he proclaimed, 'I must thank my aunt and uncle for bringing me up as if I was their own child. I would also like to express my respect for Elspeth's parents who have shown me great kindness. I know I speak for Elspeth and myself, when I say how grateful we are for all the wedding presents. And finally, perhaps the two most important thank-yous of all. Firstly, to my Groom's Man, Geoffrey. Ever since childhood we have shared practically everything.' Edwin reached out and grasped Geoffrey's hand, hanging onto it. 'And the final thanks goes to my lovely Elspeth whose generous nature knows no bounds,' and he gave her a warm smile and clutched her hand, ignored her indignant, 'What the hell are you playing at, Edwin!' and gently forced her to turn and face the congregation.

He paused, the expanse of faces before him showing amusement and tolerance. It was hardly appropriate for the bridegroom to make a speech during the service, but it seemed his intentions were noble.

He continued: 'As a token of the indebtedness I feel towards Geoffrey and Elspeth, I will no longer act as an obstacle which they have to creep around. I therefore make them a gift of each other, and remove from them the strain of making love behind my back!' With a flourish, he sacrificed his hold on their hands and, not glancing to either side, marched down the aisle, totally unaware that Elspeth had pirouetted and fainted into the arms of her lover.

Outside the church, Edwin stopped, listened to the uproar of incredulous voices behind him; then he struck off across Belgravia Square, breathing in the crisp, free air. In his pocket were the honeymoon rail-tickets for Cornwall. He decided that at least his ticket would be put to good use.

Chapter Eleven

ALL BRITAIN WAS AWASH with red, white and blue, the colours contrasting with the grey November skies. At Megstow Quay, the piano sounded continuously from *The Cherry Bowl,* nearly every cottage displayed a Union Jack, and bunting was suspended across the narrow streets. Rosena had never seen so many people looking as happy or as tipsy. The announcement of the Armistice had created an amazing sociability, and smiles and cheerful greetings were everywhere.

Outside the general store, a placard proclaimed:

HOSTILITIES CEASED ON ALL FRONTS 11 A.M. YESTERDAY!

and Rosena offered a silent prayer that Gareth would soon return.

She gratefully accepted a celebratory glass of brandy, from Mr Arnold, manager of the general stores, who himself was tipsy, his eyes glazed. Somehow Rosena persuaded him to serve her with the groceries she selected from the shelves then she left the shop, stepping around the galvanised pails on display outside. On the street, a young man, for some reason glancing backwards, bumped into her, causing her packets to fall. He turned, his rosy-cheeked face showing concern. He stooped to retrieve the fallen items and restore them to her basket. He was only slightly older than herself, and from the fine cut of his raglan coat, she could see he was gentry.

'I do apologise for my clumsiness,' he said. 'The brandy must've gone to my head.'

'Me too,' she giggled, feeling quite inebriated. "Tis a good job war doesn't end every day!'

'Once will be quite enough,' he said seriously. 'This must be the war to end all wars!'

She found herself gazing at his angelic, boyish face. He had dark hair, honest eyes and, she decided, lips that were most kissable. She censured herself. One drink, and she was ready to throw herself into the arms of a stranger!

She adopted a slightly prim attitude, nodding in agreement with his sentiments. Their eyes met.

'The least I can do,' he said, 'is carry your basket.'

She showed a reluctance, then relented. 'I suppose t'will do no 'arm,' and he relieved her of the burden and they started down the street.

'You'm a stranger 'ere?' she asked, for want of something more intelligent to say. 'You'm on holiday?'

'A sort of holiday,' he said. 'I'm staying at *The Cherry Bowl*.' He paused, frowning. 'It was to have been my honeymoon, but my wedding was cancelled at the last moment ... so I came minus my bride!'

'Oh ...' She was aghast. 'I am sorry.'

To her surprise he laughed. 'It was all rather sordid really. I ...' he checked himself. He had no right to shock this sweet Cornish girl with his woes. Instead, he slowed their pace for he was not anxious to conclude their togetherness. Her presence seemed sweet and uncomplicated.

'It must've been awful for 'ee,' she said.

'You've always lived here?' he asked.

She nodded, in no way hurrying the snail's speed of their progress. 'I've never been further than Truro, and that was some years ago.' She noted how he changed the basket to his right hand, grunting as if caught by pain.

'You 'ave a bad arm?' she enquired.

'I have a slight war wound, but it's practically better now.'

'You were at the Front?'

'Yes, but I got hit by some shrapnel and they sent me home.'

'Tell me,' she said with sudden intensity, 'did 'ee know a soldier called Williams ... Gareth Williams?'

He shook his head. 'No, I can't recall a Williams. There were so many men ...'

'Of course,' she nodded, disappointed - but suddenly he stopped.

'Oh ... Yes, I can,' he said. 'I remember a Williams. He came up with reinforcements just before we marched for that final assault.' He paused, gathering his thoughts. 'It was his first time in action and he didn't shape up very well. He had some sort of injury. Apparently he'd fallen out of a window. The others made fun of him, reckoned he had a yellow streak .' He paused, conscious that he might have upset the girl. 'Of course Williams is a very common name.'

''Twas not my Gareth,' she said. 'E'd been wounded in action.'

He nodded, relieved his criticisms of the man had not offended her. 'I personally knew no other Williams,' he said.

'Now the war's finished, I'm sure 'e'll be home soon. You see ...' She hesitated as they reached the cottage gate, taking the basket from him, 'we're to be married when 'e comes back.'

He smiled. 'Then I wish you happiness.' He held out his hand. 'It's been a joy meeting you. My name's Edwin Carter.'

She shook his hand, feeling her cheeks tingling. 'I'm Rosena Bray.'

'May we go shopping again, Miss Bray? Perhaps tomorrow?'

'I can't afford to go shoppin' every day, nor do I need to!'

'Then you must show me around the village. I'd be extremely grateful.'

'There's not much to see.' She wavered. 'But all right. I'll meet 'ee 'ere, same time.'

He laughed and doffed his deer-stalker hat. 'I'll look forward to it.' And he watched her as she walked into the cottage.

Her father drew back from the kitchen window as she entered. 'Who's the young fellow?' he asked.

'Oh ... 'e's on 'oliday down 'ere. From London, I think. 'E was in the war, but 'e got wounded and sent 'ome.'

John Bray nodded. ''E looked a pleasant man. Why don't 'ee invite 'im for tea.'

She put her groceries in the cupboard. 'I might,' she said.

Meanwhile, Edwin had continued his walk, reaching the dunes. It was a dull day with dankness in the air. He stood, gazing down the beach to the grey sea. The waves reminded him of men marching relentlessly.

The girl had cheered him up. Many of his friends would say that he was always cheerful, but that was because they did not know that he often hid behind a facade of exuberance. Today, his thoughts had frequently drifted to France. He still regretted that he had left his men and not seen the war through to its bitter conclusion. And if that wasn't depressing enough, there was the disaster of his wedding day. He felt bad about the disruption he had caused his aunt and uncle. The whole affair must have been deeply humiliating for them. He had written, trying to explain his behaviour, begging forgiveness, but they could hardly be blamed if they chose to disown him. As for Elspeth, he had no regrets.

But something else was dragging his spirits down.

He walked over the sands, the cold wind whipping at his cheeks. He had always promised that one day he would return, experience first hand the grim ambience of the waves and wind-swept shore. The prospect of spending his honeymoon here had been an opportunity to confront his past and at the same time have Elspeth with him to provide comfort.

But she was not here. So he stood alone and tears came to his eyes as he recalled long-ago events, which now overshadowed all else, even the horrific memories of the war. The shrill cries of the gulls became the voices of the dead, calling to him from beneath the waves.

'Your Gareth must be a fine man,' Edwin said as they walked up the hill towards the derelict engine-house. It was a cold day, far too miserable for sight-seeing, but he seemed not to care.

'Yes,' she said. 'I 'ope 'e comes 'ome soon.'

They scrambled through some blackberry bushes and reached the base of the old chimney. The walls were a crumbling jig-saw of masonry cloaked with ivy. Edwin appeared fascinated and they gazed up at the rusted metal attachments and the empty squares of the windows. Afterwards they peered into the mouths of gloomy galleries where low walls created a series of cubicles. Something about this place had always scared Rosena, but with this man at her side, she felt no fear.

When they emerged they paused at the cliff-edge and she pointed out various land marks. He stood for a long time looking out to sea, deep in thought.

'I'm sorry about your weddin',' she said, anxious to recapture his attention. She was inquisitive by nature and the whole mystery of his sudden appearance at Megstow Quay interested her,

'It's a long story,' he said. 'I've not told anybody so far. I'd like to get it out of my system.'

'Whatever 'ee tell me,' she said quietly, 'will be confidential.'

He glanced at her. He loved to look at her face. It was so candid and he knew he could trust her. 'Let's sit over there.' He pointed to a slab of rock, close to the ruin. 'It's out of the wind.'

'I'm in the Army,' he explained as they sat down, 'but soon I will be discharged. Then, I hope to work again for my uncle, visiting the wool mills in Yorkshire, placing orders. I met Elspeth in Yorkshire. We were attracted to each other at first sight. Her beauty took my breath away. I wondered what she saw in me.'

Rosena was gazing at him with attentiveness. She could well understand any woman being attracted to him. His keen, blue eyes were frequently lit with laughter, his rosy-cheeked face was glowing with life.

'We had,' he went on, 'what might be called a tempestuous affair. So many parties and dances. I often went up to Yorkshire, and when I wasn't there, she would come down to London, staying with her sister. I wined and dined her and we went to the theatre. I felt very proud of her. Of course she met my cousin Geoffrey Frenchcombe and he flattered her, as he does all women.' He paused, gathering his thoughts, then he continued. 'After she accepted my proposal, I joined the Army and went to France, and ...' France, he thought, had it really happened? Had he really experienced hell and survived? He had spoken to nobody about it since he'd returned.

'And?' she queried gently.

'When I came home and recovered from my wound, I learned that she'd been spending all her time in London during my absence. My uncle was most anxious for our marriage to proceed because Elspeth's father is a bigwig in the Yorkshire wool trade. Well, all the wedding arrangements were made, and then one evening I called in at my cousin Geoffrey's rooms for a brandy. He was my Groomsman. While he was in his kitchen, I spotted a letter on his writing bureau. I recognised Elspeth's writing. What I did next was quite wrong. I don't know what came over me, but I picked up the letter and had it hidden in my pocket by the time he came back into the room.'

She inhaled sharply, somehow sharing his trepidation, thankful that his cousin had not caught him red-handed.

'When I read that letter I nearly died of shock. I could have taken her to court.'

'But 'ee didn't?'

'She'd written that marriage to me would make no difference to their wonderful relationship. With me away on business so often, they would have plenty of time to themselves. And she went on to write the most intimate, passionate details. The whole thing sickened me so much, that I walked out on the wedding. Do you blame me?'

'No!' she murmured supportively.

'Thank you for listening to my tale of woe.'

She felt embarrassed and somehow honoured by his candidness. 'I must go back,' she said. 'Father'll be 'ome soon expectin' supper.'

'Of course,' he nodded, rising to his feet. 'Can I see you again?'

'I would like that,' she said.

'Tomorrow, then, same time?'

She shook her head. 'I can't tomorrow. I'm workin' up Perhaver.'

'Perhaver?'

'Yes. 'Tis a convalescence 'ome for wounded soldiers. I 'elp with the welfare. 'Tis where I met Gareth.'

'Oh ...' Her words had triggered off a memory - an incident in the trenches. Seeing the address on a letter Rifleman Williams had written, he'd asked the man if he came from Cornwall. 'No sir,' the reply had come, 'I met a young lady when I was in 'ospital down there!'

He lapsed into a silence. Rosena was so in love that he hadn't the heart to disillusion her.

'I'm busy tomorrow,' she was explaining, 'but would 'ee come to tea at our cottage on Thursday? I told Father about you. 'E'd love to meet you.'

'I'd appreciate that, Rosena.'

Somehow the mere sight of Edwin through the kitchen window had satisfied John Bray that here was a gentleman who would in no way take advantage of his daughter. And also, any person who could stop her mooning over her Welshman was more than welcome to take tea with them.

Rosena had baked a cake and some scones, cut some crab sandwiches, and prepared cream. She'd set the table with their finest tea-set. 'We must treat 'im like gentry,' she told her father, 'because that's what 'e is.'

She washed, went upstairs and checked her face in the mirror, then she put on her brown velvet dress and pinned up her hair. When she spotted Edwin walking down the street, she hurried out to meet him. After she had taken his fine coat and placed it carefully upon a hanger, she introduced him to her father, and the two men talked about the fishing industry. She noticed how Edwin was adept at encouraging others to talk about themselves. But, like many men who had been to war, he refrained from mentioning it. For some reason, Gareth had never shown such reticence. Presently they sat around the table and Rosena poured the tea.

'What a beautiful cake!' Edwin exclaimed.

''Tis saffron - a Cornish speciality,' she said.

'Saffron,' he murmured appreciatively. 'I've heard it is very expensive to buy.'

As they started to eat, John Bray said, 'Tell us about London, Mr Carter.'

Edwin painted a glowing picture of life in the big city, of people dressed smartly - he loved to talk about clothes and fine cloth - the shops, the streets and buses, the great parks and churches, the theatres, and the motor cars. Rosena listened entranced.

'We don't get many motor cars down 'ere,' she said.

'It must seem strange to be in Cornwall, bein' so quiet,' John Bray commented. ''Ave 'ee ever been this way before?'

Edwin hesitated, then said, 'Once before, when I was a toddler. In 1890 to be precise. I can't remember it at all.'

'You came with your aunt and uncle?' Rosena enquired.

'N-No,' he said, and she sensed a reluctance in him.

'Perhaps Mr Carter'd would rather not talk about it,' John Bray said.

'Yes,' Rosena said, pouring some more tea. ''Tis none of our business.'

'There's nothing secret about it,' Edwin said. 'It just frightens me when I dwell on it. It was sheer chance that I didn't drown with my family.'

'Drown!' Rosena gasped.

Edwin placed some jam on his scone. 'They were all drowned when a ship called the *Atlantic Queen* went down ...'

For some reason, Rosena glanced at her father and was shocked by his taut expression. For a moment she thought he had been taken ill again, but suddenly he spoke up: 'Terrible tragedy strikes us all from time to time, but life 'as to go on.'

'Indeed,' Edwin said, and he turned to Rosena, his face cheerful again. 'I do hope we'll have time for some more walks before I go back.'

'Of course,' Rosena said. Something very odd had passed between her father and Edwin Carter - and clearly her father had been shaken. But now his mood lifted, and Edwin talked about his uncle's business; and how he hoped to rejoin the firm after he left the Army, that was if his uncle forgave him for walking out at the wedding. She understood now why he dressed so immaculately, for his knowledge of textiles and clothes was profound. His Uncle Jeremy owned a warehouse near to St Paul's churchyard in London. Before going to war, Edwin had worked for him - travelling to the Yorkshire mills.

Rosena was glad Edwin was an easy talker. Her father was not ungracious, but she noticed how he stared at Edwin. She thought he might be tired, and perhaps Edwin sensed it too, for presently he stood up and thanked them for their hospitality. Rosena fetched his coat.

Edwin shook John Bray's hand. 'It was an honour to meet you, sir,' he said, and John Bray bowed his head in acknowledgement.

Rosena walked with Edwin to the gate.

'I'm sorry that my stories sometimes shock you,' he said.

She shook her head. 'You have suffered so much.'

'You look so pretty when you're shocked,' he said. 'Of course that's why I tell you these stories. To make you look pretty!'

'Then they're not true?'

'I'm afraid they are,' he sighed. 'Thank you for the tea. I'll see you tomorrow.'

'Yes,' she said with an eagerness she couldn't restrain. She watched him walk up the street, turning to wave once. A pang of guilt came to her. With the war over, and Gareth, please God, coming home soon, she had no right to allow another man to stir her emotions.

Once back inside, her mind kept returning to Edwin. He was gentle and kind and pleasant, but there was something in his past, some dark secret, that troubled him.

''E's a nice young man,' she said to her father.

''E is,' John Bray agreed, 'but 'e's not of our class, Rosena. 'E'd soon tire of the likes of us.'

She dried the plates and placed them in the cupboard. Her father's attitude puzzled her. He had known from the start that Edwin was from the gentry; yet he had wanted to invite him for tea. Now, suddenly, his feelings had changed. Why?

She glanced at his craggy face, and saw something there that she'd seen once before, long ago, when she was eight. She'd never forgotten that dreadful fight he'd had with the Taunton Terror. She remembered the haunted expressions of her parents, and the clam-like way they'd refused to talk about the past. Now she saw that same firm set of his jaw, as if it would take a wrench to prise it open. Even so, she didn't like to see her father disturbed. Something about Edwin's visit had given him a terrible fright.

Chapter Twelve

EDWIN WAS UNABLE TO SLEEP. His small room at *The Cherry Bowl* had assumed the characteristics of a prison cell. With its pretty chintz curtains and soft eiderdown, this should have been a lover's nest, a place of paradise, where he and Elspeth became one in body and mind. Instead, he was alone, haunted by the bleak visions of the past, in particular the young German NCO's agony-contorted face, his mouth open, pleading for death.

Another scene probed into his mind. Grenades were bursting; he had seen one man disintegrate into small pieces - and then he was gazing down into a crater where Rifleman Williams crouched over the body of Corporal Russell. The NCO was clearly finished, and Williams claimed he was wounded. Edwin had shouted at him to wait for a stretcher party.

He had confided to Rosena about the farce of his wedding day, but he knew he could not do the same about the fate of her Gareth. Of course there was the possibility that the Rifleman Williams who had died in the crater was a different man - but he doubted it.

With Gareth dead, it was wrong that she should waste herself on a dream which would never be fulfilled, yet he could not face stifling her hope, unless there was positive proof. Perhaps, if there was one service he could do her, it was to provide the indisputable truth - and then, somehow, give her the support to accept it.

Next morning, at the breakfast table, a letter post-marked London awaited him. Apprehensively, he recognised his Uncle Jeremy's business-like writing. Here was the answer to his own letter, begging forgiveness for his outlandish behaviour. Would the response be sharp and ruthless, depriving him of love, family employment and inheritance? He tore it open.

Amazingly, his uncle had seen the funny side of things. All was forgiven. It was not the end of the world. Edwin could imagine Jeremy throwing back his head, roaring with laughter, Aunt Beryl watching with warm, doting eyes. Edwin read on:

But don't be such a bloody fool next time. Once you fancy a woman, marry her and get her in the family way before she has time to draw breath! Now, the sooner you get back to work the better. With the war over, the bottom will drop out of the khaki trade - but at least you can't say the same for ladies' drawers! The demand is insatiable. That's where our future lies, my boy. We need you.
Yours affectionately
Uncle Jeremy.

Edwin had been in need of a pick-me-up. The letter provided it. When he met Rosena that afternoon, he told her that his uncle wanted him to travel in ladies' drawers, and she laughed so much they had to sit down. The day was fine they walked along the cliffs. He knew that their relationship was restrained because the Welshman was never far from her mind and he respected her loyalty.

Rosena had no doubt that Edwin was quite capable of being a wonderful lover, and under other circumstances she would have welcomed his advances. Instead, for some reason, she found herself telling him about her first days at the village school when she was five years old. 'I was so shy,' she explained, 'I wouldn't even answer my name when teacher called the roll. She got really angry, said she'd expel me if I didn't answer. She reported me to Father.'

'What did he do?' Edwin enquired.

''E made me rehearse at home. 'E pretended 'e was teacher, callin' out the names - and when 'e called out mine, I 'ad to answer 'Yes, Miss!'. We must've done it a hundred times. And eventually I got it right every time.'

'So you went back to school and answered the teacher.'

She pulled a wry face and shook her head. 'I just froze when I was at school.' They both roared with laughter. 'But one day teacher took me in 'er arms, gave me a cuddle, and said would I please 'elp her by answerin' because she didn't know what else she could do about it. And after that, I never 'ad any trouble.'

He kept chuckling to himself. He loved the story. Presently, as they walked across the cliff-top meadows, they came upon a herd of cows quietly chewing their cud. The beasts trusted Rosena implicitly and allowed her to touch their soft noses.

'They have such gentle, serious eyes,' Edwin remarked, 'and long silky eyelashes.'

'They flick their tails as if they were paint brushes,' Rosena added.

'Well if that's the case,' Edwin confided, 'I don't think much of the paint they splash around!' It was a comment of no great wit, yet it appealed to Rosena and tears of mirth glistened in her eyes as she laughed.

They passed along narrow paths through wooded bowers which smelt of earth. Presently, he told her he had to return to London in three days time. He hoped that his Army discharge would soon be finalised and he would resume employment with his uncle.

'May we correspond, Rosena?' he enquired.

'I'd like to, Edwin, but I'm committed to Gareth.'

He sighed, then said, 'Would you wish me to make enquiries about him through the War Office? Perhaps I could find out where he is.'

"Tis kind of you,' she said thoughtfully, 'but there might be a quicker way. 'Is sister-in-law at Trethomas might 'ave news. She owns a boardin' 'ouse there, but I don't 'ave the address.'

He said, 'Well, the local police station's bound to have a list of boarding houses.'

Her mood became animated again. 'Then I shall go to Trethomas,' she said. 'I've 'ad enough waitin'. I love Gareth and I've got to find 'im.'

'If you go during the next three days,' he suggested, 'I could come with you.'

'Then we'll go tomorrow.'

He was fascinated by her impulsiveness. He had never known a woman who was so ostensibly open, so lacking in pretension, or who wore her heart so openly upon her sleeve.

On the train, she gazed with entranced eyes through the carriage windows, seeing sights of the world beyond a radius of Truro for the first time. She appeared not to consider that their mission to Trethomas might end in heartbreak, nor did the fact that she had received no recent letters from Gareth diminish her conviction that his sister-in-law would reassure her as to his safety.

Reaching Cardiff, they crossed the town on the top-deck of a tram. She had never seen such busy streets, and so excited was she that she grasped Edwin's hand like a child, and it was still there as they boarded the train at Queen Street Station en-route for Merthyr Tydfil.

When they had planned their venture, Edwin had suggested that they stayed overnight at some boarding house. At first she had hesitated, suspecting that her father might disapprove - but then she realised that he would be away on an overnight fishing trip and would be none the wiser, so she agreed.

By half-past-four they were in a bus on the final leg of the journey, and when they dismounted, the conductor directed them to Trethomas police station. With dusk descending, they walked through the narrow streets; the air was thick with acrid smoke. "Tis worse than the smell of fish!' she complained.

Soon Edwin was enquiring about the guesthouse of Mrs Williams and a police-sergeant explained the way: 'In Parry Street it is, just past the chapel.' They walked on, Rosena grateful for Edwin's arm, passing a group of miners, illuminated by a street lamp, their faces black.

Ten minutes later Edwin knocked at the guesthouse door. It was now bitterly cold, but a light glowed warmly from behind the frosted window. A woman's voice sounded from inside: 'Put your dolls away, Gwenda love!' and then the door was opened by a round-bodied woman whose hair glinted russet in the hallway light.

'Is it Mrs Williams?' Edwin asked.

'Yes.'

And now Rosena joined Edwin on the step, her heart pounding with excitement. 'Mrs Bronwyn Williams?' she enquired.

'That's right, but ...'

'I'm Rosena Bray.' Rosena believed her announcement would banish all confusion.

Bronwyn looked puzzled. 'I'm sorry, I don't ...'

Rosena said, 'Surely Gareth mentioned me?'

'Gareth!' Bronwyn cried. 'You've 'eard about 'im!'

'No ... We've 'eard nothin' about 'im. That's why we're 'ere - to ask you.' Rosena paused, then she repeated: 'Surely Gareth mentioned me?'

At the sound of Gareth's name, sudden hope had flared in Bronwyn. But now disappointment dulled her voice. 'No. Why should 'e mention you?'

Pride shone in Rosena's face. 'We're goin' to be married!'

Bronwyn felt her legs go weak. 'Married!' she gasped. 'Are you sure it's Gareth you mean?'

Rosena nodded. 'I'm very worried, Mrs Williams. I've not 'eard from 'im for weeks. Now the war's finished, we wondered if you knew where 'e is.'

Bronwyn was flabbergasted. 'You'd better come in,' she at last managed.

As they entered the narrow hallway, they saw for the first time the young girl, watching them suspiciously. Her face startled Rosena for it was so like Gareth's.

Her mam sent her scuttling away. 'Go and eat your supper, Gwenda!'

Bronwyn led them into the front room, turned up the light and poked the coal fire. 'Mrs Williams,' Rosena persisted, "ave 'ee news of Gareth?'

'Yes,' Bronwyn said, straightening up, her face grave. 'Do sit down. I'll make some tea.'

Before Rosena could speak, Bronwyn had left them. The Cornish girl gazed at the two fine paintings on the walls. She reached up and touched the artist's signatures - *Gareth Williams.*

'They're wonderful pictures,' Edwin murmured. 'Rosena, you mustn't build your hopes too high.'

She hardly seemed to hear. She moved about the room, knowing that Gareth had probably sat in this very room. Somehow she could feel his presence all around her.

When Bronwyn returned with the tea, she found her two visitors sitting side by side upon the sofa. Bronwyn was anxious to find out more about this girl who claimed she intended marrying her husband. She felt the best way to draw her out was to be economical with the truth.

'Where did you meet Gareth?' she enquired, assuming a casual air as she poured the tea.

'While 'e was convalescin' in Cornwall,' Rosena responded, but now her patience was growing thin. 'Mrs Williams ... where is Gareth now? Is 'e all right?'

Bronwyn leaned back in her chair, her eyes fixed firmly on her young visitor. 'You were very much in love with each other, then?' she said.

'Yes ... yes. Is he all right!'

'I'm afraid, Miss Bray,' Bronwyn announced, taking a cruel delight in stifling the affair, 'Gareth is dead, killed in France.'

'Oh no!' Disbelief clouded Rosena's face. 'No ... no!' She glanced at Edwin, seeking assurance that her ears were deceiving her. Finding none she sobbed loudly and slumped forward, her face buried in her hands.

Edwin slipped his arm around her shoulders. This was the moment he'd dreaded.

'I heard from the War Office last week,' Bronwyn was explaining. 'I'm sorry to upset you.'

'Mrs Williams,' Edwin murmured, 'could you leave us alone for a little while? This has been a terrible shock for Rosena.'

'Of course.' Bronwyn rose. 'If you want lodgings I've got some rooms available. I'll warm the beds.' And I'll charge you the top rate, she added beneath her breath.

'That would be splendid,' Edwin said.

A moment later Bronwyn was in her kitchen, shaking with anger. If the girl was shocked, so was she! He promised to marry her, she thought scornfully, and what did he get in exchange? She stamped her foot. She fumbled in a drawer, found the buff War Office telegram ...

```
Regret to inform you ... Rifleman Gareth
Williams missing in action, presumed dead.
```

All along she'd consoled herself with the words in the letter from Gareth's Commanding Officer: 'Presumed dead' does not mean 'definitely dead.' But now in a tantrum she screwed up the telegram. She had no wish to speak with the Cornish girl again; certainly she saw no point in going through the trauma of informing her that Gareth was her husband. Instead she focused her bitterness against her husband. If the Germans hadn't killed him, she bloody would!

Meanwhile, Edwin comforted Rosena with gentle words. Sobbing, she hugged onto him and he felt the gentle nudge of her breasts and the warm softness of her body, and he knew that he loved her. But he would not take advantage of her now, though he was sure it wouldn't be long before she would welcome his advances.

Chapter Thirteen

'NOW THE WAR'S OVER,' John Bray remarked, 'at least we don't 'ave to worry about U-Boats.'

Tom Lethbridge nodded and thought: And I don't have to feel ashamed about not being in khaki!

The two men were below deck in John Bray's boat *Silver Cloud*. In the cuddy they were studying their charts. The nine craft of Megstow Quay fleet had been using Newlyn as their base, spreading their drift nets west of Land's End and reaping a steady harvest. The third member of their crew, Seth Currow, who was stone deaf, was on deck steering the vessel.

In the uncertain light of the oil lamps, John Bray looked haggard and tired. He worked hard, despite the fact that Tom tried to get him to take it easy. The heavy manual tasks were constantly repeated: shooting out the string of nets, drawing them in, shaking out the catch and, at the end of the day, stowing the nets and coiling down the warp. All the while they kept watch for treacherous weather.

Now, as they sat down in the cabin, bracing themselves against the roll of the boat, John Bray conceded his fallibility for the first time. 'Tom, I've not been feelin' so good of late. I can't go on forever. One day, I could get another attack and I'd be gone. And God willin', I can leave this world with peace of mind.'

'Well, I'm sure you'll have no problem there. You've always done your best.'

John Bray shook his white head. 'I've been tortured, Tom. Twenty-seven years ago, I did somethin' awful, and it won't rest in me.' He paused, head down.

'Some crime?' Tom prompted, puzzled.

John Bray nodded. 'Black, wicked crime - and the trouble is, if I don't confess it, other people may suffer.'

'Who?'

'Rosena ... and this fellow she's met from London, Edwin Carter.'

Tom sighed. 'I've seen them walkin' together in the village. There's a closeness about 'em.'

'That's what worries me,' John Bray continued. 'At first, I felt it would be good if 'e could make Rosena forget that Welshman. I'm sure 'e's either dead or gone off with somebody else, but Rosena grieves 'er heart for 'im.'

'I hope she'll learn the truth soon,' Tom said, 'then she can start livin' again. She's not made to spend 'er days in grief.'

'I'm worried that if she finds her Welshman is gone, she'll set 'er heart on Edwin Carter.' He gripped the sleeve of Tom's coat to emphasise his words. 'And she must never, never marry 'im!'

Tom was taken aback, but John Bray went on, his voice edged with desperation. 'Tom, if anythin' 'appens to me, if I 'ave another attack, there'll be nobody around to stop them marryin', unless ...'

'Unless?'

John Bray took a ragged breath. 'Unless you do.'

Tom showed impatience. 'Tell me what you mean straight out!'

'Promise me you won't let them marry because ... What I'm tryin' to say, is that Edwin Carter and Rosena are brother and sister!'

'Brother and sister!' Tom Lethbridge's pipe dropped from his mouth. He grappled with John Bray's startling revelation. 'What you're sayin',' he at last got out, 'is that you're Edwin's father, as well as Rosena's?'

'No, I'm not Edwin's father, and ... and I'm not Rosena's true father either!'

'What!' Tom shook his head in bewilderment, his mouth agape. After a moment, he said, 'If 'tis true what 'ee say, why don't you tell Rosena?'

'Can't you understand, Tom? I'm not 'er father. It'll capsize her world if she finds that out. But if it's the only way of stoppin' 'er marryin' Edwin, then she'll 'ave to know - but not before. Maybe their relationship'll fizzle out. I do 'ope so.'

Tom tried to think calmly. He felt staggered by the burden of being unwillingly privy to this black secret.

'You'd better tell me the whole story,' he said quietly.

'Mam!' Gwenda called. 'There's a soldier to see you!'

'Well, ask him in then!' Bronwyn was at the head of the staircase, polishing the brass rods. Now she put aside her tin of Brasso and stood up. It was three weeks since the visit of the Bray girl and her friend, but Bronwyn's blood was still boiling from what she'd learned. If Gareth was in his grave, he'd be turning in it like a pig on a spit. She went down the stairs to find an Army officer in the hallway. He was clutching an important looking briefcase. 'Mrs Bronwyn Williams,' he said in a clipped, Scottish voice, 'I'm Captain MacArthur. I'd be grateful for a moment of your time.'

There were some guests in the front room, so she led him to the kitchen. He sat down a chair, and took some documents from his briefcase. 'I'm here regarding somebody we think might be your husband, Mrs Williams.'

He produced a large photograph from his papers. 'Is this him?'

She peered at the photograph. Gwenda was craning her neck to see. 'That's Uncle Gareth for sure,' she said, 'but doesn't 'e look funny!'

The picture was just head and shoulders. Gareth's eyes were like large vacant pools. His face was scarred and there was a bandage around his head.

Bronwyn took a deep breath. 'Yes, it's 'im.'

'Well,' Captain MacArthur explained, 'he received a terrible wound on the battlefield. A bomb exploded near to him. It affected his memory. Our people found him in a German hospital they overran, but identification has been very difficult. He hasn't spoken a word, doesn't know who he is.'

Despite everything, Bronwyn felt tearful. 'Where is 'e now?' she asked.

'Cambridge Military Hospital at Aldershot. We'd like you to visit him. Seeing you might just spark off something in his memory.'

Her gaze dwelt on the photograph, then it swung to the wedding picture on her dresser. There they were, leaving the chapel arm in arm, Gareth with a satisfied smile, and her gazing up at him with adoring, trusting eyes.

'Will we go and see Uncle Gareth, Mam?' Gwenda asked. 'Give 'im a piece of your mind you can, and tell 'im what a nasty man 'e is!'

Captain MacArthur gave the child a surprised look.

'Yes,' Bronwyn said, 'of course we'll go to see 'im.'

Four days later, at Aldershot Railway Station, Bronwyn was directed up Gun Hill towards the Military Hospital. There was a bitterly cold December wind, they were tired from the long journey and Gwenda dragged on her mam's arm, making the climb even harder.

The Military Hospital had been named after the Duke of Cambridge. From its lofty position, the huge white-faced building made an impressive picture. 'Goodness me,' Gwenda gasped, 'Uncle Gareth must be very important to be 'ere!'

Bronwyn didn't speak. She felt anxious about what awaited her, wondering if she would be strong enough to cope. They entered the hospital, and eventually were dealt with by a soldier with a stripe on his arm. He glanced at a millboard, found what he sought and nodded. He called to an auxiliary standing nearby, and a moment later she was leading them down a long corridor.

They walked along highly polished linoleum, Gwenda wide-eyed, clinging to Bronwyn's hand and making retching sounds as the sharp smell of carbolic. They passed trolleys bearing semi-conscious patients, orderlies pushing them to and from the operating theatres. Through the open doorways of the wards, they glimpsed lines of white-covered beds packed closely together and all occupied. Many showed the humps of wire cages, protecting shattered limbs from the bedclothes. Everywhere, nurses, VADs and doctors were busy. 'During the war, we got hundreds in direct from the battlefields,' the young auxiliary explained. 'Even now, a lot of men are dying from the wounds they received.'

At last they reached a door marked 'Principal Medical Officer' and the auxiliary knocked and was called in.

A large, sandy-haired man in a white coat greeted them. He had been in consultation with several junior doctors, but he rose from behind his desk to shake Bronwyn's hand. 'I'm Colonel Mason,' he said as if everybody should know him. 'You must be Mrs Williams.' He was a commanding figure with penetrating eyes. He'd clearly been expecting her because a buff file marked 'Rifleman Williams' was on his desk.

'We're having an up-hill battle,' he said. 'Your husband hasn't spoken a word since he's been here. He's completely lost his memory. But these things aren't always permanent. One familiar thing can trigger the brain into action again. It's a most fascinating case. I'll take you up to the ward myself.'

Bronwyn bit her lip and nodded.

'I'm sorry, but your daughter will have to stay here. Danger of infection.'

A jolly-looking VAD took Gwenda's hand and gave her a humbug. Bronwyn thought the sight of the child would do as much as anything to jog Gareth's memory, but she was too awe-stricken to say anything.

Colonel Mason said, 'Come with me, Mrs Williams,' and she followed him out of his office, up some stairs to the first floor and through a set of swing doors. A Ward Sister wearing a smart red tippet rose from a desk, and joined them as they went through a further set of swing-doors. They were now in a small side-ward which was in partial darkness. The sister said, 'Open the blind, Nurse Phillips,' and a young nurse pulled a cord and thin afternoon light flooded into the room, revealing two patients who were lying motionless in their beds. Dizziness assailed Bronwyn and everything became green, but the colonel said: 'Far bed, Mrs Williams,' and his matter-of-fact tone somehow restored her balance.

She approached the bed and gazed into a face that seemed nothing more than a bandaged skull. The eyes were dead, showing no spark of recognition.

'Yes,' gasped Bronwyn. 'My Gareth, it is. Is 'e ... alive?'

The colonel rested a gentle hand on the man's shoulder. 'You're alive, aren't you, old boy, eh?'

Only then did Gareth Williams give his head the faintest of nods, and Bronwyn let her breath out in a thankful sigh. She reached across and took his passive hand in both of hers. 'It's me, Gareth, love. Bronwyn. Can you see me?'

Gareth's face remained blank. 'He recalls nothing,' Colonel Mason murmured.

'Poor Gareth,' Bronwyn sobbed, 'poor dear Gareth.' Despite the shoddy way he'd treated her, she wanted to press herself against him, pass the warmth of her own life into him, but instead she raised his hand to her lips and kissed it. She'd stay with Gareth ever more if she could somehow stir feelings back into him. But now she felt his fingers fluttering around hers. He was trying to pull her close. His tongue slowly moved over his lips, moistening them.

'He's trying to communicate, Mrs Williams,' Colonel Mason said, his interest quickening.

She leaned over Gareth, placed her ear to his lips. She remained motionless for an age, while those around her watched with fervent intensity. At last she straightened up, frowning.

'What did he say, Mrs Williams?' the doctor enquired.

Bronwyn hesitated, then answered, 'I couldn't catch it.'

'Well, that doesn't matter,' Mason said, elatedly 'He must've recognised you and is trying to communicate. The miracle has happened! Thank God you came, Mrs Williams. But we must be satisfied for the moment. We mustn't get him too excited. He needs you to guide him back to normality, Mrs Williams. You must visit him frequently.'

Bronwyn's glance fell on the young nurse. She was pretty and her bosom was struggling against the constraints of her uniform. 'Yes,' Bronwyn vowed whisperingly, 'I'll guide 'im all right!'

Ten minutes later she was reunited with the excited Gwenda. In a small anti-room, a nurse provided them with tea.

'Did you speak to Uncle Gareth?' Gwenda asked.

'Yes, love.'

'And did you tell 'im what a nasty man 'e is?'

'No ...'

'Why not, Mam?'

Bronwyn didn't answer.

Gwenda looked puzzled. 'What did 'e say then?'

Bronwyn's lips tightened in anger and she began to tremble so violently that the spoon in her saucer rattled. ''E said: Rosena ... Rosena Bray!'

Chapter Fourteen

JOHN BRAY FELT HIS ILLNESS more than he revealed. Bouts of breathlessness caught him, particularly at night when he would wake up gasping and he'd have to open the window to get more air. However, he had no wish to call the doctor again. He would only chastise him for working too hard or not losing more weight.

For twenty-eight years he'd felt confident that, when he died, the secret of his past would be buried with him, but Rosena's association with Edwin Carter had changed everything. That was why, in utter desperation, he'd turned to Tom Lethbridge. Even so, he prayed that Tom would never be put in the dreadful position of having to break the news to Rosena that the couple she'd loved so devotedly, down the years, were not her true parents but imposters.

But the retelling of the story to Tom had renewed its sharpness in his mind, and as he lay restless in his bed, Emma's smallpox-scarred face, frantic with fear, loomed before him. When stormy winds pounded the shore, memories of the 1890 shipwreck tormented him.

As the winter of 1919 gave way to spring, the West Country took on its mantle of sweet-scented flowers. Britain was adjusting to peace, although the newspapers still carried stories about the war, As the cost of victory was tallied, it emerged that over nine-million men had perished. In front of the church at Megstow Quay, a cross was erected with the names of thirty-six local men who had fallen. And in Paris, a peace conference opened, with representatives from all the great powers, and the seeds were sown for the new League of Nations which, it was anticipated, would solve all future international problems and so prevent wars.

Like many Cornish folk, Tom Lethbridge followed events closely and welcomed the return of the men from France. With normality restored, the fishing industry boomed and the Megstow Quay fleet ventured further afield, though John Bray now left these trips to Tom and the younger men.

Tom had no desire for any woman other than Rosena, but he would not foist himself on her. If she chose to look another way, so be it. But he would not allow her to forget him. He often brought her back gifts from distant ports, shawls, sheep skin rugs and brooches. It was pleasing that she'd spent the winter evenings knitting thick Guernseys and sea-boot stockings for him, as well as for her father.

Although Rosena seldom spoke of it, belief that Gareth was dead had taken a considerable toll of her, and for some weeks she looked drawn. She sometimes found comfort welcoming the touch of Tom's hand, or slipping her arm through his.

But as time passed, he knew that she was gaining strength from elsewhere. She was exchanging correspondence with Edwin Carter, and the mere mention of his name brought brightness to her eyes. She talked of him often, and even told Tom how Edwin had been discharged from the Army, and how he had returned to his uncle's business. As she babbled away, Tom realised that she didn't view him as a lover, but simply as a good companion. Melancholy grew in him - melancholy that he saw mirrored in John Bray's eyes, for it seemed that very soon, some awful step would have to be taken to destroy her happiness.

John wrestled with his conscience, constantly putting off the decision. 'Rosena's a truly good girl,' he told Tom, trying to reassure them both. 'I know she won't give herself to any man, not until she's wearin' a weddin' ring. I'd stake my life on that!'

If John Bray had forgotten how strong were the passions and lusts of youth, Tom had not. He repeated to Rosena advice he'd given her before: 'Don't be too trustin' with men, Rosena. They're all alike. They all want that one thing only women can give. A lot of them'll promise anythin' to get it.'

She made no comment, but he noticed this change in her reaction, and the chilling feeling was in him that already his warning might be too late.

He checked the word 'incest' in a dictionary, and the definition made him shudder.

It was quite wicked, he concluded, that Rosena should be allowed to drift into sinful ways in total ignorance. Yet what could he do? Should he take matters into his own hands?

For six weeks things ran on, then one evening when John Bray returned from sea, Rosena, waving a letter, skipped across the quay to meet him, her face unusually happy. 'I've 'eard from Edwin,' she cried. 'Oh, Father ... I'm so excited! 'E's comin' to see us again.'

Once you fancy a woman, marry her and get her in the family way before she has time to draw breath! Edwin now realised the wisdom of his uncle's advice. He loved Rosena and he was determined not to delay. He selected a handsome engagement ring of Lapis Lazuli at one of London's most exclusive jewellers. It was fortunate that his earnings from the business enabled him to afford such luxuries.

As he prepared to go to Cornwall, his mind was filled with Rosena, with her gestures, her laughter, her sweet, impulsive manner. He saw in her everything that Elspeth lacked. Of course he would have to win over John Bray who, for some reason, had shown hostility, but Edwin was confident of success. And once he had John Bray's blessing, he would propose to Rosena. The prospect of having her for his wife was like a heady wine.

The demands of business seemed relentless; he had to be in Yorkshire by the following Tuesday, selecting wools and placing orders, which meant that his stay in Cornwall would be little more than a long weekend. He motored down from London in eight hours, enjoying the power of his new motor. By the time he reached Mcgstow Quay and booked in at *The Cherry Bowl,* it was far too late to call at the Brays', so he unpacked his baggage and settled into the familiar upstairs room. But his thoughts were interrupted by the inn proprietor, William Briggs, who tapped on his door and gave him a note. It had been handed in at the downstairs bar.

Edwin was puzzled. He tore open the envelope and read the brief message. A man named Tom Lethbridge wished to speak to him on a matter of extreme urgency and would call at the inn before breakfast in the morning.

The man's name was vaguely familiar but he couldn't remember why.

That night he could not get to sleep. Finally his memory clicked into place. Tom Lethbridge had been a suitor of Rosena. She had turned down his proposal. By the time Edwin at last drifted into sleep, he'd concluded that whatever the disappointed Lethbridge wished to say to him, it would not be easy on the ear.

Chapter Fifteen

JOHN BRAY HAD TOLD TOM of Edwin's intended visit, and the two Cornish men had contemplated glumly the options open to them. John Bray feared that revelations of the past would bring the law down on him, but Tom had reminded him that unless something was done the outcome for Rosena could be catastrophic. Of course John Bray did not need reminding. Eventually they agreed that Tom would talk with Edwin in the hope that disaster might be averted. Hence, Tom arrived at *The Cherry Bowl* not long after dawn, and Bill Briggs led him up to the guest's room.

Following a firm knock, the door was opened to reveal Edwin pulling on his silk dressing-gown and looking somewhat bleary-eyed. Nonetheless he shook Tom's hand and gestured him inside, saying, 'You're early, Mister Lethbridge. The matter must be important.'

''Tis, sir.'

Tom glanced at Bill Briggs and the latter withdrew, closing the door behind him.

'Take a seat,' Edwin suggested, sitting on the bed himself. 'You have me intrigued, Mister Lethbridge. Don't keep me in suspense any longer.' Edwin reached for his silver cigarette case, offered it to Tom who declined, and proceeded to light a cigarette for himself. Despite Edwin's obvious puzzlement regarding the early visit, Tom noticed how he possessed an underlying exuberance, a zest for life. Tom had seen these same qualities in Rosena. And there was about Edwin and Rosena, he concluded, a likeness of features.

The time to speak candidly had come. 'Mister Carter,' he began, ''Tis necessary you're made aware of certain events concernin' the Brays. This may well affect your intentions towards Rosena.'

Resentment flared in Edwin's eyes but he made no comment.

'I understand,' Tom continued, 'that in 1890 you were a survivor when the steamer, *Atlantic Queen* sank.'

'That's so,' Edwin affirmed, drawing on his cigarette.

'Do you remember the exact circumstances?'

'Of course I don't,' Edwin said impatiently. 'I was a year old. All I know is what I've been told. About how a boat was washed up on the shore at Megstow Quay. Everybody else had been drowned, but I'd been placed in the boat's rope-locker, presumably by my parents, and that was the reason I survived.'

Tom nodded. ''Twas a miracle.'

'Mister Lethbridge, I don't need reminding about the awful tragedy. Every time I see the sea, I'm filled with grief. God knows why I was allowed to survive when every other member of my family drowned.'

In a quiet voice Tom said: 'Not every other member of your family was drowned.'

Edwin's eyes widened. For a second nothing moved in the room, apart from the slow drift of cigarette smoke. At last Edwin's guarded question came: 'What do you mean?'

'I mean both you and your baby sister survived.'

Edwin's head jerked up. 'What puts that preposterous idea in your head?'

'I was told by the man who found you in the washed-up boat. 'E told me there was a baby with you.'

'It's not true!'

''Tis true, Mister Carter. I'd swear it.'

'Who's telling these lies?'

Tom hesitated, then said, 'You mustn't reveal his name to anybody.'

Edwin was highly disturbed, but he made a visible effort to remain calm. 'Who is he?'

'John Bray.'

Edwin exhaled with surprise. 'You mean he was the man who found me when I was washed ashore?'

'Yes. 'E found you, and 'anded you over to the doctor, who eventually traced your uncle and made sure you were cared for.'

'And my so-called sister?'

'John Bray and his wife Emma raised and loved the child like their own. You see, they'd already lost two babies and ...'

Edwin was on his feet. 'You mean ... you mean Rosena ...?'

'Yes,' Tom nodded. 'She's your sister!'

'This is outrageous! I've never heard such a monstrous lie!'

''Tis true!' Tom said. 'You 'ad to be told.'

Edwin turned away. He stabbed his cigarette into an ash-tray and paced around the small room. He was well aware that Tom Lethbridge had had designs on Rosena, but he'd never dreamed his jealousy would drive him to such devious ends. He stopped pacing, faced the other man and said, 'Kindly leave my room, Mister Lethbridge. I don't believe this ghastly story. To spread such rumours is a crime and I'll consider taking legal action. If you weren't crippled, I'd throw you down the stairs!'

Tom did not flinch. 'All I can say, Mister Carter, is you'd better heed what I've told 'ee, otherwise there'll be terrible consequences.'

Edwin threw open the door. 'Get out!' he shouted.

With some dignity, Tom limped from the room. He went down the stairs, furious that he had not foreseen Edwin Carter's reaction, and fearful of what might now follow.

It seemed that either Edwin would believe him, go to the law, and have a charge of kidnap brought against John Bray, or, alternatively, he would dismiss out of hand the entire story and proceed to lure Rosena into an incestuous marriage!

Warm sunshine sparkled from a cloudless sky. The sight of Edwin walking down the street made her smile happily. He looked distinguished in his red-and-blue striped blazer and straw boater. She knew that the entire village, peeping from behind curtained windows, would be aware that this classy gentleman was paying her court, but she felt the more who knew, the merrier. She was standing at the door as he came through the gate.

John Bray had been repairing lobster pots at the quay, but he was well aware that Edwin had arrived, and as he saw him reach the cottage, he wondered if Tom Lethbridge had made his early-morning visit. He had hoped that Edwin would return immediately to London, but in that he was disappointed. Soon, Rosena and Edwin came walking along the quay, hand in hand. Edwin extended his hand and John Bray shook it, though with little warmth.

'Edwin's goin' to take me for a car ride,' she declared. "E 'asn't got to go back until tomorrow.'

'I hope you can spare your daughter for a few hours, Mister Bray,' Edwin said in his respectful way. Tom Bray noticed he had said 'your daughter'. If Tom had enlightened him about the true relationship, why was he speaking in those terms?

'What Rosena does, Mister Carter,' he said stiffly, 'is of 'er own choice.'

Edwin touched the brim of his boater in grateful acknowledgement.

'We'll be back in time for dinner,' Rosena smiled. She couldn't keep her elation from showing in her every gesture.

His green Pierce-Arrow was parked behind *The Cherry Bowl* and Edwin opened the door for her and helped her in.

"Ow grand it is!' she gasped.

'The latest import from America,' he smiled proudly, flicking a mote of dust from the bonnet, 'complete with four-speed gearbox.'

The morning was fine and he had thrown the hood back. This was the first time she had ever been in a motor car, and nervousness rose in her, but she placed her trust in Edwin's capable hands. As he turned the cranking-handle, the motor roared into life, and she squealed with excitement. A moment later they were speeding out of the village.

He demonstrated the car with great pride, and she was happy to share his enthusiasm, and to be sitting next to him. On the way to Talmouth, they pulled in at the roadside, a breathtaking view of a bay stretching beneath them. He switched off the engine, turned to her and smiled.

'Edwin,' she murmured, 'we've only spent a short time together, but I feel we know each other so well.'

He nodded. 'Your letters are marvellous. I count the days till the next one arrives. But ...' he sobered. 'But has your father told you why he dislikes me so?'

'Oh, 'e says you and I are from a different class; that I'm just a simple fisherman's daughter.'

'You and I are two people,' he said, 'and we will make our own rules.' He knew that Rosena's sweetness of nature would transcend any class barrier.

'I'm sure Father'll see things the way we see them,' she was saying. ''E's such a wonderful man, and 'e only wants what 'e sees as best for me. But I feel close to you, Edwin.' She laughed. 'We're almost like two peas from the same pod.'

She had meant the remark to be light-hearted, but a seriousness settled over him and she wondered how she had upset him. He re-started the engine and they motored into Talmouth. Soon he seemed his cheerful self again, telling her about how his uncle's business was flourishing. They parked the car on the street-side and took coffee at a café, sitting outside in the sunshine.

Rosena was a warm, caring person, crying out for love, and the loss of Gareth was something that had been hard to come to terms with, and now Tom Lethbridge's words kept preying on Edwin's mind. At first he had been determined to dismiss them as a pack of lies from a jealous man, but as he gazed at her lips, seeing there an open invitation to be kissed, uneasiness gnawed at him. Supposing there was substance in Lethbridge's story. The outcome would be more pain for Rosena, and he felt increasingly responsible for her.

When they returned to Megstow Quay, Edwin parked behind *The Cherry Bowl,* and she waited in the car while he went to his room to change his clothes. She sat admiring the glistening coachwork.. Her gaze dwelt on the dashboard glove-compartment and she could not resist the temptation of opening it. Her heart gave a skip as she saw inside the little box clearly marked *ST CARTIERS' JEWELLERS.* As Edwin reappeared, she closed the compartment, excitement throbbing through her.

Edwin ate that day at the cottage, but the meal which Rosena lovingly prepared was not a success because of John Bray's silence. Rosena could not understand him. But the belief that an engagement ring awaited her in the glove-compartment of the car consoled her. Edwin, of course, was his polite, courteous self, but nonetheless she was glad when the meal was finished.

In the afternoon, she took Edwin for a long walk along the beach and eventually they came to the wrecked rowing-boat where she had first given herself to Gareth.

Rosena felt excited, and arm in arm with Edwin she was hungry for his kisses, pressing her body against his, but a strange reticence was in him. For a while he seemed apart from her. Perhaps, she thought, he will wait until he gives me the ring, and then everything will be different.

He touched the weathered, rotting timbers of the old boat.

'Rosena,' he said, 'there were two lifeboats washed ashore from the *Atlantic Queen* in 1890. The one I was in at Megstow Quay, and another one that carried no survivors. Could this have been the second boat?'

The passion in her had been replaced by a sudden chill. A vision filled her mind of people clinging desperately and in vain to these timbers as the waves overwhelmed them.

'This could've been the second boat,' she said soberly.

She remained silent, not wishing to intrude on his sad memories, but hoping, in some way, that her presence gave him support.

At last he turned away from the wreck, his hand reaching for hers.

To Edwin, nothing would have been more delightful than to take her in his arms, yet, as they walked on, doubts plagued him. He was not an irresponsible man. In fairness to them both, he had to be sure of the truth.

Tomorrow, at mid-day, he would have to leave for London, and this saddened her. To cheer her up he said, 'I've got a present to give you before I go.'

Her mood immediately brightened. 'Oh, Edwin ...'

That evening, after he had returned to The Cherry Bowl, she had a long talk with her father, trying desperately to understand his attitude, but he was uncommunicative.

'Why don't 'ee tell me the truth, Father?' she demanded. 'Why treat me like a child?'

He simply shook his head, his face creased with misery. He put his arms about her, kissed her forehead.   'All I want is what's best for you,' he murmured.'

When he went to his bed, she was sickened by the knowledge that she was inflicting this misery upon him, though just how she could not guess.

Her hours with Edwin next morning passed quickly. He accompanied her and her father to St Arthur's Church. Afterwards he took her for a final spin in the car. When they returned to the inn, she knew that his visit was practically over and she was filled with gloom. But suddenly he said, 'I must give you your gift,' and her pulse quickened.

However, he did not open the glove-compartment, but reached into the back of the car and produced a parcel.

'There's enough woollen underclothes there to last you for the next two or three years. I can assure you, Rosena, they're of the finest quality.'

An iciness was in her. 'Thank you Edwin,' she said.

A half-hour later when he left, the ring was still in the glove-compartment, and the implication of Tom Lethbridge's words was gaining increased credibility in his mind. So was the prospect of employing a private detective to unravel the truth in this affair.

Chapter Sixteen

ON THE DAY FOLLOWING Edwin's departure, Tom Lethbridge joined John Bray aboard *Silver Cloud* and the two men prepared for sea.

''Is reaction took me aback,' Tom explained. 'I put things to 'im as gently as I could, but 'e blew 'is top, threatened to go to the law.'

John Bray frowned. 'If 'e does, I'm finished. But perhaps he was bluffin'. Perhaps the message sank in, and when 'e 'as time to think about it 'e'll let things drop. Could be we've seen 'im for the last time. I truly hope so.'

'You don't think 'e's told Rosena what I said, do 'ee?'

John Bray shook his head. 'No, but since 'e's been gone 'er mood 'as been black as sin. 'E must've taken what you told 'im to heart, and 'is attitude towards 'er 'as changed.'

'Poor Rosena,' Tom sighed.

'What she needs is a good 'usband, so she can put the past behind 'er.' John Bray paused, then he said: 'Tom, why don't 'ee propose to 'er again?'

Tom shook his head. ''Er mind's too full of Edwin Carter. She can't understand what's 'appened, but she's still in love with 'im.'

The two men, the old and the young, worked in silent partnership, stowing nets into the boat. Then, once everything was ready for sea, they filled their pipes and lit up. 'All we can do then,' John Bray said, 'is wait and see what the future brings.'

Tom didn't answer. He just couldn't imagine Edwin sitting back and doing nothing. He wasn't that sort of person.

Despite a euphoria of post-war activity, the winter of 1920 was a bleak one for Rosena. She tried in vain to puzzle out the reason why Edwin had brought an engagement ring to Cornwall, and then not given it to her. It didn't make sense. She still wrote to him, and he to her, but the letters became infrequent. His flame of love, which had once seemed so alive, seemed to have perished. But why?

However with the onset of another spring, a profound shock awaited her.

Bill Briggs, landlord of *The Cherry Bowl,* found himself with his fourth paying-guest in the last two years. The latest arrived one afternoon, having caught the bus from Talmouth. He was tall and strong-looking, and his shoulder-length hair hung in long straggly strands about his ears. His face might have been handsome at one time, but now it was scarred. He carried a heavy suitcase and what appeared to be some sort of easel. In a Welsh voice, he declared he was an artist who'd come to paint a portrait of a local girl. In the visitors' book, the artistic writing boldly stated the name 'Gareth Williams', but it meant nothing to Bill Briggs.

The figure standing at the cottage doorway took her aback. And then he spoke two words and their deep Welshness made her heart leap.
'It's Gareth!'
'G-Gareth ... Gar ...' She choked on the name. Her eyes widened in amazement. She tried to speak, couldn't, and suddenly green waves of shock rose about her. She was fainting as he caught her and lowered her to the cottage floor just inside the doorway.
'Ro-sena, my petal,' he murmured. He held her, making soothing noises, until her eyelashes flickered, and then he repeated, 'It's Gareth, come back after all this time, like 'e promised 'e would.'
'Gareth,' she breathed. 'Oh Gareth, I thought ... you were ... dead!'
'So did a lot of people. But I wasn't, see, though I took a nasty blow on the 'ead and I lost my memory for a while ...'
'Gareth, my dear love!' She gripped his arms, and for a moment they lay on the floor, hugging each other. She was breathless with happiness. 'Gareth,' she gasped. 'Gareth, Gareth ...' She kept squeezing his hand to make sure he was real.
As their coherence returned, he said, 'Always promised I'd come back, just as soon as I could ...'
Presently they scrambled up. They sat upon kitchen chairs, facing each other, holding hands, knees touching. She gazed into his face, and saw the record of his suffering - but deep in his grey eyes she saw the old twinkle. All the old love was in her again.
'See,' he said, leaning forward and removing his beret, 'this is what the Huns did to me.' The ugly wound, healed over with pink skin showed vividly.
'Poor Gareth.' Tears glistened in her eyes, her every sense brimming with compassion.
'But one thing carried me through, you see. I promised myself that one day I'd paint the most beautiful girl in all of England. That's what kept me alive, without a doubt. That's what I want to do more than anythin' else. It'll be my masterpiece, Ro-sena.'
'Oh, Gareth ...' And she could restrain herself no longer. She slipped her arms around his neck and crushed her lips against his.

His voice had not changed. It still had the same deep timbre, solid roundness and resonance, and an hour later as she sat on the rocking chair in the garden, the sun glinting in her hair, she drifted on a cloud of happiness, luxuriating in just hearing him talk.

For a man who had suffered so much, he now applied himself to his work with incredible professionalism. He was fulfilling his dream, he told her. He had insisted that she put on the violet-coloured dress which she had worn when he'd first met her at Perhaver Manor, and the same straw-hat with its shiny, imitation cherries. This was how he wanted to paint her. He chose the valerian-cloaked cottage as the background. She wanted to tuck her work-soiled hands away, but he would not hear of it.

'But they're ugly,' she complained.

'They are part of you,' he said, 'and you are beautiful - all of you!'

Gareth set about his preliminary sketches, working with charcoal on a pad. He had long debated whether to paint her in profile or full-face and had decided on the latter. 'So as to capture the fullness of those lovely hazel eyes,' he smiled. He made her sit in several different positions before he was satisfied. He wanted a position where the lines of the brow, the cheekbone, the jaw and neck were not symmetrical. He chose her eye as an anchor, so that if she moved, even slightly, he knew immediately.

He made a number of sketches, working from different angles. As he worked the children from the next cottage peered over the garden wall, then called to their friends so that soon there was an audience, but neither Rosena nor Gareth objected. It tickled Gareth's vanity, even when little Helen Trevick said in a squeaky voice: ''Tid'n a bit like Rosena.'

'The likeness will come later,' he called back. 'Background and surroundin's come first.'

Presently Gareth and Rosena began to talk, their voices low, almost conspiratorial, sharing an intimacy that was for no other ears. As he worked he told her about his harrowing experiences, those of them he could remember and wished to relate. He no longer talked about the trenches. 'It was so awful,' he commented, 'people back here wouldn't believe it,' and he left it at that.

After he'd been in the crater, there had been a great chunk of nothingness in his memory.

'The first firm memory I 'ad was bein' in 'ospital at Aldershot, and of Bronwyn comin' to visit me.'

'You'm lucky to 'ave 'er for a sister-in-law,' she remarked, 'but I wish I'd known. I could 'ave come and 'elped you.'

'No,' he commented. 'Wouldn't 'ave been right, not with me in the condition I was. But gradually my memory returned. Bronwyn and Deacon Evans from Trethomas came every week. Deacon Evans 'elped me to understand a lot of things, he did. Turn your 'ead a bit to the left. That's better.'

He concentrated on his work, sometimes measuring size with the handle of his paint brush. His face was filled with such delight in what he was doing, that she was loath to bring him back to less aesthetic matters, but there was something she had to know.

'Gareth, before you went away we agreed to be married.' She bit her lips with remorse as she thought of Edwin but went on. 'I don't want to wait any longer.'

He turned away to hide his pained expression. To bring disillusionment to her now would ruin his painting, and yet sooner or later he would have to enlighten her.

Bronwyn was well aware of his previous sins and had forgiven him. Once she'd understood the extent of his injuries, she'd decided that he'd already received far greater punishment than she was capable of administering. Right now, she believed he was in Cardiff, staying with his artist friend, Hugh Mansfield.

'Ro-sena, my petal,' he said, 'marriage to a wreck like me wouldn't be fair on you.'

Vexation sparkled in her eyes. 'Doesn't matter. I'll spend the rest of my life lookin' after you. I'll ask for nothin' more.'

He raised a finger to his lips. 'Keep your voice down, love. We don't want the whole village to know.'

'Then it's settled,' she said. 'We'll start the arrangements for the weddin'.'

'W-well,' he hesitated, 'let me finish the paintin', then we'll see.'

She emitted a satisfied sigh, finding something in his tone which gave her misguided reassurance.

John Bray returned from the sea in the late afternoon. After he had recovered from the shock of seeing Gareth 'returned from the dead', Rosena was delighted by the hospitality and the friendliness he showed the Welshman. When she mentioned marriage, he nodded and said, 'If 'tis what you truly want, I'll not stand in your way, me dear.'

The fact was, anything that drew Rosena away from Edwin was most welcome. He now bitterly regretted that Tom had spoken to Edwin, unlocking the door to the past. But even so, if Rosena and Gareth proceeded with wedding plans all might end well.

After supper, Rosena walked with Gareth back to *The Cherry Bowl*. The day had seemed long. He had worked hard, laying the foundations for the portrait, and he was well satisfied with his progress. But his conscience plagued him. Not only would he now have to enlighten Rosena about his true relationship with Bronwyn, but also her father, which was a shame because at last he seemed to have won the old man's respect. However there was no point in breaking the news until the painting was done. It would be quite impossible to capture Rosena's beauty, if her face was smouldering with anger. He would write a nice, humble letter to her after he returned to Trethomas, explaining everything, hoping she would be as understanding as Bronwyn had been.

Of course Rosena was blissfully unaware of his dark thoughts, putting his silence down to the awful suffering he'd undergone. The most important thing was that he was home, and this drove all other considerations into the background. With her father at last showing a glimmer of welcome to the Welshman, the future seemed to offer the promise she'd prayed for.

They stood in the shadows at the side of the inn, the clink of glasses and crude voices coming from inside. As they kissed good-night, all the old passion touched her, and she allowed him to fondle her body with his relentless hands. She was suddenly spinning in a dream-world, letting the past and the future fade from her mind. And at that moment, the firmness of his body against hers told her that his anatomy, his passion, was as strong as ever. She knew that more than the desire to paint her had drawn him back.

Chapter Seventeen

NEXT MORNING, after a short sketching session, Gareth could contain his frustration no longer. The nearness of her had him restless with desire. He suggested a walk along the beach to which she willing agreed. As they walked, his hands caressed her, exciting her. They reached the wrecked rowing boat, the place that held the most intimate memories of their relationship. And now he showed feverish delight, helping her over the gunwales. He drew off his smock and laid it for her to sit on.

The sun was warm. She lay back. She laughed, slipped off the beret from his head and gently smoothed his long hair, then she kissed his forehead. She was trembling; she, like him, was ready.

Passion rose in him with animal-intensity. 'I've waited long enough, Ro-sena.' He grasped her tightly, drawing her lips to his, stifling her words. She yielded, letting his tongue play around the inner flesh of her mouth. Now his fingers ripped her blouse open, exposing the lacy straps and top of her camisole. She rested back, smiling, her entire body burning.

'I wore the camisole 'specially for 'ee,' she whispered, but sudden fear passed through her.

There was a fierceness about him. He pulled her blouse back from her shoulders, followed by the straps of her camisole, but she was still determined to strike her bargain.

'Gareth, you said you'd marry me. Say it again, and I'll be yours.'

He was breathing heavily. This moment was golden. It might never be repeated. The sight of her pale breasts, so nearly exposed, had a white-heat flooding through his head and his loins. It was a torrent he could not resist. He'd waited so long! A flicker passed over his eyes, dilating the black pupils.

'Yes, my dear love ... I'll marry you ... of course I'll marry you ...'

And with that she succumbed. Gareth was back where he belonged - or so she thought.

Gareth toiled for three days, completing his charcoal drawings, pausing only briefly while she prepared tea and scones for him. In his note-book, he jotted down details of light, colour, composition and angles. Afterwards, he started on his colour roughs, working with crayons on a small canvas board . He told her that he would complete the painting at his studio in Cardiff. He needed to be there to mix the oils correctly.

She gave a reluctant nod. 'We'll not be apart for long. The future holds good things for us, Gareth.'

She never tired of sitting, never grew impatient at the slow and precise way he worked. Each day their love-making became more abandoned. In the evenings he took supper with them, and John Bray treated him like an old friend and the two men exchanged stories about their past - though of course each carefully tailored his own advantage. Despite what he had suffered, Gareth's wits were sharper than ever.

When Gareth rested from his easel, they would walk bare-footed along the sands. She never tired of talking about their first meetings, how their initial love had stirred. He would smile and say, 'This is what I dreamed off when I was in the trenches.'

'I still can't believe 'tis real,' she murmured almost gleefully. 'Who said fairy stories don't come true?'

'Is the convalescent 'ome still there?' he enquired.

'No. It closed when the war finished. I expect the Perhaver ghosts are up to all their old tricks again ... Like us!'

Once he had finished the preliminary tasks on his masterpiece he was consumed with enthusiasm to complete the work in his studio at Cardiff. As always, she tried to accommodate herself to his wishes, tried to make allowances for all that disappointed her. She told herself that their separation would only be short; this time there was no war to stand between them.

She went with him on the bus, helping him with his baggage, and bade a tearful farewell at Talmouth Railway Station. It reminded her of the similar occasion two years earlier, but now so much had changed.

'Paintin' somebody,' he told her as he leaned from the carriage window, 'is like a voyage of discovery. The more you know about your model, the more wondrous the portrait.'

'Well you know me,' she murmured. 'You know me like nobody else - inside and out.'

Down the platform, the guard blew his whistle and called, 'Stand back, miss!'

'Good bye, my love,' she murmured, clinging to his hand till the last possible moment. 'I'll count the minutes until your letter arrives.'

He forced himself to smile. Gareth the actor was stretching his talents to the extreme. If there had been a way of achieving his ends without hurting her he would have chosen it. But to paint her, to capture her genuine beauty, her happiness, had long been his ambition - an ambition equalled only by his burning lust to possess her body.

'Letter for you!' Harry the postman called, seeing Rosena shaking a counterpane from an upstairs window. 'Can't stop for lemonade today, me dear. I got out of bed late this morning.'

Gareth had been gone for three days. Harry left the envelope on the door-mat, and Rosena rushed downstairs.

'Oh ...' The post-mark was not the expected 'Merthyr Tydfil', but 'Paddington, London'. With disappointment she recognised Edwin's hand-writing. Surely, Gareth could have written by now. For so long a letter from Edwin had been her highlight, but now, as she opened it, an odd, mixed feeling was in her.

It was the warmest, the most intimate letter Edwin had written for a long time. He had done a great deal of thinking and had reached certain conclusions, though she couldn't understand why so much soul-searching had been necessary. Edwin was pleading for her forgiveness and apologising for the coldness that had spoiled their relationship. But he begged her to trust him and to understand that he wanted to do what was right for both of them.

That same morning, Rosena sat at the kitchen table. With a heavy heart, she wrote the briefest response. I'm truly sorry, Edwin. I do thank you for your love ... but Gareth's come back ...

She'd posted it off before noon.

For a further week, she watched for the postman every day, a growing sense of uneasiness in her. Why was he taking so long to write?

For several days Gareth lost himself in his work, knowing that he was creating the most miraculous painting he had ever done. The inspiration had come from within Rosena herself. Making love with her had intensified his creative instincts.. But he also knew that he could not lose himself in his work for ever. The past had taken its toll, the price had to be paid, not only by himself, but by Rosena also.

One afternoon he tore himself from his painting and struggled to put words on paper. Hugh Mansfield, the artist who owned this Cardiff attic-studio where they worked, was twenty years older than Gareth and was wise in the ways of the world. He admired Gareth's talent and sought to nurture it at all costs. For Gareth he had been both mentor and confessor, and he had listened with a patient ear as Gareth related his experiences with Rosena.

'And you're writing to her now, eh?' Hugh asked.

'Not gettin' very far. It's not easy, breakin' somebody's heart ... but I've got to.'

'And then what?'

'I've talked things over with Bronwyn. She says if I'm unfaithful again, she'll leave me. She's quite firm about what I must do. And she knows what she wants to be.'

'What's that, Gareth Boy?'

'She wants to be a pastor's wife.'

'What?'

'You see Deacon Evans from Trethomas says that 'e will recommend me to the council, and 'e feels sure that they'll approve me, with my knowledge of the Bible and all.'

'Good God, man!' Hugh had a great temptation to roar with laughter, but he resisted it. 'Surely,' he said, 'you have to spend years at college, studying theology. You can't become a pastor just like that.'

'Deacon Evans said I was a graduate of the University of Life,' Gareth explained. 'No other formal trainin' is necessary. And 'e told me 'e's very influential with the Board of Deacons.'

Hugh Mansfield was amazed. 'You can't be serious, Gareth.'

'I'm deadly serious. I've led a sinful life, Hugh. Got to do an awful lot of repentin' and good deeds to make up for it, I 'ave. This is the only way.'

'So you'll let the deacon put your name forward?'

'When I've finished this paintin'.'

'If you become a pastor,' Hugh said, 'it'll be a great loss to the art world.'

'I've achieved my masterpiece. Anythin' else would be an anti-climax. But I'll still do some paintin'.'

Gareth focused his attention on the letter he was trying to write. Now, finally, the words seemed to flow:

> *Dearest Rosena*
> *The time has come for me to be honest with you, and to tell you that I am already married - to Bronwyn - and have been since before I met you ...*

After he had posted the letter, a deep depression descended on him. Fine words about giving up his sinful ways maybe convinced other people, but they didn't change his feelings, didn't stop Rosena from being mixed in with every thought that entered his head. At night he dreamed of her lying back, smiling and naked and wanting him. Sooner or later he knew that he would have to return to her and possess her again.

At last Harry Ansell came with the letter the post-marked 'Cardiff'. A perverseness prevented her from immediately opening it. She held it like a valuable document that would be damaged beyond repair if she carelessly tore it open. Instead she slipped it into her apron pocket and walked with Harry to the gate. As he was moving off along the quay, she slit open the envelope.

Harry was some yards off when he heard her strange half-scream, half-cry-of-anger. In surprise he turned and saw her raise her hand to her forehead, totter on her feet and collapse. As he rushed back to her, Nora Trevick, the neighbour, ran from her kitchen, clearly having been watching from her window all along. Together they knelt alongside Rosena and struggled to revive her.

Nora noticed the letter, lying on the ground. She picked it up, her eyes widening as she scanned through it.

She pushed the letter into Rosena's pocket, and helped the groaning girl onto her feet and into her kitchen.

'Must've been bad news in that letter,' Harry said.

'You could call it that,' Nora responded.

Life for Rosena seemed like a bleak tunnel without any opening. Even when she had believed Gareth dead, her days had been warmed by memories of the love she thought they had shared. Now everything had been stripped away; the relationship and the intimacy she had surrendered seemed cheapened beyond redemption. She felt bitter and cheated and wasted.

Of course John Bray was well aware that she was totally crestfallen, though he never suspected the extent to which their intimacy had gone. Being aware of this made her feel ill, for she knew she was not worthy of her father's trust.

For the time being, John Bray saw no point in revealing the truth of Rosena's birth to her. It would only increase her burden of disillusionment. He prayed that Edwin would stay away from Cornwall and not investigate matters further. If he did, terrible problems would arise.

The weeks slipped by, and although each concealed inner secrets from the other, John Bray gave Rosena the strength to yet again face a world without Gareth Williams. They loved each other as truly as any father and daughter - and perhaps the past might have drifted into obscurity, but it was not meant to be because Rosena missed her course.

As alarm spread through her, she tried to convince herself that the mental anguish to which she had been subjected had upset her monthly balance. But a second month passed without the issue of blood, and soon her worst fears were confirmed by an onset of morning sickness.

She was plunged into mental turmoil. Her foolishness would be revealed for all to see. If Jenny Killigrew had been dubbed a trollop, she would now be deemed to have taken her place. At night she sobbed into her pillow. She recalled reading how women had tried to bring on miscarriages by drinking bottles of gin or sitting in scalding hot baths, but she suspected that such measures were useless. She became drawn looking, lack of sleep adding to her discomfort.

One morning her father, taken aback by her appearance, said, 'You should see the doctor, me dear.'

'No, Father!' she exclaimed, her eyes wide with an alarm he could not understand. 'I'll be all right in a week or so, you'll see.'

He shook his white head in puzzlement, but he didn't press the matter further.

As autumn waned and winter crept in, she felt desperate. The memory of the wretched Killigrew girl haunted her. If the girl had been pregnant she could understand her chagrin, and the despair felt by any woman who had misplaced her trust.

Agonising through the lonely nights over her own daunting circumstances, listening to the downstairs clock chiming the hours away, her mind often swung to the Truro woman who specialised in terminating unwanted pregnancies. She recalled how the suggestion of abortion had once been repugnant to her. Yet there was another side to her problem. Her father's heart was not strong. Knowledge of her shame might be enough to induce another attack.

She longed for support in her predicament. If only she could have gone to Tom, but she knew his feelings about abortion, and furthermore he had warned her so many times about the untrustworthiness of men. Her pride would not allow her to seek his support. And then there was Edwin. But having rejected him, she knew it would be totally unfair to approach him now.

So, whatever she did, she would have to do it alone.

Chapter Eighteen

EDWIN MADE A CONSCIOUS EFFORT to turn his mind away from Rosena. He knew that his love for her could never be fulfilled. It was a wound he must carry for evermore.

'Going down to Cornwall, seeing where the shipwreck happened, was a weird feeling,' he said as he took supper in the dining room of his Uncle Jeremy and Aunt Beryl. In the fireplace a cheery fire glowed, creating a glint on the silver candlesticks and fine cutlery which adorned the mahogany dining table. 'It was just a quirk of fate that I survived.'

He paused, wiping his lips with his napkin while the maid removed the plates. 'Sometimes I think about my family,' he said. 'It's an odd feeling. I never actually knew much about them.'

Uncle Jeremy carefully smoothed his waxed moustache. 'Well, your parents had fallen on hard times; their business at Plymouth had failed. But your father was a qualified engineer in plumbing and waterworks, as I'm sure you know. But he couldn't get his inventions patented in England. He reckoned he'd have better luck in Canada. I tried to talk him out of it, but he wouldn't relent.'

'That was the biggest mistake he ever made,' Beryl commented as she placed custard onto plates.

'So,' Edwin said, 'Father, Mother, little Jane and me boarded the *Atlantic Queen* and all his plans amounted to nothing.'

'Shocking navigational error by the captain,' Jeremy said. 'He lost his way in the storm, foundered on the Barnacle Rocks.'

'Tell me,' Edwin said, 'did you ever see my baby sister?'

Beryl nodded sadly. 'We saw her when she was two weeks old - a bonny little girl, so like her sweet-natured mother.'

'And my parents' bodies were recovered from the sea, but not Elizabeth Jane's.'

Aunt Beryl gave a visible shudder. 'Such a tiny little body,' she sighed. 'I suppose it was just ... swallowed by the elements.'

Edwin was well aware that his uncle and aunt wanted to let the matter rest, just as they always had, thoughts of the tragedy too awful to dwell on. All he had ever been able to glean was that he had been found by Cornish fisher-folk, no doubt, as Uncle Jeremy explained, long since dead and buried. It had taken

Tom Lethbridge to enlighten him that the nebulous 'Cornish fisher-folk' had been John Bray. He had handed him over to a Doctor Carey.

'This man Doctor Carey?' Edwin persisted. 'He traced you as my relatives and made contact.'

His uncle swallowed a spoonful of custard tart. 'Yes. He consulted the ship's passenger lists, contacted friends of your parents in London and eventually got in touch with us. It was a great relief when you appeared safe and sound.'

'I owe Doctor Carey a considerable debt of gratitude,' Edwin said. 'I must pay him a visit.'

'You'll have difficulty,' Jeremy remarked. 'He died years ago.'

They finished the meal in silence. Edwin knew he had treated Rosena badly, arousing in her a love which he had so eagerly wished to reciprocate. He had given her the impression that his feelings had cooled, but nothing had been further from the truth. He was burning with love for her - but every day Tom Lethbridge's warning had assumed greater credibility. He realised how badly he'd behaved towards Lethbridge. Full of remorse he had written to him, apologising.

And now what seemed the final blow to his relationship with Rosena had come: Gareth had returned from the dead to dominate her affections.

The matter would not rest in Edwin. He loved Rosena, nothing would ever change that. No other woman could ever take her place. He had discarded the idea of employing a private detective. That would disturb too many skeletons. But he knew he couldn't continue to exist as he was. He would have to tell his uncle and aunt everything Tom Lethbridge had told him - and then would come the time for a drastic decision.

One of Edith Polgaze's patients had nearly died after the probe had pierced her bladder, but the war, with its atmosphere of 'there may be no tomorrow', had ensured that there was no lack of business - and even now it was over, there were plenty of girls who were so glad to have the menfolk home that they forgot to take precautions.

So Mrs Polglaze, a rotund widow, sat her girls down and explained the disadvantages of keeping a child and how many destitute mothers, shunned by society, turned to the streets for a living. Today, as she launched into her usual motherly 'chat', it seemed that the pretty girl who sat in the Truro parlour was more preoccupied with her own emotions than she was with homely wisdom.

The overhead gas lamp made Rosena appear wan. She glanced at the iron bedstead, its mattress covered, for her benefit, with a freshly laundered sheet. Its cleanliness was superficial. She could see bloodstains ingrained into it.

Coming to this place had taken all the courage she possessed, and doubts still filled her mind.

"Ow far gone are you, me dear?' Mrs Polgaze enquired.

Rosena cleared her throat nervously. 'Since July.'

Mrs Polglaze sighed. 'I usually like to get 'em earlier. Sometimes the baby's difficult to shift at this stage, but that doesn't mean to say it can't be done.'

'What exactly do you do?' Rosena asked in a quiet voice.

'Let me show 'ee, then you'll know what to expect.'

Mrs Polgaze stood up and beckoned Rosena over to a table in the corner of the room. The tools of the trade were neatly laid out - a long steel probe, a large, brown bottle labelled 'CARBOLIC', a funnel, a coil of pink rubber tubing and an enamel basin containing some water. Alongside, was a bottle of brandy.

'I always make sure everythin' is very clean,' Mrs Polglaze said reassuringly. 'There's nothin' to be afraid of, me dear. I just pump some carbolic fluid into your womb, and then, very gently, I insert the probe and dislodge the baby. All I ask is that you have a little brandy before we start, That's just to settle you ... and then you can leave the rest to me. I'll do my best to make sure you'll be all right. I've had many years' experience, so you're in the best possible 'ands. Now I've been quite honest and told you everythin'.' She unscrewed the brandy bottle and poured a stiff tot into a glass. 'If you're 'appy about proceedin', drink this, and then slip your knickers off and lie back on the bed.'

For a moment Rosena felt dizzy, almost as if she was already intoxicated. She imagined she felt the baby kicking inside her, as if desperately struggling for its right to live.

'There'll be very little pain for 'ee,' Mrs Polglaze was saying, soothingly. 'Drink all the brandy if you want.'

Rosena felt she was swimming against the tide of her uncertainty - but all at once she was fighting back. ''Tis not my pain that concerns me,' she cried out. ''Tis what my baby suffers as it's stabbed with the needle.'

'Oh come!' the older woman laughed. 'The baby feels nothin'. It's already drowned in the carbolic. Now, let's get on with it.'

Revulsion swept over Rosena. What on earth had made her come to this place, conspiring with this awful woman in the murder of part of herself? She started to tremble.

'I'll not do it,' she gasped. 'I only came for advice, Mrs Polglaze.' She fumbled in her handbag and took out her purse. She knew the woman didn't believe her. She didn't believe herself.

She couldn't blame everything on the fear of shocking her father into another heart attack. That had just been a convenient peg on which to hang her weakness. But now suddenly other emotions had been unleashed inside her.

'I'm grateful for your advice,' she said, her voice growing firmer. 'I'll pay for your time.'

Mrs Polglaze's expression had hardened. 'It's your choice, me dear. I 'ope you realise that havin' a baby is a tremendous responsibility. Being a mother with no 'usband 'as driven more'n one woman to suicide.'

Rosena did not relent. She repeated her thanks and a moment later was hurrying down the street, utter relief blinding her to the challenges that she would now have to face.

That evening John Bray seemed more relaxed than she had seen him for a long while. He had not noticed how her body was beginning to show the signs of her pregnancy, but she knew her condition could not go unnoticed for much longer. She had decided that after supper she would tell her father. She knelt in her bedroom and prayed that the shock would not be too much for him.

She cooked a fine meal of his favourite herby pie, and when she had cleared away the dishes and he sat in the rocking chair, smoking his pipe, she drew up a chair opposite him.

'Father,' she said softly, 'there's somethin' I 'ave to tell 'ee.'

He hardly heard her words. 'I've been thinkin' a lot about you lately, Rosena,' he said. 'The war cost this village too many of its young men. If you won't take Tom for a husband, there's not many left to choose from.'

She didn't say anything. She knew she could never go to Tom now that she was carrying Gareth's child. She wished she had accepted his proposal last year. Her father would be happy now, Tom would be happy and she wouldn't be in her present predicament.

'Father,' she whispered.

He glanced across at her, his face and whiskers ruddy in the firelight. 'Rosena, I do love you. I want to know that after I've gone, you'll be secure with a good man to take care of you. You'm a good lass and you'll make a good wife. You mustn't waste any more time takin' care of me. Maybe you should get away from Megstow Quay.'

She suddenly felt close to tears. 'I'd never leave you, not from choice.'

He reached out, took hold of her hands. 'Why not marry Tom?' he said. 'You'd make a good pair. 'E'd look after you, Rosena - and you 'im. Think on it.'

She felt in a pit of despair, but she gave her head a slight nod, and he squeezed her hands and stood up. 'Now,' he said, 'I'm for bed. We're off tomorrow to Mount's Bay.'

'You drive yourself too hard,' she murmured.

'I can't shake off a lifetime of 'abits, just like that. Anyway, I'd die of boredom if I 'ad to sit around and do nothin'. When my time comes, I'll be glad enough to join Mother, and we can carry on arguin' like we always did.' He laughed, tapped out his pipe and put it down.

'Don't talk like that,' she said. 'You're not ready for the next world yet.'

He hesitated. 'Rosena ... there was somethin' you wanted to tell me?'

She gazed at him. His eyes were bright and he looked in better health than at any time since his heart attack. 'You're a good maid,' he murmured and as he smiled, there was a contentment about him, and she felt it would be wrong to mar his well-being. She decided to put off her confession until the morrow. She went to him, slipped her arms about him and gave him a hug. 'There's nothin' to tell you that won't wait,' she said, and he nodded, kissed her forehead and went up to bed.

As she stood in front of the dying fire, she felt the baby kick inside her. She was thankful that she had not allowed that awful woman in Truro to stifle the tiny life. When she was in bed, her mind returned to the problem of confiding in her father. It would be a shock for him, but she prayed that he would be understanding.

Next day, John Bray was not due to take his boat out until the evening, so Rosena did not set her alarm clock. It was eventually the screeching of gulls outside her window that roused her. She got up and dressed in the cold, grey light, conscious of her swollen breasts. She went downstairs, stoked up the range and took the cover off Cedric's cage. She put the kettle on. When the water boiled she made the tea, filled two mugs and took them upstairs. It had long been a habit on the mornings when her father was not at sea, for her to take him tea in bed, and sit for a few minutes to talk.

She opened the door and went in and he seemed to be asleep. She put the mugs down on the chest-of-drawers. His stillness frightened her and she went quickly to him and she saw at once the blueness in his face. His eyes were staring at the ceiling, his mouth open.

He was dead.

In a daze she stumbled down the stairs, out of the cottage door. She hammered on the Trevicks' door. It seemed ages before Nora Trevick answered, and she was in poor humour until Rosena stammered out the sad news. She agreed to go down to *The Cherry Bowl* and telephone for Doctor Tancred. He arrived an hour later, pressed his stethoscope against John Bray's chest and listened, after which he shook his head. 'Died in his sleep,' he announced. 'He didn't suffer anything, me dear. Tell me, was he well yesterday? Did anything happen to give him a shock?'

'Nothin',' Rosena murmured, overwhelmed with a thankfulness that nobody else would understand.

Doctor Tancred put his instruments back in his bag. 'This'll be a difficult time for you,' he said, and then noticing the fullness of her body he added: 'in more ways than one, I do believe. I'll get a woman from the village to come and lay your father out.'

'Thanks,' Rosena said.

'You come in and sit with us,' Nora Trevick said. "Ave a little drop of brandy.'

'Brandy?' Rosena shook her head. She seemed totally vague. 'I'll ... I'll just stay 'ere for a little while. I want to sit with 'im.'

The others nodded, though Nora looked affronted, but then she'd always considered the Brays a stuck up lot. Still, now the girl was left alone with a child in her belly, jilted by its worthless father, maybe she'd become more sociable.

When Maggie Pollock and her daughter arrived twenty minutes later to do the laying out, they found Rosena slumped over her father, her eyes red with tears. Proud of their skills, they showed her what they had brought - a shroud, a white cap and a pair of clean white stockings.

Rest assured, me dear,' Maggie said soothingly, 'we'll have your father clean and fittin'ly dressed by the time he meets his maker.'

Chapter Nineteen

THE WEATHER WAS BLEAK on the following Sunday. Rosena had never realised her father had so many friends, and neither, during his lifetime, had he realised. All work in the village had been suspended for the day, and as the coffin was borne slowly through the winding streets and up towards the church graveyard on the hill, many emerged to join the procession. Rosena wondered if it was the prospect of free ale after the funeral that attracted them. She noticed that even Silas and Martha Killigrew were amongst the mourners. Strangely, she found some comfort in the steady tread of so many feet.

To Rosena, it had always seemed stupid to have a graveyard high on a hill, for it was hard work carrying a coffin up the final steep slope. All six fisherman straining beneath its weight were sweating despite the cold. They frequently paused to catch their breath and adjust their hold. In fact the overweight Zack Dowlyn looked on the threshold of a heart attack himself as they reached the top.

In black and veiled, she walked just behind the coffin. Her lips moved to form the words of the hymn *Rock of Ages* but no sound emerged. However the rest of the mourners were more than making up for her silence, singing in slow, harmonious tones. Tom was at her side, holding her arm. She was glad of his solidity, for, in her pregnant state, she found the climb wearying. She had thought every tear she possessed had been shed, but now her eyes were moist again and she was thankful for her veil.

Her father had left a copy of his will in the cottage. He had completed it after his first heart attack and made certain Rosena knew where it was amongst personal documents. With it, she found some faded newspaper cuttings, all relating to the 1890 shipwreck.

Scanning through the faint print she was reminded of the story she already knew ... of how the *Atlantic Queen* had sailed from Plymouth only to founder in the gale, all left aboard perishing. Earlier, two overcrowded lifeboats had been launched from the doomed vessel. These had eventually come ashore on the Cornish coast - but all who had been aboard them had been washed overboard and drowned, with the exception of a one-year-old boy. Somehow he had survived and was subsequently claimed by relatives.

Poor Edwin, she thought. What a miracle he's still alive.

She wondered who had actually found him, and what had become of the boat in which he had been discovered? Probably chopped up for firewood by the villagers of Megstow Quay, she concluded.

She felt convinced that the second boat was the one beached against the cliffs below Perhaver Manor, as Edwin had suspected. She was ashamed that she and Gareth had made love upon boards where others had faced terror and death. Perhaps Fate deemed pregnancy as her just punishment.

From John Bray's will, she had discovered that everything he owned had been left to her, even his fishing-boat *Silver Cloud*. Tom had made a generous offer for this and she'd accepted. He'd paid cash on the nail, and this had eased her immediate financial problems.

Tom had been of great support since her father's death. He had made all necessary arrangements, sending out notification of the death in black-edged envelopes and booking *The Cherry Bowl* for the after-funeral gathering. It was a matter of prestige to provide ample fare after a funeral. Burying folk did wonders for the appetite.

Inside the church, the coffin was rested before the altar and the congregation knelt in prayer. Afterwards, the Reverend Trevellen spoke of the great respect he had held for John Bray and how good his church-attendance had been. Rosena scarcely heard the words for renewed grief assailed her and Tom's hold on her arm tightened as she swayed. Two more hymns were sung before everybody moved to the graveyard and the coffin was lowered into the cold grey earth.

When it was over, Tom paid the burial fee, and they all went down to *The Cherry Bowl* where tables were heaped with food. But eyes went firstly to the drink and the majority partook of poker beer. Soon a sing-song started, and Isaac Lugg, the coffin-maker, expressed the general opinion that a good burying was better than any fair.

As the mourners did full justice to the occasion, Rosena found herself meeting the stare of a man standing just inside the doorway. His mouth was sagging open. She could not tear her gaze from him. There was something familiar about his burly figure. He had strangely high cheekbones and eyes which had a slight lift at the edges. This made him look almost devilish. His shoulders were stooped. She turned to Tom. 'Who's that standin' near the doorway?'

Tom took a swing from his tankard. 'Said 'is name was Amos Kirby - an old friend of your father's.'

'Amos Kirby?' The name meant nothing to her, but uneasiness spread through her. She stared at the man, meeting his eyes - and suddenly realisation came to her and her blood turned cold.

'Friend!' she exclaimed. ''E was never Father's friend. 'E was a wrestler called *The Taunton Terror!*'

The memory of his fight with her father flooded back to her. But she had no time to muse because Kirby moved across the room towards her. She noticed how his left arm hung limp.

'Miss Bray,' he said in his low voice, his stare still fixed upon her face, 'sorry to 'ear about your father. I was passin' by and felt I must come and pay my last respects.' He reached out, grabbed Rosena's reticent hand and held onto it.

'It was k-kind of you,' she stammered. 'I'm sure Father would've appreciated you bein' 'ere. Please make the most of the refreshments.'

Kirby nodded. 'I remember John Bray so well. My arm still hangs limp from the contest we 'ad. Ruined my career, it did.' He still held Rosena's hand. His eyes were bloodshot yet they possessed a chilling power. She remembered how he had fought at the fair, brutally crushing his opponents into submission, being jeered by the crowd, basking in their hatred.

The years had not been kind to him. He looked ill. The foulness of his breath touched her nostrils. Now, she wondered if he'd returned to inflict some sort of revenge for the humiliation he'd received.

At he released her hand and stepped back. 'Thanks for your hospitality,' he said. 'I must be on my way, but I'm glad I've seen you. We must meet again.'

She swallowed hard.

He bowed his head, turned away, disappeared into the crowd. She did not see him again that afternoon. The fear that he had instilled in her all those years ago had not diminished. He had spoken of seeing her again. With her father in his grave, Tom frequently at sea, and her pregnancy developing, she would be highly vulnerable.

John Bray's presence pervaded the cottage. His bedroom remained as always, his clothes in their normal places, his pipe, his mug, on the side table - all as if tomorrow would see him home again. On the evening of the funeral, she stood alone, gazing at the room by lantern light, grief frozen tight inside her. All the mourners had tottered home from *The Cherry Bowl*, Tom had at last left her, having impressed upon her that he was available at any time when she needed help. She did not speak the thought that was in her head ... if there's an emergency, the few miles to St Mags might just as well be a thousand.

She had sensed the villagers' gossip, the whispers behind raised hands, but Tom had still not commented on her pregnancy. Perhaps, she thought, he refuses to accept it as a reality. As she went to bed that night, she still felt the pressure of Amos Kirby's stare and smelt his breath.

She awoke at first light. Frightening images were racing through her mind. She felt feverish.

She rose, dressed and went downstairs to stoke up the fire. The cottage felt damp and cold. She made some tea and sat in the rocking chair, sipping it. She wished there was some friend in Megstow Quay she could turn to, but there was not. She wondered where Kirby was now? Had he left the village, or was he still loitering around, intent on committing some vengeful deed against her? If he came to the cottage, she would have to fight him off. She contemplated getting a gun, but dismissed that. Instead, she took the carving knife from the drawer and placed it within easy reach.

All through that day, her spirits remained low. In the afternoon she put on her shawl and walked to the village pump for water. The wind was bitter-cold.

The village streets were quiet, most of the menfolk would be in bed, snatching their rest before going to sea on the evening tide. Glancing ahead, she saw a man walking ponderously over the uneven cobbles, and there was something familiar in the slant of his shoulders and bulky figure ... and she thought, My God, it's him!.

She felt panicking pressure of fear in her every sense. But when she glanced ahead again, she realised how foolish she was. Her imagination was fashioning every man into Amos Kirby.

'Afternoon, Miss Bray,' Frank Bines the cobbler called. "Tis a bitter-cold day.'

When she reached the cottage she sensed that something was wrong. In the kitchen, she placed the pail down, then she removed her shawl. The feeling of unease persisted. Then realisation dawned in her.

She went to the parrot's cage. Cedric was lying on its floor, a bundle of red and blue feathers amid the shell-husks and droppings. She lifted him out, feeling the coldness in him. His neck and head hung limply. For a moment she hugged him against her, praying that her warmth might restore his life - but it did not. For half-an-hour she sat, holding the body, her eyes blurred, unable to believe that the fierce spirit had left Cedric for ever. Presently she rose, placed the bird gently down, and took some tissue paper from the dresser. She carefully wrapped the bird, then, taking a shovel, she went to the back garden and, with the cold wind whipping at her, she buried the little bundle. She imagined that somehow Amos Kirby was responsible for this death. Perhaps he had placed some curse upon her.

Loneliness gnawed at her. She felt that if Kirby did come for her, she would not have the strength to defend herself.

That evening, she made a decision. She would have to seek help. There were only two people she could turn to. She didn't want to face Tom, despite his offer of help. That left Edwin. She must swallow her pride. She had to escape from the cottage, from any place where Kirby might seek her out.

Next morning she left a message with the neighbouring Trevicks in case Tom should enquire; then, carrying a suitcase, she caught the nine o'clock bus to Talmouth. An hour later she was aboard the London-bound train. This was the furthest journey she had ever undertaken alone. She took no interest in the changing scenery beyond the carriage window; her mind was too full of other concerns. She had the address of the Carter-Wilson warehouse, and that is where she would go, praying that Edwin was not away on business. What would she say to him when she found him? And more to the point, what would his reaction be?

At Paddington she dismounted from the train, walked up the platform to the bustling concourse. There she asked a flower vendor the way to St Paul's.

'Best take a cab if you can afford it, dearie. You'll find 'em outside the station.'

She expressed her thanks and in the street she found a line of cabs. 'Can 'ee take me to St Paul's?' she enquired, and a driver nodded, smiling, she felt sure, at her accent.

'First time in London, darlin'?' he asked, holding the door for her. She nodded, climbed in.

They started off, threading their way between double-deckered buses. Rosena doubted that she would feel safe on such transport, for they seemed dangerously top-heavy.

She felt she was being drawn headlong to a confrontation that perhaps she was insufficiently prepared for. What would Edwin's reaction be?

The cab driver drew open the glass partition and took it upon himself to point out all the sights as they passed along. At first she felt indifferent, but gradually his enthusiasm spread to her.

'This is the West End of London, darlin' - Regent Street. At the end is Piccadilly Circus. Watch out for Eros, the statue of love.'

Her cheeks tingled. Her condition was obvious, but at least her guide wouldn't know she had no husband. A moment later she was gasping at the sight of Nelson's Column, rising to breath-taking height in the sky.

The cab driver cleared some dawdling pedestrians from his way with a loud blast of his horn. They motored along The Strand, past the very grand *Savoy Hotel,* and presently they were climbing a hill at the end of which loomed St Paul's Cathedral. 'Carter Lane, you wanted?' he enquired.

'Yes. The Carter-Wilson Warehouse.'

'I know it,' the cab driver nodded. They turned off by the large churchyard and shortly stopped outside an imposing brick building. It was three storeys high, its windows and doorways embellished with artistic stonework. As she stepped from the cab, the driver lifted out her luggage.

She fumbled in her purse and gave him a generous tip.

'Thanks and Merry Christmas, Missus!'

She gasped. Merry Christmas! She'd been so full of her troubles that she'd forgotten Christmas was only a week away.

Nervously, she climbed the steps to some high doors which stood open. Upon the wall was a shining brass plate proclaiming: Carter-Wilson (TEXTILE WAREHOUSEMEN). Plucking up courage, she crossed an inner-porch and pushed her way through some frosted-glass doors. A commissionaire in a smart navy-blue uniform appeared and enquired as to her business.

'I've come to see Mister Carter,' she said.

'Is he expecting you, ma'am?'

'Not exactly.'

The man gave her swollen figure a hard look, then he said, 'I'll take you to his office. But he's very busy today. You'd better let me carry your case.'

They moved down a corridor and across a large store room. Hundreds of bolts of cloth were stacked on slatted shelves. She heard a man saying, 'I'd like to order fifteen yards of this green shade.'

She was led up a flight of stairs to a closed door. The commissionaire knocked, cocking his head to listen. It was then that Rosena noticed the name plaque on the door - MISTER JEREMY CARTER.

''Tis Mister Edwin Carter I want to see,' she explained quickly.

'Oh, Mister Edwin isn't here now ...'

'But ...'

'Come in!' a voice boomed from inside, and the commissionaire opened the door to reveal a portly man in a high-winged collar, silk tie and black morning-coat. He put down some pattern-books he'd been examining and moved out from behind a large baize-topped table.

'A lady to see Mister Carter,' the commissionaire announced.

Rosena felt utterly confused. ''Twas Edwin I wanted to see,' she repeated.

Jeremy Carter gave her a warm smile. He had a fine waxed moustache and there was a twinkle in his eye. 'Come in ... Rosena Bray, isn't it?'

Rosena gasped. ''Ow did 'ee know my name, sir?'

He stepped towards her, took her hand in both of his and gave it a warm squeeze, 'Sit down, my dear.'

When she was perched on the edge of a chair, Jeremy said, 'I'm Edwin's uncle. He told me about you ... Rosena Bray from Cornwall. Your lovely accent gives you away, my dear.'

She was lost for words.

'I know Edwin is intending to write to you,' Jeremy went on. 'I suspect his letter is in the post. I'm surprised that you've come to London - but you're very welcome. Have you anywhere to stay?'

She shook her head. 'I know there are some good lodgin's near Blackfriar's Bridge.'

He smiled. 'You must stay with us and meet Beryl my wife. Stay for the Christmas if you want.'

'Oh ...' she hesitated, unused to such conviviality.

'It will be no trouble, Rosena.'

She relented. ''Tis very kind of you. But where's Edwin?'

He paused to light his cigar. 'Edwin's gone to Australia. He's working in Melbourne - at a wool broker's office.'

'Oh …' She looked utterly crestfallen. 'I was hopin' to see 'im, to talk things over. We were ... very good friends.'

Uncle Jeremy raised his eyebrows. 'Edwin's not the father of your child?'

Her cheeks flushed. 'No,' she said emphatically. ''Twas another man. I'm afraid I've been foolish, Mister Carter. I ...'

'Would it be Gareth William's child?'

She could hardly believe her ears. He seemed to know everything about her.

'Yes,' she admitted ... 'but I thought we were goin' to be married. I didn't realise 'e already had a wife.'

He eased her embarrassment with a wave of his hand. 'These things happen, Rosena. I hope perhaps we can help you. Edwin told me all about you, and all about your Gareth, but of course he knew nothing of the baby.'

Rosena lowered her eyes, misery taking hold of her. When she looked up again, she said, 'You are so kind to me. I can't understand why. I felt desperate for 'elp. I came to see Edwin ...'

He took a watch from the pocket of his waistcoat and checked the time. 'You must be tired. We'll go home now, but on the way, I want to show you something.'

She was totally bemused. She stood up, lifted her case, but he took this from her and a moment later they left the building and went to the yard at the back where he had his shiny green car. He helped her to a seat, and she couldn't help noticing how frequently his hands touched her. He stowed her bag in the back and soon they were moving along the city's busy streets towards the Mansion House district.

Presently he drew up outside a high, domed building. Above the entrance was a gold-lettered sign: WHITWORTHS ART GALLERY.

He took her arm and led her into a hall. The walls were covered in magnificent framed portraits and landscapes. Jeremy appeared to know numerous people, exchanging greetings as Rosena followed him to the far end of the gallery - and there they paused. She felt dizzy for she was gazing up at a fine painting of herself. Beneath it the caption said A CORNISH MAID, and written at the bottom right of the canvas was the artist's name ... *Gareth Williams.*

'It's a beautiful work,' Jeremy murmured, 'but no more beautiful than its subject. Now perhaps you will understand why I recognised you so instantly. The painting's likeness is breathtaking. I've made an offer to buy it. I've written to Gareth Williams, care of St Godfrey's Chapel, Trethomas. I understand he's the pastor there.' He allowed himself a small, hollow laugh. 'Perhaps he'll save the souls of a few sinners. They say it takes one to know one.'

She made no comment. She knew that whatever else Gareth might be, he was certainly an artist of very great ability.

They stayed in the gallery for perhaps ten minutes, then he took her arm again and they returned to the car and motored on. They crossed the Thames and a half-hour later they reached the Carters' home in Beckenham. The house was of mock-Tudor design, set in its own half-acre, and was approached through formal lawns. It was double-fronted with a wing for the servants above the garages. Jeremy had instructed a telephone message to be passed to his wife, so they were expected.

Beryl, a well-built, friendly person, welcomed Rosena with the same hospitality her husband had shown. She led her up the stairs to a bedroom, which was pretty with frilled curtains and pink wallpaper. Next Rosena was shown the water-closet with its flush, and the bathroom. Hot water could be run directly from the shiny brass taps into the porcelain hand-basin and bath. Such luxury was completely new to her.

'Dinner will be ready in half-an-hour,' Beryl smiled. 'Meanwhile make yourself at home.'

Rosena was speechless.

Chapter Twenty

SHE HAD NEVER EATEN SUPPER on such a grand table. She was fascinated by the assortment of cutlery but was not sure what she should use and when. She overcame the problem by copying her hosts. When they picked up a certain knife, fork or spoon, she did the same a few seconds later. Had they eaten their napkins she would have done likewise. Presently she forgot her inhibitions and began to enjoy the meal.

Edwin's sudden departure puzzled her, but Beryl assured her that he was in good health and he had left to take over an excellent job in Melbourne. Rosena sensed that there was more to it than that.

'After the meal, my dear,' Jeremy told her, 'we'll have a long chat, and rest assured we'll do everything we can to help you. We'll find you somewhere to go for the birth of your baby.'

'I appreciate your kindness,' Rosena said, 'but I can't understand why you're goin' to so much trouble.'

Jeremy exchanged a glance with his wife. She seemed to dote on his every word, her eyes rarely leaving him.

'Families have to stick together, Rosena,' she said.

'Families?' Rosena queried, her puzzlement deepening.

'Patience, young lady,' Jeremy cut in, his eyes twinkling. 'Let's enjoy our meal and not give ourselves indigestion. All will be revealed in a minute.'

Gently admonished, Rosena asked no more questions, although they were crowding her mind. At last the dessert, peaches and cream, was served and consumed, and they got up from the table and went into the drawing room. As the maid followed them in with a tray of coffee, Jeremy motioned Rosena to a comfortable chair, and his wife seated herself opposite.

'Now then, we must talk business,' he pronounced. 'Let me tell you, Rosena, that Edwin will be writing to you. The letter is probably already in the post. But I will forewarn you about its contents. He left for Australia because he loved you to distraction. And yet he knew, and we all know except perhaps you, that marriage was impossible.'

'Impossible?' Rosena queried. 'I know 'e brought an engagement ring when 'e came down to Cornwall. I would gladly have consented, but 'e didn't propose.'

Jeremy nodded understandingly. 'He couldn't propose. While he was in Megstow Quay he learned something that came as a great shock to him ... and

I'm afraid it will come as a great shock to you, Rosena. That's why I felt it wise to finish our meal first.'

Beryl came and sat next to Rosena, taking her hand gently in hers.

Jeremy moved across the room to a writing desk and extracted a document from its drawer. He handed it to Rosena. She glanced at it, puzzled. It was a birth certificate.

'What Edwin learned,' Jeremy said, 'was that he was not the only child that survived the wrecking of the *Atlantic Queen*. He was washed ashore with his baby sister - and they both survived.'

'But 'e always told me 'e was the only survivor of 'is immediate family ...'

'That's what he believed, until he learned otherwise.'

Rosena felt bewildered. She could not understand where all this was leading. 'What 'appened to 'is sister, then?' she enquired.

'You are his sister! What you have in your hand is your own birth certificate.'

'That can't be true!' Rosena exclaimed. 'My parents were John and Emma Bray ...'

'They were your adoptive parents,' Jeremy persisted. 'Your true mother and father were emigrating to Canada with you and Edwin when the ship sank. They were drowned, but you and Edwin survived and were washed ashore. John Bray rescued you both from the shore and in due course passed Edwin to the local doctor who traced us. We brought up Edwin as our own. We always believed that you were dead, drowned with your parents. But the truth is that John Bray kidnapped you and kept you as his own.'

Rosena could not believe her ears. 'Why ... why would 'e do a thing like that?'

'Because, my dear,' Jeremy said, 'he and his wife Emma had just lost their own child at birth. They thought a baby coming out of the storm was a gift from Heaven.'

Rosena was choking with disbelief, but Beryl was nodding and saying, 'This has been a great shock for us all. In fact your true name is not Rosena Bray, but Jane Elizabeth Carter, as you can see from your birth certificate.'

Rosena was shaking her head. 'I can't believe this. It must be a lie. 'Ow did Edwin get this ... story?'

'John Bray, the man you thought was your father, told his friend Tom Lethbridge. He told Edwin.'

'Tom! It can't be true. 'E would've told me.'

'No ... he couldn't. John Bray made him swear to keep it a secret from you. The reason he told Tom was because, in the event of his death, somebody would have to ensure you and Edwin never married, being brother and sister. Tom told the truth to Edwin. That's why he never proposed to you.'

'Oh Lord!' Rosena was trembling. She was trying desperately not to believe this preposterous story, yet the whole thing frightened her because it had the ring of truth about it.

'But I can assure you that Edwin never stopped loving you,' Jeremy continued, softening his tone. 'His love for you was driving him crazy. He had to do something, make a fresh start. That's why he went to Australia. And Rosena, whatever you do, you must not breathe a word of this conversation - not unless you want your father's - your adoptive father's - name to be blackened.'

Rosena raised her glistening eyes to meet Jeremy's.

'Can't you understand?' he said. 'If the whole affair hadn't been kept secret, he'd have been charged with kidnapping and gone to prison. That's why he never told a soul ... until he saw the awful implications his deed could bring about.'

'So you see,' Beryl cut in, 'we are your uncle and aunt, and we will certainly help you all we can. In fact Jeremy will speak to our family doctor, Angus McMahon, and make an appointment for you. He'll make sure things are going along all right. And after the baby's born ... well, we'll discuss the future another time.'

'You may wish to have the child adopted,' Jeremy said.

'No ...'

'I don't think there will be any alternative, but we won't worry about the future now. I would suggest that an early night will be the best thing. You must be very tired.'

Rosena nodded. She gazed at the formal looking document in her hand.

CERTIFIED COPY OF AN ENTRY OF BIRTH.
REGISTRATION DISTRICT - ENFIELD

Jane Elizabeth Carter born 7 May 1890 at Enfield. Father: William John Carter - Rank or Profession: Plumber.

'I'm afraid,' she murmured beneath her breath, 'I don't believe any of it.'

But that night as she lay between silk sheets, Jeremy's words gained credibility in her mind. No wonder her father had acted curiously towards Edwin. Events from the past, the mystery that had shrouded her childhood - now it all seemed to fit together.

She felt the world had been whipped from beneath her. It seemed she had lost everything - or almost everything. At least she appeared to have found two good friends in Jeremy and Beryl Carter. Or to put it more precisely: two very good relatives.

Rosena stayed with the Carters for a almost a month, sharing their quiet but ample Christmas and New Year's celebrations. They treated her with kindness. Beryl tried to persuade her to rest - but she couldn't sit around doing nothing, so she helped the cook, marvelling at the selection of fine foods the larder boasted.

When she visited Doctor McMahon, Beryl went with her and sat in the waiting room while she was ushered by a nurse into the big surgery. She felt apprehensive, but the doctor was a worldly man. His manner was so matter-of-fact that she almost forgot her embarrassment. She answered his questions candidly and he made notes. Presently he checked her blood-pressure, after which the nurse led her behind a screen and helped her to undress. It seemed strange that she was allowed some privacy to take off her clothes, yet within a moment she would be obliged to display her most private parts. Wearing only her shift, she was assisted onto an examination couch.

Doctor McMahon was holding a metallic trumpet-like instrument. Rosena's blue eyes widened with alarm, but he laughed. 'Don't worry,' he said. 'We call this a Pinard's Stethoscope. It's for listening to what's going on inside your tummy.'

She tried to relax as he held it against her abdomen in several different places, placing his ear at the other end. He drew back, putting the instrument aside, and scribbled notes onto his pad, then he pressed his dry, confident hands onto her abdomen. For what seemed an age he continued, until sensing her impatience he explained, 'Just confirming the position of the baby.' When he eventually straightened up, he said to the nurse, 'I thought so,' but he didn't explain what it was he had thought. Finally, as his gentle fingers explored inside her, she felt a pang of gratitude that she had not allowed Mrs Polglaze's steel probe the same intimacy.

But now she noticed his grim expression. 'There's somethin' wrong?' she asked.

'Please get dressed,' he said, 'then we'll have a talk.' .

A moment later and Rosena, still buttoning her cardigan, was occupying a chair. He finished his notes and looked up, giving her a reassuring smile. 'It's not an unusual condition. Many women experience it ... but I'm sure you will want me to be frank.'

'Yes ...'

'The baby is resting in the breech presentation position. It probably means that the head will be born last. Your labour may last longer than normal. The birth may be difficult.'

She nodded nervously.

'Your uncle mentioned that he was making arrangements for you to go into St Mary's Home at Wimbledon. It's a voluntary church organisation run by holy nuns - The Sisters of Compassion. They're very experienced and there's always a consultant on call. I shall pass my notes to them. Meanwhile, you'll probably get some discomfort and a lot of indigestion. You see, the baby's pressing against your digestive organs. But if all goes well, you can expect the baby in March.'

'Thank you, doctor,' she murmured. 'Thank you for tellin' me everythin'.'

During the next week she tried to put aside concern over the complications of her pregnancy. That was a bridge she would have to cross when she reached it. Now, gradually, she reconciled herself to the unusual circumstances of her early childhood. Beryl gently enlightened her about her true parents. How her father had been a talented plumber with modern ideas concerning drainage.

At first Rosena resented the fact that the couple she had respected as her parents had deluded her - but soon she realised that this made no difference to the depth of her love for them, even in memory. Jeremy enlarged upon his own knowledge of the circumstances, as relayed through Tom and Edwin, and her initial bitterness gradually dissipated. She thought of John Bray, living in torment all those years, fearful lest his secret be revealed and bring the law down on his head - and tears filled her eyes as she understood what he had suffered. In her mind he would always be her father

At night as she enjoyed the luxury of her bedroom at the Carters' house, thoughts of the past and the future tormented her. She felt profound gratitude for every man who had suffered in the war, but beyond this she felt contempt for Gareth. He had so nearly destroyed her. The prospect of ever seeing him again was repulsive to her. She would do what was best for the child without his help. Let Bronwyn have Gareth.

She felt angry with Tom for not being open with her. It was hurtful to know that he had been hiding so much, yet she had to admit that his hands had been tied.

'I'm not Rosena Bray,' she told herself over and over, 'I'm Jane Elizabeth Carter.' She no longer doubted that it was true, but it didn't rest easily in her. It was a profound shock to learn that you were no longer yourself.

Overriding everything were her feelings for Edwin. Gareth's return had blinded her to the fact that Edwin was the finest man she had ever known? She wept into her pillow and cursed the quirk of fate which rendered theirs a forbidden love.

Next day Jeremy suggested that he might be able to find employment for her in his firm after the baby was born. 'And I would only ask one condition, my dear.'

'What's that?' she asked.

'That you have the child adopted.'

She felt fear flutter through her body. It was almost as if the baby growing inside her sensed that fear.

She shook her head, but Jeremy had turned away, taking it for granted that she agreed with him.

By mid-January, she was telling herself that she must not overstay her welcome, though the warmth of the Carters' hospitality remained unstinting. Indeed Beryl was treating her like the daughter she'd yearned for but never had.

Rosena decided she must get back to Cornwall, pack up the cottage and pray that Amos Kirby had receded into the past. At the due time, she would go to the nursing home in Wimbledon - and concentrate on the future and whatever it held.

Jeremy drove her to Paddington Railway Station. As he went to kiss her good-bye, she turned her cheek towards him, but he murmured, 'On the lips, my dear. Just this once. Nobody'll know.' After she had succumbed, he said, 'I'll start to make enquiries about having your child adopted, my dear. It'll be the best way.'

'No, Uncle Jeremy,' she said. 'I wouldn't agree to that.'

'But ...' It was his turn to show surprise. 'Life will be impossible for you if you keep the child.' She didn't answer, but as the train carried her home she wept.

At the cottage she found a letter on the doormat. It was post-marked 'Taunton'. She did not recognise the hand-writing. She hesitated, unease sweeping through her - then she asked herself: Why am I afraid of an envelope? And she tore it open.

> *Dear Miss Bray*
>
> *My husband Amos is ill. The doctor has warned us that he may not have long to live. He is sorely troubled by some event in his past and he has asked me to write to you and ask that you to visit him as a matter of EXTREME URGENCY. He has some information that is most*

important to you. I do not know what it is, but he is most concerned that you come before it is too late. Our address is at the top of this letter, and Amos repeats PLEASE, PLEASE COME.

Yours sincerely
Nesta Kirby.

Rosena's immediate reaction was to tear up the letter. But instead, she placed it on the dresser and set about bringing warmth to the cheerless cottage.

Nora Trevick knocked at the door and told her that Tom Lethbridge had called round and been very perturbed when he'd learned she'd gone to London.

Rosena prepared her supper, though bad indigestion troubled her, robbing her of her appetite. She needed to draw together some sort of plan. She felt frightened of the past and frightened of the future. She knew that she needed the support and love of a man.

While she sat sipping tea, her gaze drifted Nesta Kirby's letter on the dresser. Why should that dreadful man be so desperate to see her? The urgency of Nesta's words, of her plea, haunted her. By the time she went to bed that night, she had realised that this was something she could not ignore, despite the fact that the harrowing prospect of again confronting Amos Kirby petrified her.

Chapter Twenty-one

'YES,' NESTA KIRBY REMARKED as she poked her kitchen fire, "e's been very poorly. I thought 'e'd passed away last week.'

Rosena had been directed to a shabby backstreet which led down to the River Tone; its decrepit terraced houses were of sombre granite. She'd found No. 7. Nesta Kirby, a dumpy looking woman with a wilful slant to her jaw, had invited her in and explained that the doctor was upstairs with her husband at that moment, so Rosena was waiting in the kitchen, sitting in a chair from which a large black cat had been shunted.

'This must be a terrible time for you,' she said, taking a sip from the tea she'd be given.

'Terrible time?' Nesta snorted. 'I don't know. It'll be a happy release if 'e departs for the next world. 'E's a most difficult man to live with, Miss Bray. I don't know 'ow I've put up with 'im. I can 'ardly blame 'is first wife Molly for what she did, though it didn't do 'er no good.'

'First wife?' Rosena queried.

'Well, they weren't actually married ... but Amos always called 'er 'is wife, and 'e fathered 'er babies.'

'What happened to 'er?'

'Oh, she ran away. She was terrified of 'im. 'E used to beat 'er up, 'e did. God only knows why she went with 'im in the first place. Unbeknown to Amos, she'd booked a passage to Canada. But the ship she was on got wrecked in a storm and sank near where you live, down Cornwall ... everybody drowned ... That was over twenty-five year ago.'

'The *Atlantic Queen?*' Rosena gasped.

'Yes.' Nesta looked surprised. 'You knew about it?'

Rosena nodded.

Nesta went on. 'Of course Amos tried 'is bullyin' tricks with me, but wrestler or not, I gave 'im as good as 'e gave me. I hit 'im with a broom handle once, but it didn't make life any happier ...'

Rosena's thoughts were racing. She was sure that Kirby's first wife going to her death on the *Atlantic Queen* was somehow significant - but why? The stairs creaked and the doctor came down, fastening his bag.

'I've given him some extra pills, Mrs Kirby,' he said, 'I'm afraid he isn't for this world much longer.'

Nesta Kirby nodded. "'Tis all 'is years of wicked ways that's comin' home to roost.'

After the doctor had gone, she led Rosena up to the bedroom. It reeked of sickness, and there were several half empty medicine bottles on a side table. Amos Kirby lay propped up on pillows, his eyes showing the dullness of death, but the sight of her brought a smile to his cracked lips. 'Glad you've come,' he murmured weakly, and then to Nesta he added, 'Fetch the photographs ... I want 'er to see 'em.'

As his wife left to do his bidding, Kirby wheezed, 'I may not be around much longer, my dear, but ... but I wouldn't be 'appy goin' to my grave with you ignorant of what happened all those years ago. Shall we say ...' He hesitated as a bout of coughing shook him. He wiped spittle from his lips with his hand. 'Shall we say, my first wife Molly didn't behave like a good wife should. She ran away.'

Nesta Kirby returned carrying a leather bag. 'Rosena knows what 'appened,' she cut in, 'I told 'er.'

'Oh ...' Kirby rested back, wearied by talk, but shortly he roused himself and reached for the leather bag. He fumbled inside and dragged out an old, post-card sized photograph. 'Take a look,' he said, holding it out for Rosena.

Rosena gazed at the photograph, then she blinked hard to make sure her vision was not playing tricks - but nothing could change the face that was smiling at her from the picture.

It was the most difficult letter Edwin had ever written. He expressed his sorrow at John Bray's death, then, as gently as he could, he related to Rosena the complicated events which had occurred in 1890, and he asked her not to be unkind to Tom for concealing the truth. Edwin explained how his love for her had remained, despite his efforts to allow their relationship to fade. Even now he loved her so much, it hurt him - especially as he realised they could never marry. Had I stayed any longer in England, he wrote, knowing that you were only a few hours away, I would have gone mad!

He described his life in Australia, and how vast the country was. Melbourne, where the climate was mild and the rainfall light, was the capital of Australia. It was surprisingly sophisticated, with its bustling harbour, parks and elegant buildings. In the post-war boom, the wool industry was growing fast, with demobbed servicemen exploiting the land, flooding the green hills of Victoria with sheep.

But soon his pen returned to his feelings for the Cornish girl.

> *I love you, Rosena, with a yearning which is not brotherly. Fate has inflicted a bitter blow upon us, and we must each now go our separate ways. Please, please understand that what I have done is for the best. Do not think ill of me. I love you and always will. God, how I wish circumstances could have been different.*

The past burned inside him like an ulcer. Sometimes at night as he lay in his bed, he imagined he heard Rosena's rich, warm Cornish voice, or her gentle laugh. And after sleep overtook him, he would dream that she was with him, her lips hungry for his, her breasts and warm body crushed against him. Soaked with the sweat of passion, he'd awake with his heart pounding. Then would come the crippling realisation that he was dreaming of his sister.

Each moment they had spent together haunted him, seeming to grow more vivid as time passed. She was everything he'd ever longed for. Had she been dead, he might have reconciled himself to the loss, but the fact that she was alive, alone, left him feeling bereft.

'What you need,' Bill Luxton his manager had told him, 'is another woman - and a randy one at that.'

Edwin had smiled and shaken his head.

He'd tried to lose himself in work. Brokerage of prime wool was big business, and his knowledge of wool trading was greatly appreciated by Luxton. In the warehouse, he prepared catalogues and sorted the wool sent in by sheep-farmers under contract to the company. Interested customers would view the bales prior to auction. There would also be enquiries from overseas mills. But he was not confined to inside tasks. Part of his work was to tour the far-flung outstations, discussing business with the farmers. On horseback and beneath blue skies, he crossed rolling grasslands, sometimes seeing groups of kangaroos leaping away before him.

On the day after Edwin had posted the letter to Rosena, Bill Luxton looked up from his desk and said, 'I'm worried about you, Edwin. This is where you belong now. Don't waste your life moping for the past. Get yourself a nice little Aussie woman. There's plenty looking for husbands.'

Edwin closed his ledger. 'Perhaps you're right, but it's not easy.'

'Look,' Luxton persisted. 'I'm going up to the Gippsland Hills this weekend for a picnic. You should smell the eucalyptus trees up there! My girl friend's bringing along her cousin, Kathy Briggs - a right little bewdie from all accounts. Why don't you make up a foursome?'

'I've got too much work to do.'

'Oh, come off it, mate. I'm your boss, anyway. I've met some crazy Poms in my time, but you take the bloody ticket. This weekend, okay?'

Edwin hesitated. It was true he couldn't go on being a social outcast, nor could he go on making love with a memory. 'Okay ...but I hope this Kathy girl won't expect too much from me.'

Luxton's craggy face creased into a satisfied smile. 'Wait till you see her, mate. She'll rush you off your feet.'

It was the day following her visit to Taunton, and she had walked the cliff-path to St Mags. Struggling on the slopes and battling the wind had exhausted her. Now she was in Tom's parlour, recovering her breath and grateful for the warmth of his fire. The fullness of her body troubled her, but her mind was centred on more important matters. Breathlessly, she'd told Tom of her experiences.

'I nearly fainted with shock when I saw the photograph.'

'Why?' Tom asked. He was sorry that Rosena had learned of her past, not from him, but from Jeremy Carter's lips - and from Edwin's letter which she'd received that very morning, early post. But now at least the whole affair had come into the open.

'Why was it such a shock?' he repeated.

'Amos Kirby insisted that I kept the photograph,' she said and now she reached into her handbag, took it out and placed it on the table.

His eyes widened. 'This is ... you!' he gasped.

She nodded. 'That's what I thought at first. But tid'n me.'

'But the likeness ... If it's not you, who is it?'

''Tis Kirby's first wife - Molly,' Rosena explained. 'She wasn't really 'is wife, but they lived together, and he fathered 'er children. That's why 'e kept starin' at me when 'e came to Father's funeral, because I was so like 'er. 'E thought she'd come back to haunt 'im.'

'She's dead then, this Molly?'

'Drowned in the 1890 shipwreck. She'd run away from 'im, was goin' to Canada. She took 'er two babies with 'er - twins they were. Do you see what this means? The likeness between 'er and me?'

Tom shook his head, as if to drive away the truth, but he knew there was but one explanation. 'She's your mother,' he gasped.

Rosena whispered, 'Yes, Tom,' and she paused while he absorbed the startling fact, then she went on, her voice trembling with revulsion: 'And even worse ... Amos Kirby is my true father!'

'My God!' Tom clicked his tongue, frantic comprehension struggling in his eyes. Again there was a pause, then he murmured, 'Well one thing's clear, you didn't inherit your sweet nature from 'im. Your mother must've been a truly lovely person. It was a tragedy that she drowned.'

Rosena nodded, slipped her arm through his and hugged him close. 'I don't believe my mother did drown,' she said.

He gave her a puzzled glance.

'You know that wrecked boat along the beach below Perhaver? I'm convinced it was the second boat washed up after the *Atlantic Queen* went down.'

'Yes,' he nodded, 'washed up empty. All the poor souls 'ad been drowned.'

'They weren't, Tom. I believe that Molly survived with one of 'er babies - the boy. Somehow, somebody else was caring for the girl. I was that girl! I was taken into a separate boat. That was the one that was washed up at Megstow Quay. The fact that Edwin and I were together, gave the impression that we were brother and sister. But we weren't. 'Is real sister perished with the rest of 'em.'

'What are you sayin', Rosena!'

'I spent all last night reasonin' it out. This morning I walked along the beach and sat in the boat, and when I closed my eyes, I could sense the past, 'twas so strong about me.'

'But if your true mother survived, what 'appened to 'er - and the child?'

'I believe she climbed up the cliff path to Perhaver Manor - and Squire Perhaver took 'er in. She lived at Perhaver until she died two years later - and she never ventured out or showed 'er face because she was terrified Amos Kirby would find out she was still alive and come for 'er!'

Tom had stiffened, breathing heavily. Rosena went on, speaking slowly so that the implication of her words could sink in. 'There was one other thing Kirby told me. The boy-twin had been crippled at birth. 'E had one leg longer than the other ...'

Tom Lethbridge came to his feet, a muscle twitching in his face.

It was then that Rosena drove the final bolt home. 'Before I left Kirby's 'ouse, 'is wife told me Molly's full name. 'Twas Molly Lethbridge!'

His mouth hung open, his face working with emotion. At last he voice came huskily in a statement of fact. 'So 'tis you and me who are brother and sister - twins. And all these years we never realised.'

She rose, went to him and their arms were suddenly around each other.

'No wonder I always loved you, Rosena,' he murmured. 'You were the image of our mother, but neither of us were old enough when she died to remember 'er.'

Later, they sat in silence, each trying to mentally adjust to their newly discovered sibling relationship. Eventually Tom said, 'You'll 'ave to let Edwin know.'

'No!' she exclaimed. ''E must never know.'

'But, Rosena ... You're free to marry 'im now!'

'I've another man's baby in my belly, Tom. I could never marry in these circumstances.' Her voice showed a bitter edge: 'No man wants another man's leavin's!'

He showed a flash of rare anger. 'You'm bein' selfish, Rosena! You'm just thinkin' of yourself. You've got another life to consider now.'

'You don't need to tell me that!' she retorted. 'My whole existence has been knocked topsy-turvy - but nobody's stolen my pride. I'll not burden any man with my problems and that's final! Now I must go.'

He watched in a sort of daze as she put on her coat and the shawl he had once given her. For a moment it seemed she would leave without further ado, but suddenly she relented, her eyes softening, and she came to him and kissed his cheek. Passion rose in him like a high wave. He pulled her against him, crushing his lips to hers, kissing her with fierce hunger, and the resistance left her and all at once her mouth was as yielding and warm as his. When she at last drew back, he gasped, 'I should've done that years ago, Rosena.'

She smiled. 'Just as well you didn't, Tom Lethbridge. If you 'ad done, we'd probably be man and wife today. Just think of that. Twins marryin' each other!'

Reluctantly he released her from his arms. 'I love you, Rosena, always will.'

'Thanks, Tom,' she murmured softly. 'Thanks for bein' you.'

When she had gone, he slumped onto a chair, his face filled with bleakness. There were tears in his eyes, a half-hour later, when he found pen, ink and paper and started a letter.

Dear Edwin

We only met once, and that was under strained circumstances. I do hope any ill feeling is long forgotten. I know you are a good man from what Rosena has told me. If, God willing, you receive this letter, you will know that I have managed to get your address from Rosena and I shall have done so without her suspecting that I am contacting you. She would not forgive me for such action, but I am convinced in the fullness of time what I am doing will be for the best - although so much depends on you. You will not be aware that Rosena is expecting Gareth Williams' child, and he has deserted her for the wife she did not know he had. Nor will you be aware that other staggering information has come to light ...

He paused, renewed frustration gnawing at him. He was fooling himself. He allowed the pen to drop from his fingers. There was no way he could get Edwin's address in Australia without arousing Rosena's suspicions. And she would never, never condone such high-handed action.

Chapter Twenty-two

THE CHILD HAD A TRIANGULAR FACE and narrow chin, but there was something of the father about his eyes, but it was as just as well that the resemblance was not too obvious. Conceived in a bloody broom cupboard, Jenny thought, no wonder the poor little sod looks so shifty!

Her own mother believed that Jim Turnwell was the father and that was why Jenny had run away with him.

'Davie's a healthy enough little'un. 'Tis only natural 'e should 'ave trouble teethin'.' Martha Killigrew's eyes were red from the onions she was peeling at the kitchen table. She placed a piece of bread in the child's hand, watched him ease his sore gums on it.

Jenny had arrived in St Mags on the mid-day bus, the first time she'd returned since she'd eloped. After she'd married Jim Turnwell, he'd gone back to the Army in France and she'd found lodgings in Manchester. When Davie was born Jim had never doubted that he was the father.

'Does Tom Lethbridge still live in the village?' she enquired.

'Yes,' her mother nodded, 'Why? Do you want to see 'im?'

'No, I don't,' Jenny said. 'I'm glad I scared 'im that time. Too stuck up for 'is own good, 'e was.'

Her mother didn't comment. She glanced at the clock on the dresser. 'Your father'll be back from the pub soon. Better be sweet to 'im, if you want some money.'

'Just enough to tide us over till Jim gets some work,' Jenny said, bouncing the child on her knee, well aware that he needed changing but feeling too tired to do it. 'Did Tom Lethbridge ever take that Bray girl for 'is wife? 'E was keen enough on 'er.'

Martha Killigrew shook her head. 'She got 'erself in family way. The father was some soldier who'd been up at Perhaver ... Gareth Williams. 'E fancied 'imself as a painter. Maybe 'e was up Perhaver when you worked there. Maybe you knew 'im.'

'I knew 'im,' Jenny confirmed, inwardly smug that she hadn't been the only female stupid enough to fall for his glib talk. 'That must've pulled Rosena Bray down a peg or two. 'As she 'ad the baby?'

'Gone away somewhere to 'ave it. Probably thinks she can keep things quiet for a bit. But all of Megstow Quay and St Mags knows what she's been up to.

Nora Trevick's seen to that with 'er quicksilver tongue. She got sight of a letter.'

Jenny fanned a fly away from Davie's eyes. 'Should think Miss 'igh and mighty Bray'll be ashamed to show 'erself around these parts now.'

Her mother nodded. 'Don't know what 'er father would say if 'e was still alive, especially as the vicar's sermon last Sunday was all about the evil sins of the flesh. 'E didn't mention Rosena's name, but it was clear what 'e was gettin' at. Thank God your 'usband fathered your babies. At least you can 'old your 'ead up when you walk down the street.'

'Yes, Mum,' Jenny said rather meekly. 'Wouldn't want to be in Rosena Bray's shoes.'

Both women heard the rattle of the street door latch. 'Must be Silas,' Martha said. 'Remember what I said - be sweet to 'im!'

'You haven't got much money, Rosena,' Jeremy said, keeping his voice low.

They were sitting in the patients' rest-room of St Mary's Home for Unmarried Women, an austere Victorian house with windows which faced Wimbledon Common. Across the large room, a waif of a girl was breast-feeding her baby. Jeremy sniffed disdainfully. The atmosphere of hospitals had always made him feel ill. Here, the pervading redolence of antiseptic could not mask the establishment's other smells - babies, milk, food and beeswax polish.

His attention returned to the Cornish girl. She was lying on a leather couch, looking quite mountainous in a pretty pink dressing-gown that Tom Lethbridge had given her. The baby was ten days overdue. Rosena kept shifting her position in a vain effort to ease her discomfort. 'If you keep the child,' Jeremy went on, 'things are going to be virtually impossible. Not fair on it; not fair on you. You must have it adopted - just a question of signing these papers and I'll see to the rest. The child will go to an excellent orphanage and be well looked after until a suitable family is found.'

Beryl had been fidgeting. She leaned close to Rosena. 'My dear, where is the lavatory?'

Rosena nodded to the far end of the ward. 'Through the door.'

As Beryl hastened gratefully away, a twinkle returned to Jeremy's eye. 'Rosena, my love, the future can be good for you, once the child is adopted. There'll be work for you in my warehouse. I'll make sure you have a nice apartment to live in, enough money, and I'm certain we can make an ... arrangement.'

She gave him a puzzled glance. 'An arrangement?'

He smiled conspiratorially. 'Beryl and I ... well, we don't ... A man has certain needs. You're an attractive woman, Rosena. Nobody need know. You understand, I'm sure. And you'd have no worry about money.'

Her mouth sagged with astonishment. The words seemed to burst from her of their own accord. 'Uncle Jeremy ... I'm not a prostitute ... not for you or any man!'

Jeremy blanched. 'Keep your voice down.' Further discussion on the matter was stifled because Beryl returned, and his voice resumed its former, hard tone. 'Once the child is adopted, you'll be independent. You can make a fresh start.'

'It breaks my heart to say it,' Beryl said, 'but I'm sure Jeremy is right. Later on, you're bound to meet somebody who'll make you a nice husband - but not if you've got a little one trailing along.'

Jeremy placed the formal looking papers on the table in front of Rosena, and offered her his gold fountain-pen.

Rosena felt desperate, trapped. How could she explain her feelings to him? She repeated what she'd told him before. 'Uncle Jeremy, I don't want to give up my child.'

He looked exasperated, clearly annoyed at the rebuff she'd given him. 'Then you'll have to find your own way. There's nothing more we can do.' He became brusque. 'We'll leave the papers with you, Rosena. Let me know if you come to your senses and sign them ... and about the other matter.'

'I'll ... I'll think about it,' she said coldly.

Jeremy and Beryl stood up. Beryl reached out and touched Rosena's hand and murmured, 'Good luck, my dear.' Jeremy simply gave her a curt nod, then they left. Two minutes later, in the hallway of the nursing home, they encountered Sister Edna, her serene face framed by the pale blue habit of her order. She was in charge of the home. She beckoned them to one side.

'Rosena's birth will not be easy,' she told them in her calm Irish voice. 'With the baby overdue, Doctor Weaver the consultant may decide to induce labour.'

'Sister,' Beryl said, 'is there any risk involved - to her life I mean? And how about the baby?'

'Breech birth can be an ordeal, Mrs Carter. The baby's buttocks instead of the head are in the cervix, and the legs are stretched upward. It may be a forceps delivery - but Doctor Weaver is a very good man. He will do whatever is humanly possible - and we must pray that the Good Lord will do the rest.'

'But the Lord moves in mysterious ways,' Jeremy murmured, half to himself.

Sister Edna gave him a questioning glance, fingered the tiny silver crucifix at her throat and offered no contradiction.

When they were in their car, speeding towards Beckenham, Jeremy was deeply silent. Eventually Beryl asked what was in his mind.

'I'm thinking that it might be best for everybody if the baby died,' he replied.

'Oh Jeremy, you shouldn't say that.'

'But it's true, my dear.'

Beryl sighed. She opened her handbag to find her handkerchief and dab a tear from her eye. 'It's all so sad.' As she replaced her handkerchief her glance rested on the yellow envelope of the cable Edwin had sent them from Melbourne. 'Jeremy ... why don't you want to tell her that Edwin is on his way home?'

'The last thing we want to do is raise the girl's hopes only to be dashed. If she'd agreed to have the child adopted, things might have been different. We don't want her to think that Edwin's coming back to marry her.'

'But I'm sure he is, Jeremy.'

Jeremy snorted. 'Not if I can talk some sense into his head first!'

Rosena was in great discomfort, had been for days. She felt as if a huge grapefruit was pressing against her midriff. With the baby's birth already overdue, she had the woebegone feeling that the Carters' interest in her might wane. Beryl's because she now realised that Rosena was not related - and Jeremy's because she had embarrassed him. Despite this, she was also aware that she owed them a great deal. Even the fact that she was here in this nursing home was thanks to Jeremy, even though he was expecting to be re-paid in a way she'd never suspected. Disillusionment settled over her.

Her gaze rested on the adoption papers that Jeremy had left. He had left his pen. Much of what he had said was true. The money she had was fast running out. She had the expenses of her confinement to meet. The prospect of returning to Megstow Quay, facing local folk, was daunting. Furthermore, her wantonness had inflicted on a helpless, yet-to-be born baby, the stigma of illegitimacy which would have to be carried for ever.

Panic churned inside her. Perhaps she had no option but to walk steadfastly into the trap that awaited her. Her hand touched the pen. One quick squiggle, she told herself, will alter my life and my baby's for ever ...

After she had put her signature to the form, agreeing to the adoption, Sister Edna asked her if she was quite sure this was what she wanted, and when Rosena nodded, the nun enquired if she would wish to hold the baby for a little while before it was transferred to St Bernard's Orphanage and Adoption

Society. Again Rosena nodded, although she was now in such discomfort, easing herself from one haunch to the other, that she scarcely knew what she was doing.

Next morning she still showed no sign of going into labour. Doctor Weaver checked her blood pressure, found it high, and decided to induce the birth. Soon, a porter arrived and helped Rosena into a wheelchair - and she thought, Oh God, what's happening? Is there a monster inside me!

Edwin felt that the rail journey from Southampton would never end. He changed at Woking, and thereafter the train stopped at every possible station on its way to Wimbledon.

Over and over, since leaving Australia, he'd read Tom Lethbridge's incredible letter. Never in his wildest dreams had he imagined that the Cornishman would reverse his advice never to marry Rosena. Now everything had turned around. Tom had begged Edwin to come to England, to propose to Rosena, and pray that she'd forget her stupid pride.

The fact that the letter had reached Edwin was a tribute to the mail service, for the address had been scant, simply:

EDWIN CARTER (ENGLISHMAN)
c/o THE WOOL BROKERS ASSOCIATION, MELBOURNE ...

Edwin had immediately discussed matters with the understanding Bill Luxton. The latter's match-making between Edwin and Kathy Briggs had proved a pleasant diversion but no romance had ensued. Luxton had willingly given Edwin leave of absence in the hope that he would get his affairs sorted out and return to Australia complete with a wife. So Edwin had booked a passage to England, cabling his uncle and aunt that he was on his way.

Now, as he glanced at his watch, wondering how many more stops there would be before Wimbledon, he felt even more frustrated than he had during the weeks of the sea voyage. Admittedly, there'd been interesting sights to intrude upon his longings for Rosena: The paradise-islands with their palm-fringed beaches, scattered across the turquoise sea like a terrestrial Milky Way. And later, when the ship left the Pacific Ocean, the Panama Canal. Fifty miles of water-way were curbed to man's will by six great locks, each partitioned to allow for two-way traffic. As they entered the Caribbean, he watched from the stern-rail the arching playfulness of dolphins cavorting in the wake of the ship, leaping to catch the sun.

He hoped that soon he'd be returning and sharing these wonderful scenes with Rosena and the baby as they voyaged to a new life in Australia. Please

God, he'd prayed, may she accept my proposal - then we can escape from the past.

When he telephoned his uncle from Southampton, Jeremy gave him a long lecture to the effect that it would be quite wrong to consider marrying the girl, and that he would be making an even bigger fool of himself than he had in walking out on his wedding day. Jeremy asked Edwin to come home so that they could discuss matters before he made any attempt to contact Rosena, but having fed all his loose change into the coin box, Edwin's patience was running out, although just before the line went dead he extracted from the grudging Jeremy the one snippet of information he wanted above all else: Rosena was in a maternity home at Wimbledon. It seemed he couldn't have reached England at a more vital moment.

At Wimbledon Station he found a taxi and enquired the whereabouts of the maternity home. The cabby thought for a moment, then drove him to an establishment on the east side of town. In response to his anxious enquiries, he was told that there was no Rosena Bray there, but they directed him to a second nursing home, run by nuns, on the edge of Wimbledon Common near to Kings College School, and kindly arranged another taxi for him. Twenty minutes later, he arrived, mounted the steps of the Victorian house three at a time and entered its deserted hallway. Nobody was in sight, but he could hear babies crying, a burble of upstairs voices, rushing footsteps and the clink of plates. He pressed a push-bell on a side table, was startled by the sharp sound that was unleashed. Through a doorway came an elderly nun. She looked at him with enquiring eyes.

'Is Rosena Bray here?' he enquired.

'Yes, she is,' Sister Edna replied in her Irish voice. 'But I'm afraid she's ... well, there've been complications. The consultant's with her now.'

There was a commotion behind Edwin and he turned to see an enormously pregnant girl, looking no more than sixteen, helped through the main door by an older woman, panic stamped across their faces. 'Water's broken,' the older woman cried. 'Weren't due for another week ...'

The girl suddenly howled, standing legs astride, clutching her swollen abdomen, and Sister Edna moved forward to help her. Another nun appeared, and for a moment Edwin thought the girl was going to give birth immediately. But her cries subsided and the group passed into the inner regions of the home. He was left alone, desperate to know what was happening to Rosena, wondering if he had been forgotten in this moment of urgency. However, shortly a young nun appeared, smiled sweetly and said, 'Sir ... would you care to wait in the parlour? I'll get you some tea.'

'But Rosena Bray ... is she ...?'

'We're praying for her. We'll let you know as soon as there's any news.'

The nun, Sister Helen, disappeared, leaving Edwin in a small side-parlour. He paced the polished linoleum, glancing disinterestedly at the huge potted aspidistra and pictures of a haloed Jesus and angels. Sister Helen eventually returned with a tea and some biscuits.

'You must try to relax,' she advised. 'Are you the baby's father?'

'No,' Edwin said. 'I've just come from Australia. I ...'

'Oh ... Australia? That's a long way. Well, sir, you have your tea, and we'll come and tell you just as soon as there's any news.'

In the delivery room, Rosena had lost hope of ever reaching the end of her long tunnel of suffering. Contractions swept over her like a raging tide. She had become completely disorientated during the relentless hours of labour, exhaustion depriving her of the will to go on, but the two midwives kept repeating, 'Won't be long now, dear ... You're doing well!' and their faces loomed above her, guiding her through a red haze of agony. An enormous stretching sensation made her feel that her body was bursting.

Suddenly, somehow, she seemed above it, her screams almost those of another person. The midwives shepherded her, cajoled her, and at long last the patience of Doctor Weaver was rewarded. The baby's buttocks and legs slithered into the world, and he used the forceps to ease the hard bud of the head clear.

'It's a girl!' a midwife said.

Later, after she'd ejected the afterbirth, Rosena lay back, totally exhausted, her eyes shining, her cheeks flushed, her hair damp and tangled. In her was a glowing sensation of achievement, of creation, far beyond anything she had ever known.

'See,' the midwife was persisting, 'she's a little beauty!' and held the moist red body in front of her.

With supreme effort, Rosena raised her head and saw the baby. Its eyes were closed, its face puckered with disdain and swollen red. It was greeting life with innocent rage, arms flailing, tiny, star-fish hands unclenching, sturdy little thighs and heels churning. Rosena smiled weakly. She reached out, took the baby in her arms. She felt victorious. She knew that she would rather die than surrender its upbringing to another person.

Chapter Twenty-three

EDWIN WAITED. The outside light faded and rain splattered against the window. Presently another nun came and turned the gas-light on, but she had no news for him. Anxiety clogged his veins. He sat head-slumped, half dozing, aware that the hours were slipping by. Then, at last, Sister Edna's Irish voice sounded: 'Mister Carter!'

He was on his feet immediately. 'Is Rosena all right?'

Sister Edna held up a calming hand. 'Our prayers have been answered,' she said. 'Mind you she's very weak. The birth was difficult for her, but the Lord helped her. She's resting now, under sedation.'

'Does she know I'm here?'

The nun shook her head. 'She knows nothing apart from that she has a little girl ... and that she's changed her mind about adoption.'

'Adoption?'

'Yes, she'd signed the paper for adoption, but when she saw her baby, she begged us to tear the paper up. So we did, in front of her eyes.'

Edwin sighed with relief. 'Can I see her?' he asked.

'Not now. Any excitement would set her back. It'll take time. Give her two days, then she'll be ready.'

'Of course.' He was annoyed with himself for not showing more consideration.

She touched his arm. 'The baby's not yours, is it, Mister Carter?'

'No,' he said, 'but it doesn't matter. If Rosena agrees to marry me, I'll love the baby as much as any true father.'

Sister Edna gave him a serene smile. 'We've taken her away from her mother for a little while, to give them both some rest. We'll put her back in her mother's arms later on. But, if you want to see the baby, I'll take you to the nursery now.'

'Oh yes,' he nodded, his eyes brightening. He felt clammy with perspiration and exhausted with relief. He followed Sister Edna down the corridor and up a stairway, she turned and said, 'You can leave a note for Rosena if you wish.'

Edwin nodded gratefully. But a moment later when he saw the child for the first time, saw the ugly, red facial marks and the huge upper lip that extended almost to the nostrils, he groaned with dismay.

'Be my wife, Ro-sena, and I'll love you and the baby with all my heart.'

It was the following day, and Rosena had made an incredible recovery, her Cornish fibre tougher than anybody had expected. So delighted was Sister Edna, that she had relented and allowed an early visitor, feeling sure that a man of the cloth would not over-excite the patient. She did not notice the stunned expression with which Rosena greeted this man.

'But Gareth,' Rosena whispered, noticing that he'd shaved off his moustache. She kept her voice down to avoid being overheard by the three other patients in the ward, 'I don't love you. 'Ow can I, after the way you behaved?'

'The way I behaved? Don't worry about that, petal. You see, the Good Lord 'as made me understand I wasn't to blame about what we did. Let me explain. You were like my Eve - temptin' me with your carnal apple. But I'd been wounded. My defences were weakened by fightin' for my country, fightin' the just war ... no wonder I didn't 'ave the strength to resist.'

'So you'm sayin',' she bristled, ''twas all my fault!'

'I forgive you, Ro-sena. That's why I'm 'ere ... sent by the Lord.'

How sanctimonious he looked in his white Baptist collar! And his charm, his infectious Welshness, his apparent sincerity ... they all meant nothing. She'd been stupid not to see through him in the first place.

'Does Bronwyn know you're 'ere?' she asked.

He shook his head. 'My dear Bronwyn ... died in my arms, six months ago. A seizure, it was. I ...' He paused, a tear trickling down his cheek.

'I'm sorry,' she said. 'Sorry for Bronwyn.' He shot her a pleading glance. He wants my sympathy, she thought, but I have none to give him.

Gradually his grief subsided. His eyes settled on Emma Jane. ' She'll carry those scars for life,' he whispered, 'but she's got your eyes, Ro-sena - slanting up at the edges, I mean.' He made a conscious effort, knowing the part he had to play. 'Ro-sena ... let me 'old 'er for a moment. Let 'er dad 'ug her in 'is arms ...'

He reached forward and she reluctantly allowed him to take Emma Jane from her, to make soft cooing sounds which didn't come naturally to him. 'Good girl, she'll be,' he murmured, anxious to pass her back. 'Emma Jane ... you'll make a wonderful sister for Gwenda.'

''Ow did you know I was 'ere?' she asked.

'I 'ad to see Mister Jeremy Carter ... your uncle, isn't 'e? 'E's bought my paintin' of you - offered a good price, and paid me in cash, 'e 'as.' He patted the bulging pocket of his jacket. ''E thought I might be interested to 'ear about you. I should say I was. I caught the first train. I never realised you were in the family way, Ro-sena. You should've told me.' Holding the baby precariously on one arm, he reached across and placed his hand over hers.

'I've thought about you so much, about when we first met, the good times we had at Perhaver, those glorious walks along the beach. And do you remember the concert? Didn't we laugh? Oh, my dearest, 'ow sweet it was. And now we're together again. I know the Good Lord's planned it. I always said I'd marry you, remember?'

'Let me have Emma Jane back before you drop 'er,' Rosena said. As she took the baby, she thought: Poor little girl. She needs a father just the same as everybody else.

She doubted she would ever bring herself to feel love for Gareth again, but did it matter? She remembered words Tom had spoken: You'm being selfish, Rosena! You've got another life to consider now.

Maybe, she thought, maybe this is the way it's meant to be after all. Gareth and Rosena ... and now Emma Jane as well.

'Be my wife, Ro-sena,' he repeated.

'A cup of tea?' young Sister Helen asked, unaware of the intensity of Gareth's words. She stood beside Rosena's bed, a tray in her hands.

'Oh, yes,' Gareth said, anxious to hasten her on her way.

But Sister Helen was in no hurry. She turned to Rosena. 'You've made a wonderful recovery,' she said. 'Won't be long before you can go home.'

Home, Rosena thought, what home!

'Did Sister Edna give you the letter?' the young nun enquired.

'What letter?'

'It was left by the gentleman who called yesterday. He wanted to see you, but you weren't well enough. Sister Edna said he could leave a letter and she'd give it to you when you were well enough to read it. It must still be in Sister Edna's office. I'll fetch it for you.'

Gareth suddenly spoke up, rising to his feet. 'I know where Sister Edna's office is. I'll get it and save your tired legs, sister.'

Sister Helen hesitated. At that moment one of the other patients called for urgent attention. Sister Helen nodded, 'Thank you, sir.'

Gareth smiled at Rosena. She sensed a strange desperation in him.

'Shan't be a minute, petal,' he said. 'While I'm gone, you make up your mind about what I asked.'

'Gareth ... this time there would be no doubt? We'd definitely be married?'

Gareth lowered his voice. 'That'll be a true promise. We'll get married tomorrow, if that's what you want. It'll be for the baby's sake ... and for your sake, my love.'

Rosena nodded and Gareth left the ward.

He found Sister Edna's office at the end of the corridor. The door stood open, but nobody was inside. He entered, glancing at the assorted papers on the desk, cursing at his failure to find what he was seeking.

Jeremy had told him that Edwin had returned from Australia and Gareth felt sure that it was he who had left the letter. Perhaps Sister Edna had already taken it to deliver to Rosena. He cursed. Then his frantic gaze swung to the room's ornate mantelpiece. Leaning against a clock was an envelope addressed to 'Rosena Bray'. He snatched it down and slipped it into his pocket.

'Did you get the letter?' Rosena asked as he returned to her bedside.

''Twas all a mistake, petal. Wasn't for you at all.'

She sighed with disappointment. 'I thought it was strange.'

He leaned forward and took Rosena's hand in his. 'Now my dear, lovely Ro-sena. Say you'll be my wife, and we'll make our plans, we will. You'll be so 'appy. I promise you.'

A smothering resignation settled over her. She gazed at her baby, sleeping peacefully, unaware of her mother's turmoil. It will be for Emma Jane's sake, Rosena told herself. She needs a father, just like every child. I've no right to deprive her.

Gareth glanced furtively around, then lowering his voice, he said: 'I won't ask much of you, my petal - nothin' that you don't want to give, I mean. But there's just one small favour.'

'A favour?'

'Yes. It's ...' He hesitated, shaping his words. 'It's just that I don't have much time. Very urgent business, you know. I'll explain later and you'll understand. What I'm askin' is when I walk out of this place, you come with me. We can be married tomorrow.'

'But Gareth, I'm still weak. I've got stitches in me, and the baby ...'

A frightening impatience flared in Gareth's eyes, the black pupils expanding. He wasn't going to let anything stand in his way now. Infatuation, lust, obsession for this woman burned in him. 'I don't 'ave much time, I told you. There's a doctor where we're goin'. You've got to get out of that bed and come with me now. I can't make it any clearer!'

Chapter Twenty-four

WHEN EDWIN REACHED his Uncle Jeremy's house, he telephoned the nursing home. He was greatly relieved to learn that Rosena and the baby were doing well. He spoke to young Sister Helen and she assured him that within a day or so the Cornish girl would be strong enough to receive visitors. As he rang off, he reminded himself that he must be patient and do nothing to jeopardize Rosena's health. She would need plenty of strength when they voyaged across the world to face a new life in Australia. The prospect filled him with joy. But that evening, as they finished dinner, Jeremy gave him some surprising news.

'That Welsh painter Gareth Williams, the fellow who fathered Rosena's child, he called here this morning to collect the money I owed him for his painting of Rosena. Insisted I paid him in cash. He seemed positively furtive, desperate to get the money. Didn't stay long after he'd checked it.'

Edwin frowned. 'Does he know Rosena's in the maternity home at Wimbledon?'

'I told him.' Jeremy took a draw on his cigar. 'But really, Edwin, you don't have to worry about Rosena now. She's not your concern. She's cut herself off from this family.'

Edwin didn't reply but his mind was racing. He glanced at his watch. It was too late to go to Wimbledon tonight, but he would go first thing in the morning.

On arrival at the maternity home, Edwin was ushered quickly into Sister Edna's office. The nun was pale and distraught. 'It was a terrible thing, Mister Carter. The Reverend Williams insisted he would make sure she got all the medical attention she'd need. I protested strongly, but they wouldn't listen to me. The poor girl hardly had enough strength to walk up the ward, let alone into the street. And the child ... just a day old!'

'You mean Rosena's gone with Gareth Williams?' The blood was draining from Edwin's temples.

Sister Edna nodded miserably. 'He said it was God's will.'

'Oh no!' Edwin was desperate with fear. 'Where were they going? Did they say?'

'No, Mister Carter. They left no word - just walked out. It was awful.'

He tried to steady himself, to force coherence into his emotions. 'When did they leave?'

'About noon yesterday.'

Edwin shook his head in dismay. 'He may have taken her to Wales. I've got to find out.'

'I pray for the girl all the time,' Sister Edna assured him.

Edwin nodded and left, a sense of intense urgency quickening his stride.

Gwenda awoke screaming. She lay upon the narrow bed in the garret room at her Auntie Megan's, her bedcovers knotted on the floor, the moon sending a shaft of silver through the sky-light above her head. She hated this room, and now her young body was trembling and moist with fear. Gradually her heart steadied. She was angry with herself for screaming. Big tears rolled down her cheeks. She wanted her mam - but her mam wasn't with her any more, and nor was Uncle Gareth, and she didn't know when they would come back.

Presently she recovered her bedcovers and wiped her eyes with the sheet. Her mam had once told her that it helped to go to sleep if you thought about something nice, so she did ... Her mam coming back, giving her a cuddle and a big kiss, and them going home to Parry Street to live.

It was the same dream which always haunted Gwenda. Even when she was awake, she only had to lower her eyelids to see the vision of her mam's face bristling and red, her eyes sparking with anger as she glared at Uncle Gareth.

'Gareth, you bastard,' she'd screamed, 'you promised me, on the bible, there'd been no more philanderin'!'

Uncle Gareth had been putting on his parson's collar, but he hurled the stud onto the kitchen floor in temper and said, 'Why can't you keep your nose out of things. Always bloody pryin'.'

'That little trollop! Ooh, it makes my blood boil!'

'It's all lies,' Gareth shouted. Gwenda had never seen him so furious.

'No it's not, Gareth Williams,' her mam shouted. 'Man of the cloth or not, 'tis you who's lyin'.' And it was then she picked up the carving knife from the kitchen table, outrage making her knuckles white upon its handle. 'I'm tempted to do away with you. You're an evil man.'

'Don't you call me that, woman!' Uncle Gareth cried. 'God will strike you dumb!'

'No He won't!' her mam shrieked - but Uncle Gareth seized her by the shoulders, shaking her till her russet hair swung loose around her head.

The sight of them struggling, their awful shouting, had Gwenda screaming with horror and running from the kitchen and out through the front door, down darkened Parry Street, pummelling her eyes with her fists, trying to blot the image of the scene from her mind. She'd run blindly, her feet carrying her to her Auntie Megan's in the next street but one.

'You make so much fuss,' Megan had grumbled as she wiped the tears from Gwenda's face with a towel. 'Your mam always 'ad a fiery temper. You know there's been lots of rows before. When people are married, they sometimes think they 'ate each other, but they get over it. You'll see that when you grow up, you will. Anyway, you can stay 'ere tonight if you want. I don't expect your Uncle Huw will mind.'

And so Gwenda had gone to bed in the high, lonely garret room, and early next morning the brass knocker on the front-door thumped, echoing through the old house. It must be Mam, she thought. In her borrowed, too-large nightdress, her face red-puffy with crying, Gwenda crept down the stairs to the first landing, and peered into the hallway. Auntie Megan had opened the front door, letting in a cold gush of air.

It wasn't her mam who'd knocked; it was Uncle Gareth. Stubble like smeared ash showed on his jaw, and his hair was awry in the wind.

'We guessed she'd come round 'ere, silly child,' he was saying, 'so I brought a few of 'er things. Anyway, Bronwyn and I 'ave decided to go away for a few days ... a sort of 'oliday you could call it.'

'What's wrong with you, Gareth Williams?' Megan demanded. 'Look as though you've seen the Holy Spirit, you do. You better come in, 'ave a cup of tea.'

'No ... no. Won't stop now. Won't keep Bronwyn waitin'.' He thrust a bundle of Gwenda's clothes into his sister-in-law's arms. 'We'll let you know when we're comin' back.' And with that he'd turned and gone, and Auntie Megan had stood in the hallway, grasping the bundle, speechless and taken aback by Gareth's behaviour. Eventually she closed the front door and went into the kitchen.

That afternoon, Gwenda ran home to the guesthouse in Parry Street, hoping she might be able to get some dolls from her room, but everywhere was locked up and deserted, with the curtains drawn across the windows, and the sign **NO VACANCIES** displayed.

A week later a postcard arrived in Uncle Gareth's handwriting. We're having a lovely holiday. It's just what we needed. We won't be back for a while yet. Don't worry about us - we're fine. Love Gareth and Bronwyn.

On the day the card had arrived, Auntie Megan had pursed her lips angrily. Gwenda's eyes had dwelt on the great knife her aunt had been using to slice bread, its wicked blade catching the sunlight from the window. It reminded her of the knife her Mam had been holding the last time she saw her.

'Bloody rich, that is,' Uncle Huw now remarked for the hundredth time, 'Gareth and Bronwyn dumpin' their kid on us, leavin' all their cares behind an' ... clearin' off to enjoy themselves.'

Auntie Megan frowned. 'Can't understand it. Isn't like Bronwyn to go off so sudden.' She gazed at the postcard, then turned it over. 'Postmarked Cardiff.'

Gwenda had never been to Cardiff. It sounded a nice place.

Uncle Huw looked at Gwenda, his tufty eyebrows arched, his striped butcher's apron smeared with blood. He'd been at his shop since six o'clock that morning, cutting up the meat. Now he'd come home for his breakfast. 'You say they 'ad a big row the night before they left?' he asked.

Gwenda took a long, shuddering breath. She didn't want to think about it. Uncle Huw had asked her the same question before. She wished he could look inside her head and see the dream, then he would know exactly how it had been. 'Yes,' she said quietly. 'Mam was very angry with Uncle Gareth, she was.'

'Why was she angry?'

'Mam was annoyed about a little trollop,' Gwenda explained.

Uncle Huw shook his head in puzzlement. 'Don't mean nothin' to me.'

'Nor me,' Auntie Megan sighed.

To Gwenda it seemed a lifetime ago that the card had come. Since then, she had wandered time and again back to Parry Street to stand gazing up at the silent guesthouse. She had peered through the letter-box and caught a whiff of the staleness from within. She strained her eyes through the narrow slit, but with the curtains pulled, all she could see was blackness. She noticed how the coal-dust grime was thickening on the windows, how her mam's holystoned doorstep was turning a dirty grey, how the once-gleaming brass of the door-knocker had tarnished. It would have made her mam gasp with shame.

Gwenda would shudder, sensing but not admitting that this place was the ghost of her childhood, a childhood that was never to return.

Chapter Twenty-five

'TAKEN ILL ON THE TRAIN, she was, comin' up from London.' There was an impatient edge on Gareth's voice. 'Sort of fainted, I think. 'Tis nothin' really.'

Rosena had collapsed into an armchair. Through a haze of weakness, she could see Gareth outlined against the Georgian-window of the doctor's surgery, the baby held carelessly in the crook of his arm like an unwanted doll. Beyond Gareth, through the window's leaded glass squares, she could see a market place, bright in afternoon sunshine, and a large wooden-framed building with overhanging upper floors. She knew they were in Carlisle, for she had heard a porter shouting as Gareth had at last told her that they were to leave the train. Why they had come to this place, she had no idea - but she had pleaded with him that she must see a doctor.

Doctor Maldruth was an elderly, white-haired man with a haughty manner. His thin face revealed some distaste at having to deal with this case. 'When was the baby born?' he asked.

'Three days ago.' Rosena didn't have the strength to raise her voice above a whisper. Even baby Emma Jane seemed exhausted. She had cried during the long hours of the train journey, but now, as Gareth held her, she was asleep. Rosena noticed that Gareth was no longer wearing his clerical collar.

'Goodness me, young lady,' the doctor said, 'you should be resting, not travelling the country.'

'Doctor,' Gareth said abruptly, 'we had to come for the child's sake. We have to formalise our marriage. 'Twas all at short notice.'

Maldruth smiled. 'You mean at the 'Smithy'?'

Gareth nodded. He glanced at his watch anxiously. 'That's why we're in a hurry.'

'Oh you needn't worry,' Maldruth said. 'They keep doctor's hours over there.' He turned back to Rosena. 'Now, I'd better examine you. We can't have you fainting again - especially on your wedding day, eh?'

She endured the examination while Gareth stood gazing out of the window, holding the baby as he might have done an item of baggage. Rosena wondered how she could ever have loved Gareth so trustingly. Of course the awful wound he'd received had changed him. He now possessed a pitiless streak, along with a strange furtiveness. The gentle side of his character, if ever it had been more than an act, had gone.

After leaving the nursing home at Wimbledon by a taxi-cab, they had paused only to purchase cotton-squares for the baby, then they had pressed on to Euston Station. Gradually it dawned on Rosena: they were not going to Wales as she'd anticipated. With her legs weak and her head swimming, Gareth had virtually carried her onto a north-bound train, obsessed with the wish for haste.

The seemingly endless journey, sitting in a crowded carriage, had been utter torment for her. The stitching felt like red-hot needles being pressed into her most sensitive parts, and she knew that her clothing was moist with blood. 'How much longer?' she pleaded with Gareth. 'Where are we goin'?'

'Wait an' see, Ro-sena!'

She clenched her teeth in misery, knowing that in coming with him, she had made a ghastly mistake. And now she had no alternative but to submit to him because she didn't have the strength, nor even the will, to escape.

As Emma Jane's crying persisted, Rosena had unbuttoned her dress to feed her, partially exposing her milk-swollen breast. She was conscious of the disapproving gasp of the woman sitting opposite, and the shuffling feet and lowering of eyes of male passengers.

''Ave you no shame?' Gareth whispered, leaning close. 'Your breasts are for my eyes alone.'

'Baby must be fed,' she insisted as she pressed her nipple between the tumid lips of the tiny, red-scarred face.

Doctor Maldruth washed his hands in a bowl and carefully dried them. He had placed a fresh dressing on Rosena but he insisted that it was too early to remove the stitching. 'You must come back in a week's time. Where are you living?'

Gareth cleared his throat quickly. 'Oh ... local. We'll come back.'

Maldruth eyed the Welshman disbelievingly, but he nodded. 'Better let me check the baby.' He took the child from Gareth, wrinkling his nose for she needed attention.

Embarrassment gave Rosena strength. 'Let me change 'er. I 'ave some towellin'.'

The doctor nodded. 'There's water in the bowl if you need it.'

Afterwards, he tested the baby with his stethoscope, then nodded approvingly.

'The scars on 'er face?' Rosena enquired anxiously. ''As she got them for life?'

Maldruth touched the red marks with his finger, peering close. 'The little lass had a rough time at birth. They're not scars on her face. They're blisters. Give it three weeks and they'll be gone.'

'Thank God,' Rosena gasped as she took Emma Jane back.

Gareth had put his hat on, anxious to leave. 'Doctor,' he said, ''ow far is it to the Old Blacksmith's?'

'About ten miles,' the doctor said.

'Is there a train?'

'Yes - to the Junction,' Maldruth nodded, 'but the village is a long walk from there through the water meadows. If you must be married today, with the lass in her condition, you'd best not think about a train. It'll have to be a taxi, unless you want her to flake out.'

Gareth nodded, then he held out a five-pound note to Maldruth. 'Keep the change,' he said, 'but please say nothin' of our visit - not to anybody.'

The surprised doctor shrugged his shoulders and took the money. 'As you wish,' he said.

The more Edwin agonised over things, the more certain he became that Gareth Williams would have taken Rosena and the baby to Wales. For Rosena to leave hospital so soon after the birth was utter madness. He wondered what sweet talk Williams had given her to make her agree to such lunacy. The man's sanity was in doubt. There was something evil about him, and for him to be a minister of the church was total hypocrisy. The knowledge that Rosena was in his clutches made Edwin groan out loud.

From the nursing home, he went directly to Paddington and spent a wearisome two hours waiting for the next train to Wales. If the wait was frustrating, the rail journey was even more so, with its change at Cardiff, and slow train from Queen Street to Merthyr Tydfil. He kept recalling the last time he had been to Wales. Then, Rosena had been at his side, her hand in his, and later, when she believed that Gareth was dead, she had hugged him, sobbing. Now, the conviction that he could never truly love anybody else, was more profound than ever.

From Merthyr Tydfil, he caught a bus, and just before seven o'clock, when he dismounted, he was breathing the coal-gritty air of Trethomas.

He walked through the gloomy, deserted streets, trying to recall the way to the guesthouse. It was growing dark, and lights showed through the curtained windows of the terraced houses. The belief that he might now be close to Rosena had his pulse quickening. Would she be ill and weak? What would her reaction be when he suddenly appeared out of the blue? Was the baby all right? And what would Gareth Williams' attitude be?

Edwin had long ago dismissed any prospect that Rosena might not be here. That was why, when he finally found Parry Street and stood before the guesthouse, his heart sank. Not a chink of light showed at the windows, and when he climbed the steps, found the brass knocker and thumped loudly, emptiness echoed back at him like mocking laughter. The place had about it the unmistakable shabbiness of desertion.

The house stood alone. He went down a side-alley and peered over a wall. In the gloom he could just make out the small garden, overgrown with weeds. The back of the house was as black and silent as the front.

He was unsure what he should do next. He cursed his stupidity. He'd been so certain she'd be here.

He decided to make enquiries. The neighbours must know something. But when he returned to the street, he noticed for the first time light gleaming from the windows of the adjacent chapel. Hope rose in him. The Reverend Gareth Williams If anybody knew where he was, this was the place to ask.

The chapel door was half open; the interior, with its neat pews, was brightly lit. As he entered, he realised that the only person present, was an elderly woman sweeping the floor. At first, she was unaware of him and nearly dropped her broom when he cleared his throat.

He smiled to put her at ease. 'I'm sorry to startle you, but I'm looking for the Reverend Williams.'

'Reverend Williams?' Her mouth dropped. She was still taken aback by this city-dressed stranger - a rare sight in Trethomas. She had to admit he was a handsome young man, though he looked rather anxious. She smiled back at him.

'Reverend Williams,' she repeated. 'Been gone for nearly six months. Resigned, 'e did - all sudden like. We've 'ad awful trouble 'ere, with no minister. But a new reverend's comin' next week, so we've 'eard.'

'Reverend Williams has been gone for six months?' he murmured, his brain filled with alarming implications. 'And his wife too?'

She nodded. 'We 'eard they'd gone on a long 'oliday, though it seems really queer, 'specially as they left their little girl behind with Bronwyn's sister Megan.'

'Where did they go?' he asked.

She shook her head vaguely. 'Never knew, though Bronwyn's sister may 'ave an address.'

'Does she live locally?'

'Yes ... number six Morgan Street. Turn left at the end of Parry Street and it's the next street but one.'

Edwin thanked the lady, slipped some coins into the collection-box and hurried from the chapel.

'Gareth was at a maternity home in London, just a few days ago, you say?' Huw leaned back in his chair and blew on his steaming mug of cocoa. ''Tis unbelievable.' He was a burly, red-faced man, well suited to his trade of butcher.

'And when he left he took with him a lady called Rosena Bray and her baby,' Edwin went on. 'Gareth was the child's father.'

Megan shook her head in perplexity. She'd never trusted Gareth Williams. He'd led poor Bronwyn a merry dance right from the start.

They were sitting in the small parlour of number six, Morgan Street, drinking cocoa and eating digestive biscuits which young Gwenda had obediently brought round on a plate. Earlier, the couple had been surprised by a knock at the door, and an even more surprised when the night-time visitor turned out to be a well-dressed gentleman with a cultured English voice.

At first, standing at the door, Edwin had met with suspicion from Bronwyn's sister and her thick-set husband, particularly when he explained the purpose of his visit, but after he mentioned Gareth Williams' name for the second time, Huw said, 'You'd better come in and sit down,' and it wasn't long before a ginger cat had climbed onto his knee, and Megan had made the cocoa. Soon, the couple's suspicion had given way to bewilderment as Edwin quietly related his grim story.

Now deep concern was clouding Megan's eyes. 'If Gareth's run off with this Cornish girl, where's Bronwyn?'

'Yes,' Gwenda piped in, eyes wide. 'Where's my mam?'

'Hush.' Huw frowned at the girl. 'Be quiet when grown-ups is talkin'.'

Gwenda lowered her eyes. She remembered seeing Mister Carter when he had come for the first time to Trethomas and she felt sure he was a nice man. But she wished he would tell them where her mam was.

'Be a good girl and go to bed,' her aunt said. 'Say good night to Mister Carter and Uncle Huw.'

The girl sighed, but she came to Edwin and he shook her small hand, and saw the sadness in her eyes. 'I hope your mam comes home soon, Gwenda.'

She nodded, smiled shyly, then moved away and kissed her uncle.

'It's been an awful shock for the child, 'er parents runnin' off like that,' Megan was saying. 'Every day she goes round to Parry Street to see if they've come 'ome.'

'But they're never there,' Gwenda said from the doorway. 'Sometimes I peep through the letter-box, but there's nobody inside ... just an awful stink.'

"'Tis staleness,' Huw explained. 'Old 'ouses always smell when they're closed up, what with the damp and all.'

The child nodded and went to bed.

Edwin was uneasy about what he'd heard, though he tried not to show it in his manner. Huw and Megan suggested that he stayed for the night, but he told them he must be on his way. They assumed that he was travelling by car and he did not enlighten them. Before leaving, he gave them Uncle Jeremy's address and asked them to contact him if there were any further developments.

Once outside, he did not delay. He knew exactly what he must do as he hurried back along the deserted cobbles. Reaching the guesthouse, he mounted the steps, stooped down, thrust the letter box open with his fingers ... He stumbled backwards, nearly gagging

All along he'd longed for some justification to go to the police, but Gareth's removal of Rosena from the maternity home, supposedly with her consent, had not been a criminal offence. Now, however, there could be no doubt.

What he had inhaled was the sickly sweetness of rotting cadaver.

Her despair deepening, Rosena had plied Gareth with questions ... Where are we going? Why have we travelled so far? Why are you not wearing your clergyman's collar?

But the only answer she got was an impatient, 'Wait and see.'

How different his manner was to that he'd shown when he'd pleaded with her at the maternity home to be his wife. Now other things were brooding in his mind.

As they waited for a cab to arrive, he was pacing up and down the doctor's waiting room, pausing frequently to glance through the window.

She had settled gratefully into a chair, glad of the respite to feed the baby. Even so a further question rose to her lips: 'What are you afraid of, Gareth? Why are you so ... furtive?'

He stopped in his tracks, swung round to face her, and for a moment she saw fear in his bloodshot eyes, then he said, 'Rosena, trust me. I've 'ad a lot of problems, bad problems, but I'll explain everythin' when we reach 'ome.'

"Ome?' she gasped. 'Where's 'ome?'

Before he could respond, the cab hooted from the street and Gareth gathered up her case and was bustling her to make haste.

Rosena felt as if she were trapped in a whirlpool, too weak and ill to fight it. She no longer cared for herself but centred her whole being on the tiny scrap of humanity she held in her arms - the scrap that, once the knot had been tied with Gareth, would at least avoid the life-long stigma of bastardy. In the cab, the silent Gareth beside her, she was aware of every shuddering bump on the rough road, pain stabbing upward through her body. For the moment Emma Jane slept, her poor little red-marked face pinched. Rosena clutched her protectively, aware that the only haven the baby had, in a world full of jeopardy, was in her arms. Gritting her teeth, she prayed silently that God would give them strength to face whatever lay in store.

As she lifted her eyes, she saw flat, green meadowland, dotted occasionally by farmhouses and cottages. Presently they crossed over a river bridge and suddenly, quite incongruously, the road was passing grim-looking barrack and factory buildings.

Rosena now had no illusions about where they were heading. From romantic novels, she had learned of the different marriage laws existed in Scotland. North of the border it was possible, subject to certain conditions, for two consenting adults to be wed by verbal contract.

All at once she had an urge to get it over with. The fact that there was no romance in her heart seemed of little consequence.

Another five minutes brought them to the village with its church and cottages. The cab drew up near a cross-roads, outside a single-storey, white-washed building with a fine decorative window at its centre. Above the window in bold letters was painted *'Marriage Room'.* Upon the window's turned-back shutters was more wording: *'Old Blacksmith's Buildings, Famous for Runaway Marriages', 'Books, Romances, Post-Cards, Relics of Old Priests & Other Antiquities.'*

Sitting on a wooden seat in front of the place was a couple who looked no more than teenagers, dressed in their Sunday best and looking sheepish in the afternoon sunshine. The girl was clutching a prayer book. Rosena felt ashamed of her own dishevelled appearance, of her shapeless, pink cotton dress soiled and crumpled by the journey. Beneath it her body felt equally shapeless. She was thankful she had no mirror; she felt sure that a glimpse of her face, pale with all she had suffered, would have sickened her beyond recall. She wondered if her eyes were as bloodshot as Gareth's. She unpinned her hat and gathered in the strands of her dark hair. She thought of the lovely bathroom at Uncle Jeremy's with its scented soaps, and wished she could submerge herself in warm, soapy water.

Gareth turned towards her and there was excitement in his expression. For the first time in hours he was smiling. 'Told you we'd be married today,' he murmured. He climbed from the cab and walked across to the couple on the seat. After a brief conversation he returned. 'The priest's attendin' a funeral,' he said, 'but 'e'll be back soon to perform the ceremonies. You do understand, Ro-sena? We 'ad to come 'ere, for the child's sake. If we'd got married south of the border we would've 'ad no end of fuss with banns and everythin'. You can't get married in England or Wales at a day's notice, you know.'

She realised she had to humour him, for she understood now the brittleness of his moods. Perhaps in due course he would honour his word and tell her the truth, though she doubted it.

After he had paid off the cab-driver from his thick wad of notes, he took her case and led her to the seat, and the other couple moved over to make room.

'Mister MacGregor told us he'd be back at four o'clock,' the young man commented. 'It's gone five now.'

Rosena guessed that Mister MacGregor was the so-called 'Blacksmith Priest', not an ordained priest of the church, but nonetheless fully qualified to solemnise marriage under Scottish law.

'Well I 'ope 'e 'urries up,' Gareth muttered. 'Don't want to wait all night, do we? Got better things to do, eh?'

The other couple laughed self-consciously.

Gareth rested his hand on Rosena's, gave it a squeeze. 'Wait here a minute, petal.'

He rose to his feet and started down the street.

Rosena's heard the sound of young voices. She noticed some children peeping at them from the side of the building, their whisperings so broad in dialect that she wondered how anybody could understand them.

She leaned back, lowered her eyelids, conscious of the baby's warmth against her. She smelt the soothing sweetness of roses in the air, heard the homely buzz of a bumble bee, and for a moment felt she was floating above herself and had escaped the throbbing pain in her body. She imagined it was Edwin instead of Gareth she was about to marry.

But her pretended happiness made her sadness even sharper as her mind returned to reality. My wedding day, she thought, I never dreamed it would be like this. What would my dear father have thought, with me clutching a baby? And Gareth Williams about to be my husband? Don't trust 'im, her father's warning haunted her. 'E's far too glib. Mark my words. 'E'll use 'ee if 'e can, then be off. ... I just don't want to see 'ee 'urt, that's all.

A tear overflowed and strayed down her cheek.

She saw Gareth returning, and there was a jauntiness in his stride. At least he wasn't leaving her in the lurch as her father had suspected he would - not yet.

''Ere you are, Ro-sena. Only right you should 'ave some flowers.' The four red roses he slipped into her hand were fragrant. 'Bought 'em from the cottage down the street.'

'Thank you, Gareth ...' She even managed to smile. Perhaps, she dared herself to hope, perhaps I've judged him too harshly.

'Here Mister MacGregor comes now!' the girl with the prayer book exclaimed, and they all looked around to see a ruddy faced, bearded man wearing a smart kilt and polished leather sporran rushing down the street.

Sorry to keep you waiting, lads and lassies!' he cried cheerfully. 'Now then, who's first?'

After the other couple went in, the children came forward and stood peering through the windows of the Smithy. As the minutes ticked by, a bright yellow charabanc drew up, and about twenty tourists streamed off and were quickly hushed into silence by their guide as they waited at the roadside and on the pathway leading to the building's doorway. Presently the young newly-weds emerged, beaming with happiness, to be greeted with a burst of applause. The bridegroom tossed some coins into the air and the children rushed forward, hands raised to catch them.

Gareth stood up, grasping the case with one hand and Rosena's arm with the other. He pulled her up and dragged her stumblingly through the crowd into the marriage room for their own ceremony. Rosena glanced at Gareth. 'Could've done without all these busy bodies, we could,' he scowled.

The marriage parlour, or forge, was a rectangular room decorated with farm implements and bellows, and the walls were covered by old paintings, lucky-horseshoes, newspaper cuttings and photographs. One photograph showed King George and Queen Mary on a visit to this very room.

Many of the tourists had followed inside and stood blocking the doorway. This was for them the highlight of the trip from Blackpool - a real wedding to watch. A quietness settled over them as they waited for the ceremony to commence, but into the hush a woman's tactless whisper carried: 'Poor girl, doesn't she look ill?'

True enough, Rosena was feeling faint, and, as nausea gripped her stomach, she swayed on her feet. The room, hot and packed with people, seemed to be closing in on her. She felt she was suffocating; but she forced herself to breath deeply and gradually the faintness subsided.

'So you want to be married?' Mister MacGregor asked in his kindly voice, unaware of the battle she had fought.

'That we do,' Gareth answered confidently.

Rosena realised that they were standing before a big black anvil which rested on the top of an old tree stump.

MacGregor asked their names which they gave. 'And have you lived in Scotland for at least twenty-one days?'

Again Gareth showed no hesitation: 'Yes, sir.'

'Even more important,' MacGregor said, 'do you love each other?'

'With all our hearts,' Gareth replied, smiling, and now all his old charm was flooding back, 'and our little baby too, who will be made lawful today.'

MacGregor nodded. 'We have an old custom,' he said. 'If the baby is held beneath the mother's apron during the ceremony, it will be legitimised.'

There were several sentimental 'oos' from the women watching. Somebody murmured, 'Tied to her mother's apron strings, eh?' and there was a ripple of laughter. Clearly an old hand in such matters, MacGregor produced an apron from a drawer at the side. Rosena took it and wrapped it around Emma Jane. Next, the kilted 'priest' asked for two volunteers to act as witnesses and a man and woman were soon forthcoming from the visitors. The woman, her eyes shining, took Rosena's roses so that she could follow MacGregor's instruction to hold Gareth's hand across the anvil. The ceremony then began, with MacGregor reading solemnly from the prayer book, and afterwards he looked at Gareth and said, 'Have you a ring?'

For a second Rosena wondered if the marriage would be called off through lack of a gold band, but she needn't have worried. Gareth reached into his waistcoat pocket and produced a ring which he slid onto her finger. It was about two sizes too big and it was badly scratched, but that didn't seem to matter to him.

'Do you take this woman you hold by the right hand to be your lawful wedded wife?'

'Yes,' Gareth nodded.

'And do you, Rosena, take this man to be your lawful wedded husband?'

Emma Jane started to cry so loudly that MacGregor didn't hear Rosena's confirmation. When he looked at her, she was busy gentling the baby, but he assumed she had said yes and continued: 'Before God and these witnesses, I declare you married persons and whom God hath joined let no man pull asunder,' and he clanged his hammer down on the anvil. 'Now you may kiss your bride, Gareth!'

Gareth did just that. He seemed not to notice the coldness of her lips, and all around people were clapping and calling out congratulations.

Mister MacGregor took both their hands in his. 'Good luck, Mr and Mrs Williams!' he beamed heartily, but Gareth shook his head.

'Our name will not be Williams. We shall take my wife's name - Bray.'

MacGregor looked surprised, but he nodded. 'As you wish. It's quite legal to do that.'

Rosena was not consulted, but she had no wish to question Gareth's actions now. All she wanted was to escape from this stifling room.

MacGregor set about completing the necessary paper-work and the wedding certificate which was on pale blue paper with a picture of the Smithy printed on the top. This was signed by the bride, groom, and the two witnesses. Finally MacGregor himself signed with a spectacular flourish.

Miss Bray thus became Mrs Bray. MacGregor charged Gareth three guineas, but Rosena suspected that the real cost lay in the future.

Chapter Twenty-six

TRETHOMAS POLICE STATION was in a room of an end-of-terrace cottage in Towyn Street. Young Constable Dave Jenkins and his wife occupied the remainder of the cottage as living accommodation.
It was gone 11 PM and the constable had just removed his tunic and brewed a pot of tea. A moth fluttered about the low-wattage bulb that illuminated the room. PC Jenkins was settling down behind his desk with a cross-word puzzle, when his evening peacefulness was shattered by the well-dressed stranger bursting in with his preposterous story.

'You'll understand,' PC Jenkins explained as he recovered from his shock, 'we don't get much crime in Trethomas.'

'All I'm asking,' Edwin said, 'is that you come and smell for yourself.'

The policeman gave a resigned nod and stood up. He assumed a manner of calmness and deliberate slowness which exasperated Edwin.

It took Jenkins all of five minutes to replace his tunic, button it up to the throat and put on his helmet. He felt sure that his visitor was exaggerating the situation; possibly he was deranged. What well-dressed city-gent would turn up in a place like Trethomas at this time of night, unless he was off his rocker?

Accompanied by the impatient Edwin, he plodded along the dark streets to the Parry Street guesthouse.

But one sniff through the letter-box changed his attitude noticeably. 'I don't like it, Mister Carter ... Bloody 'ell, I don't! Better inform Sergeant Lewis.' They hurriedly returned to the police station.

Edwin's brain was racing. It was obvious that there was somebody very dead at the guest house ... and whoever it was had been there a considerable time. His immediate fears had swung to Rosena, but he knew that the corpse could not be hers. She had been at Wimbledon only yesterday.

Who else could it be? He remembered the child Gwenda talking about her mam and uncle Gareth having a tremendous row and even struggling together. The possibilities slotted into his mind. He suspected that Gareth must have murdered Bronwyn and then fled ... and, now he had Rosena in his power. And she, no doubt, was unaware that behind the glib, false promises of her companion, lurked the calculating mind of a killer on the run - and that she herself might be the next victim ... Edwin sucked air into his lungs in anguish. He felt utterly frustrated. Gareth could have taken her and the baby to anywhere in the country by this time. They might even have embarked for the Continent.

He wondered why his note of proposal and love, left with Sister Edna, had brought no reaction. Had Rosena's love for Gareth surmounted all her other emotions despite the sinful way he had treated her?

Edwin was certain of one thing. He would not rest until he had traced Rosena and discovered her fate - even if it proved the worst.

Back at the police station PC Jenkins called the operator and asked for the number of Sergeant Lewis, who lived on the north side of town. 'Come on, Sergeant,' he groaned, waiting for the response, gripping the receiver tensely. ''E never was one to leap out of bed in the middle of the night.' It seemed ages before the telephone was lifted at the other end.

As PC Jenkins blurted out the news, his calmness long gone, Edwin paced up and down, remembering little Gwenda's plaintive words: 'Where's my mam?' Poor child. How on earth would the awful truth be broken to her?

Sergeant Lewis at last arrived, clearly irritated at being awakened. He was a sharp-featured Welshman with a know-all manner. He nodded curtly to Edwin, then listened as his constable repeated the evening's events. 'Better go and see for myself,' he decided.

Edwin and PC Jenkins followed him, sometimes blundering against each other along the dark streets. Within ten minutes Trethomas's senior police officer was left in no doubt as to the gravity of the case.

They checked the front door and windows and found everything secure. Then they went down the side-alley, and climbed over the brick wall of the garden, PC Jenkins emitting a gasping, 'Bloody 'ell!' as he crushed his private parts against the unyielding tiling on top of the wall. There was no pause for sympathy. Scrambling through a jungle of weeds and prickly thistles, they tried the back door, but it was as firmly locked as the front entrance. Sergeant Lewis peered through the kitchen window but could see nothing.

'Smash the pane, boy,' he said and PC Jenkins somehow found a chunk of coal. Shortly there was a crash of glass as the window was shattered inwards. Directly, the familiar, sickly stench burst out, poisoning the night air with its putridity.

'Bloody 'ell!' PC Jenkins gasped, choking on a sudden bout of coughing.

With one hand shielding his nostrils, Sergeant Lewis hoisted himself onto the window ledge, and taking care not to cut his hand, reached through the broken glass and loosened the latch. Edwin helped him force up the lower section of the sash-window, fighting a desire to vomit. With the window open, they stepped back, the way before them as inviting as the Black Hole of Calcutta. Lewis was inwardly fuming. It had taken the stranger's arrival in

Trethomas to uncover something that had, literally, been under their noses for months. He turned to his constable. 'Whatever's causin' this stink, must be there in the kitchen.' And then his voice dropped to a whisper as he added: 'In you go, boy!'

Once my most precious dream was to be the wife of Gareth Williams, she thought. Now I am - and I feel nothing. Perhaps I should feel sorry for him. He was wounded in the war ... and afterwards he lost Bronwyn. But I can only wonder what will happen to us now.

She now realised that there were two sides to this man. Firstly, the charming, dear, lovable Gareth - fast to display emotion, even tears. But all this was a facade which concealed a ruthless, cruel schemer, quick to grasp any compassion shown to him and twist it into gaining what he wanted.

She lay fully dressed in the middle of the double bed, the hotel room dimly lit by the small table lamp on the writing desk. It was dark outside, and rain pattered against the window. Exhausted and still greatly discomforted by her surgical stitches, she had been glad enough to take refuge in the hotel close to the blacksmith's. After a quick meal, she had slept for an hour, and for another hour she had remained unmoving, feigning sleep, toying with the loose wedding ring upon her finger. Who had last worn it, she wondered? Bronwyn? Had he taken it from her lifeless hand?

She was fearful that the slightest show of being awake would rouse Gareth from his armchair near the window. To her he seemed like a volcano and the slightest cause would make him erupt. In her state, the prospect of any physical attention filled her with abhorrence. She'd hoped he would leave her for a while, go out, but he'd shown no such desire. Instead he'd uncorked the bottle of wine left in the room along with a card 'To the Newly-weds, with the Compliments of the Management,' and she'd heard the repeated gurgle as the wine was poured. Even had he offered her some, she would have refused - but he did not. Now she felt Emma Jane stirring, and knew that her own pretence of sleep would be interrupted by the baby's hunger-cries. Soon she sat up and unfastened the front of her dress. Immediately Gareth came to his feet.

'So you're awake, my love,' he said, 'refreshed and ready for our weddin' night, eh?'

She made no reply. She slipped her nipple into Emma Jane's tiny mouth.

He drew a tremulous breath. 'You make a pretty picture in the soft light. Mother an' child.'

'Gareth,' she said, ignoring his attempts at charm, 'where are we goin' to live?'

'Before anythin', I'm goin' to give you the honeymoon you deserve.'

Anger edged her voice. 'Tell me. Where are we goin' to live? Are we goin' to Trethomas?'

'No.' He started to pace the room. 'I need your trust, Ro-sena. There's a lot I've got tell you ... a lot for you to understand.'

'Start tellin' me now, Gareth.'

He stopped in his tracks. 'My dear, right now I want to shield you. I ...'

'Gareth!' she cried in exasperation. 'I want to know everythin'. Now!'

A look of resignation came over his face. 'All right. You're my wife. We'll have to face this thing together.' He drew an anxious hand across his lips. 'I'm in a very difficult position. You see ... six months ago somethin' awful happened. Somethin' so awful that ... I had to resign from the church and leave Trethomas. It was ...' He appeared to break down, emotion choking his words, but she was not deceived.

'You mean Bronwyn's death?' she said coldly.

'Yes ... Bronwyn's death, that's it.' He looked up, his eyes full of sadness, then he went on. 'My God, how cruel fate can be! I went to pieces after I lost her. I just wanted to leave everythin' behind. I can never go back to Trethomas.'

She waited while he went through the act of regaining his composure. How had Bronwyn put up with him? Perhaps it had been too much for her. Died of a seizure, he'd told her. No wonder!

'Can you understand,' he sobbed, ''ow I missed 'er? I needed somebody else to share life's path with. You were the perfect choice, my love ...' He reached out, caressed her hair between his thumb and forefinger. 'Put the baby down, Ro-sena. Let me hold you in my arms. It was so good before ... you remember, don't you?'

'I remember.'

'Then put the baby down. It's our weddin' night. This is what you always wanted.'

Gareth felt the lust burning inside him, the lust that had nearly driven him mad, even before Bronwyn had gone. Since that last time he'd made love to Rosena in Cornwall, his every thought had lingered on the memory of her perfect body, of possessing her completely. Even in his dreams, she had haunted him - her lips, her mouth, her breasts, her perfection. Now at last she's mine, bound by marriage vows. Nobody will ever take her away from me.

Rosena deliberately rubbed Emma Jane's back until a noisy bubble of wind was brought up, then, murmuring soothing sounds, she placed her down in the side of the bed and gently wrapped her in the sheet. As she turned back, Gareth emitted a throaty laugh, his breathing heavy. 'My God, I've waited so long. This is what I always wanted.' His fingers hooked into the front of her dress with rough urgency, pulling it open to expose her swollen, tender breasts. Before he could bury his face between them, her revulsion erupted and she slapped his cheek, causing him to jerk back with an oath on his lips.

'When I'm ready, Gareth ... not before!'

'Ro-sena,' he cried, 'I ...'

'No ... no!'

Frightened by their raised voices, Emma Jane started to cry. Despite the dim light, Rosena saw violence flare in Gareth's eyes, glimpsed the throb of a pulse in his temple. She flinched away, averting her face, fumbling with trembling fingers to fasten her dress, terrified that his angry hands would seize her. She hadn't the strength to fight him off. Oh God, he might kill her ... and then what would become of Emma Jane? She should not have put the baby at risk by angering him. But suddenly she realised that the uneven rasp of his breathing had become steadier. He swallowed loudly. She waited, her heart thumping. Then in a quiet, patronising voice he said, 'Don't ever hit me again, Ro-sena. A woman must respect 'er 'usband. In the Lord's eyes, and bound by your vows, you're mine, Ro-sena, body and soul. Always remember that.'

As he turned away from her, black doubts flooded into his mind. He had taken a profound risk in emerging from hiding, but had had needed the money Jeremy Carter owed him Overshadowing this however had been his desperation to find the Rosena Bray of his dreams. Now the sickening thought was in him that she no longer existed.

PC Jenkins' wife Meg was a pretty and hugely pregnant girl. Soon after midnight when Sergeant Lewis and Edwin returned to the Towyn Street cottage-cum-police-station, she realised that unusual events were afoot and quickly rose from her bed. She pulled a glum face when she learned that her husband had been left at the guesthouse to stand guard until the morning. Sergeant Lewis motioned Edwin to a chair, then he telephoned the Criminal Investigation Department at Cardiff. Once more Edwin listened while events were related. Lewis finished by saying: 'We reckon the body's under the kitchen floor. Must've been there for weeks.'

All the while, Meg Jenkins had been listening, her mouth rounded into an awestruck hole. At last she managed a hoarse whisper: 'My word ... Who'd 'ave believed it? Whatever has the Reverend Williams been up to?' But despite her shock it wasn't long before she had the kettle on and tea brewing. 'I'll take a jug of tea up to Dave,' she said. 'Must be really creepy up there.' Meanwhile Sergeant Lewis had replaced the receiver. 'CID'll be here first thing in the mornin',' he said. 'They'll pull up the boards in the kitchen. Won't be a pleasant task. We'll 'ave to get a doctor along to certify death, though I don't think that'll be very difficult.'

'I'm very anxious about Rosena Bray,' Edwin said. 'I believe she's with Gareth Williams wherever that is. They may have gone to her home in Cornwall. I've got to find her as quickly as possible. I'm sure she's in terrible danger .'

Lewis assumed his most pompous manner. 'I'm afraid, Mister Carter, we shall require you 'ere tomorrow mornin' while the investigation proceeds. There'll be questions to answer an' a statement for you to sign.'

Edwin ran an exasperated hand through his hair, but he sighed and resigned himself. 'Doubt there's a train to Cornwall before mid-day anyway.'

Meg filled a jug with tea and spooned in five sugars, then she cut some cheese and prepared a door-step thick sandwich.

'If you want, I'll take that up to your husband,' Edwin volunteered.

'That'd be much appreciated,' the woman nodded gratefully. 'It's really creepy knowin' that somebody's lyin' dead there at the guesthouse.'

Sergeant Lewis wasn't so sure. 'I don't know about you goin', Mister Carter.'

'I won't run away,' Edwin glared at him. 'Surely you don't think I committed murder!'

At first Lewis didn't answer, but as Edwin took the steaming jug, he scowled, 'Make sure you're back 'ere in ten minutes. Any longer an' I'll issue an arrest warrant!'

Meg had prepared her second, tiny bedroom for the baby she was expecting, but she kindly made up a bed in it for Edwin and he was able to snatch a few hours' rest. Surrounded by teddy bears and woolly toys, he was reminded of another baby, a baby with red marks on her face. What sort of room did she have, what toys?

During the remaining hours of the night, there was little sleep for him. His brain was too full of awesome probabilities concerning the fates of Rosena and poor Bronwyn ... and of the dreadful news which would have to be broken to little Gwenda. How did you tell a child that the decaying body of her mam had been found beneath the kitchen floor? Were there any words gentle enough to soften such facts?

Come morning he could have slept on, but he was disturbed by the voices and footsteps of men passing beneath his window on the early shift at the mines. Presently the sizzling aroma of frying bacon tempted him and he forced himself from the bed. He refreshed himself in the bowl of water Meg had left on the wash-stand. He had no razor so was unable to shave. He wondered what horrors the day would reveal. He dressed, then went down the narrow staircase. Soon, along with a morose Sergeant Lewis, he was tucking into a hearty breakfast.

As they wiped their plates clean with bread, a police van braked to a halt outside, and soon a Detective Sergeant from the Criminal Investigation Department, Cardiff, together with three constables, was snatching a cup of tea before tackling the grim business of the day. Meanwhile Sergeant Lewis summoned the local doctor. When the latter arrived, complaining vociferously that his morning surgery would be delayed, the party set out for the guesthouse. Left behind, Edwin helped the good-natured Meg with the washing up, despite her protestations.

A half-hour later he made his way to the guesthouse, having no wish to enter but contenting himself with standing amid the throng of a dozen or so housewives in their curlers, pinnies and slippers, who had gathered in the street outside. Some were holding children. He listened to the incredulous burble, the unanswered questions, of their Welsh voices. One women kept saying, 'An' 'im a minister of the church, an' all!' Standing to one side was Gwenda's Auntie Megan, her face as white as alabaster. She caught Edwin's eye and gave him a grim nod.

The crowd was kept at a respectable distance by the stern gaze of the policeman posted on the steps outside the slightly ajar front door. On the kerbside, the police van was parked. A pushy young man, obviously a newspaper reporter, forced his way through the throng. With pad and pencil poised, he started to question the policeman who appeared totally uncooperative.

It wasn't long before a shocked gasp and murmurings of, 'Oh, my God!' replaced the speculations of the women. The front door had been pulled fully open, and two policemen appeared carrying a stretcher. On the stretcher was what was obviously a corpse, completely shrouded in a blanket. The stretcher and its grisly burden were carefully loaded into the back of the police van, the doors slammed and locked. Soon, the van's engine roared into life and a way was cleared for the vehicle to move off down the street. When Edwin returned his gaze to the guesthouse, he noticed that the newspaper reporter had somehow slipped inside.

He felt a gentle touch on his arm, and turning met the tearful eyes of Megan. 'It's Bronwyn, isn't it?' she murmured.

'I hope not,' he said. 'I hope not for poor Gwenda's sake.' He tried to put a confidence into his voice that he was a long way from feeling.

'It would've been her fortieth birthday next Tuesday,' Megan murmured, her face brimming with sadness.

Edwin escorted the woman back to her house in Morgan Street. They walked in silence, each deep in their own thoughts, but on the doorstep she asked, 'What shall I tell Gwenda when she comes 'ome?'

'Wait until you're sure,' he advised. 'Wait until the police make the official announcement.'

She gave him a bleak smile. 'Thank you, Mister Carter. Thank you for everythin'.'

He nodded and wondered what reason she had for gratitude. Had he not come to Trethomas, they would all still be blissfully unaware of the tragedy.

'Will you come in for tea?' she enquired.

He shook his head. 'I must be on my way. The police want me to sign a statement.'

Touching his hat, he left her. A moment later, as he took a circuitous route back to the police station, he stopped at a small general-store and drapery. Inside he found a shelf devoted to toys. A pretty doll caught his eye. It had rosy cheeks and wore an orange-coloured crepe dress. He bought it, had it wrapped, and then returned to deliver it to Megan. 'For Gwenda,' he told her, feeling how inadequate his gesture was.

At noon he sat in the police station, answering the questions put to him by a bleary-eyed PC Jenkins. In concise terms he related all he knew. He was glad when he had finished and able to put his signature to the statement. PC Jenkins then wrote down his contact address at Jeremy's and told him he was free to go.

By the time he had taken the bus to Merthyr Tydfil and travelled by rail to Cardiff, he had missed the last train to Cornwall where he was determined to continue his search for Rosena. The next train was at 10.15 tomorrow. To fill in time, he found a barber and was refreshed by a shave and trim. Later he took a meal in a restaurant, after which he decided to find a hotel for the night. As he turned into St James Street he noticed a news-stand and bought a copy of *The South Wales Gazette*. He scanned the front page in vain. Was it too early for the story of the Trethomas tragedy to be in print? But then, turning to the inside page, he found it. An insignificantly short column headed:

BODY FOUND AT GUESTHOUSE. He read on.

Following a tip-off, police in Trethomas have discovered a body at the local guesthouse, owned by former church minister Gareth Williams and his wife. The house has stood empty for some six months. It is believed that the body had been there throughout that period. The present whereabouts of Williams is unknown. The body, said to be that of a female, was removed to the mortuary at St Annes Hospital, Merthyr Tydfil, for post-mortem examination. Police are anxious to contact Williams to assist them with their enquiries.

Tucking the newspaper under his arm, he walked on and soon found a suitable hotel. From the telephone in the lobby, he tried to contact his Uncle Jeremy. Beryl answered. Jeremy was working late. In as calm a way as possible, he informed his aunt of events and listened to her dismayed gasps. He told her not to worry, that things would sort themselves. As he rang off, he found himself wishing that he'd not told her, though sooner or later she'd have to know. She, like him, would spend a restless night in frustrating speculation.

That evening, after a meal and bath, he retired early. As the sleepless hours passed, he was aware of the traffic noise in the street below dying to nothingness. Later he heard a cat meowing but presently it quietened too.

He tried to think rationally. He wondered what Gareth's true motives were in absconding with Rosena and her baby. Being on the run, desperate to obscure his tracks, why had he burdened himself in this way? Could it be an inexplicable desire to paint her again? Or perhaps his twisted mind harboured thoughts of love. Or was it a wanton greed to possess? Was he driven by raw, lustful hunger for her body?

Rack his brains as he might, Edwin had no answers, only fears. At least, he consoled himself, with the small fortune Jeremy had paid Gareth for the picture, there would be sufficient money to meet their immediate needs - or perhaps to escape from the law.

What were Rosena's feelings? She must have felt some affection for Gareth to have left the maternity home so soon after the birth, ignoring the offer of marriage that he, Edwin, had made in his letter. Did she imagine that she loved Gareth, despite everything? And what would her feelings be once she discovered the dreadful fate of poor Bronwyn? Even worse, would the Welshman's unstable behaviour turn to violence again? One murder or two made little difference to a man who faced the hang-rope.

Edwin was depressingly conscious of time passing. Each minute lost, even as he lay in this hotel bed, increased his awareness of helplessness, of his lack of any firm information. Perhaps, he told himself, the answer to everything would be found in Cornwall. And thoughts of the West Country brought an image of Rosena's smiling face into his mind, the gentle warmth of her Cornish voice and laughter to his ears, and feeling close to her he fell asleep.

He awoke next morning with thoughts of Bronwyn on his mind. What on earth had she done to warrant such a macabre end? He couldn't face breakfast, so he paid his bill and left. On his way to the railway station, he picked up the morning edition of *The South Wales Gazette.* This time the Trethomas story had made the front page, though still only a short column near its foot. But brief though the report was, its content made his jaw go slack with shock.

> *Police have been unable to identify the body discovered yesterday beneath the floorboards of a guesthouse in Trethomas, although a post-mortem examination has revealed that death occurred through stab wounds. The victim was stated to be female ... and in her early twenties.*

He felt stunned. So the corpse hadn't been Bronwyn's. He'd felt so sure. He ran his eyes again and again over the words, seeking an alternative meaning but finding none. At last he composed himself. So where was Bronwyn? And who was the murdered girl?

Chapter Twenty-seven

CLOUDS WERE BUILDING AND BREAKING, sending sunlight dancing across the hills and the sea in ever changing patterns. The bus deposited them at Cullipool, the tiniest of hamlets nestling in a remote cove at the foot of rolling green hills. To Rosena, it seemed ages since they had last seen habitation. Shading her eyes against the glare, she gazed to her left, seeing the yellow, gleaming sands and beyond, the dark hulks of several small islands rising from the shimmering sea. As the bus moved away along the coastal road, its receding sound was absorbed by the brooding silence. No gulls shrieked from the heavens; the languid sea made no sound as it touched the beach. Not even a breeze whispered to blunt the hush. 'Seems the whole world is asleep,' Rosena commented, but Gareth did not answer.

Picking up their baggage, he started towards some red-stone cottages which lined a rough cinder-track. Rosena followed, feeling stiff and weary after sitting cramped in the bus for so long. Emma Jane, still feather-light, was asleep on her arm, blissfully unaware of the turbulence which surrounded her first few days of life.

A large black dog eyed their approach with suspicion but didn't bother to get up or bark. As they passed along, Rosena could see that the first two cottages seemed derelict and unoccupied, but Gareth knocked confidently on the paint-flaked door of the third cottage, humming softly to himself as he awaited a response. Footsteps sounded from within and a young, well proportioned girl opened up, smoothing unkempt fair hair back from her face. There was a smudge of flour upon her cheek. Her dirty blue-cotton dress was tattered and about three sizes too large. It scarcely restrained her ample bosom, and she was barefooted. But it was her eyes that attracted Rosena's attention, for they were large and lavender-blue. Her sensuous lips widened into a smile. She gazed at Gareth, knowingly, but said nothing.

'Is your dad 'ere?' he enquired and she nodded. Her wide eyes swung to Rosena, briefly taking her in from head to foot, then lingered for a long moment on the baby. Again she smiled, then she spun round and disappeared inside.

'That's Kathy,' Gareth explained. 'Poor soul 'as been deaf and dumb since birth. She lip reads. 'Er father, Frank Mansfield, 'as been very good to me ... at a price.'

A minute later Kathy returned with her father. Frank Mansfield was a short, barrel-like man of about fifty, clad in an open-necked vest and work-stained britches. His straggly hair hung thick about his neck, and his face was black with stubble. He made no effort to remove the pipe from his mouth but exchanged nods with Gareth and gazed at Rosena enquiringly. His eyes were the same vivid colour as his daughter's.

Gareth took his arm and led him a few yards down the track. There they stood talking, perhaps arguing, their voices out of earshot. Gareth loomed over the short man like a giant. Eventually Mansfield shrugged his shoulders and the two returned. Rosena realised her presence had somehow been explained and accepted - albeit with reservation.

Quite boldly, the girl Kathy reached across and touched the red marks on Emma Jane's tiny cheeks with her fingers, making a sound in her throat which Rosena construed as commiseration.

'Let 'er 'old the child,' Gareth murmured. 'It'll give 'er pleasure.'

Rosena hesitated, then with great reluctance handed over her precious bundle. Kathy, her lavender eyes shining, grabbed the baby with frightening eagerness, but once in her arms, she held her gently enough and rocked her from side to side, her face filled with ecstasy, a low 'cooing' sound coming from her throat.

Mansfield led the way down a narrow path to the shore, where a boat with an outboard motor was moored. He loaded their few possessions into the stern, then helped them aboard, Kathy and the baby coming last. The engine was started and soon they were chugging across the smooth sea and the cottages on the shore had shrunk to doll's house proportions.

During the last twenty-four hours Gareth's spirits seemed to have lifted, though Rosena felt that his darker moods were never far away and could quickly return. Again and again, he had spoken of the wonderful honeymoon he was giving her - a place where they would find all the peace they needed. But Rosena had not shared his enthusiasm. She was too steeped in her own melancholy, her own fears. There were so many questions plaguing her mind, but she had not pressed him to provide answers. She sensed that he would only fob her off and she lacked the energy to persist or face his inevitable anger. She would have to bide her time.

Having committed herself to him in that fateful moment at the maternity home, she now had no alternative but to follow his bidding. After all, what could she do in this wild place without him? She reminded herself that she was his wife, just as Emma Jane was his daughter, and there seemed no option but for them all to face the future together, whatever it held.

'Anybody been to Mansfield Island since I left?' she heard Gareth enquire, raising his voice above the throb of the engine. Mansfield Island, she thought, the same name as the man. That's odd.

Frank Mansfield at last removed the pipe from his mouth. 'Only Megson goes there. He grazes his sheep there. You've met him, I'm sure. Nobody else goes anywhere near the place. They're too afraid. You know the island's history? About the deaths, I mean?'

Deaths, Rosena thought, what deaths?

Gareth was nodding. 'Doesn't worry us.'

Mansfield handled the boat with the skill of long experience. The sky was losing its brightness; the sun relinquishing its fierceness, burnishing the island hills and the sea to the west. A forlorn sense of isolation was growing in Rosena. She felt they might just as well have been the only inhabitants on a far planet. The sea around them seemed unnaturally calm, its leaden surface unblemished by other craft. They had encountered no other human beings, apart from Mansfield and his mute daughter, since leaving the bus.

Mansfield guided the boat through a string of small islands. On one Rosena noticed some gaunt ruins. Gareth turned to her. 'That's an old monastery, but the monks gave it up years ago. Their burial ground's on Mansfield Island.'

'Mansfield Island?' she enquired.

He nodded. 'You'll love it there, you will. Get your strength back in no time. Just you, me, the babe and ...'

'And who, Gareth?'

He smiled. 'And Kathy. She'll keep 'ouse, do the chores, 'elp you with the baby and make life easy for you.'

Rosena glanced at the girl sitting in the stern of the boat. Her entire attention was focused on the baby she held.

Twenty minutes later, Gareth called to Rosena and pointed excitedly to the island they were approaching. 'Mansfield Island, my love. The perfect place for a perfect 'oneymoon!'

Rosena gazed ahead and saw the towering redness of sandstone cliffs, dotted with grassy ledges, and the yellow sandy beach. Back from the beach, nestling between two hills, was a small white cottage.

'I've stocked your larder,' Mansfield was explaining. 'Otherwise, you'll find the place as you left it.' He stopped talking, concentrating as he cut the engine and brought the boat alongside a primitive, limpet-encrusted jetty. The craft secured, he jumped out and Gareth passed the baggage up to him, then the rest of them clambered ashore. Rosena noticed how some huge pebbles littered the sands; they were like giant sugar-almonds. She turned to Kathy, anxious to reclaim the baby, but the girl waved her aside. Mansfield led the way, his boots sinking into the sand, and as they followed, Gareth picked up a handful of green seaweed. 'Good to eat, this,' he said.

They passed through some low trees, the ground marshy beneath their feet, and soon they were climbing to the small cottage. This looked nowhere near as white as it had done from a distance. Its walls were weather-stained and cracking with age; its roof was green with moss, and many tiles were missing, no doubt ravaged by countless storms over the years. Gareth reached the front-door and pushed on its unsecured latch, causing it to swing open, and a moment later they were inside.

The living-room in which they found themselves had a flagstone floor and was quite large. There were benches let alcove-like into the thick, rough walls, a gnarled table, some chairs, a discoloured dresser with three drawers - and a fireplace with a heap of peat alongside. The place smelt musty, damp and stale, and Gareth pulled back the faded curtains and opened one of the sash windows.

Mansfield dumped their baggage on the floor and turned to Rosena, addressing her directly for the first time. 'The larder leads off the kitchen at the back. There's a couple of paraffin lamps on the shelf. The lavatory's out the back, but watch out for spiders.' He gave her a malicious grin. 'Not many luxuries here I'm afraid, but you won't be disturbed by prying neighbours, that's for sure. You're quite cut-off. You may not think you are when the tide ebbs - but if you try walking across those sands, you'll sink without trace. If there's an emergency, if you're taken ill or something, you'll have to fire off a flare and hope somebody spots it from the shore. Gareth'll show you how the flares work.'

'There'll be no emergencies,' Gareth cut in.

'Where's the nearest doctor?' Rosena asked.

'At Oakport,' Mansfield replied. 'Ten mile up the coast.'

She followed him into the kitchen where there was a cooking range, a sink and a primitive shower. 'Not much privacy,' he said, 'but with just the three of you, that won't matter much.'

'Three of us?' Rosena queried.

'I told you,' Gareth explained. 'Kathy'll be 'ere to 'elp with the chores.'

'There's no need for 'er to stay,' Rosena said. 'I can do all that needs doin'.'

'She's stayin',' Gareth retorted, an impatient edge showing in his voice. 'You're too weak. You'll need 'elp.'

Rosena turned away, feeling angry. She went back into the living room. Kathy was sitting on one of the bench seats, rocking the baby. When Rosena reached out to take Emma Jane, the girl swung around, turning her back. Rosena felt her cheeks flush with anger. She reached around the girl and grasped the baby, pulling quite hard before Kathy, her great luminous eyes blazing resentment, released her. Akin to a rope in a tug-o'-war, Emma Jane objected strongly, crying in staccato bursts.

Rosena soothed her, then gathered up her case and climbed the narrow wooden stairs that led, creakingly, from the living room to a large bedroom. Here she found a double-bed, with blankets and sheets folded on a mattress. The ceiling had exposed beams. One small window jutted outward beyond the eaves. The glass was thick with encrusted salt, but as Rosena peered through she could distinguish sheep grazing on the surrounding hillsides. She was puzzled at first by the sight of numerous mounds on the flat ground behind the cottage - and then a grim realisation struck her. This must be the monks' burial ground that Gareth had mentioned. It seemed odd that it was so near the cottage.

She spread the blankets and rested the baby down; she noticed a further doorway in the bedroom. As she went to investigate, Emma Jane started to cry again, quite determined to let the world know it was feeding time.

Glancing through the second doorway, Rosena discovered another bedroom - a tiny box-room that was almost completely filled by a single bed.

'That's where Kathy'll sleep.'

Rosena jumped, unaware she had company.

Gareth had spoken loudly so as to be heard above the baby's cries, having just come up the stairs. 'She'll be close at hand if we need 'er,' he added.

Need her, Rosena thought, need her for what?

Frowning, she sat on the bed and picked up Emma Jane. She said nothing as she began to feed her, nor did she look at Gareth. She hated the thought of Kathy sleeping so close, even though she could neither speak nor listen. Something about the girl's eyes, their lavender-blue wantonness, their unbridled sensuality when she looked at Gareth, and about her obsession with Emma Jane, sent a shudder through her.

As the baby sucked, Rosena heard the roar of an engine from outside and Gareth said, 'Frank is on 'is way back. 'E calls over every few days to bring us supplies.'

Shifting her position slightly as she sat on the bed, Rosena winced with discomfort. 'Gareth, I'll 'ave to see a doctor soon. To 'ave these stitches taken out.'

He looked displeased. 'I think we could take them out ourselves.'

'No,' she said firmly. 'I must see a doctor.' He made no response so she went on. 'There'll be things for the baby too - a cot, a dummy and some clothes. I need a change of clothing too.'

His frown deepened but he gave a reluctant nod.

'Gareth, why do you show so little interest in Emma Jane? After all, she is your daughter. I don't think you've cuddled 'er since that day at the maternity 'ome.'

He forced himself to smile. 'I'm not much good with babies. Never been used to them. You see, Gwenda was quite grown up by the time I married Bronwyn.'

'Gwenda ... where is she now?'

'Stayin' with 'er aunt and uncle in Trethomas. She's right as rain there, she is.'

Rosena glanced around, then asked, ''Ow long will we stay on this island?'

He shrugged his shoulders. 'For a while ... until it's convenient to leave.'

'And 'ow will 'ee know when it's convenient to leave?'

'When my friend Hugh Mansfield, Frank's brother, writes to tell me, then we'll move to Cardiff and I'll get a job, sell some paintings, earn some money.'

She was not reassured. 'You've committed some crime, 'aven't you?'

He turned his back on her, stood gazing through the window. 'No,' he said.

'I don't believe you, Gareth. When will 'ee tell me the whole truth?'

He did not reply. Perhaps, she thought, perhaps now is the time to stand up to him.

'When will 'ee tell me the whole truth?' she repeated.

He unleashed a grunt. 'When you open your legs for me, like a true wife. I'll tell you everythin' when we're together like we were before.' He looked straight into her eyes. 'That's a promise, Ro-sena.'

She nodded resignedly. 'Then you must take me to a doctor.'

Chapter Twenty-eight

'MY GOD,' Tom Lethbridge gasped, 'and all along I'd been tellin' myself that she was all right. I felt sure she'd write to me as soon as the baby was born. After that I thought she'd stay with your uncle and aunt for a while.'

Edwin gave his head a melancholy shake. It seemed a hundred years since he'd last seen Lethbridge, so much had happened in between - and the Cornishman seemed to have aged considerably; the lines on his face and around his eyes etched darkly. The two men were sitting in the living room of Tom's cottage at St Mags. 'She's run off with Gareth Williams, Tom, the day after she gave birth. Now, heaven knows where they are. But there's even worse for you to know.' He spread two torn-out newspaper pages on the table in front of Lethbridge. 'I felt sure the body was his wife's ... until that final sentence hit me in the eye.'

He paused, sipping from a mug of cool water, while the other man read. After his walk across the cliff-tops in the fierce noon heat, the drink seemed more refreshing than any he'd ever had. That morning he'd gone to Megstow Quay to the Brays' cottage, praying that he might find Rosena there, but one glance at the silent place with its curtains drawn dashed his hopes. And as he'd stood before it, Nora Trevick from next door had appeared. She soon confirmed his suspicions that Rosena had not been back for weeks. 'Left to 'ave a baby, 'er did,' she told him. 'We understood 'er was stayin' up in London with some posh folk, but I don't 'ave no address.'

'You've no idea where she is now, then?'

'In London, I s'pose.' The woman pondered for a moment, then added: 'The only person who might know definite, is that Tom Lethbridge in St Mags. They two used to be pretty thick.'

'Tom Lethbridge,' Edwin said, his senses seizing onto faint hope. 'Yes, perhaps he'll know something.' He thanked the woman, touched his hat and departed.

Nora Trevick stood watching him walk briskly across the quay. Such a handsome young man, she thought, then with a sigh she returned to the drudgery of her kitchen.

Tom was speechless. He could hardly believe the words he read. He stood up, stepped into his open doorway where the light was brighter, and re-read the newspaper pages.

'All that happened six months ago, Tom,' Edwin explained.

'And where's Williams been since?'

'I wish I knew. He must've been lying low somewhere, hoping that the body would go undiscovered. What a hope!'

'But why did he suddenly appear at your uncle's?'

'Getting desperate for cash, I should think. You see my uncle had taken delivery of the painting from the art gallery - the portrait Williams did of Rosena. I'll give the Welshman his due. It was a magnificent piece of work. Anyway, Uncle Jeremy owed him the money for it - a small fortune by all accounts. Williams was no doubt hard up, so he risked showing himself in London. And that's when he heard about Rosena and ... well you know the rest.'

Tom was clucking his tongue in dismay. 'To think she's with 'im - a murderer. Edwin ... she's in terrible danger. There's no tellin' when he'll turn on her ...'

'I know,' Edwin nodded glumly. 'The thought's driven me mad ever since I found out. If only I knew where they were. If only there was some clue. I'll move heaven and earth to get her back, but I need something to work on.'

For a moment the two men were silent, their breathing heavy as they considered the implications. At last Tom said, 'I wonder who this girl was. What she did to anger Williams into stabbing her, poor lass?'

Edwin was shaking his head from side to side. He had no answers - nor did it appear he would find them in Cornwall.

He glanced at his watch. By the time he got to Talmouth, it would be too late in the day to catch a train to London. 'I'll go back to Megstow Quay, stay at the pub. The room there will bring back memories. You and I almost had a fight, remember?'

Tom managed a smile. 'No need to go there. There's free board and lodgin' in this cottage any time you want. You're more'n welcome to stay the night.'

Edwin's arrival had stirred in Tom many of the old emotions - emotions which he knew he must suppress, and which must remain locked away, deep in his soul, for ever. But resigned to the knowledge that his relationship with Rosena could not go beyond that of any brother and sister, his love for her remained - and so did his profound concern. With John Bray in his grave, he felt the responsibility for her fell upon him, and now he was frantic with worry.

After Edwin had gratefully accepted his offer of a room for the night, Tom went to his own bed, his mind full of images of Rosena, of Gareth ... and of a knife being plunged again and again into human flesh. His breath came in great gasps; he felt desperate to reach out, to seize the Welshman by the throat and take revenge for his monstrous crime, and for what he was doing to the sweet Cornish girl - the girl whom Tom had once dreamed would be his to love and cherish. He sat up in his bed, head gripped between his knuckles, trying to think of a way forward. The whole situation, the whole mystery, seemed like the ebony darkness of his bedroom, with no light immediately apparent through the drawn curtains. Yet somehow, somewhere, there must surely be a glimmer. And true enough, as he strained his eyes, he distinguished the faintest chink. So, too, there must be some weakness in Gareth Williams' trail of deceit. A weakness that could be exploited and expanded to reveal everything. But where was that chink?

Inside his brain everything Edwin had told him whirled, like pieces of a jigsaw caught in a vortex ... Gareth's sudden appearance after six months of absence, Rosena's ordeal at the maternity home, their apparent disappearance into thin air - and before all that the bizarre events at the Trethomas guesthouse - the murder of a young girl who had fallen foul of a man who was no more fit to be a minister of the church than was Satan himself.

And gradually a possibility seeped into Tom's mind. At first he gave it no credence, but the idea would not leave him, nor allow him to find any rest in what remained of the night. By dawn he knew he had to prove the matter, one way or the other. He rose from his bed, dressed hastily and pulled on his boots. He glanced into Edwin's room and saw that he was asleep. He did not disturb him. He scribbled a note and placed it prominently on the kitchen table. Then he stepped out into the thin light of early morning, his limp not diminishing the steadfastness of his stride.

Tom glanced at two-year old Davie Turnwell, as he sat chewing on a crust of bread at the kitchen table. The boy, who had a strangely triangular-shaped face, had lived with his grandparents for over six months.

Martha Killigrew had been taken back by Tom's early visit, but she'd invited him into her shabby kitchen where the smell of stale cooking lingered thick enough to cut with a knife. She offered him a chair and poured him tea into a cracked mug. It was clear from his expression that he was on serious business.

Tom was glad he'd arrived before Silas Killigrew went off to work. He was anxious to hear what both husband and wife had to say. Killigrew sat pulling on his sea-boots, keeping his eyes down in a shifty way. He'd not spoken to Tom since they'd almost come to blows over the supposed rape of his daughter Jenny. At that time he'd threatened murder on any man who suggested Jenny was anything less than the purest damsel ... but since then he'd been made to eat his words.

'But why,' Martha said, wiping her hands on her apron, 'why are 'ee askin' such questions?'

Tom hesitated. He knew he had to choose his words carefully. 'I 'ave a visitor from London. He may 'ave some news of 'er. You say she came 'ere just over six months ago?'

'Yes,' Martha said, 'She came 'ere askin' for money from 'er father ...'

'But I threw 'er out,' Silas interrupted angrily. 'I told 'er she'd made 'er own bed, so she could bloody well lie in it!'

'Soon after that, we got a letter from 'er 'usband,' Martha went on. "E'd walked out on 'er. Found out young Davie wasn't 'is at all. In a fit of temper, Jennie 'ad told 'im it were Gareth Williams' child, conceived in a broom cupboard up Perhaver.'

'The little slut came back 'ere,' Silas said. 'Tried to get money out of us ... but I weren't 'avin' that, by God no. I told 'er to come back when she'd sorted 'er life out, and not before. I told 'er if she wanted money, that Gareth Williams was the one to see.'

Martha had begun to sob, the memory of it all too much for her. 'Jenny's a wicked girl. Where she got it from I don't know. When she left, she said could we look after Davie, just for a week or so, till she could sort things out? So we took 'im, and we ain't seen 'er since. Not a word to ask 'ow 'e's gettin' on. No doubt she's taken up with some other man ...'

'You've not 'eard from 'er for six months, then?' Tom was anxious to make sure.

Silas shook his head. 'Not 'ad the decency to let us know what she's up to. We don't know where the little slut is.'

Tom drained his tea and rose to his feet. 'Then we best tell the police.' The couple gazed at him in surprise.

'Why the police?' Martha gasped. 'She's not done some crime, 'as she?'

'No,' Tom said, ''tid'n that.'

He left the Killigrews gazing at him in puzzlement. What needed to be told them was best left to the police once they had definite proof. But in Tom's mind all doubts had been banished. The corpse found at the Trethomas guesthouse had been that of Jenny Killigrew.

Dear Tom,

I am keeping my promise to write to you as soon as I had news. Please forgive me writing in pencil. I have no pen. I do hope everything is all right with you. As for me, I am well and you must not worry. Much has happened since I left Megstow Quay. Firstly, I gave birth to a sweet little girl, Emma Jane. You will love your niece when you see her. Shortly after she was born, I was visited by Gareth whom you will understand is Emma Jane's father - and he proposed to me, and I accepted. Gareth did not waste time. He whisked me up to Scotland, and at Gretna we were married and our baby was legitimised, so she will not have to grow up with any stigma of her mother's sinful ways hanging over her - thank God.

Before I went to hospital, the Carters were very kind to me at their home in London - especially Aunty Beryl, and I will be writing to them to let them know what has happened. I will also write to Edwin in Australia. I hope he is making a success of his life. He is a good man and deserves the best.

For our honeymoon, Gareth has brought me to a peaceful island. It is in Scotland, It is very remote and primitive; no other people live here now. But it is a place of beautiful sunsets and tranquil days. We are staying in an old cottage and our water comes from a stream beyond an ancient cemetery. It is piped up a nearby hill to an open-topped tank on its summit. As it is filled a float appears. When the float disappears we know we've got to pump more water into the tank.

The island is made up of small valleys and hills. Rabbit warrens are everywhere. The valleys are clogged with shrubs and low trees, and there are tufts of grass that we use as stepping stones across the boggy areas.

When I was walking the other day, some deer poked their heads up from the heather. They stood very still and I was six feet from them before they raced away.

But despite everything, I long for the day when I will see you again - and Megstow Quay, for I have now realised that there is nowhere in the world more beautiful. Gareth has said we will probably live in Cardiff when our honeymoon is over. But now I must finish. Baby is crying and she needs changing.

Fondest love
Rosena.

She knew that she had not mentioned any details of the island's location. To have done so would have greatly displeased Gareth. Later, as she re-read the letter, correcting a couple of spelling mistakes, she could feel tears forming on her lashes. She wiped her eyes, annoyed with herself. She hoped the letter did not reflect her unhappiness. She did not deserve any sympathy. She had nobody to blame but herself. She knew that Gareth was concealing something from her, something dreadful, and she did not believe much of what he told her. But she was his wife, and there was a marriage certificate to prove it.

Once her desire had been to get away from the narrow existence of life in Cornwall - but now that dream had been fulfilled, memories of her childhood, of her years caring for her father, of Tom's gentle fondness for her, filled her with remorse and home-sickness.

She straightened up, determined not to submit to melancholy. She heard Gareth's voice, his laughter, and glancing through the window saw him coming up the valley from the shore, the scales of the silver-blue herrings he carried glinting in the afternoon sun. His other arm embraced Kathy. Her skirt was held high to reveal legs which still glinted from sea water, and her head was resting against his chest in unmistakable intimacy. Rosena turned back from the window, feeling the blood draining from her face. She tried to tell herself that this was Gareth's way of tricking her into responding to his ardour - giving a husband his rights, as he put it. Perhaps he would succeed, for if it wasn't jealousy boiling in her now, what was it?

When they entered the cottage, Kathy took the fish into the kitchen and started to prepare supper. Gareth stood in the living room. He looked flushed and fulfilled, pleased with himself, but not sufficiently to blind him to what she was doing - slipping her letter into an envelope.

'What's that?'

'I've written to my brother Tom. I'd like to post it tomorrow. You said Frank was comin' and we'd go back with 'im, and we'd visit this place Oakport and see the doctor, remember?'

His smugness disappeared. 'Oh, I don't think there's a post office there. I'll see to the letter for you. I'll get Frank to post it ...'

'No,' she said firmly. 'I want to post it myself.'

'Ro-sena ...' He stepped towards her and before she could turn away, he plucked the envelope from her hand. As she tried to recover it, he danced back, toying with it in his palm, grinning at her triumphantly. 'I said I'd see to it for you, my love.'

Everything seemed suddenly very clear to her. 'You won't,' she snapped. 'You won't post it ... because you don't want anybody to know where we are. That's why you chose the name of Bray at our weddin', to confuse anybody who comes lookin' for you ... like the police! You've committed some terrible crime, maybe murder, 'aven't you!'

All humour had drained from his face. His eyes were smouldering with sudden fire, his lips trembling. 'No ... no, that's not true!'

'Then you're a liar as well as a criminal, Gareth Williams!'

'Damn you, Ro-sena. If that's what you believe, to hell with your bloody letter!' And with furious hands he tore it into tiny pieces and stamped from the room.

Chapter Twenty-nine

THAT EVENING they ate their herring supper in morose silence, their mood only briefly lightened when a mouse scuttled across the flagstone floor.

Rosena noticed the secret glances that Gareth exchanged with the mute girl. She'd combed her hair, washed her face, and Rosena had to admit that she looked pretty, with her large lavender-eyes catching Gareth's frequently.

At night the baby slept between Gareth and Rosena, for she had no cot as yet, and Emma Jane would awake once, sometimes twice, to be fed. Little wonder, Rosena thought, that my eyes are red and I'm forever tired. No wonder he finds the girl more attractive than me.

On her way to and from the box-room, Kathy would pass through their bedroom as if it was her own - and Rosena had little doubt she had shared the double bed with Gareth before she had arrived. How she must resent her presence! The girl had no modesty or shyness. She would undress with her door wide open, sometimes turning her nude back as if to taunt Rosena.

On the fifth night of her marriage, Rosena was awakened by the quickening pant of the girl's breathing, coming from the box-room, followed by a groan of ecstasy. She did not reach beyond the sleeping baby to check for Gareth's presence in the double bed. Instead she lay listening, and as the girl quietened, she became aware of the bleating of sheep from outside, and entwined with this was another sound: her husband's breathing no more than a few inches from her ear. Whatever ecstasy the girl had enjoyed had been in her dreams. Rosena grated her teeth. She thought: she must be dreaming of him, remembering the last time he took her. And then her thoughts swung to herself. Was she turning into a jealous shrew? Kathy, with her terrible affliction, scarcely more than a child, should be treated with pity, not scorned as a rival in love.

Next morning, when Frank Mansfield came over from the mainland, Gareth wanted to leave the baby on the island with Kathy, but Rosena said, 'No. She's got to see the doctor at the same time as I do.'

They reached the mainland and were soon on the crowded bus to Oakport, the road following a shoreline fringed with cliffs and bays. Gareth stuck to her like a limpet, placing himself between her and other persons.

'You don't need to worry,' she told him. 'I won't run away.'

'Nor talk to anybody?'

'Only the doctor,' she said.

But still he did not trust her. Even when they were at the surgery, he remained close, the most devoted of husbands. The doctor himself was immensely old and so thin and pale he looked ready for his coffin. In addition, he was deaf and used an ear-trumpet. Although he asked several questions, Gareth's soft-spoken answers were intentionally vague and made little sense, but the doctor nodded and smiled pleasantly. However of most importance to Rosena was the fact that the old man's fingers were as gentle as butterfly wings as he inserted his instrument. At last, to her immense relief, the stitches were removed and she was assured that all was healing well.

Little Emma Jane gurgled happily as she was examined and given a clean bill of health. Rosena was greatly comforted by the fact that the red marks on the baby's face were fading, though as yet not completely gone. She understood, more than ever, the misery her mother had suffered with her facial blemishes.

'Another few weeks,' the doctor confirmed, 'and the marks will have disappeared, my dear.'

Gareth allowed her no time to respond. 'Thank you, doctor,' he said brusquely, producing his purse, clearly anxious to conclude the consultation.

Afterwards, in bright sunshine, they walked through Oakport, where it was market day. The town was about the same size as Talmouth, though very different in style, with a multitude of cheap cafés. Back from the quayside, its granite houses were crowded together in the narrow, cobbled streets. Mingling with the throng, were many soldiers from the grey barracks which was on the outskirts of the town. Seeing army uniforms reminded Rosena of the days when Gareth had been in khaki. Then, she had been overwhelmed by his handsome appearance. Now, with his moustache shaved off, his hair long and shaggy, a thick coating of stubble on his jaw, and his shirt sagging open at the throat, only his tall, powerful body made him stand out from other men. Nobody would recognise him as an ex-military man, and certainly not as an ex-minister of the church. More important still, nobody would recognise him as Gareth Williams.

At a drapery she selected a few items of clothing for the baby and a blue-cotton dress for herself, and in another shop they purchased a blanket and a Moses-basket that would take the place of a cot until they went to Cardiff. Emma Jane fitted snugly into the basket, and they walked with it between them, each holding one handle, though there was little weight involved.

With the shopping done, Gareth had no wish to linger and in the early afternoon they caught the bus back to Cullipol and shortly afterwards Mansfield took them over to the island in his boat.

On arrival it was evident that Kathy had been busy, for washing hung on a line, drying in the hot sun, and the cottage had been swept and dusted. The girl gazed at Gareth, her big eyes pleading for his appreciation. He smiled and nodded in her direction and she immediately turned and began preparing a meal. Her father did not wish to stay and soon left them.

After they had eaten, Gareth said that he would like to sketch Kathy in the soft evening light, and the two of them wandered out. They walked through the grave-yard mounds, then mounted a hill, scattering the sheep as they progressed. A moment later they had disappeared over the crest.

Rosena cleared the table and washed the dishes, then she fed the baby and settled her into the Moses-basket which she took up to the bedroom. She felt that Gareth and the girl would have gone to a picturesque, rocky cove about five minutes' walk beyond the hill. She decided to join them. Emma Jane was sleeping peacefully; it would not hurt to leave her for a few minutes.

Rosena had guessed accurately. From the crest of the hill, she saw Gareth and Kathy on the rocks below. He had completed his drawing and had placed his pad aside. She, completely naked, had risen from her statuesque pose and with an expression of unmistakable glee, jumped into the sea. Coming to his feet, Gareth tore off his shirt and trousers and plunged after her and they frolicked in the waves, ducking and wrestling with each other, his laughter sounding clearly, and then quietening as he embraced her, pressing her young body against his.

Rosena turned back; she had no desire to watch. She realised that now, more than ever, she had a rival - and if the girl wanted to behave with wantonness, then she would match her.

Once back at the cottage, she took off her dress and refreshed her body beneath the primitive shower in the kitchen. Her breasts were large and tender, the nipples prominent, and her body was still cumbersome from the pregnancy. It would be some weeks before her true figure returned. Even so, once she had dried herself, put on her new dress and spent ten minutes drawing a brush through her dark hair, a glance in the mirror confirmed that she had nothing to be ashamed of.

When Gareth and Kathy returned, their hair wet, the girl went directly upstairs to her room. There was about Gareth an arrogance. It was as if he knew that Rosena was aware of his behaviour - and he was challenging her to make an issue of it. But she in no way reproached him, not even with her eyes. Instead she was at her most coquettish, flirting with him, and once she touched his ear with her lips and whispered, 'Thank God the stitches are out.'

He warmed to her, a sparkle coming into his eye. He complemented her on the new dress, and hardly seemed to notice when Kathy came downstairs, giving him a resentful stare before stepping outside into the twilight.

A few minutes later, Rosena went up to the bedroom. She slipped out of her dress and was lying naked upon the bed when he too climbed the stairs. As he saw her he made a strange, hungry sound in his throat; she saw him as a stallion brimming with lust; then her name came to his lips in a hoarse whisper. 'Ro-sena ... Oh, Ro-sena.'

She felt his big hands touching her. She gritted her teeth. Soon, she told herself, I will remind him of his promise to tell me everything.

Once the merest thought of him made me moist with excitement. His touch was like magic, whirling me into the heavens. Why is it so different now? He has not changed; he still makes love with the same passion. Yet his hands, his lips, his tongue, his body no longer unleash in me the rapture I once felt.

As he penetrated her, she cried out with the sudden pain, not with the ecstasy he imagined, but she had no wish to disillusion him. For a while she proved she was as good an actor as him, feigning hunger, even desperation, in her lovemaking, half smothering him with her body as they play-wrestled in the wetness of their own sweat and juices - and then gradually it came upon her that she was acting no longer; with eyes closed, a roaring entered her head and there were seagulls screaming above and she was back in the wrecked row-boat on the Cornish beach, crying real tears, digging her nails into his flesh ... and the rest of the world whirled away and everything was lost in a sea of carnal fulfilment.

Neither of them noticed or cared that Kathy slipped in, only briefly casting a sullen eye in their direction before closing the door of her own room.

Rosena lost count of the times he entered her that night, but she knew she had given him all he desired, and she eventually slept with her head nestled in his armpit. When she awoke, hours later, to feed the baby, he did not stir from his heavy slumber. Her entire body was throbbing with pain and tenderness; her private parts were on fire, but she was beyond caring.

As Emma Jane guzzled contentedly, Rosena wondered if her mind had exaggerated the gravity of their circumstances. Making love had given her a strange sense of release, a feeling that, after all, life would go on - and perhaps everything would begin to make sense.

She settled the baby back into the Moses-basket, moving easily in the moonlight which shafted through the uncurtained window, then she lay down alongside Gareth, hearing the restful sibilance of his breathing. She sensed that he would not need the girl again. She did not sleep. She gazed at him, waiting for the first sign of wakefulness. Her mind dwelt on the closeness of the burial ground and of the corpses beneath the mounds. She shuddered and snuggled closer to Gareth. She remembered Mansfield mentioning 'the deaths' and Gareth had shrugged it off as unimportant. But was it?

The island was an alien and weird place, full of secrets and ghosts. It did not somehow belong to the modern world, but to the past. No wonder few people came here. She wondered how long it would be before Gareth decided to move to Cardiff.

As the sky paled with the soft pinkness of dawn, his eyes opened and he smiled as she brushed his cheek with her lips. She pressed her heavy breasts against his chest. Then she whispered, 'Gareth, dearest.'

'Uhhm?'

She smoothed his brow with caressing fingers. 'You promised you'd tell me everythin' once we were truly lovers again.'

He sighed. 'Ro-sena, my love, let's sleep a while longer. It's so early.

'Gareth ... you promised.'

He laughed, his hand finding her breast, his breathing quickening, his maleness rising. 'After we've ...'

'Before,' she said firmly, pushing him aside. 'Tell me now.'

He gave in suddenly. He lay back, his breathing growing steadier. He had prepared himself for this moment.

'It was Bronwyn,' he murmured. 'She started it.'

'Bronwyn ... 'ow?'

'She was caught stealin', stealin' from the shops. Caught red-handed, she was. I'd suspected it for a long time, but I never realised it was so bad. When the police came, they searched her cupboards ... they found all sorts of goods. It was terrible. You see, business at the guesthouse had been droppin' off. She thought stealin' was the easy way of keepin' up 'er standard of livin'. Always liked the good things. Anyway, she was charged with theft of goods with a value in excess of one-hundred pounds. The wife of the minister, charged with theft! It was so ... humiliatin', oh God it was. In the Bible it says a good wife is the crown of 'er 'usband, but she who brings shame is rottenness in 'is bones.'

He paused to draw breath, shaking his head from side to side, his face a picture of remorse. 'Ro-sena ... 'ow could I preach to the people on the virtues of 'onesty and good livin', when my own wife ...?' Emotion clogged the words in his throat.

'So you ran away, both of you?'

'That's it. I suppose it was sinful, but we couldn't face the accusin' faces of those people. It was too much. Bronwyn suggested that we closed up the guesthouse and went away for a while. She promised she'd never steal again. So, we went to my friend in Cardiff, Hugh Mansfield, and explained everythin'.

'E 'elped us, like the good man he is. 'E sent us up 'ere, with a letter for 'is brother. Frank is 'is brother, you see. Hugh said 'e owed 'im a favour or two. Way back, their family used to live on this island. A really grand house, they had, on the other side of the island - but it was destroyed by fire. Anyway, Hugh said if we wanted somewhere to lie low for a bit, this island was the ideal place.'

He rested back, seemingly exhausted from the stress of repeating the sorry tale.

'And Bronwyn?' Rosena prompted him. 'What 'appened?'

'Poor Bronwyn, oh my God!' He was sobbing now. 'She never found peace. She was tortured by remorse. She just couldn't forgive 'erself for the shame she'd brought on us. It drove 'er mad. What was in 'er mind killed 'er. She ...'

'She died 'ere on the island?'

'Died in my arms.' Tears were running down his cheeks. 'In this very ... room.' He could speak no more; he was choking with emotion.

She lay back, not speaking, allowing him to recover his composure. Eventually he whispered, 'Now you know everythin', my love. Now you'll understand why I can never go back to Trethomas.'

Next morning the weather continued fine. Gareth took his fishing rod and disappeared to a favourite cove beyond a low headland. He hadn't spared Kathy a glance. The girl, clearly sulking, indulged in a frenzy of work, scrubbing the kitchen floor as if her life depended on it. Afterwards she took Emma Jane from her Moses-basket, bathed her in the kitchen sink, waving Rosena away when she went to help. Presently the girl sat nursing the baby in the sunshine outside the back door, making sounds like a broody hen.

Rosena was annoyed with herself because she could feel no gratitude for what the girl did. Instead she resented the way Kathy took charge of the child, behaving as if it were her own. Admittedly she couldn't ask permission, but she could have been far less aggressive in her manner.

Rosena curbed her impatience, but she felt she must reassert herself. She fetched the Moses-basket, then she went to the girl and indicated that she should put the baby in it. Kathy shook her head stubbornly, but now Rosena showed aggression. Reaching out, she pulled Emma Jane from the other girl's arms and settled her into the basket. Then, without looking back, she lifted the basket and walked off.

She passed quickly through the burial ground, wondering if Bronwyn's final resting place was close by, but she shrugged off the gloomy thought. She climbed a hill and walked along its crest. From this high vantage point, she had a wonderful view of the surrounding sands, miles upon miles of them, through which channels of water flowed. With the tide out, it seemed that it might almost be possible to walk to the mainland on foot, but then she recalled Mansfield's grim warning of being caught in the quicksand.

She could see too the surrounding islands, all much like Mansfield Island with red sandstone cliffs, hills clothed with low, wind-disfigured trees, purple heather, bracken, grass and naked rock. As usual, she was struck by the deathly silence and solitude of everywhere. The whole area seemed to lack a spark of human life. She wondered why people were reluctant to come to Mansfield Island. Was the place so evil that it frightened everybody away. Was it haunted by witches like the caves in Cornwall?

The day was pleasantly warm; the heather smelt sweet; bees hummed around the rich-yellow honey-suckle, and Emma Jane, no burden at all, lay contentedly in the basket, soothed by the motion of her mother's steps. Rosena decided to explore the far side of the island. She was fascinated by Gareth's words of a grand old house, now in charred ruins.

As she descended into a valley, a heat haze was rising above the heather. She followed the tracks that sheep had made. The ground was soggy, water springing up about her feet, forcing her to move slowly. As she started to climb again, some beige-coloured deer poked their heads up. For a moment they froze, then as she got nearer they exploded into life, crashing off, dragging saplings with them. She walked on, presently disturbing sheep as they grazed. They watched her suspiciously, but some of the smaller lambs showed no timidity, allowing her to touch their soft noses. She wondered how long they had before they were taken to market.

She had no idea of the exact position of the old house, but, ten minutes later as she topped a hill, she saw it at the head of a valley, blackened by fire, half concealed by the foliage that had run riot over the years.

The house had been square in shape, with alcoves and terraces. Still standing was one small tower with pantiled roof and a balcony topped by a semi-circular arch. Elsewhere some of the tiled flooring remained. Inside the crumbled balustrades, several bronze statues survived, as if in defiance of the devastation inflicted by flame and time.

She rested the basket down, lifted Emma Jane out and sat with her on a small hillock, gazing upon the remains of what had once been a residence of regal elegance. Presently Emma Jane began to cry. It was time to be fed. Rosena opened her dress and for a while she was oblivious to everything, apart from satisfying her daughter with the flow of milk.

Suddenly the voice came: 'The house is *Glencannon* ...'

'Oh!' She jumped with fright, nearly losing her hold on the baby. 'I ... I thought I was alone ...' Her heart was beating like a hammer.

The man was standing some ten feet from her, a large collie dog at his heel.

'A fine titty you have, madame, if you don't mind me saying.'

She could feel his eyes burning into her. She hurriedly drew her dress together.

He was unshaven and had shaggy, oily hair poking out from his battered hat; his clothes were torn and filthy, his left cheek disfigured by an ugly, purplish cicatrix. He carried a shepherd's crook.

'I comes here from Oakport on Tuesdays and Fridays,' he said. 'Grazes my sheep here, you see.'

His gaze was roaming over her body, indolent yet persistent, and there was a leering smile dragging at his lips.

'You must be Megson?' her voice quivered.

He nodded, his eyes not leaving her. 'And you must be Gareth's woman ... his new woman? He's a strange one, he is, but he has an eye for a pretty woman, that's for sure ... And a fine little young'n you got there.'

She hugged Emma Jane protectively against her. She wanted him to go away. His very presence made her tremble. She felt he might make some advance, so she attempted to draw his attention to other things. 'The house ... what 'appened to it?'

He wiped his nose between thumb and finger, and dried his hand on his britches. He turned to look briefly at the ruin, then he dropped to his haunches beside her, the collie resting its head on its forelegs, tongue lolled. 'The house was struck by lightning and burned to the ground. That was just after the ...'

'After what?'

'After the ... deaths.' He paused, enjoying the impact of his words. He enjoyed shocking her. As if affected, some sheep started bleating from beyond the valley. 'It all happened thirty year ago. This island belonged to the Mansfield family. Ship builders they was, really wealthy. They had this house built. It was crazy, being so remote here, but that's the way Stephen Mansfield wanted things. He was a giant - and strong with it. And was really jealous about his wife Laura. She was a real looker. I've seen pictures of her. He brought her here to keep her away from other men, so the story goes.'

He stopped talking and Rosena glanced at him anxiously, but he was only gathering his thoughts before going on. 'It was said that his jealousy drove Laura to unfaithfulness. Several times she tried to escape, but he caught her. God knows what punishment he inflicted on her, but it must've been hellish. She eventually bribed a servant to get a message to one of her lovers on the mainland ... a fellow called John McVey.'

'Go on,' Rosena whispered.

'The McVeys were in shipping too. There'd always been bitter rivalry between the two families. One night, with a friend, McVey landed on the island, determined to rescue Laura. Mansfield somehow found out. He and his men ambushed them as they came ashore, dragged them up to the clifftop over at North Point. He got Laura there as well, told her that unless she confessed her unfaithfulness, he'd throw McVey over the cliff. She confessed all right, begged on her knees for mercy, but Mansfield went mad. He and his men threw McVey to his death, then his companion went the same way - and then Laura herself.'

''Ow terrible!' Rosena gasped.

'Their bodies were washed up at Oakport a month later ... and Mansfield was arrested and charged with murder. He was convicted and sentenced to death. He was hanged screaming vengeance on all McVeys and swearing that he'd haunt Mansfield Island for ever more. That's why most folks are too scared to come near the place.'

'But you're not scared?'

He smiled. 'It's peaceful grazing here ... and I don't believe in ghosts ... do you?'

His story had left her strangely chilled. 'Yes, Mister Megson. I think I do.'

'Stephen Mansfield's sons, Frank and Hugh own the island now. Hugh sometimes comes up from Wales to paint pictures and Frank ... well, I'm sure you know him.'

She nodded. For a moment neither of them spoke, then she looked up and met his stare. She noticed crustings of stale food about his mouth. 'Mister Megson,' she said. 'Would 'ee do me a favour?'

He ran his tongue over his lips. 'I'll do anybody a favour if they'll make it worth me while.'

Her mouth had gone dry, but she pressed on. 'If I was to give 'ee a letter, would 'ee post it for me?'

'You mean a letter you don't want your husband to know about? And newly wed and all?'

She silently cursed his perception. She bobbed her head. 'If I bring it here, next time you're on the island, will you post it for me?'

He seemed to like the idea. 'Next Tuesday, same place, same time. I'll be here. And like I say, my dear, I'll help anybody ... for a favour in return.'

He rose to his feet, gave her a farewell wave and departed with the dog at his heel.

Chapter Thirty

ON THE WAY BACK the sky darkened and a wind blew up. She wondered again and again if she had done right to ask Megson to post her letter. She did not wish to deceive Gareth, but she knew that Tom would be worrying about her. And there was Beryl too. After all their kindness, it was not fair to simply disappear and not keep them informed. She decided she must write to both Tom and Beryl.

She walked along the cliffs on the island's north side, the wind billowing her skirt. She gazed down at jagged rocks so reminiscent of the Cornish coast. At last she reached a high point. She stood on the very edge, seeing the dark slab of rock fifty feet below her, the sea licking greedily across it. She shuddered. She didn't need to be told. This was the very spot where Hugh Mansfield had committed ghastly murder.

That night in bed, Gareth made love to her as the rain drove against the windows and thunder rumbled in the heavens. Afterwards, she clung very close to him, listening to his breathing grow steady as slumber overtook him. She wondered if he really loved her, or was it raw lust which had made him bind her to him in marriage.

She had, of course, not dared to mention her meeting with Megson. It was clear that the shepherd was acquainted with her husband, though to what extent she couldn't be sure. Supposing, she thought, Megson betrays me; I have no reason to trust him; he might not post the letters; he might even tell Gareth. She groaned aloud. He'd go berserk with rage, perhaps become violent. He'd never forgive her. At least, she decided, I will make him one concession. I will not mention where we are ... just that I am all right.

But now another thought preyed on her. If it had been Bronwyn with her thefts who had brought all the trouble onto Gareth, why did he have to remain in hiding? With Bronwyn dead, he might feel shame for what she had done, but he himself had committed no criminal offence. So why ... why did he spend his days behaving like a hunted animal?

Again the answers eluded her. She wanted to trust him, to believe in him, and once she had despatched her letters, she would do her best to honour and support, even obey, her husband as he faced the world and attempted to make a fresh start.

But still her brain whirled around. She wondered what 'favour' Megson would require for his services. Would it be double the price for two letters?

There were three pound notes in her case, the last money she had. Please God, she thought as she drifted into troubled sleep, please God may that satisfy him.

The next two days were dull, with a leaden sky and wind which whipped the sea into anger. Gareth remained at the cottage, so close to her in fact that she was only able to snatch brief moments alone, amid the spiders in the lavatory, to scribble her letters, which by necessity could be little more than notes.

Tuesday dawned with a pinkness that heralded a brighter day. She rose early. Gareth was only half awake. She dressed, making sure that the letters and three pound notes were in the deep pocket of her dress. She was about to go downstairs when Gareth stirred. 'You're up bright and early, my love. What are you goin' to do?'

A tenseness was in her, but she forced herself to relax. She stretched her arms with a show of lethargy. 'Oh, I fancy a walk,' she yawned. 'Some fresh air to drive the cobwebs away.'

'Then I'll come with you.'

She stemmed back her confusion. 'L-let me get your breakfast first. I'll bring it to 'ee in bed.'

He smiled and lay back.

She returned fifteen minutes later with a mug of tea, two boiled eggs and bread. He was dozing again, but he immediately roused himself. 'I've been thinkin',' he said, as he tapped his egg with a teaspoon. 'You 'aven't seen the ruins of *Glencannon*, 'ave you?'

She shot him a worried glance, fear clawing at her stomach. 'No,' she said.

'Then we'll go there this mornin'. It'll make a good walk for us.'

Her legs seemed to melt. She felt sure he knew, that Megson had already somehow betrayed her, that Gareth was toying with her like a cat with a mouse.

Panic was surging through her, but she steadied herself and picked up Emma Jane from her basket. 'Baby needs changin',' she said.

'Would you like to see the old 'ouse?' Gareth repeated.

'Yes ... unless there's somethin' better to do.'

'Such as what?'

She smiled at him. 'Eat your breakfast. I'll show 'ee when I come back,' and she carried the baby down the stairs.

After she had changed and washed Emma Jane, Kathy appeared in the kitchen looking bleary-eyed and dishevelled, but her lavender-eyes brightened as she saw the child. The Cornish girl motioned her to take her, which she did with her usual eagerness. Rosena left them in the kitchen and re-climbed the stairs. Her nerve was returning. Megson couldn't possibly have contacted

Gareth since Tuesday. It must have been just coincidence that had made him mention 'Glencannon' ... albeit a cruel coincidence. But one thing was certain; the last thing she wanted was Gareth's company when she met the shepherd. And another truth she had learned: her most potent weapon, in bending Gareth to her will, was her body.

'Somethin' better to do?' he asked, his eyes twinkling with lechery.

She didn't answer. She unfastened her dress, allowed it to slip to her ankles. For a moment she allowed him to feast his gaze upon her nakedness, hearing a growl, like a hungry wolf's, growing in his throat as she moved her breasts seductively.

She leaped upon him, tearing off his nightshirt, forcing his mouth open with her tongue, drowning him in a torrent of kisses until he was gasping, laughingly, for air. She gave him scant respite; his passion needed no stoking; soon he was responding feverishly. He came again and again in a plethora of slippery passion, but still she drove him on and on. Eventually he was completely spent. 'No more, Ro-sena. No ... Jesus ... no more.'

She smiled and finally relented. She caressed him soothingly, covering his entire body with tender criss-cross kisses, lulling him into a sleep of utter exhaustion.

She waited for five minutes, then, convinced that he wouldn't wake for hours, she carefully disentangled herself and slipped from the bed. She drew on her dress, making sure the letters were still safe, then she tip-toed towards the door.

Twenty minutes later, coming to the hill overlooking *Glencannon*, she saw the collie first, loping diagonally across the slope. Shuffling behind the animal at much slower pace, was the scruffy figure of Megson.

And as she stood, waiting for the shepherd to reach her, her blood froze because she heard Gareth's voice come softly from behind her. 'Thought I'd catch you up, petal. Show you the old 'ouse!'

She was certain that he had followed her, knowing what she was up to. This was a game he was playing, taunting her into a humiliating trap.

Gareth slumped to the ground, cursing as he appeared to notice Megson for the first time. Megson, glancing up, spotted Rosena and waved his crook. His steps quickened as he mounted the slope towards her, calling the dog back. His face was red with effort when he reached her, then he saw Gareth and his mouth hung open in speechless surprise.

'Didn't expect to see you 'ere,' Gareth said. He looked at Rosena. 'This is Megson, the local shepherd ... if you didn't know already.'

Very quickly she said, 'Pleasure to meet you, Mister Megson. I 'eard Frank mention your name the other day.' And inwardly she was praying that the man would join in the bluff.

He hesitated, then dipped his forehead as a sign of greeting. 'Come to look around *Glencannon*, have you?'

She nodded. She longed for Gareth to turn his back, so that she could hand the letters over, but he was at his most companionable, linking his arm through hers.

'Looks like another fine day,' Megson remarked, 'perfect for honeymooning, eh?'

'Indeed,' Gareth responded. 'Pity it can't last for ever.' At last he relinquished Rosena's arm, starting down the slope, not showing any inclination to linger with Megson. 'Let me show you around *Glencannon*, like I did around Perhaver, remember? Won't find any beautiful paintings 'ere, though.'

She acknowledged the comment with a nervous laugh, at the same time catching Megson's bloodshot eye. In a flash, she had taken the letters and money from her pocket, but simultaneously Gareth was turning. She immediately pretended to slip on the grassy slope, hearing Megson's gasp as she inadvertently dragged her skirt above her knee. When she scrambled to her feet, brushing her dress down and dismissing their expressions of concern, she had left the envelopes and pound notes concealed in the thick moist stems.

Once again she attempted to catch Megson's attention, pointing to the hiding-spot, but he did not acknowledge her, and she was left uncertain as to whether his lascivious eyes had noticed anything more than her exposed leg. He simply called to Gareth, 'Don't let the lady get frightened by no ghosts!' and with that he whistled to the collie and made off over the hill.

Over the next few days, a foulness came to the weather. Low cloud and mist hung over Mansfield Island, coating everywhere in moisture, and obscuring even the closest islands, and the sea was grey and restless. The cottage, its walls already damp with mildew, was illuminated by paraffin lamps, the smell of which seeped deeply into the lungs. Gareth lit a fire in the living-room hearth and spread peat before it to dry, and Rosena spent much of her time comforted by the warmth, nursing her baby, singing over and over the nursery rhymes she had learned as a child. She had convinced herself that what Gareth had told her about his departure from Trethomas was true, but she yearned for the day when they would leave this place and go to Cardiff as he'd promised.

Kathy prepared the meals, made the beds, and looked at the baby so longingly that Rosena felt compassion for her and allowed the girl to hold her.

Rosena's old industrious nature was stirring in her again. She hated to watch others work while she did nothing. Accordingly she cleaned the oil lamps. Hoping to reduce the fumes given off, she trimmed the wicks, and cleaned and polished the glass tubes and bowls.

Gareth seemed in good spirits. The consummation of his marriage had obviously driven the moroseness from him - at least for the moment.

Two afternoons later, despite the rain, he took Rosena to a grassy cleft in the centre of the island which was partially hidden by silver birch, and showed her the piled stones and cross on which was simply inscribed

Bronwyn (1883-1922) - God Bless Her.

As they stood before it, the rain dripping through the trees dismally, Rosena asked, "Ow long ago did she die?'

Gareth cleared his throat. 'Six months. Soon after we got 'ere, it was.'

Rosena recalled the red-haired, vital woman she'd met at the guesthouse - and now all that remained was a rotting, worm-eaten corpse a few feet below the earth.

'Gareth,' she murmured, 'the weddin' ring I wear ... did it belong to 'er?'

He looked startled by her question, but he nodded.

As she gazed at the heaped stones and the clean, unmildewed cross, there seemed a freshness about the grave which was not somehow compatible with some six months' of harsh elements. For a moment the thought crossed her mind that the body didn't rest here at all, that this was another one of Gareth's shams ... but then she reproached herself. Perhaps he'd recently renewed the cross. Was she forever to remain a suspicious, untrusting wife who was constantly seeking falsehoods in what her husband told her? Even now she should be sharing his quietly-spoken prayer instead of hatching up evil thoughts.

They arrived back at the cottage sodden and bedraggled, but they stripped and dried themselves and their garments in front of the blazing fire, and seeing Gareth naked, the brightness of the flames emphasising his strong body and muscles, another seemingly stupid thought took hold of her ... if he ever turns violent in a fit of temper, I won't stand a chance.

But Gareth appeared to have no such thoughts. His expression was almost exultant and he said, 'Thank God I found you, Ro-sena. Thank God you're my wife now.'

'Gareth,' she murmured, 'the blackness in your pupils. It's almost disappeared.'

That evening their meal consisted of sliced corn-beef and boiled potatoes, and afterwards Kathy served a dessert which Rosena could not recognise. 'Deep-fried seaweed,' Gareth explained, 'sprinkled with sugar.'

'It looks like shredded lettuce.' She tentatively tried a small piece. It was crunchy, like spun sugar, and very rich.

'Well?' Gareth asked.

'Delicious,' she said.

Next morning he went out to check the water-pump which was giving trouble. While he was busy, Rosena heard the engine of a boat, and shortly afterwards Mansfield walked up to the cottage, carrying a box of provisions. He exchanged a brief undemonstrative nod with his daughter and dumped what he'd brought on the table. He then reached into his pocket and took out an envelope. 'Letter for Gareth,' he said.

Rosena took the envelope, noticing how light it was; there was scarcely the thickness of paper inside. The postmark was 'Cardiff', and her heart quickened. The envelope was addressed to Frank Mansfield, but there was a small circled 'G' in the top left-hand corner. Perhaps this was from Gareth's friend Hugh, writing to say that at last it was 'convenient' for them to return to Cardiff ... perhaps, she thought excitedly, he's been refurbishing a home for us and it's finally ready. She longed to open the envelope but knew she mustn't. She placed it on the table.

Gareth returned a minute later, breathing heavily from his exertion and obviously glad to see Mansfield.

'A letter for 'ee,' she said, sliding it across the table.

He grasped it, hesitated, then slit it open with his index-finger and peered inside, but he did not extract the contents. He put the envelope in the pocket of his jacket.

'Aren't 'ee goin' to read it?' she exclaimed in frustration. 'Maybe it's from Hugh to say we can go to Cardiff.'

'No,' he said. 'It isn't that,' and immediately he turned to Mansfield and said: 'Could do with some 'elp, fixin' that pump.'

Mansfield nodded and the two men turned their backs and walked out of the cottage.

Rosena stamped her foot with annoyance. Why did he have to be so secretive? Had he still got so much to hide? She wanted to believe in him, to trust him ... why couldn't he be completely open with her? But then doubts came to her. She had gone behind his back in her attempts to post letters to Beryl and Tom. It seemed that deceit was a contagious disease.

Gareth hardly spoke a word for the rest of the day. After Mansfield had left, he came back into the cottage, kicked off his boots and slumped onto a chair, his face set in a deep scowl. Nor did the midday meal brighten his mood, for he hardly ate anything.

'Are you sick?' she enquired.

'No.'

She waited a minute, then said, 'It was that letter from Cardiff, wasn't it?'

He glared at her. 'Don't pester me with questions ... not now. Just give me time to think.'

From that moment on, an atmosphere of sullen depression descended upon them - a thick silence that only the baby occasionally broke. Gareth shuffled around listlessly, his head down. In the afternoon he walked out alone. From the window she saw him standing on the hill, like a statue silhouetted against the dark sky. He was gazing seawards and the rain was sweeping into him.

She glanced at Kathy who, for the first time, gave her a smile. Rosena wondered if the girl was mocking her. How much did she know ... did she know more about Gareth than she herself did? The answer was locked behind Kathy's wordless lips.

When Gareth came back, his mood was as black as ever; he declined supper and went to bed.

Rosena spent an hour playing with Emma Jane in the firelight, and Kathy soon came to join her, sticking her tongue out in a simple idea of play. The baby watched them with wide, unresponsive eyes, but she waved her arms and legs vigorously and clenched her tiny fists. Before long, Rosena thought, you will learn to smile. Please God may you have something to be happy about.

After she had fed, winded and changed her daughter, she crept upstairs, settled her in the basket, lay down beside the unmoving Gareth and listened to the dismal drum of rain on the cottage's tiles.

What would tomorrow bring?

Chapter Thirty-one

BY DAWN, THE SKIES HAD RELENTED. The rain had stopped and as the sun rose, warmth seeped into the day. But Gareth's mood was no brighter. He ate his breakfast in silence, then taking his fishing rod he left the cottage. From the bedroom window Rosena watched him strike out towards his cove. She moved about the room, tidying. Presently she noticed his jacket hanging on the back of a chair beside the bed.

For ten minutes she resisted temptation, but her glance kept returning to the jacket and at last her inquisitiveness got the upper hand. The jacket was still damp from the rain. She slipped her fingers into the pocket where he had placed the letter. She sighed. The pocket was empty. Perhaps it was best this way; after all she had no right to delve into his things - even so she checked the remaining pockets. All she found was a tiny key ... until she reached into the inside pocket and touched something else. She hesitated. It was not too late to leave it untouched. But her hand seemed to move of its own accord and she extracted the envelope and felt into it. She groaned with disappointment. There was nothing in it.

She returned the envelope to the pocket and sat on the edge of the bed, allowing her trembling to subside. She thought about the key. She knew where it belonged. It had always been in the unlocked dresser-drawer in the living room. Perhaps ...

Downstairs, she inserted the key and strained to force the drawer open. The wood was old and swollen, but it gave with a jerk, opening just a crack, and inside she saw the folded newspaper cutting. She glanced apprehensively around to make certain she was alone, then she drew the flimsy cutting out, her heart hammering fiercely.

Across the top, somebody had scrawled: Thought you might wish to see this. For God's sake stay hidden.

Her gaze seized upon the words printed below:

TRETHOMAS GUESTHOUSE BODY IDENTIFIED

Police have identified the girl found stabbed to death at the Trethomas guesthouse as Jenny Turnwell whose parents live at St Mags in Cornwall. The body, hidden beneath the kitchen floorboards, was discovered when an unpleasant smell was noticed. The guesthouse has stood empty for the past six months and police are anxious to trace the owner, former church minister Gareth Williams, who is wanted for questioning.

The words swam before her eyes, the print merging. She felt faint; she swayed on her feet. The clipping slipped from her fingers, fluttered to the floor. She stooped unsteadily to recover it. As she began to straighten up, she saw his boots, not ten feet from her, and the drips of water coming from the fish that dangled from his hand; then she was looking into his face, seeing his lips drawn back, twitching with anger, and his eyes, wide and harsh like a stranger's. She tried to speak, but her voice was all strangled. The room swirled about her as if flooding with green water. She felt sick. She couldn't breathe. She fainted.

The spider was quite large. It looked grey against the dark background of the ceiling's beam. It moved in short sharp bursts until, exhausted, it disappeared into a crack.

She could hear Emma Jane crying from downstairs.

Awareness was seeping into Rosena's head. She still felt intensely sick. She was in the bedroom, propped against the bolster on the bed. She remembered seeing Gareth's boots and the dripping fish, and ... 'Oh, God!' Where was he now? She tried to force herself up, but the pain in her head made her slump back. She must have bumped her head on the flagstone floor. She reached up and felt the swelling with her fingers. Suddenly she remembered the newspaper cutting and she groaned.

It was then she realised that Kathy had come into the room, was standing over her, the baby in her arms. The girl nodded towards Rosena's breast. It was feeding time for Emma Jane. Gritting her teeth against the pain, Rosena forced herself into a sitting position. She took the baby and, still half dazed, started to feed her.

Like a pebble sinking to the blackest depths of a pond, her mood plunged. She was married to a murderer - a man who had stabbed a young girl to death - a man who would go to the hang-rope if they caught him.

But why had he done it? She recalled the Killigrew girl standing forlornly at the cottage gate in Megstow quay, a waif of a girl with windswept hair and a strange, fluttery voice. She had pleaded for help then ... and now she was beyond help. But why?

Turning her head so her lips could be seen, she asked, 'Where is 'e?'

Kathy pointed through the window, then shrugged her shoulders, and Rosena imagined that her husband had stormed from the cottage, and was now probably striding across the hills, plotting up some dreadful means of punishing her. Her mind brooded on Megson's grim story, about another murderer, Stephen Mansfield, venting fury on his young wife by throwing her over the cliff.

When Emma Jane was once again satisfied, Kathy lifted her from her mother's arms and went downstairs to change her. Rosena had risen shakily to her feet as she returned and placed the baby in the basket. The two women then descended to the living room. Rosena glanced at the old dresser, seeing that the drawer was closed and the key re-inserted. No doubt Gareth had decided that it was pointless to conceal its contents any longer. She slumped wearily into a chair. Her feeling of nausea had relented.

Sooner or later he would come back and then ... what?

She had dozed but as the latch of the door sounded she awoke with a start. She wondered if he intended to kill her. She made no effort to rise. He loomed over her, standing against the brightness of the window so that she could not see his expression.

'Ro-sena,' he said, his voice strangely calm. 'I'm sorry for what 'as 'appened. But I've walked for two 'ours, prayin' for guidance ... and the good Lord 'as spoken to me.' He paused, stepping towards her, then he spoke again, louder and full of righteousness. 'Rosena ... you must be punished for what you've done.'

'Punished,' she repeated wearily, a tone of inevitability in her voice.

'Yes, my dear, punished ... but not now.'

He said no more but walked into the kitchen and she heard the tap running as he washed himself.

Over the next three days his mood was one of pious superiority, as if he was acting out the Lord's will. She made no effort to question or to accuse him. She strove to avoid him, fearing that she might do something to stir his anger, or incite the blind violence he was clearly capable of. At night he used her body, satisfying his hunger with scant consideration or tenderness. She endured his hands upon her, hands that had killed, and she submitted to him with terror in her heart, knowing that only when he was spent would there be any respite.

But by the fourth morning, she tentatively hoped that his intention to inflict 'punishment' was fading, that he'd decided his attitude of cold harshness would be sufficient to discourage her from further acts of, what he called, 'betrayal'.

After breakfast that morning, Mansfield arrived, dumping his usual box of provisions on the kitchen table. Later, he stood talking to Gareth out by the water pump. Rosena had busied herself clearing the table, while Kathy gleefully splashed water as she undertook the chore she loved - bathing Emma Jane.

Gareth returned to the cottage and for the first time in four days smiled at his wife. 'I'd like to sketch you, Ro-sena, sittin' on the rock over at the cove.'

She wondered what he had in mind. She didn't trust him, but she nodded. She removed her apron, then, checking to see that Kathy and the baby were all right, she followed him from the cottage, tidying her hair with her hands.

Ten minutes later he had her sitting, her head turned in profile, on the same rock where Kathy had posed naked, with a background of sea and sky. He went to work, frequently glancing up at her and grunting with satisfaction, sometimes murmuring, 'Keep still, my love.'

His gloom had lifted and she wondered why. Was it some news that Mansfield had brought him?

He finished the drawing an hour later and showed it to her. In the past she would have been impressed and flattered by the beauty his pencil created, but now her inner feelings, her fears, prevented her from showing any enthusiasm. She gazed at his big hands - murderer's hands.

As she followed him back over the hill, she thought about the letters and wondered if they were still in the grass where she'd left them ... or had Megson posted them? If he had, her bitter regret was that she hadn't been more specific about the location of the island.

They crossed the burial ground to the cottage. She sensed an eerie stillness about the place. Mansfield had departed. She overtook Gareth, ran into the living room, finding nobody present. Terrified, yet not knowing why, she dashed into the kitchen, but neither Kathy nor the baby were there. She climbed the stairs two at a time. The bedrooms were deserted, the Moses-basket gone.

When she came down, Gareth was gazing out of the window, his back turned. He reminded her of a big, black crow.

'Kathy must've gone walkin',' she blurted out, 'with Emma Jane.'

Gareth slowly turned. Her eyes were pleading with him for confirmation. He shook his head. 'She's not walkin'. She's gone with 'er father, taken the baby to the mainland, she 'as. That's your punishment, Ro-sena; that's the Lord's will. And remember I'm doin' it because I love you. If you do anythin' more behind my back, anythin', you'll never see the child again. And that, my love ... is a promise.'

Chapter Thirty-two

DUSK WAS TAKING HOLD as Edwin stopped at a roadside café ten miles beyond Manchester. He rapidly consumed a hot pie and peas, washed down with rather bitter coffee; he needed some refreshment because he had eaten nothing since the breakfast served by Aunt Beryl eight hours earlier. Yet he begrudged any time wasted, any delay, in his race northward, despite the fact he might be following a false trail.

On his return from Cornwall, he'd stayed with his uncle and aunt in Beckenham while he considered his next course of action.

Sudden joy had shot through him that morning when Beryl had shown him the letter she'd received - the handwriting as familiar as his own. But the shock of what he'd read had shattered his hopes.

His long passage from the other side of the world; his desperate, grisly search in Trethomas for the girl he loved, and the revelation that his visit to Megstow Quay had subsequently unearthed ... All his endeavours seemed to have crashed about his ears with Rosena's simple statement: *Gareth and I were married just three days after our baby was born.* What madness had driven her to become the wife of a man who had treated her so contemptuously - a man who's true sins, once revealed, would prove more despicable than those in her worst nightmares?

Choked with dismay, Edwin had scanned the note for some indication of the island's location ... but apart from mentioning that it was in Scotland, there was nothing. And then he'd turned his attention to the envelope; it had been franked 'Oakport' by the Post Office.

The name of the town triggered only the vaguest recollection in his mind, but he immediately went to the big Blackstone's Library nearby and thumbed through a Bartholemworth's Gazetteer of Scotland. There was no mention of Oakport. In exasperation he turned to a map of Scotland and the far north of England, gazing over it on the off chance of finding some clue. He knew he was clutching at straws ... but he was rewarded; he found what he sought. Oakport was on the Solway Firth, a few miles inside the English border.

Edwin had found Jeremy's attitude towards Rosena puzzling. At one time there was nothing too much he would do for her; now he seemed completely indifferent to her fate and not remotely interested in Edwin's determination to continue his search. It was only thanks to Beryl's persuasive powers, that he'd grudgingly lent Edwin one of his cars - the green Lanchester.

Now Rosena's letter was in the glove compartment of the car. Edwin didn't need to look at it to recall its words; their image was branded into his mind. The letter, scribbled in pencil, was painfully brief. He'd tried to read between the lines for some secret message, but there was nothing beyond the devastating news of the marriage and the fact that she and Gareth were now staying on some quiet island in Scotland.

As Edwin left the café and resumed his journey, roaring on through the summer night, he was glad of the car's powerful engine and bright headlights. He wondered how much longer it would take to reach the Solway Firth. It occurred to him that he should have informed the police of Rosena's letter. So desperate was he to set off, that he had not given it a thought. Undoubtedly, he should have contacted the constabulary in either Trethomas or Merthyr. Even now he could stop the car, find a public house and telephone, but it was getting late and he decided against it. There must be a police station at Oakport, and that would be his first point of call. Perhaps he would glean some information there, some further evidence to send him in the right direction.

In the small hours, after several wrong turnings, the road swept round some dunes and he at last reached Oakport, braking to a halt on the sea-front. He switched off his lights. His eyes ached from the strain of driving, so he leaned back in his seat and dozed off. He was awakened, much later than he'd intended, by the screeching of sea-gulls wheeling over a choppy sea. Already the harbour was coming to life, with men loading oyster pots and baskets onto their small boats and chugging away. The sea-front smelt of fish, reminding him of Megstow Quay, but the sea lacked the Cornish blueness, looking grey and sullen.

Leaving the car, he found a small snack bar and enjoyed a sausage sandwich and a mug of coffee. He also obtained directions to the police station. The thought of sleepy police stations with sleepy, sceptical constables to whom he would have to explain the long chain of events which brought him here, didn't imbue him with enthusiasm, but he knew he had no alternative. He glanced at his watch. It was seven-thirty.

After he'd found the familiar blue lamp above a doorway and stepped inside, he was surprised. There was nothing sleepy about the station; the three police officers therein were in a high state of agitation, consulting maps and talking in animated voices. He had to wait nearly five minutes before a grey-haired sergeant condescended to glance in his direction, his head cocked on one side enquiringly.

Edwin sparked into action. He spread on the counter the newspaper page from *The South Wales Gazette,* giving details of the Trethomas murder and the hunt for Gareth Williams. After the sergeant had impatiently scanned through it, Edwin passed him Rosena's letter. The policeman's expression changed from impatience to one of mild interest. 'And who, might I ask, are you, sir?'

Very briefly Edwin gave details of himself and his search.

The police-sergeant raised his bushy eyebrows incredulously. Meanwhile a young constable was looking over his shoulder. 'I remembers that case, Sergeant,' he said. 'We got the case-report through last week.' He turned and started to rummage in a drawer, but the sergeant placed a restraining hand on his arm. 'No time for that now, son. Just take a statement from this gentleman and we'll get round to it as soon as we can.' He looked at Edwin and added, 'You caught us at a bad time. We've had a spate of burglaries in Oakport - three last night. Catching the guilty parties is currently top of our priorities. But once we get time, we'll certainly follow up your case.'

Edwin gave a despondent nod. 'I wonder if you could give me some idea of any islands near here.'

The sergeant pointed with his pencil. 'See, there's a map on the end wall. Have a look for yourself.'

The constable, tall and thin as a drain-pipe, had appeared with pencil and pad, and he painstakingly took down Edwin's statement, blowing out through his lips in shock as the story unfolded. Once he'd signed, Edwin moved across and studied the map. There were no islands in the immediate vicinity of Oakport Harbour, but off the coast to the west, he noted some small islands with such names as Monastery Island, Death Island, Mansfield Island, Harvelloch ... The map told him little, apart from the names. He wanted to question the constable about the local geography, but the young man had rejoined his sergeant and they were busily shuffling through statements relating to the burglaries. Edwin swung his gaze back to the map. The nearest mainland point to the islands was a tiny village or hamlet whose name only warranted the tiniest print. Peering close he could just make out the faint letters ... Cullipol.

It had now gone nine o'clock. With Oakport's main street stirring to life, he found a stationer's shop and purchased his own map of the district. Cullipol wasn't marked; clearly it was the tiniest of hamlets and of scant importance, but he remembered its location from the police map and pencilled in a cross at the appropriate point ten miles along the coastal road.

An hour later he parked the Lanchester up a hillside-track and walked down to the straggle of decrepit cottages which lined the cinder track. He placed his feet carefully to avoid disturbing the big, black dog sprawled beside a half-gnawed bone. The animal's snoring was the only sound to break the silence which hung like a shroud over the hamlet. He reached the first two cottages, seeing the doors splintered inward, hanging on rusted hinges, and the broken windows and gaping holes in the roofs. He peered inside and glimpsed a mass of old bottles, tin cans, smashed furniture and decaying rubbish. But suddenly a tingling in his spine warned him that he was being watched. Turning, he saw that the dog had raised its head, was gazing at him from dull, rheumy eyes. After a moment the animal decided that it was all too much effort and once more rested its head down onto its front paws.

Edwin wondered if the canine was the only inhabitant of the hamlet ... but he concluded that somebody must have given the bone to it. He turned his gaze towards the sea. The tide was far out, and it was a misty day with low cloud, but he could see the darker smudge of an island rising from the murk, and he knew that there were more islands beyond. A fleeting excitement touched him. Could it be that Rosena was somewhere out there?

His attention swung back to the cinder track; it was then that he noticed curtains hanging at the windows of the third cottage.

Stepping forward, he rapped against its weathered door with his knuckles, the sound challenging the stillness. He waited, then tried again, achieving nothing apart from confirmation that there was nobody at home. Frustrated, he was pondering on what to do next, when he realised that the dog had at last lifted itself from repose and was standing a mere yard behind him, the grey hairs of its ears and jaws indicating its advanced years. Fastened to its ancient collar was a dull, metal disk.

Edwin dropped to his haunches, reached out, clicked his thumb and index-finger, and called in a gentle but hearty tone: 'Come on, old boy!'

The dog shuffled forward on stiff legs, its tail wagging from side to side. Edwin's fingers closed over the disk and he saw the inscription: Mansfield, 3 Cullipol Cottages. He gave the dog a friendly pat on the head and straightened up. For a moment, the fact that he knew the name of the family, or individual, who lived in Number 3. seemed of little consequence, but then he recalled that one of the off-shore islands was called Mansfield Island. Could this have any significance? It might be that the island was a private one, owned by the occupants of this cottage. A private island ... what a perfect hideaway for a murderer on the run!

He cursed under his breath, wishing there was somebody around to answer his questions. He decided to return to his car, wait an hour or so, then come back.

Through the windscreen of the Lanchester, parked on the elevated side-track, he had an excellent view of the hamlet. He felt, that in all his life, he had never encountered habitations, albeit partially derelict, so ghostly silent, so resentful of intrusion. Even in the deserted shell-shattered cottages of France, there had lingered a greater sense of human life, human warmth, than here.

He reached into the dashboard glove-compartment, took out Rosena's note, savouring the feel of the paper, knowing that her fingers, only a few days earlier, had experienced the same touch. He re-read the words, pausing on the last sentence: Gareth has said that after our honeymoon we will go to live in Cardiff. He sighed in bewilderment. Did she really imagine that anything Gareth Williams said could be believed?

He must have dozed, the long hours without proper rest taking their toll. He awoke an hour later, still feeling drowsy and stiff in his limbs. He allowed himself a smile; he knew how the old dog felt. He decided to return to the cottages, though instinct told him that nothing had changed. Even so, he needed fresh air and a stretch of his legs.

He was almost at the foot of the hill, when he saw a lone figure walking slowly along the road - a woman. His pace quickened, and he was only a few yards behind her as she turned down the cinder track towards the cottages. Although his steps sounded quite clearly, she made no attempt to glance over her shoulder. He even called, 'Excuse me!' but she made no response; she seemed in a world of her own. At last, catching her up, he reached forward and touched her arm. She unleashed a weird, gasping sound and jerked around, a young woman, scarcely more than a child, her lavender eyes fixed on him, wide with fear.

He tried to reassure her with a smile, stepping back, but her alarmed expression didn't relent. 'I'm awfully sorry to startle you,' he said, 'but I'm wondering if you can help me. I'm trying to ...' His words trailed off as he heard a gentle gurgling sound. He smiled again, for the first time noticing that the girl was clutching a tiny baby, wrapped in a tartan shawl, against her ample bosom. 'I'm trying to contact a friend of mine,' he repeated. 'I think he's staying around here. His name is ... Gareth Williams.'

The girl jumped visibly, the abrupt movement causing the shawl to fall away from the baby's face. She made no reply apart from a vigorous shake of her head, then she turned, ran down the track and disappeared through the door of number 3.

Edwin closed his eyes; he felt stunned. The brief glimpse he'd caught was vivid in his mind ... so was the moment when Sister Edna had allowed him a view of Rosena's baby at the Wimbledon maternity home. Despite slight fading, the baby's oddly shaped birth-scars were unmistakable.

'Mansfield Island?' Police Sergeant Webber met Edwin's blue eyes. 'Certainly I know it. As you understand, it's not the most popular place in view of what happened there. Most people leave it well alone. Anyway, it's privately owned.'

Edwin was impatient. He had the feeling that the painstaking progress of the investigation was conspiring against him.

'What I'd like to know,' Webber continued, 'is why the baby was in the care of Frank Mansfield's daughter. Could it be that the mother is ...'

'Dead?' Edwin supplied the final word. 'I hope and pray she's not, but one thing's certain. Every second she remains with Williams she's in mortal danger.'

The policeman studied the cutting from the 'South Wales Gazette', then turned to Rosena's pencil-written note and said, 'You've got no positive proof Williams is on the island?' .

'Not positive proof,' Edwin's voice was edged with anger, 'just a very positive hunch!'

Startled by the other man's intensity, Webber glanced up. Despite his sceptical manner, he'd formed a healthy respect for the well-spoken Southerner.

He turned the pages of his note book, found a telephone number; then he made a call. Soon he was discussing the availability of marine transport. Giving a satisfied nod, he replaced the receiver. 'Tonight,' he said, 'we'll give the island the once over.'

Edwin grunted with satisfaction. 'I'd like to come with you.'

Webber looked dubious. 'It's not usual ...' but then he changed his mind. 'All right. Maybe we'll need your help for identification purposes. You be here at midnight, at high tide. Seems as if there's a bit of a storm blowing up, so come prepared for a rough passage and some scrambling over muddy ground. And remember, if you're not here on the dot, we'll go without you.'

'I'll be here,' Edwin confirmed.

On leaving the police station he returned to his car and tried to snatch some more sleep, but his mind was too active. He spent two hours aimlessly wandering the cobbled streets of Oakport, constantly checking his watch, amazed by how slowly the seconds ticked by. Presently he found a fish and chip café and while he was eating some young uniformed soldiers entered, and seeing their exuberant faces, he hoped they would never have to face such battle-front horrors as he had experienced.

Come the evening, he dared not go to sleep in the car for fear of not awaking in time. He bought a newspaper and sat reading on the quay until it began to spit with the rain that had been threatening all day. The wind came up very quickly, rattling the rigging on the boats drawn up on the tide-exposed silt of the harbour.

Edwin thought about the sea, his old adversary. Soon the tide would come sweeping in, perhaps on the back of a storm, and waves would crash against the quay-side and have the boats bucking against their moorings like frightened horses. He thought of his parents, his little sister and the others who had drowned when *The Atlantic Queen* had foundered over a quarter of a century ago - and the old uneasiness spread through him. He asked himself a question that he'd asked a thousand times before: Why was I chosen to survive when so many died? And why was Rosena chosen? Certainly her precious life hadn't been spared so that she could become the victim of a callous, evil killer.

Back in the Lanchester, he watched the weather worsen. As the light faded, he listened to the lash of rain against the windscreen and the creak of the car's springs as the wind buffeted it. A mixture of disappointment and fear settled over him: disappointment that the weather might cause tonight's trip to be cancelled. But even stronger, a fear that if the boat did set out, they might suffer the same terrible fate as that of his parents and baby sister. As the hours dragged by his anxiety increased.

By eleven-thirty he'd changed into a thick jersey and the oldest clothes he could find in his case. He then put on his raincoat, realising how inadequate it was, but he had nothing else. A minute later he was on his way to the police station, battling wind and rain, splashing through puddles, and doubting that the trip would go ahead. But he found Sergeant Webber and the young and lanky constable, Swain, dressed to face the elements in oilskins and high boots. The trip was obviously 'on'. When the two officers saw Edwin, they burst out laughing and Swain said, 'You should've brought your brolly, sir. You might get wet.'

Edwin shared their mirth, acknowledging how ridiculous he must appear. Sergeant Webber came to the rescue, producing a spare set of waterproofs and helping him into them.

'Thought the weather would put you off,' Edwin said as he pulled on the boots he'd been loaned.

Webber laughed. 'Catching criminals isn't like cricket, you know. Summer showers don't stop play!'

Once they were out into rain and darkness, their laughing ceased. Moving down the street towards the harbour, they all felt that one thing seemed certain: if anybody was on Mansfield Island, surely they would not be expecting visitors on such a foul night.

Twenty minutes after midnight, the launch pulled away from the protection of Oakport Quay, and nosed out into the turbulent water of the harbour. As the engine roared up to full throttle, the vessel seemed to hurl itself into the waves as if enjoying the challenge, not caring a whisker for the souls on board. Edwin turned green beneath his oilskins, crouching in the cabin and grasping a handrail to brace himself against the leap and fall of the vessel. He could see the whiteness of foam frisking past the cabin windows, and already queasiness was agitating his stomach. If he survived tonight, he promised himself he would never again take to water in anything less than an ocean-going liner.

This powerful craft was some twenty feet long, steered from the cabin, and crewed by two army corporals who clearly knew their navigational skills. Apparently it was the custom of the local constabulary to hire boats from the military on the rare occasions when it was necessary to patrol the islands.

What irritated him particularly was the way in which the two crewmen appeared to enjoy the challenges that wind, rain and sea threw at them, their voices and laughter rising with excitement as an extra large wave was encountered, or they were plunged downward into a valley of black water. On the latter occasions it felt to Edwin as if the boat-bottom was hammering against solid brick instead of compressed water. Glancing sideways, he saw that the two policemen, though not overly amused, seemed to be taking the hazardous venture in their strides.

He tried to suppress his immediate fears of capsizing by lifting his voice above the engine's roar, and asking Sergeant Webber why, even in fine weather, Mansfield Island was seldom visited.

Webber relished the opportunity to tell the story, and against the noisy background he related the gruesome history of Stephen Mansfield, his beautiful young wife and John McVey. He concluded by saying that the island was now jointly owned by Stephen Mansfield's sons - Frank who lived at Cullipol, and Hugh who was an artist in Cardiff.

Edwin was so affected by the story that he momentarily forgot how sick he felt. He realised that his own circumstances were not unlike those of John McVey, who had landed by night on the island in an attempt to rescue his lover. McVey's brave efforts had ended with not only his own death, but with those of his companion and his tormented lover - all hurled from the island's highest cliff. Edwin whispered a silent prayer that his own fate would be kinder.

To his surprise, his stomach had still not erupted by the time the engine was cut. Webber called that they had almost reached their destination and to make ready. The wind had now dropped, the rain ceased, but the sea was still turbulent. The overhead cloud was low, completely obscuring moon and stars.

In almost total darkness, the crew allowed the craft to drift into a small cove. It took them a further ten minutes of skilful manoeuvring before they were moored at a crumbling jetty. 'We'll be back soon after dawn,' Sergeant Webber informed the crewmen. 'If there's any change in plan, we'll let you know.'

As they scrambled onto the jetty, leaving the two crewman on board, Webber turned to Edwin. 'The other landing-place is on the far side of the island - opposite Cullipol. The only use this jetty normally gets is when old Megson brings his sheep over from Oakport. He's the only devil who'll come near the place. Rest of the locals wouldn't come here if you paid 'em.'

'Don't blame them, after what happened ...' Edwin's words came to an abrupt stop as he jerked out a supportive arm to catch PC Swain who had slipped on the jetty's rotting wood.

Soon their steps were making unavoidable crunching sounds as they crossed shingle towards the looming, uninviting murkiness of higher ground. 'D-devil's Island would've been a better name for this place,' Swain remarked in a voice so tremulous that Edwin shot the tall constable a sidelong glance; in the darkness he couldn't be sure whether he was playing the fool or not, but concluded that he wasn't.

Webber was leading the way. 'Must admit I'd rather be in bed with the missus.' His voice had dropped to a stealthy whisper. 'Better be worth it, after all this.' At the head of a narrow cleft, he called a halt, the others almost blundering into his back in the gloom, then he said: 'I was counting on there being some moonlight, but so far as I remember Mansfield's old house *Glencannon* is in a valley beyond the next hill, and we've got to skirt it on the west side and follow along the coastline. We're bound to get lost or stuck in a bog, if we try cutting straight across.'

'And where do you think Williams'll be, if he's here?' Edwin enquired.

'There's only one inhabitable place on the island now. That's the cottage on the far side. With any luck, Williams will be fast asleep, and we'll walk straight in and shake him by the shoulder.'

'Unless he's been tipped off we're on our way,' PC Swain suggested.

'In which case,' Sergeant Webber responded, his teeth showing a slight glimmer in the darkness. 'He'll probably set up a nice little booby trap for us!'

They moved on, their boots squelching and sucking in the spongy ground, but as they climbed the going got firmer and the noise of their progress diminished. When they crested a hill, they were startled by a frantic, scurrying movement - but then they heard the bleating of sheep and as they relaxed, Webber was chuckling. 'Don't know why we're so nervous. This place isn't exactly infested with head-hunting cannibals waiting to ambush us.'

'Just ghosts,' Swain commented. 'Or Gareth Williams maybe.'

They pressed forward, sometimes having to claw their way through low shrub and heather, but presently they reached what appeared to be a sheep or deer track and they were able to make faster progress. They emerged onto a hillside, and as they moved across it, bracing themselves against the steepness, Webber pointed to their right. 'The old house is down there somewhere - at least what's left of it.'

They all stared downward but could see nothing in the darkness. 'We'll have to take your word for it,' Edwin said.

Fifteen minutes later they were standing on the cliff tops, hearing the roar of the sea.

'This must be the place where Mansfield committed his murders,' Webber remarked grimly.

The wind was blustery as they followed the cliff-tops southward, taking care not to blunder near the edge. Now excitement was growing in Edwin. He refused to give any credibility to the thought that Rosena might be dead, despite the presence of her baby with another woman. There must be some reasonable explanation. He hurried on. Within twenty minutes, he might be face to face with the girl whose smiling eyes had lured him from the other side of the world.

But what would her reaction be? Was it possible that she was still in love with Gareth just as desperately and devotedly as ever; and, no matter how he had treated her and how wicked his crime had been, she would remain loyal to him? Maybe any warmth or love that she once felt for me, he thought, will turn to hatred when she learns that I've tracked her husband down and brought the police in. Will she really come to me if Gareth ends up with a noose around his neck?

And there was something else: was he scrambling across this god-forsaken island because he had an inborn sense of justice, a desperate desire to search out and punish an evil man? Or was it simply that he wanted to steal another man's wife?

He convinced himself that neither question related to his true motive. He loved Rosena. He always had done; he always would. If, once he found her, she again rejected him for her beloved Gareth, his respect for her, his love, would leave him no alternative but to leave her for ever more, and return, heavy-hearted, to an empty life in Australia.

'We're almost there.' Webber pulled them up as they reached the summit of yet another hill. They were all breathing heavily from the latest climb. Edwin was soaked with sweat beneath his oil-skins. The sky was showing an eastern-paleness, its first agitation of pre-dawn. In this weird, shadowy world, they could just see the cleft of a valley below them. Half way down, a pin-point of light showed. Starting their descent, they realised that the light was coming from the window of a small cottage.

'Paraffin lamp,' Edwin whispered. 'There must be somebody there.'

Webber turned to Swain. 'Have the handcuff's ready, lad.' They continued forward, their pace quickening on the incline. Soon they were passing through the eerie mounds of the monks' burial ground, Webber gesturing anxiously for silence as the unevenness of the surface had them stumbling. When they were some twenty yards above the cottage, the sergeant signalled them to wait. Then, gripping his truncheon and bent almost double, he gingerly approached the lighted window.

With baited breath, Edwin and PC Swain watched him reach the cottage and from beneath the sill-line, cautiously raise his head to look through the glass. Seconds later he was backtracking to rejoin them, crouching down breathlessly. 'Nobody's in the room ... but it looks lived-in ... and the lamp's standing on the table.' He paused, gathering his thoughts, then he turned to Swain. 'Mister Carter and me'll go round the front and try a polite approach. You stay here at the back. If anybody tries to escape, grab 'em!'

'Yes, sergeant.'

Edwin doubted that the constable's lank frame would be any match for Gareth Williams in full flight, but he followed after the sergeant.

It took them three minutes to circle around the cottage and walk up to the door. Without hesitation Webber hammered against the flaking wood with his fist. To their astonishment the door swung open; it hadn't been latched. The living room was revealed, with its flagstone floor, shadowy alcoves and scattered furnishing, all illuminated in the yellow glow of the lamp. Edwin followed the sergeant in. For a second they hesitated, then Webber moved towards the kitchen.

Edwin noticed the stairs, ran across and climbed them two at a time. He emerged into the main bedroom, but the only light came from downstairs and in the dimness he could see very little. He blundered forward, stumbled across the bed and fell face-first onto the soft mattress. Flailing with his hands, he realised that he was sprawled amid crumpled blanket and sheets. The bed was unmade; it was also empty.

At that moment Webber climbed the stairs, the paraffin lamp he held sending weird shadows dancing across the beamed ceiling. He saw the doorway to the second bedroom and checked inside. When he reappeared, he was shaking his head disgustedly.

Edwin had come to his feet. He noticed that there were two pillows on the double-bed, side by side ... also, there was a woman's blouse hanging on the back of a chair. Rosena's? He touched it and was surprised by its dampness. Turning, he noticed a sketch pad on the chest-of-drawers. Some impulse had him picking it up, holding it to the light. His pulse quickened. It was an unmistakable drawing of Rosena, the sky and sea in the background.

Webber was swearing softly to himself. 'The birds have flown, Mister Carter.' He gazed around the room at the scattered clothing, the untidy bed, the half open drawers. 'And in a hurry too. Must've got word we were on our way - but how?'

Chapter Thirty-three

IT WAS ONLY MINUTES EARLIER that Frank Mansfield had pushed his boat off from the jetty, allowed the current to take hold, and the ebb of the waves to draw him silently away. He was glad that the wind and rain had relented; he was also glad that the clouds were still low and the night pitch black; if anybody was about, the craft's departure would go unseen.

Gareth and Rosena were crouched in the stern with the few clothes they'd managed to carry with them. Gareth had reacted with frantic energy when Mansfield had arrived on Mansfield Island with the news that the police were on their way. 'Lucky for you my army drinking pal overheard the police booking a boat for tonight,' he'd said.

Gareth had rapidly dressed, motioning Rosena to do the same, and within minutes they were scrambling down to the jetty and into the boat.

''Ow did they find out we were there?' Gareth gasped.

Mansfield shook his head, bracing himself against the movement of the boat. 'Must be something to do with that stranger who was snooping about Cullipol. He gave Kathy quite a start, poor girl. Mentioned your name, as well.'

'Damn the bastard,' Gareth snarled.

Rosena listened to their words, but she could not concentrate. She was in utter misery. She had hardly spoken since the abduction of her baby. The swelling of her unsuckled breasts was agonising, and there was a constant seepage of milk soaking her clothing. She had bound a towel around to relieve the pressure, but it was of little help.

Now as they left the island, Rosena broke her silence. 'Gareth, where are we goin'?'

'Frank'll drop us a few miles down the coast. We'll catch a train from Workington. We'll ...'

'But Emma Jane,' she exclaimed. 'We've got to take 'er with us!'

Gareth had turned away, was gazing towards the receding shore. 'Sorry, my love. No chance. Kathy'll see she's cared for. Baby'll come to no 'arm where she is, unless you do anythin' stupid. If you try runnin' away or sneaking' behind my back, I'll not be responsible for what 'appens to 'er.'

'Gareth Williams ... 'Ow can you be so cruel!'

If he made any reply, it was drowned out by a sudden roar as Mansfield started the engine; the boat surged forward. They moved from the bay into the rougher waves of the open sea, and Rosena gripped the gunwale, her knuckles white, to avoid being hurled overboard. The sharpness of salt burned her throat and nostrils. The black, glinting waves loomed perilously close, their spray lifting like white whiplash. The boat was tossed from one trough to another, but now as Mansfield opened the throttle its bow cut through the sea like a lance.

On Rosena's cheeks, her tears were mingling with the wetness of salt-water. She sobbed aloud as the distance between her and Emma Jane lengthened. She despised Gareth, despised him so bitterly that her mind brooded on murder. Had there been a knife or a gun at hand ... Her anguish boiled to black, venomous hatred, then gradually was forced aside by the question that forever tormented her. Would she ever see her baby again?

It was the next day and Frank Mansfield was expecting a visit from the police. Not that he was overly concerned. He was confident he had answers for any questions they might throw at him. Furthermore, he was determined not be intimidated by the likes of Sergeant Webber and his side-kicks. The police had tried to pin a charge on him a couple of years ago over some contraband goods, but he'd outwitted them and he could do it again if necessary.

In the early afternoon, when he saw their van and another green car stop at the top of the cinder track, he sent Kathy into the back room and told her to keep the baby quiet. When an officious knock sounded on the cottage door, he took his time, lighting his pipe and tamping it down before he opened up.

The day was already hot, and Webber and Swain looked red faced and sweaty in their high collars. In addition both were bleary-eyed from a sleepless night - but the sergeant got straight to the point. 'Mister Mansfield, we're anxious to question a certain Gareth Williams, and we understand he was residing on Mansfield Island until last night.'

'Was residing?' Mansfield exclaimed. 'I bloody well hope he's still there. He owes me a couple of weeks' rent!'

'We have reason to believe he moved out last night - and in a hurry. We've got a few questions you might be able to help us with.'

Mansfield looked suitably puzzled but after a moment he nodded and said, 'You'd better come in, though I've not much time this afternoon.'

The policemen stepped over the threshold, removing their helmets. The cottage's front room was far from hospitable, and little better in truth than the derelict rooms of the first two cottages, though it did have tattered, grimy curtains at the windows. Webber could feel the dust of the place turn gritty between his dentures. There was a rancid odour of stale food going off in the heat; and a reek of tobacco mingled with a smell that Webber, being a family man, immediately associated with young babies. The room was littered with cast-aside clothes, boots and odd bits of fishing tackle, and the table was covered in plates of half-eaten food over which two blow-flies busied themselves. Mansfield did not offer his guests seats or refreshment, but asked, 'Why should he have left in a hurry, like you say?'

'We were hoping you'd be able to tell us,' Webber commented. Meanwhile PC Swain had produced his notebook and was making notes.

'I've no idea.' Mansfield took a draw on his pipe. 'He wasn't due to go yet.'

They all heard the sudden cry of the baby from the next room, but nobody commented.

'When did you last see him, Mister Mansfield?'

'Let me think ... It was last Thursday when I took supplies over. Are you sure he's left? He may still be on the island.'

Webber shook his head. 'I had men searching the island this morning.'

Mansfield showed annoyance. 'I might remind you, it's private property ...'

'That's right, Mister Mansfield. That's why we took the precaution of taking out a search warrant. Yes, Williams has gone all right. I presume he must have had a boat.'

Mansfield nodded, content to let them reach that conclusion.

The policeman continued his probing: 'When did you first meet Williams?'

'He and his wife got off the bus about six months ago, wanted a nice peaceful place to stay.'

'Why was that?'

'Apparently Mrs Williams had been in some trouble in Wales - stealing and suchlike. He'd been a church minister and the disgrace was too much for him. Couldn't face his congregation any more. All he wanted was to get away and find some peace while he decided what to do.'

'I see.' Webber took a handkerchief from his pocket and mopped the back of his neck. 'But what happened to Mrs Williams?'

'Well, apparently she left the island, went off somewhere.'

'Rather strange, wasn't it?'

'That's what I thought. They must've had a bust-up or something.'

'Anyway, Williams stayed on the island?'

'Yes, until he went away for a week and came back with his young lady.'

'And her baby?'

'And her baby,' Mansfield concurred.

'Is that the same baby we just heard crying?'

'Yes, my daughter's looking after it, worst luck. You can see this place is like a pig-sty. She never does any work. Just moons over the baby, nothing else.'

223

'Why should she be looking after it?'

'Gareth Williams asked me to take the child off his hands. The mother was sick. It was too much for her.'

Webber paused while PC Swain scribbled his notes, then he asked, 'Did your brother know that Williams was here?'

Mansfield was growing impatient. 'Why all these questions? What's going on?'

'All I can tell you is that the police in Wales want to question Williams in connection with a murder.'

'Murder!' Mansfield allowed his mouth to sag. 'Gareth's not the guilty party, is he?'

'I wouldn't know about that,' Webber responded. 'Now tell me: did your brother know that Williams was here?'

'Hugh?' Mansfield shook his head. 'No reason why he should. Williams and his missus turned up needing accommodation. People don't usually want to go anywhere near the island, but it seemed just what they wanted. I was glad of the money. But I'm bloody annoyed if Williams has legged it without paying!'

'Do you know where he might've gone?'

Mansfield shook his head, but then he said, 'Wait a minute. I did hear him say something about the Orkneys once.'

Webber nodded. He seemed to have run out of questions. 'Well, thank you, Mister Mansfield. We may be in touch again.'

The policemen replaced their helmets and departed. As Mansfield stood in the doorway, watching them walk up towards their van, he allowed himself a faint smile. In view of all the trouble he'd gone to, the least his brother could do was forget about the money he owed him.

Edwin, sitting behind the wheel of the Lanchester, had opened the doors and windows to allow the air to flow. The sun seemed almost as overbearing as he'd experienced in Australia. Time dragged after the two policemen had gone down to the cottage. Of course Edwin had wanted to accompany them, but Webber had insisted that this was a police matter and he should wait outside until they'd finished. What he did afterwards was entirely up to him.

When he saw them returning up the cinder track he breathed a thankful sigh and got out of the car. A moment later and Webber was explaining what had occurred. He concluded by saying, 'I don't believe a word of what the devil says, though.'

Edwin was disappointed that no firm evidence of Gareth's and Rosena's new destination had emerged. Like the policemen, he dismissed talk of Orkney as a red herring. 'Was the baby all right?' he enquired.

Webber nodded. 'Sounded all right, but we didn't actually see it. But that place is not fitting for any child. It's filthy and it stinks.'

Edwin frowned. 'Well, I'll see what can be done.'

'It's most likely that Williams has left the district altogether now. He'd be mad to stick around here. There's no telling where he's gone. We'll be sending our report to the police in Wales and they'll no doubt carry on with the investigation.'

'I'm grateful for all you've done,' Edwin said, then he reached out and shook both men's hands, wishing them well. He had shared a night's adventure with them which he would never forget. If he was needed again they would know how to contact him.

After they had driven off, he took a deep breath, then walked down to the cottage. This time, as he knocked on the door, he could hear noise from inside - Emma Jane's cries.

Mansfield opened up, a look of annoyance on his surly face. He'd had enough visitors for one day. Standing behind him, holding the baby, was the girl. As she saw Edwin she made a strange clicking sound in her throat and pointed at him accusingly.

'You're the one who was prying round here yesterday,' Mansfield stated.

Edwin nodded. 'I'd like to discuss something with you, Mister Mansfield.'

'Who are you?' Mansfield's voice was belligerent.

'My name is Edwin Carter - a friend of Rosena Bray.'

'Gareth's woman?'

'You could say that,' Edwin reluctantly admitted. 'Anyway, I'd like to relieve you of the responsibility of the child.'

'You mean ... take the baby?'

'Yes. Rosena would want me to take it. It would be well looked after.'

'It's not mine to give, Mister Carter. I wouldn't do such a thing, not without Gareth's permission ... and my daughter dotes on it.'

'But Gareth may never come back,' Edwin argued. 'You're probably landed with the child for the rest of your life.'

He saw a glint of doubt in Mansfield's eye.

'I understand about your daughter's affection for the child,' Edwin persisted. 'I'm sorry if she will be upset, but I'll pay her well for all the trouble she's been put to.'

'Pay?' Mansfield's ears perked up. 'How much?'

'Twenty-pounds,' Edwin said, taking his wallet out.

Mansfield licked his lips at the sight of money. 'Twenty-five, no less ... and you can take the basket as well.'

Edwin nodded and counted out the notes.

A moment later he was aware of the girl's big lavender eyes, wide with horror, as Mansfield unceremoniously tugged Emma Jane from her arms and placed her in the basket.

'Now you can start doing some housework again,' he shouted.

Kathy was on the verge of snatching the baby back, but her father's glare had her cowering away. He gestured for her to put a recently prepared bottle of milk into the basket and, sullen faced, she complied.

As Edwin walked back to the car, carrying the basket, a surge of joy spread through him. At least, he felt, he had part of Rosena to cherish. He gazed at the baby's tiny face and gently kissed her head. He was pleased to see that the red marks were getting fainter, but as she started to cry he realised that he had taken on a tremendous responsibility.

Once in the car he fed her, then, after she had grown quiet, he returned her to the basket and started the engine. They had a long journey ahead of them. He knew he would be unable to care for the baby himself. If necessary he felt certain that Sister Edna at Wimbledon would help until Rosena could resume her maternal duties - but firstly he had another option to try.

At Oakport he paused briefly to telephone his Aunt Beryl and inform her of events. When he mentioned that he had Emma Jane, he heard a gasp from the other end - and then silence. For a moment he thought they had been cut off, but the truth was that the news had stunned his aunt; she could hardly believe her ears. At last she laughed excitedly. 'Oh Edwin, how wonderful. I'll be able to take care of her. I can't wait. It's like a dream come true. I'll ... I'll get a room ready. I'll go out and buy a book on baby-care. Oh ... do drive carefully!'

Edwin was smiling gratefully as he replaced the receiver. He'd been deprived of his true mother from a tender age - but with Aunt Beryl as a substitute, he could never have asked for greater kindness, love and understanding.

As he resumed his journey southward his mind, like a compass needle returning to magnetic north, swung back to Rosena. Would he ever find her?

Chapter Thirty-four

GARETH HAS SAID that after our honeymoon we will go to live in Cardiff. The final sentence of Rosena's note haunted him. It seemed the only clue left for him to follow up, though, knowing the dubious reliability of Gareth's word, it was likely to be just as much a red herring as Frank Mansfield's mention of the Orkneys probably was. And anyway, the desperation of the Welshman's hasty flight might well have altered all previous plans.

Uncle Jeremy reminded Edwin that he had responsibilities in Australia and could not remain absent for too long. But thoughts of Cardiff would not go away, and having ensured that Emma Jane was safely lodged with a delighted Aunt Beryl at Beckenham, Edwin snatched a night's sleep, an early breakfast, filled the Lanchester's tank with petrol and set off for Wales. The importance of establishing contact with Hugh Mansfield, Frank's artist brother, now seemed paramount.

By mid-afternoon he reached Cardiff, driving past the tram depot and Municipal Power Station into the bustling shopping centre of Queen Street. He had no idea in which part of the city Hugh Mansfield lived, but luck gave him a welcome boost. He noticed *'The National Art Gallery of Wales'*, an impressive white building, and on entering discovered two masterly oil paintings by 'the local artist Hugh Mansfield'. The helpful lady behind the desk provided him with the artist's address, being under the impression that he was anxious to purchase the pictures. He couldn't have asked for a better start.

On leaving the gallery, he followed his usual practice of buying a map of the local streets. A half-hour later he knocked on the ornate front door of an elegant terraced residence in the Cathedral Road district of Cardiff. Glancing around at the finely curtained windows, the well preserved paintwork and the hanging flower-baskets, he got the impression that Hugh Mansfield was not a struggling artist striving for survival, but a highly successful painter who was not short of a penny or two.

The door was opened by a neatly-dressed maid. She gave him a pleasant smile and enquired what his business was.

'I am interested in buying one of Mister Mansfield's paintings.'

She glanced at her watch. 'Mister Mansfield's due to finish his art class in a few minutes. Would you like to come in, sir?'

Edwin nodded and stepped over the threshold into a hallway decorated with several tasteful sculptures, and where three magnificent scenic paintings hung upon the walls. It seemed incredible that the fortunes of two brothers could have diverged so widely.

The maid took his hat, invited him to take a seat and departed, saying, 'He won't be long, sir.'

As Edwin waited, the sound of a voice came to him from a room that led off the hall. Rising to his feet, he stepped towards the open doorway and immediately saw a neat triangle of pubic hair and a pair of pert young breasts. A dark-haired girl, completely naked, was posing on a pedestal. Around her, busy at canvases and easels were some half-dozen students of both sexes. The voice he heard came from their tutor who was beyond Edwin's field of vision - obviously Hugh Mansfield. He was extolling the exquisite fragility of feminine beauty, the virtues of good brush-work, the attention that was necessary to lighting and angles - but even as Edwin listened, the session was concluded, bringing forth disappointed sighs from the students, and shortly the girl was wrapping herself in a gown.

There was much chattering as the students set about cleaning their brushes and putting away their paints. It was then that Hugh Mansfield strode from the room, dressed in his artist's smock and wiping his hands on a cloth.

'Hugh Mansfield?' Edwin enquired, though there was no doubt in his mind.

The artist bowed in acknowledgement. He was a tall silver-haired man, with a profile as elegant as those of his sculptures.

'I'm interested in buying a picture or two,' Edwin said. 'I was very impressed with your work at the gallery and wondered if I could see some more.'

Mansfield's eyes narrowed slightly, but then he smiled and said, 'I've got some work displayed in my studio upstairs. Would you like to wait a moment while I check to see what pictures are available.'

'Certainly.' Edwin watched the artist move up the staircase and disappear into the higher regions of the house. Five minutes later he returned.

'That's fine. Would you like to come this way?'

Edwin nodded and followed him, their feet making no sound on the thick stair-carpet. 'A lovely place you've got here, Mister Mansfield.'

Mansfield turned and nodded. 'In the main, it's thanks to the art lessons I give. I make as much money from the lessons as I do from selling my work. But I believe we have a responsibility to the future. Real talent is so rare. It must be nurtured at all costs.'

'I agree,' Edwin said. 'And there are so many beautiful scenes in this country that can be perfectly preserved on canvas. This one for example.' He gestured to a painting as the reached the first floor.

'That's the Solway Firth,' Mansfield said. 'I painted that a couple of years back.'

Edwin studied it, noting the familiarity of the island-dotted seascape and the wide expanse of yellow sand - even the derelict straggle of red-stone cottages. 'Beautiful,' he commented, and followed Mansfield across the landing to another staircase. A half-minute later they were in the studio which had been built into the attic - a large room, bright with the light streaming through fanlights and smaller side windows. The studio was crammed with easels, pallets, paints, brushes, a posing couch and various other paraphernalia associated with art. Painted canvases were stacked against the walls.

'Now then, Mister ...?'

Edwin had been prepared for this question. 'Johnson. Edward Johnson.'

'Now then, Mister Johnson, what sort of work are you interested in.?'

'Scenic ... scenes of Wales.'

They spent a good half hour in looking at various works that Mansfield had done - all quite magnificent, but Edwin noticed that there were paintings by other painters in the studio. 'Before I make a final decision,' he said. 'Could I have a browse through the rest of these pictures?'

'Of course,' Mansfield nodded. 'Take your time. I'm doing a sketch. I'll carry on working while you have a look around.'

Edwin slowly examined the remainder of the paintings, stooping to peer at the artists' names. At last he found what he sought: A scene of great beauty - Snowdonia in the spring, complete with snow-tipped peak, foothills and green lower meadows. Before speaking he double checked the artist's sprawling signature: Gareth Williams.

'This is magnificent,' he remarked enthusiastically. 'Just what I wanted.'

Mansfield was immediately at his side. 'It's a fine work.'

'Do you know the painter?' Edwin enquired, conscious that his heart was beating faster.

Mansfield was hesitant. 'Y-yes. The most precious and outstanding talent. He was a student of mine ... some years ago of course.'

'Of course.' Edwin gazed at the picture, his eyes bright with genuine admiration. 'Do you know how much he's asking for this?'

'Five-hundred pounds.'

Edwin whistled through his lips. 'Couldn't go above three-hundred - but I really would like the painting. Is there any way I could contact Williams and make an offer? Do you have his address?'

Edwin never expected an answer. He was more interested in the type of reaction it might evoke in Mansfield.

Fleeting confusion passed across the artist's face, but then he regained his composure. 'No ... I don't have his address, but ...'

'I might go up to four-hundred,' Edwin prompted.

'Come back this time tomorrow. I'll see if I can get an answer for you.'

'Oh dear,' Edwin frowned. 'I shall be leaving Cardiff at lunchtime.'

'Well ... make it tomorrow morning then. Ten o'clock.'

'That'll be ideal. I do hope he accepts my offer.'

As he left, Edwin was aware of an oddness in the artist's manner. The charm had vanished. It was as if he regretted his impulsive reaction never to turn away the prospect of a sale. As he shook hands in farewell, the pleasantness in his eyes had been replaced by wariness.

Edwin was well satisfied. He had set a trap and Mansfield had walked straight into it. If he was able to check so quickly with Gareth as to whether the price offered for his painting was acceptable, the Welshman couldn't be far away.

When his visitor seemed well clear of the premises, Hugh Mansfield, his face creased in a frown, climbed the stairs to his attic-studio. From here he went along a narrow passageway and up a further flight of steps to a small landing from which a door led off. He knocked on this and called, 'Gareth, he's gone now. You'd better come down. It's time we had a talk.'

Mansfield was waiting in his studio when Gareth Williams appeared. He looked dishevelled and tired. 'Who was 'e?' he enquired.

Mansfield shrugged his shoulders. 'I don't know, but he certainly didn't seem like a policeman. He caught me off guard. He said he wanted to buy your Snowdon picture ...'

Gareth swore. 'What did he look like?'

'Pink cheeks, round face, good clothes ... and well spoken.'

'Sounds like the devil who was pokin' around up at Cullipol ...' and then in a whisper he added, 'Edwin Carter, damn him.'

'Well, one thing's certain,' Mansfield said. 'You can't stay here. The police'll come in next, then we'll all be in trouble.'

Gareth gave a glum nod. 'But where can we go?'

Mansfield scratched his chin, thinking. 'I know where you'll be safe for a few nights, until you make up your mind. After that, I think you should go abroad.'

'You're right,' Gareth murmured. 'The further the better. Maybe Australia.'

As he left Hugh Mansfield's house, Edwin was already forming a plan. He felt convinced that Gareth, and please God, Rosena, were now close at hand, though the fact that they might be hidden in the artist's attic did not enter his mind. He did however suspect that Mansfield would try to contact Gareth in order to ascertain the price for the picture. With an answer promised by ten o'clock tomorrow morning, Edwin found himself banking on the hope that Mansfield would leave his home and go to wherever the Welshman was hiding. Surely, then, it would only be a matter of following him.

He debated whether or not to contact the police at this stage, but decided against it, being reluctant to interrupt his vigil of the artist's residence. Even a minute away, could enable the trail to be lost. Once the present whereabouts of Gareth Williams was established, he would hand matters over to the police for them to make the necessary arrest.

With his car parked some fifty yards away in a cul-de-sac, he stationed himself around a street corner, finding a low brick wall on which to sit. From here, he had an adequate view of Mansfield's front door without being obvious himself. He glanced at his watch. It had just gone 5 PM. He might have a very long wait on his hands, but if his vigilance bore fruit, then it would be worth every tedious second.

Apart from the arrival of a student, complete with canvas, and his subsequent departure two hours later, there were no comings or goings through the front entrance of the Mansfield house. Edwin began to wonder, with sickening intensity, if the artist might make use of a back door to slip away to his secret rendezvous. Why hadn't he thought of that before?

As the evening dragged by, he became more and more convinced that he'd bungled the situation, possibly missed an incredible opportunity to bring his search to a conclusion. He should have gone to the police in the first place. This time his normal ardour to see things through when the trail became hot, might have misfired.

An assorted stream of pedestrians coming from nearby houses eyed him with varying degrees of inquisitiveness. Several dogs came along and sniffed him, and a gypsy lady sold him a bunch of lavender 'For good luck, my luv!' Presently, he took to pacing up and down the side-street, but his gaze was never far from the front-door in question. At last the light started to fade, the street lamps came on. There were lit windows in various rooms of Mansfield's house, but the curtains were drawn, and as time went by the lights were turned off - except one, an apparent fan-light, near the very top of the roof.

It was near midnight, with the street's activity having dwindled and a soft rain moistening the cobblestones, that Edwin's senses were brought to a state of alertness. A car with just its sidelights on had drawn up outside Mansfield's house. Edwin edged closer, taking full advantage of the shadows. He recognised the car as a new-model Wolseley. To his surprise, Mansfield himself got out, quietly closed the car door, mounted the steps to his front door and entered the house. Clearly he had left earlier by some rear exit to fetch his car which must have been garaged elsewhere.

With eager anticipation Edwin awaited developments. His patience was not stretched. Within a couple of minutes, Mansfield reappeared, followed by two shadowy figures. All three got into the Wolsley. Edwin didn't delay. He was sprinting away, down the street, towards his own car, by the time Mansfield had settled himself into his driving seat. With desperate haste he cranked the Lanchester's engine and was edging into the main street as Mansfield's rear light disappeared to the right. Driving with his own lights off, he followed, praying that an alert policeman wouldn't stop him - and that Mansfield wouldn't suspect he was being trailed. He was thankful for the soft, sweet purr of the Lanchester's engine.

Keeping as close to the other vehicle as he dared, Edwin felt convinced that the two people accompanying Mansfield were Gareth and Rosena, and his heart was pounding with excitement. He realised that they were travelling into Cardiff's poorer district, close to the docks. The cobbled streets were deserted, poorly lit, the tram-lines glistening in the rain, and on each side the old buildings were crammed closely together. The Wolsley turned to the left. Edward took the same turning, and then groaned. Ahead, the road forked - and there was no sign of the other car. He gambled, took the right fork, and after ten minutes cruising the dreary, darkened streets he was forced to admit that his quarry had disappeared. Either Mansfield had intentionally taken the alternative direction, or had deliberately shaken him off.

Totally sickened, he patrolled the dismal streets, widening his field of search, his disappointment deepening. Twenty minutes later he stopped his car close to an old office building. Upon its wall he could just make out the sign: MORGAN - SHIPPING & COAL AGENTS. He tried to marshal his thoughts. He was convinced that he had been within a stone's throw of Gareth and Rosena as they had been whisked away from Mansfield's house. By this time, having thrown him from their trail, they were probably speeding out of Cardiff altogether. Clearly Mansfield hadn't been as gullible as he'd hoped. He wondered what condition Rosena was in. Was she ill? Or had she meekly accepted the need for retreat - perhaps in the same way as she had from the Solway Firth. What power did Gareth have over her? Or was she still deeply in love with this man, struggling with him to escape the terrible fate that awaited if the law triumphed. But surely, no matter what, she could never condone what he'd done.

Edwin realised he would gain little by sitting out the night in this depressing corner of Cardiff. He would have to seek lodgings somewhere, and then tomorrow morning go to the police and hope that they would take up the trail in a more professional way than he had.

Wearily, he slipped into gear and allowed the car to move forward. He was still angry with himself for allowing his quarry to escape. He turned around the side of the gloomy office block, found himself in a square and passing a row of high, tenement-type houses, relics of the Victorian era. Suddenly his eyes widened with disbelief.

Parked at the kerbside outside the very last one ... was Mansfield's Wolseley.

Edwin lingered only long enough to ascertain the name of the square - Rothsay Square; then, whispering a thank-you to his bunch of lucky lavender, he accelerated towards the city centre - towards the police station in City Hall Road.

Chapter Thirty-five

AFTER HUGH MANSFIELD had left them, Gareth tried to calm Rosena with his usual groundless assurances. They unpacked their few possessions in the small, dimly-lit garret-room in Rothsay Square, and presently she lay down on the bed, his words driving her into exhausted sleep.

Mansfield had promised that nobody would discover that they were here. The land-lady was an old friend of his and he'd paid her well.

But early the following morning, when Gareth rose, bleary-eyed, and gazed from the small window, he realised that this hiding place was a trap. Although he had a good view of the square and the adjacent shipping agent's offices, it would do him little good. By the time the police appeared, his escape would be cut off. They would block the narrow staircase. The only other way out was through the window, and there was a drop of forty feet to the pavement below. Furthermore, close against the old house were railings like upturned spears. He shuddered, then he looked up, saw the rusty guttering within hand-reach. If it would support his weight, he might just stand a chance of escaping across the roofs.

Turning away from the window, he regarded Rosena as she slept. He knew she hated him - but she had betrayed him and he had to have some leverage over her to prevent the same thing happening again. She placed the baby's safety above all else. An important aspect of his salvation lay in keeping her fears alive. If necessary he could live with her hatred ...

But for a moment he recalled the way she had looked when he had painted her at Megstow Quay. She had seemed like a goddess, a Cornish Aphrodite, with an expression of enchantment spread across her face, her eyes gazing into a future full of promise. How different she was now, not yet fully recovered from her pregnancy; with gaunt, sunken cheeks and darkness beneath her eyes. Yet at night she did not shirk her marital duties, nor deny him his rights. He knew he had to shield his Cornish wife from the outside world, just as he himself had to remain hidden. Once either of them were recognised, the authorities would swoop in and their chance of escape would be finished. More and more he was haunted by the gruesome prospect of the noose. At night he would dream that he was choking, bathed in sweat, clawing at his throat, too late to release it from constricting rope.

Next day passed quietly, with sunshine streaming into the little room. The window was left open to catch any slight cooling breeze and once a sparrow swooped in, then, sensing the room's confinement, departed. Rosena sorted through what possessions they had, but Gareth was insistent that everything was kept within easy reach, ready for a quick getaway if such became necessary.

He had ventured out once. He had crept down the three flights of dilapidated stairs, passing doorways from which he could hear a mixture of profane voices and babies crying. From the ground-floor room had come the smell of frying onions which made his mouth water. He was thankful that the inmates were far too involved with their own affairs to spare him a glance or ask embarrassing questions. With his cap pulled low, he reached the street and found a small grocery shop around the corner. He purchased food, drink, and some Epsom Salts to help ease the discomfort in Rosena's swollen breasts. He had once done the same for Bronwyn and she had said it had helped. Now, pleased with himself, he retraced his steps to the room.

Rosena could not understand him; how could he at one moment be cruel beyond imagination, and at others appear so considerate? It was almost as if he could not help himself from committing the most loathsome deeds - nor afterwards prevent his conscience from tormenting him - although never sufficiently to make him confess his sins or attempt to redress them. He found strength in his piety; in his belief that the Lord spoke to him and guided him along the paths he must take. But such guidance seemed to take scant account of the feelings and sufferings of others.

Throughout the day, he spent long hours pacing the room, his brow creased with anguish. When he grew tired he would hurl himself upon the bed, sometimes lapsing into restless sleep, muttering incoherently to himself. On other occasions he would reach for her to make love, grunting, animal like, until he was sated. She did not resist him; she surrendered in the hope that it might afford them, in their different ways, some respite.

Once she asked him how long they would stay in this room. 'I told you,' he retorted. 'Until Hugh arranges somethin'.'

After that, they seldom spoke; she felt that there was nothing more either could say. She would doubt the truth of whatever he might tell her; and she had already vented her feelings to him with regard to her baby. Further conversation seemed pointless.

But she did have cause to speak shortly after midnight. He had lapsed into his usual, agitated slumber - but she had remained awake, mentally and physically too fatigued to sleep, thoughts of Emma Jane and what might have happened to her forming an unrelenting pain in her head.

When she heard the stairs of the old house creaking, instinct had her sitting up in alarm, gasping, 'What's that!'

Gareth needed no further rousing; he was out of bed in an instant, crouching naked and listening in the darkness. They both heard the sound again, the cautious, unmistakable tread of feet on the landing outside - and then a hammering on the door, bludgeoning their ears, almost splintering the wood.

'Open up. It's the police!'

Gareth's hand clawed into her shoulder. His lips so close to her ear, she felt his spittle touch her. ''Old 'em up long as you can!'

He had no time to gather his clothes. He blundered across the dark room, stumbling over his boots. At the window, he climbed onto the chair he'd left in readiness, forced his leg over the window-ledge and got his head and shoulders through. He gazed at the dimly lit pavement forty feet below. He steadied himself against a sudden wave of giddiness, but then he heard the room's door being hammered again and he knew he had no alternative.

He drew his knee up to his chin. He forced his other leg over the window-ledge, pulled the casement window closed behind him, and, reaching up, clawed onto the rusty guttering. He was relieved by its solidity. Gripping tightly, not looking down, he levered the bare soles of his feet against the rough brick wall and hauled himself upward. Seconds later he was over the guttering and inching his way up the roof. This was far steeper than he'd anticipated. Between clenched teeth, he prayed that his movement would not sound in the room below. By now the police must have forced their way in.

Beneath his naked body he was aware that the slated roofing was old, even crumbling in places. The smell of its decay, its dampness, filled his nostrils. Any rash movement could send an avalanche of slates clattering down into the street - and himself with it. He could feel the sweat beading out on his body, trickling down his back, chest and legs. He remembered the upturned spikes of the railings, and groaned. Thank God the night was moonless. Not even a star pierced the heavens. Without the darkness, passers-by, or policemen posted near the front entrance, would have spotted him.

Clinging like a wingless fly, he sucked in breath, pleading that his lungs wouldn't erupt into coughing. He could hear the murmur of voices from the room below; he even heard somebody open the window, but he knew that if they looked up, the out-thrust of the guttering and roof would conceal his prone body from view. If they climbed up after him, he would push them off.

Flattened against the slates, he lost count of time. It seemed like hours. His fingers, his toes, his every muscle, ached from the long cling. He lapsed into stupor, coming awake suddenly as he felt his grip slackening.

With relief, from beneath him, he heard the bedroom door close with a bang and the receding clump of boots on the staircase. Presently, too, the slam of the front door sounded, seeming to make the entire house shudder, and then the murmur of voices moving away down the street. He allowed himself a smile. Rosena had fobbed them off, but for how long?

He forced his numbed limbs into movement - and that was when the slates slid from under him. He clawed frantically, seeking something to grip ... there was nothing. He was slipping, slipping. Loosened slates slid down the roof, gathering speed, clattering over the guttering, plunging downward. A roaring was in his head; he felt suffocated by the proximity of his own death.

His body had slewed into a horizontal position. His downward momentum was increasing as he flung his arms ahead of him.

Suddenly, his right hand closed over the surprising firmness of the guttering. By a miracle his grip held, his rigid arm arresting his slide. He eased his other arm across to reinforce his hold. For a moment he sprawled there, gulping in air, feeling the wild pump of his heart. He could hear slates shattering on the pavement below, and knew, but for the grace of God, his body could have been amongst them.

At last, slowly and with infinite care, he worked his leg over the guttering. With his bare toes, he kicked open the unlatched window, noticing that the gas lamp had been turned on from inside.

Within a minute he was back in the room, sprawled exhausted on the floor, panting with relief. But then he realised that he was not yet out of danger. The smash of tiles on the pavement must have alerted his pursuers.

He raised his head to see Rosena in her nightdress gazing down at him, her face deathly pale in the gas-light. He had never seen such an expression of mixed emotions. When her lips moved, her voice came strangely taut, and her words puzzled him: 'I'm sorry, Gareth. You gave me no option.'

His puzzlement increased, but he had no time to question her meaning. Instead, he was grunting with shock as iron-like hands seized his arms from behind. A hard knee was slammed into the small of his back, driving the breath from his body. Simultaneously, handcuffs clamped over his wrists. 'Worked like a bloody treat, it did!' a gruff voice announced triumphantly.

A detective and a police sergeant had positioned themselves beside the window, waiting for their prey to drop through. The ruse of departing footsteps had worked perfectly.

Rosena gazed down with wide eyes and flared nostrils, her fingers raised to her lips. The trap had been her idea.

There was something pathetic about Gareth flattened face-down, naked, helpless, winded, held by the two burly police-officers. All at once he looked much smaller than ever before. And now, after all his frenzied efforts to escape, tears were flowing uncontrollably from her eyes. They were not tears of thankfulness; they were not tears of happiness; nor even tears of relief. In that moment she did not hate him. Instead, she was swept with inexplicable remorse. Circumstance had forced her to destroy this man who had once lifted her to heights of ecstasy, subsequently plunged her into an abyss of wretchedness, and with whom she had shared these days of furtive retreat - the man she had married.

But she expressed nothing of this. She simply sobbed out four words: 'I want my baby.' And then, as further footsteps sounded on the stairs and more jubilant police officers crowded into the room, she swung round and could hardly believe her tear-filled eyes.

Edwin was standing before her.

She had no control over her movement. She had no consciousness of going to him, of reaching out for him. All she knew was that suddenly she was in his arms, sobbing his name, feeling the strength in his body, sensing, like a drowning swimmer, she had struggled for survival - and found a rock.

'You're safe now,' he was murmuring, 'safe now.'

'Australia,' she heard her voice gasp. 'I thought 'ee were in Australia ...'

'I came back for you, my love. You're all I ever wanted.'

Chapter Thirty-six

'ROSENA ... DO 'EE TAKE THIS MAN, Edwin John Carter, here present, for your lawful wedded husband?' The Reverend Godfrey's question hung in the expectant hush of the small Megstow Quay church, St Arthur's. Not a cough or a sigh sounded from the congregation, not the shriek of a gull from outside. It seemed to Rosena that even the waves, far below on the Cornish shore, were holding back, waiting for the response.

It was three months to the day since Gareth had been charged with the murder of Jenny Killigrew.

Now, Rosena, the full bloom of her beauty and health restored, stood in the elegant green-silk paleness of the dress Beryl had helped her choose at Harrods. A loop of raven hair escaped fashionably from her neat cloche hat, showing the same lustre as the black, patent-leather shoes buckled at her ankles. About her neck was the double row of pearls that Edwin had given her. Edwin was wearing a suit of finely woven tweed, his brown shoes glistening like mirrors.

Rosena breathed in the familiar smells of the old church - the mixture of tar, brine, fish and age. Here it was that her father John Bray had knelt so many times in prayer. Here it was that he had been finally laid to rest, unaware of the awesome experiences that were yet to befall his daughter. But today, as the future beckoned her, like a rose opening to the sun, she wanted to cherish this moment, yet she was momentarily fearful that everything might be no more than a dream, that she might suddenly awake to find herself plunged into the horrors of the past. She touched with her thumb the gold band, glistening, new and cold upon her finger, felt its solidity, its strength - and she knew she was not dreaming, that nothing could take away the reality of this day. She thought: this is the second time, within four months, that I have stood before God in an act of marriage. I must be truly worthy of this second chance. She raised her eyes and gazed into Edwin's loving face, saw the gentle smile at the corners of his mouth, the happiness in his blue eyes, the anticipation. Her next words would be the prize, the hope for which had drawn him back from the far reaches of the world, had driven him in relentless and finally fruitful search.

'I do,' she said firmly, and then on the whisper of her breath she repeated, 'I do ... oh yes.'

Edwin's expression relaxed into radiant joy.

'Then each take the other's right hand,' the Reverend Godfrey murmured, and when they had complied, he continued in a louder voice, 'You have declared your consent before the church. May the Lord in his goodness strengthen your consent and fill you both with his blessings. Before God, I declare you married persons and whom God hath joined together let no man pull asunder.' And then, as the congregation murmured, 'Amen,' he smiled at Edwin. 'You may kiss the bride now.'

Edwin needed no second bidding. He took his wife in his arms, his lips finding hers, feeling the soft acceptance and promise that was his at last.

There came the sudden gush of exhaled breaths from the congregation, the satisfied murmuring as the most beautiful part of the ceremony was completed.

A minute later, Rosena, whirling through a dream world, felt a tentative touch on her shoulder and she turned towards Tom and saw a tear glistening in his eye. It seemed but a second ago that she had walked up the aisle on his arm, conscious of the fact that he was wearing his Sunday-best suit - the very same as he had worn when he had come to the cottage to propose to her. She knew, with all the weight of the past upon them, what a noble sacrifice it was for him 'to give her away', yet he insisted that there could be no other. Now she kissed him with tenderness, and whispered, 'I love you, Tom. I always will,' and there was no disloyalty to Edwin in her words, for her feelings towards her brother would always be precious.

In the front pew, Jeremy and Beryl stood. Jeremy, immaculately dressed in pin-strip suit and spats, had consented at last to give his blessing to the marriage, having obtained privately from Rosena her forgiveness for the proposition he had once made. She had made little of it, expressing the immense gratitude she felt for all the kindness that he and Beryl had shown her. Now, emotion was welling up in Beryl and she dabbed at her moist eyes and plump cheeks with a lace handkerchief.

The villagers of Megstow Quay and St Mags had turned out in force for the wedding; even the bereaved Killigrews were present, standing quietly at the back, concealing their own thoughts and regrets.

The recriminations of the past had been replaced by the knowledge that Rosena Bray was the first real celebrity ever to come from Megstow Quay. Her photograph had appeared on the front pages of all the national newspapers. She had given evidence in court, and the incredible story of Gareth Williams, former church minister, had unfolded in gruesome detail. Women had lined the streets, raised their fists and jeered at him as he'd been led into the Assize Court.

It had been during the trial that Edwin had made a discovery that was unrelated to the murder, but was enough to lift his spirits to the heavens. He had delved into books about marriage customs, and in particular about the different wedding ceremonies held in Scotland. At the library he discovered a history of Gretna and therein read that one of the conditions necessary to legitimise a blacksmith marriage was a three week residence in Scotland prior to the ceremony. Suspecting a possible loop-hole, Edwin had placed the matter in the hands of his solicitor. The latter established that Williams had not in fact lived north of the border for the requisite time, Mansfield Island being in England.

This being the case, it took only a fortnight before Rosena's marriage to Gareth was annulled. Strange emotion deep in her soul had brought tears of remorse to her eyes. Gareth had implanted in her the seed of their mutual passion, a seed that had grown into her beloved daughter. There would always be part of him with her. But he had betrayed her and taken from her something that could never be restored, her innocence and her trust.

At first she had felt unworthy of venturing into marriage again, that she was betraying herself in the eyes of God. But Edwin's love, his kindness, his hope for the future - and Tom's blunt advice to see sense, for Emma Jane's sake, as well as your own! - had stemmed her doubts, and provided the first steps towards re-building her pride

The wedding service concluded with a rousing rendition of *All Things Bright and Beautiful,* and soon the happy couple and their witnesses, Tom and Aunt Beryl, moved to the small vestry and the marriage certificate was completed, signed and witnessed. As, with her arm linked through Edwin's, Rosena walked down the aisle, she held her head high and her face was exultant. Edwin knew that she had never looked lovelier or happier. In the bright autumnal sunshine and speckled with confetti, they enjoyed the ritual of photographs. Even the London press was present.

Afterwards, they did not directly enter their white-ribboned car. Instead, they turned towards the hillside graveyard and Rosena placed her bouquet of white irises, primula and roses against the headstone of John Bray. With gentle fingers she traced each letter of his name, feeling a closeness with the man who had cared for her as lovingly as her true father would ever have done. Standing back, she said a silent prayer of thanks for his life and that of her adoptive mother, Emma. She knew that, things as they now were, John and Emma Bray would have been proud to see her at last married to Edwin Carter, whose love she would cherish for the rest of her days.

They had come to Talmouth's grandest hotel for their wedding night. Rosena had never known such a romantic bed, with its four decorative posts, floral canopy, pillows trimmed with lace, and silk sheets. She had bathed and slipped into the shimmering ivory gown Edwin had given her, enjoying its smooth coolness against her skin. She rested back on the softness of the eiderdown and allowed contentment to flood over her. When booking, Edwin hadn't mentioned that they were on their honeymoon. Whatever must they have thought of us, she wondered, arriving with confetti in our hair, and a baby in tow! She smiled as she listened to Emma Jane's satisfied gurgling. Edwin had been insistent that the little girl shared their honeymoon. 'After all,' he'd laughed, 'she's as much part of the family as I am ... and nobody's going to leave me behind!'

From where Rosena lay, she could see her husband silhouetted against the window as he rocked the baby in his arms, humming softly. He had bottle-fed her, even changed her, and now he was lulling her gently to sleep. She heard him whisper, 'Thank goodness those nasty scars have disappeared. You'll be as beautiful as your mum soon.'

For a moment Rosena's mind drifted happily - but then, like a rock looming out of the mist, the memory of her last wedding night, scarcely four months ago, intruded - and she frowned. She imagined Gareth now, gaunt and white, a look of madness in his eyes. Each night, as his trial reached its final stages, he would be led back to his cell; then would come the suffocating clang of the door, and the merciless click and jangle of keys. And all the while the terrible black prospect of death was looming over him.

It seemed his shadow would forever darken each shaft of happiness which came to her. After they had placed the rope around his neck, as surely they must, could she ever live at peace with herself knowing that she, as much as anybody else, had been instrumental in bringing him to his death?

She shuddered, closed her eyes, hoping that at this moment, when she should be supremely happy, Gareth would stop haunting her. But he did not - and she groaned.

Hearing her, Edwin placed the baby in the hotel cot. He lowered himself carefully onto the bed beside Rosena and slipped his arm around her shoulders.

'I know the past worries you, my love ... but soon we'll leave it far behind and time will soften the way you feel.'

She turned, gazing into his face. 'You always know what I'm thinkin'. Edwin ... am I so transparent?'

He smiled. He smoothed her cheek with his fingers, feeling the moistness of tears. 'There's no wall between us, my love. What you suffer, I suffer. We share everything, the good and the bad.' He drew himself up, regarding her admiringly. 'Your tears look like tiny diamonds on your cheeks.'

Her lips quivered, then relaxed into a smile. 'Oh Edwin, I love you.' She kissed his fingers, one by one, lingering over his wedding ring on which their initials were engraved.

'Today is the happiest day of my life, Rosena. I feel I want to sing out loud.'

She shook her head. 'You can't. You'll wake the baby.'

He kissed the tip of her nose. 'Being with you is what I always dreamed of, always lived for.'

He drew her lips to his, tasting the saltiness of her tears, feeling the tender, yielding acceptance of her mouth.

'Love me,' she murmured. She unbuttoned his shirt, slipped her hand inside, feeling the hair and muscle of his chest. 'Love me now, Edwin. Make me part of you.'

He unfastened her gown and drew it back from her breasts and shoulders. 'I chose this gown,' he murmured, 'because it unfastened more easily than the others.'

She laughed, then she said, 'My turn,' and she made him stand up, pushing his hands away as he attempted to help her undo his collar stud. As she proceeded to the remaining buttons of his shirt and trousers, he said, 'Shoes and socks first.'

When they were completely naked, he lifted her in his arms and gently rested her down on the bed. He pressed his face into the softness of her breasts, breathing in the perfume of the soap she had used, then he kissed her cheek and touched the lobe of her ear with his tongue; she giggled and said, 'You make me burn all over.' He moved to her hair, enjoying its fragrance, losing himself momentarily in its dark strands.

Undulating slowly, she pressed herself against him. A moment later she was sighing contentedly as she felt his tongue tantalising her body.

He did not hurry. He wanted to savour every second, every taste. His fingers wandered to her pubis. She groaned with ecstasy, begging him to stay, to go deeper, but before she could trap him by clenching her thighs, he moved on, teasing her laughingly, his tongue finding her nipples.

At last, when he had explored every part of her body, he gazed into her face again. 'In all the world, in all the heavens,' he whispered, 'there is no one more beautiful, more perfect, than you, Rosena, my love.'

Her hazel eyes were wide and alight with desire, energy, urgency, then she lowered her eyelids, smiling, feigning surrender. She was trembling, her breath quickening.

He entered her, whispering her name over and over; she curled her legs around his back, gripping him tightly, casting aside her disguise of abjectness. They were both gasping, laughing, crying out incoherently as their love overflowed, lifting them to a paradise neither had known before ... and the past was a million miles away.

Next morning, she was awakened by the screeching of gulls from outside the window. She opened her eyes to see him gazing smilingly into her face. 'My tigress,' he whispered, 'welcome to our first full day of marriage.' She could see the hairs bristling on his chin, the faint rosiness in his cheeks. His lips descended to hers in a lingering kiss. Hugging him against her she felt his hardness, his strength and she yearned to absorb every part of his body into hers.

After they had made love, they lay back in each other's arms, happy in their exhaustion. 'Do you know,' she presently murmured, 'the Cornish have a custom. Sometimes on their weddin' night, the bride and groom are visited by a 'shallal' - a band of infernal music. They blow whistles and horns, and bang kettles and pans and tea-trays.'

'Were you afraid they might find us here?'

'Maybe they did,' she smiled. 'I wouldn't 'ave noticed.'

He laughed and kissed her - but then Emma Jane began to cry for her breakfast. Edwin climbed from the bed. 'I'll get some boiled water from downstairs.' He pulled on his clothes and checked his buttons. 'Better make sure I'm respectable.' He kissed the tip of her nose and left her.

While waiting for water to be heated, Edwin went to the hotel reception desk and bought a morning newspaper.

When he returned to the bedroom, carrying a jug, Rosena was sitting on the bed, rocking Emma Jane back and forth, singing a nursery rhyme to her. 'I've ordered breakfast served in our room,' he said, 'on a silver tray with a bottle of champagne.'

'You mustn't spoil me, my love,' she smiled.

It wasn't until she had made the baby's bottle, had allowed it to cool in a bowl of cold water, and had pressed the teat between Emma Jane's tiny, grateful lips, that Edwin scanned the front page, his attention immediately drawn to the short column near the foot:

> ### *TRIAL OF FORMER*
> ### *CHURCH MINISTER CONCLUDED*
>
> *At Cardiff Assize Court former church Minister Gareth Williams was yesterday found not guilty of the murder of Mrs Jennie Turnwell, there being insufficient evidence for conviction. He was accordingly acquitted and walked from the court, a free man ..*

Chapter Thirty-seven

Dear Tom

I hope all is well and that King Neptune has been generous to you and the other fishermen. I think of Megstow Quay often, and of the happy years I spent there, and of the people I loved. Thank you for selling the cottage on my behalf; I hope the new family will be happy there.

I was very sorry that following Gareth's trial and my return to and from Mansfield Island, there was no time to see you again and explain what had happened. We sailed for Australia within two days. Now the arrival of the newspaper cuttings from Aunt Beryl has brought the past back to us.

The voyage out here was something I shall never forget. We sailed from Southampton and came via Gibraltar and the Mediterranean. We called at Port Said (where I rode a camel!) and then went through the Suez Canal into the Red Sea. It was so hot, but it was lovely. Edwin and I took full advantage of the swimming pool on board the ship, and we had great fun playing deck games and enjoying the ship's social life. Even so it was nice to disembark at Melbourne and know that we had finally arrived.

Edwin's employers were delighted to see him back and they have made me very welcome. We now have a roomy house on the outskirts of the city, and I am getting used to the Australian way of life. I hope that one day we will visit England, but meanwhile I am very content with my life and am so thankful that I made the right decision in marrying Edwin; thanks in no small measure to your 'gentle' persuasion as well as his!

Edwin is very busy and is clearly well respected by everybody he has dealings with. The textile trade seems to be booming, and I have been out riding with him, visiting the far-flung sheep stations. The country is so big, and we often see kangaroos, or 'roos' as the Aussies call them.

We are very fortunate to have an excellent income, and our standard of living, though basic, is far higher than I thought it would be. Emma Jane has flourished and is a good little girl. She is desperately trying to talk, but as yet she cannot form the words, but I'm sure it won't be long. She loves Edwin - and he is a real father to her. And I am glad to say that she is to have a brother or sister - all being well. They tell me that the second birth is easier than the first.

Memories of the trial still haunt me, though not as vividly as before. I hated standing up in court and answering all those questions, and seeing Gareth watching me. I had no way of knowing what was in his mind. Thank God Edwin stayed close by to give me strength. Gradually of course the story came out ... of Jenny Turnwell finding him in Trethomas and turning up at the guesthouse. No doubt Gareth gave her lodgings to try and pacify her, but she kept demanding money for her child ... and when Bronwyn found out, she was furious that he had betrayed and deceived her yet again.

Edwin and I were on our honeymoon when we heard of Gareth's acquittal, hardly believing that the jury had accepted his version of events - that it had been Bronwyn who had stabbed Jennie to death in a wild frenzy - and not him. And afterwards, he and Bronwyn had fled, on Hugh Mansfield's advice, to the remote Solway Firth. Gareth never mentioned to me that it was Bronwyn and not himself who had committed murder. He knew I wouldn't have believed him. I could believe nothing he said. Of course he always claimed that it was remorse over petty theft and shame that gave Bronwyn the seizure. The whole business is so awful. It makes me shudder just to think of it.

It was only a couple of days after Edwin and I returned from our honeymoon and we were in the middle of our preparations to sail for Australia, that detectives called on us at Beckenham. They wanted me to return to Mansfield Island and lead them to the spot where Bronwyn's grave was.

I don't think I could have done it had Edwin not come with me. It was weird going back to that ghostly island where I had been a virtual prisoner. I even visited the cottage, and stood in the rooms where I had endured so much. Every nook and cranny reminded me of Gareth.

I led the police to the spot where he had shown me Bronwyn's grave. You can imagine my shock when we found no piled stones, no cross. But I knew it was the right place because I recognised the odd shape of the trees. The police dug down into the earth, but they found nothing. Gareth had faked the grave for my benefit, no doubt hoping to quell my suspicions and make me more amenable to him, as well as muddying the waters if anybody should attempt to track him down.

Both Edwin and I felt relieved to see the grave empty and wanted to believe, for Gwenda's sake, that Bronwyn still survived. But then we realised that even if she was alive, she would be found, arrested and charged with the murder of Jennie Turnwell. Poor Gwenda. How awful for a child to have such parents.

So we set sail for Australia not knowing what to believe, and wondering what Gareth would do now that he was free again. We heard nothing of him until today, when Aunt Beryl's newspaper cuttings arrived in the post. I suspect you have seen them.

No doubt Gareth thought he had succeeded in escaping the law until Megson's collie unearthed the corpse on the far side of the island, and the police confirmed that it was Bronwyn's. She had been stabbed to death in exactly the same way as Jennie. But from what I read, the damning thing was that Kathy broke down when the police questioned her, and revealed that she'd seen Gareth kill Bronwyn. Gareth must have cried with anguish. Now he has been re-arrested and charged with Bronwyn's murder, and is standing trial again.

Tom, I know it is foolish, but having lived with him, the thought of him being hung frightens me. However wicked he has been, I cannot wish that on him. I pray that the court will take into consideration the awful blow he received on his head in the service of his country. This must have affected his brain. Greedy and unscrupulous as he was, I do not think he would have committed murder before he received that terrible injury. Perhaps the judge will grant him the mercy of imprisonment rather than death.

But now to happier matters. Edwin has just come home from work and says he will add a few words to my long rambling effort; Emma Jane is gurgling for her supper and tomorrow, Sunday, we are going to the beach for a picnic. Life is very kind to us - and Emma Jane will grow up in a home full of love. The future promises much, and hopefully memories of less pleasant things will fade into the past.

Edwin and I hope that one day you will come and stay here for a holiday. Good bye and God bless you for now.

Fondest love,

Rosena.

The Author . . .

ANTHONY LEWING is a versatile writer, being a novelist and short story writer. Much of his work has appeared under the pen-names of Mark Bannerman and Rowena Carter (for women's magazines). He was educated at King's College School Wimbledon, served for thirty-five years in the Royal Army Pay Corps and is married with two grown-up children, a Yorkshire Terrier and a cat. He lives in Surrey, where he writes extensively and teaches creative writing to adult students.

Other works by the same author, published by Pipers' Ash include:

FRANK RIDDLE FRONTIERSMAN

Seventeen-year-old Frank Riddle flees from his tyrannical father and heads west to seek his fortune in the goldfields of California. In turn he becomes a prospector, gambler, womaniser, army scout and government interpreter.

When he marries a Modoc Indian woman, he finds his destiny linked with that of her people who, in the fall and winter of 1872-73, are involved in a desperate fight for survival as soldiers and settlers strive to dislodge them from their ancient refuge in the Lava Beds. Here the terrain is so awesome, so godforsaken, that it is likened to Hell ... with he fires out.

Mark Bannerman vividly recreates the Modoc War, with all its heroes and cowards, in a story of breathtaking adventure, romance, passion, action and tragedy..

> 'Frank Riddle - Frontiersman' is an excellent Western novel written by a British author who has a genuine love of the era, and the ability to convey its excitement and emotions to the reader
>
> *John Paxton Sheriff, author and historian*

'Goose Pimples' by Mark Bannerman   *ISBN 1-902628-03-9*

A cocktail of nerve-tingling tales of mystery and the macabre, brilliantly told by the internationally recognised master craftsman himself.

'Ride into Destiny' by Mark Bannerman   *ISBN 1-902628-42-X*

A gripping story of the Wild West, which stripped of its veneer of civilisation, shows the thoughts and feelings, passions and fears of the early pioneers in the land of the native Americans.

'Bridges to Cross' by Rowena Carter   *ISBN 1-902628-45-4*

A dozen tales exposing momentous relationships in the lives of women, their challenges and triumphs, their frolics and misdemeanours.

'Short Story World' by Mark Bannerman   *ISBN 1-902628-32-2*

The guide to short story writing for beginners, based on the personal experiences of the author, which have served him well and made him an internationally recognised story writer.